DEADLY DEPARTED

FLETCHER & FLETCHER, PARANORMAL
INVESTIGATORS: BOOK TWO

DAVID BUSSELL

For Mum.
Thanks for sticking with it.

DEADLY DEPARTED

CHAPTER ONE: IT'S ALL DOWNHILL
FROM HERE

THE HOUSE LOOKED ALL RIGHT at a distance: bricks and mortar topped with slate, same as any other. It wasn't until I pushed open the stubborn front gate and drew nearer that I realised what a wreck the place was. The porch was so run down that it looked as if it was wilting under the onslaught of the afternoon's unsympathetic down-pour. The windows were spidered with cracks and held in place by termite-infested frames. The front door had barely a few scabs of paint left on it. And then there was the low hum of menace the house gave off: the queasy vibration that seeped into my bones and got my down-belows clenching. Something was wrong with this house. Very wrong.

I rang the doorbell. The sound it gave off was tinny and grating; simultaneously a long way away and right inside my ear. While I waited for an answer, I shook the rainwater from my umbrella and folded it up. The front door opened with a sound like a dying animal and an old woman peered out at me with rheumy eyes, her face scored with more grooves than a walnut. She wore makeup—so much makeup that if she were a passenger in the back of your car and you had to make an emergency stop, you'd have ended up with her portrait on the back of your headrest. This wasn't your typical tarted-up old biddy, though: the kind who spunked away her pension at the bingo hall and always smelled of travel sweets. No. Despite her arthritic joints, I could tell from her surefooted stance that this was the kind of golden-ager who could wait tables in an army mess hall if need be.

'Just the one of you then, is it?' she asked, her voice a rusty hinge. 'The ad said Fletcher *and* Fletcher.'

'My partner's not feeling his best,' I replied, 'but don't you worry, I can manage. I'm a real one-man band.'

The old woman scratched her thistly chin. 'Come on in before you catch a death, then.'

She beckoned me inside with a bony finger. I instinctively went to wipe my feet on the doormat but found nothing underfoot across the threshold but rotten floorboards. The hallway in front of me was dim and uninviting and appeared to be held together by cobwebs.

'Sorry about the mess,' said the old dear as she led me deeper inside.

'Don't worry about it,' I said. *All this place needs is a lick of paint, a spritz of Febreze, and a direct hit from a short-range ballistic missile* is the part I didn't say.

We arrived in a lounge that was empty except for a threadbare floral sofa. There was no other furniture in the room, no pictures on the wall, no TV set.

'I'm guessing you don't do a lot of entertaining,' I said.

She snorted. 'Everyone I know is dead.'

There's a cheery thought.

'So,' I said, moving things along, 'what is it you need my help with exactly?'

The old woman dumped her wide behind on the sofa, which responded with a great belch of dust. 'I need something gotten rid of.'

'I see. And what's that exactly?'

She cast a furtive look to the Artex ceiling. 'Something up there.'

It was obvious what she was getting at. I felt it before I stepped through the front door. 'You think this place is haunted.'

'I know it is, and I need you to put a stop to it.'

'Stop it how?'

'I don't bloody know, do I? You're the expert. Get out your holy cross and tell it to bugger off.'

'Miss, there's been a misunderstanding. I'm an investigator, not an exorcist.'

I didn't tell her that an exorcist is exactly what I used to be, back before I got a tag put on my toe.

She showed me a folded-up piece of paper torn from the Yellow Pages. 'Says here you're a *paranormal* investigator.'

'Correct. Meaning I look into unexplained phenomena. The transmundane.'

'Nothing mundane about the thing lurking up there.'

'Maybe not, but that doesn't give me the right to destroy it.'

The old woman sat forward. 'No one's asking you to *destroy* anything. All I want is for you to shoo the thing away and send it off through the pearly gates.' Her voice cracked and her eyes took on a watery sheen. 'Please, Mister Fletcher, I'm begging you. I can't carry on like this. You have to help me.'

I was under no illusions. I knew full well that she was playing the "poor old dear" card, but knowing it didn't make it any less effective.

'Okay, don't get yourself all wound up, luv. I'll take a look, but I'm not making any promises.'

She returned a dented smile and deflated back into the sofa. 'Thank you, that's all I'm asking.'

I patted down my pockets to make sure I had everything I needed.

'Before I get to work, why don't you tell me exactly what's been going on up there?'

'Lots of things. Footsteps that don't belong to anyone. A weird voice whispering through the walls. Saw a white figure just floating there one time, bold as brass.'

She sounded genuine enough.

'One last thing. I've seen these things get dicey fast, so before I go, are you absolutely sure you're telling me everything I need to know?'

'Dead sure,' she said.

'Nothing missed out?'

'Nothing.'

'Okay then. I'll have a shufty and let you know what I find. You wait here, all right?'

Two quick head bobs. 'The room you want is at the top of the stairs, first door on your right.'

I followed the line of her crooked finger to the source of the supernatural presence and felt an icy tickle along my spine like a key dropped down the back of my shirt. Leaving the old woman behind, I trudged up a flight of creaky steps and pushed open the door she'd directed me to.

The room was small and meat-locker cold. Dubious fingers of daylight clawed through a gap in a ragged set of curtains but didn't make it far before they recoiled from the darkness like a hand from a flame. The only furnishings on display were more cobwebs and dead flies littering the floor. Even the slimiest of estate agents would have struggled to make this room sound aspirational.

Compact design! A blank canvas! Great flow!

I closed the door behind me, held my breath, and waited a few seconds to make sure the old lady hadn't followed me up. Certain she was downstairs still, I stepped out of the body I was occupying and became two people.

For those of you playing catch-up, let me colour in the details. Reader's Digest version: I'm a ghost who works with, and is able to inhabit the person of, my own reanimated corpse. Yeah, that old cliché. Jake and Frank—that's me and my corporeal counterpart—twin halves of the intrepid Fletcher & Fletcher super-team. Two dead folks who co-run an investigation agency. Together, we put the P.I. in R.I.P.

'Thanks, big man,' I told my partner. 'I know it ain't easy, lugging me around in your noggin.'

Frank gave me a lopsided grin and made a sloppy OK sign. 'S'all-riiight,' he slurred.

His speech was really coming along. I suppose I shouldn't be surprised that I'm rubbing off on the feller. Since he showed up, the two of us have been closer than two bollocks in a ball bag.

'Let's get cracking, shall we?'

Frank lumbered off and I parted the curtains, burnishing the room with amber. Even lit up, there wasn't much to look at. The only features present were a cheap mirror splotched black and dotted with greasy fingerprints, rusted staples on the walls pinning ripped corners of torn-down posters, and a tatty white nightdress hanging from a hook on the door. No sign of an otherworldly presence. No disembodied whispering. No eerie footsteps.

I started to wonder if maybe I'd been mistaken; if the frigid, sinking fear I felt earlier had been in my head. Was I imagining things? Her downstairs, too? Could be she was just a bit batty from old age, saw a white nightdress hanging on the back of the door, and mistook it for a phantom. Or maybe her brain was addled some other way. Back in the day, I dealt with more than one ghostly manifestation that turned out to be nothing more sinister than a knackered boiler. A carbon monoxide leak combined with a screaming radiator can easily get your mind running. Next thing you know you're hallucinating tortured spirits and voices from nowhere. No shame in it, just a chemical reaction.

I turned to my partner. 'You smell gas?'

I couldn't, seeing as I don't have a physical body, but my other half had the nose of a bloodhound and the drool to match.

Frank gave the air a sniff and shook his head, dislodging a cloud of dead skin cells that briefly caught the light before drifting lazily to the ground. But his nose caught something besides gas. Something that had him circling the room like a dog looking for a place to take a dump. After a couple of circuits he lurched to a stop and pressed his face against the wall decorated with the old mirror. With rigor mortis hands he began to paw at the faded wallpaper.

'What is it, Lassie? Did little Timmy fall down the well?'

Whatever was going on inside that wall, it had Frank's undivided attention. Maybe the old lady was right. Maybe she was on to something when she said she heard voices coming through the plaster.

I was about to poke my head through and take a look inside the wall cavity (a doddle when you're a phantasm) when Frank growled, raised his fists, and put them both through the brickwork. He tore into the wall as if it were made of shortbread, bringing down a door-sized chunk of masonry with an apocalyptic crash.

'What the bloody hell is going on up there?' the old lady cried from downstairs.

'Mirror came off its hook, that's all,' I said, feeding her some flannel. 'Bit of a mess but nothing to worry about. You can deduct it from my bill.'

I was about to shoot Frank a filthy look, but my eyes had already settled upon something poking out of the jumble of bricks spilt across the floor. Breaking up the powdery mess of orange and grey was a shiny white dome: the crown of a skull—a human skull—sat atop a pile of assorted bones.

CHAPTER TWO: REMAINS TO BE SEEN

'WHAT THE HELL HAPPENED HERE?' I asked.

Frank didn't have any answers, but then I don't really look to my partner for his penetrating insight. Frank's the guy I go to when heads need bashing in; I'm the brains of this operation.

I dropped to my haunches to get a better look at the skeleton. Was the person those bones belonged to hidden in the crawlspace post-mortem, Fred West style, or were they bricked up alive? More importantly, would desecrating their grave stir up the lingering soul of an angry bogeyman welcome in neither Heaven nor Hell?

From the gloom of the exposed cavity came my answer. Creeping through the demolition cloud came curling silvery wisps accompanied by a sound that no living thing could make. A sickly dread furred my tongue as the immaterial tendrils tangled and solidified to form a pair of arms that gripped the cratered edges of the wall and hauled through a body. A creature rendered from pain and malice sprang from the hole, a monstrous dead thing that existed only to plague the living. This wasn't a ghost like me: the earthbound imprint of a former person concocted from ectoplasm. This was a wailing horror movie banshee, a revenant, an unquiet spirit who refused to go softly into the night.

The ghost shot forward like a film strip skipping its sprockets—over there one moment and right on top of me the next. I felt its anvil weight across my ribcage and realised I was on my back, feet pedalling air. The revenant leered over me, eyes burning like hot coals, its mouth hung open in a silent scream. It raised a pair of gangly arms, sending golden razors of sunlight filtering through its oversized claws. I was about to get my face raked off when a confused expression crossed the creature's face, then off it went, reeling back like a fish yanked away on an angler's line.

Frank hoisted the revenant up by its neck and slammed it into the deck beside me. It thrashed around like a mammoth sinking into a tar pit, but Frank wasn't taking any shit. With the no-nonsense efficiency of a tired mother dealing with a toddler's supermarket tantrum, he bundled the creature into a manageable shape and pinned it to the ground.

'Nicely done,' I said.

Frank wouldn't be able to hold the bastard for long, though. I had to act fast. From the inside of my jacket I removed a claw hammer, specially treated for my phantom hands. I don't like to carry a shooter unless it's absolutely necessary, but it never hurts to have a bit of iron in your pocket. The hammer wasn't for the revenant, though, it was for the remains it had left behind. From another pocket I produced a nail. This wasn't the sort of hardware you'd find at B&Q, mind you. This was an ancient relic, a holy nail, the kind the Romans used to pin Jesus to the cross.

Now, you might think—top whack—there'd be maybe three holy nails in this world, four at a push, but you'd be wrong. Just like Christ's foreskin, there are double digits scattered among various monasteries and cathedrals around the globe. What this says about organised religion I'll leave you to figure out. For my purposes, the authenticity of the holy nails wasn't all that important. The fact that they were venerated and sanctified provided them with an Uncanny potency that served my needs perfectly.

I pinched a nail between forefinger and thumb, raised the hammer above my head, and pounded it into the top of the skull lying amongst the rubble. The effect was instant. The second the nail drove home, the revenant Frank was pinning transformed from a feral monster into a person. A young woman. She looked to be in her late teens and was dressed like someone from decades ago.

'Let her go,' I told Frank.

He took his weight off her and she scrambled backwards into the corner of the room, leaving behind a pitter-patter of ethereal tears. She shivered and shook, a bundle of frayed nerves.

'It's okay,' I said, 'I'm not going to hurt you.'

'What about him?' she said, pointing at Frank, who stood there like a loyal attack dog awaiting a command.

'Don't mind my partner,' I replied. 'He's harmless.'

Frank would never hurt someone who didn't deserve it; he had too good a heart. Technically, it was my heart, but it didn't burn with the same world-weary cynicism as the cold stone I carried around these days.

'What's your name?' I asked the girl, still keeping my distance.

'Mary,' she replied, avoiding my gaze. 'Mary Connor.'

'Nice to meet you, Mary Connor. How did you end up here?'

Her eyes stayed anchored to the ground. 'I got stuck. In the wall.'

I brought myself to her level, sinking down beside her whilst maintaining a respectful span between us. 'I see. And how did that happen?'

'Something went wrong. I went in but I couldn't get back out.'

'Hold your horses...' I said, realising that *"I got stuck"* implied some degree of culpability, '... are you saying you went into that wall voluntarily?'

She stashed a stray strand of hair behind her ear. 'I was an assistant.'

'An assistant what?'

'Spiritualist. I hid in there while my partner held a séance out here. It was my job. The punters thought they were talking to the dead, but it was just me knocking on the wall.'

Frank gave me a look. He knew how I felt about spiritualists: con artists, one and all. But I had a job to do, and I couldn't let old animosities cloud my judgment. I gave Frank a nod to let him know I had this.

'When did you pass?' I asked the girl.

'It was January 26th, 1946 when I got trapped.'

That tracked. The spiritualism racket had been about since the 1800s but membership really swelled after a big dust-up. The aftermath of the Great War and its sequel, WW2, were boom times for wall-rappers and table-knockers. Shameless hucksters would use their wiles to fleece war widows and milk grieving parents. Like I say, nasty pieces of work.

'How did you manage to get stuck?' I asked.

'We were in the middle of a session. Betsy was using the ruler hidden in her sleeve to make the table jump when the rozzers kicked down the door and carted her away.'

'Betsy being your partner?'

A shallow nod. 'That's right. Cleared out the punters too, they did. They would have had me away an' all, but I was hidden in the wall.'

'I don't get it. Why did you stay there after the pigs left?'

'I tried to get out—course I did—but the door was stuck.'

I figured it must have jammed somehow and stayed that way while her body turned to bones. The remains probably went unnoticed and got plastered over by the folks who moved into the property next.

'Go on,' I urged her. 'What happened then?'

For the first time since she'd appeared in her earthly form, the girl raised her head to meet my gaze. Her stare went right through me.

'I shouted for help but no one came. I screamed the place down. There was no food, no water. Eventually, I just went to sleep and that was the end of me. I've been stuck in this place ever since, trying to get the people who pass through to listen, but only scaring them away.'

'And that made you angry.'

'Yes. And then it made me something else.'

A revenant.

A ghost can only stay sane for so long beached on the material plane. I seem to be the exception to this rule, but there's no telling when I might go ballistic and start clawing people's eyeballs out. I just had to hope I could get right with Him Upstairs before that happened, and freeing this tortured girl of her Earthbound shackles was a step towards doing that.

'What happened to Betsy?' I asked. 'Why didn't she come back for you?'

'That's what I want to know,' she said, lips stretched thin, her eyes burning with the same otherworldly glow they had before I hammered a nail into her bones. 'We were a team. Why did she leave me to die?'

'Calm down, okay?' I said, fearing I was about to lose her. If she gave into rage with the holy nail in place, she'd be snuffed out like that. I needed her at peace if I was going to walk her to the next step. 'I'm here to help you, but I can only do that if you work with me. Understand?'

The embers in her eyes cooled and were replaced by silvery tears that welled up and spilled down her cheeks. 'I understand.'

A raw sobbing shook her whole body. Frank pulled a hankie from the top pocket of his jacket and handed it to her. She took it with a crooked smile and dabbed her wet cheeks.

I couldn't say for sure what had happened to Betsy, but I had a pretty good idea. Her profession tended not to attract the most trustworthy of people. When their operation was busted and the dust finally settled, I expect Betsy made for the hills and never looked back.

'You have to help me,' pleaded the girl. 'I can't stay here any more.'

Despite being the architect of her own downfall, I couldn't help but feel sorry for her.

'It's hard, I know,' I said, doing my best to empathise. 'I mean, talk about unlucky. You pretend to be the voice of the dead and end up becoming exactly that.'

'Is that supposed to help?' she asked, giving me a look that could have curdled milk.

I held up my hands in surrender. 'Not knocking you, luv. I'm no stranger to irony. I used to be an exorcist and now look at me,' I pointed at myself, then at my reanimated corpse. 'My own worst nightmare.'

The girl sat up sharply. 'You were an exorcist? Then you can help me. Help me pass through. Help me get to the other side.'

I shook my head. 'It doesn't work like that. If I exorcise you, you'll be obliterated. I'm talking permanent midnight. Trust me, I learned that the hard way.'

'Then why are you here? What are you going to do?'

'I'm not going to do anything. Your fate isn't up to me. If you want into Heaven, you're going to have to talk to the Governor.'

'You mean…?'

'Yeah. Go to Him willingly, ask for absolution, and who knows, you might just get the key to the clubhouse.'

The girl looked at me as if I'd asked her to join me for a quick dip in a slurry tank. 'You're asking me to face The Almighty? Do you know what the Bible says about spiritualists? Leviticus 20:27: *"A man or a woman who is a medium or a necromancer shall surely be put to death".* Does that sound like I'd see a fair trial?'

I took a shuffle in her direction, closing the gap between us. We were navel-to-navel now, just an arm's-width apart.

'There's a lot of iffy stuff in that part of the Bible. You know Leviticus also forbids drinking alcohol in holy places? If that's gospel, that's every churchgoing Catholic on the planet fucked.'

She laughed.

'Look, all I'm saying is, maybe the Big Man's chilled out a bit since then. Could be He was having a bad day when He passed those little nuggets along. Point is, your choices are: confess your sins to the Almighty, or spend an eternity here as a tormented poltergeist. So what's it going to be, Mary?'

She folded her arms. 'I don't get it. You're dead, too. If Heaven's the place to be, what are you doing down here?'

I sketched out a smile. 'Me and the Author have a deal: before I get to go Upstairs, I have to clear some debts. That's what this little visit is about, the latest stop on my Road to Redemption tour. If you want atonement, you're going to have to ask for it, and I recommend asking nicely.'

She hung her head. 'How would I even get His attention?'

I gave her a paternal cheek-cup. 'If I were you I'd start with the Lord's Prayer. After that, you're on your own.'

She looked to Frank as if he might provide a second opinion, but my partner had nothing to offer but a sympathetic nod.

The girl's shoulders sank and her face assumed a frown so pronounced that it appeared to end below her chin. 'All right,' she said. 'I hear what you're saying and I've made up my mind. Thank you.'

'No need to thank me,' I replied, 'just make sure you—'

That was as far as I got before she made the lunge past me, past Frank, and across the room to the dusty cranium with the holy nail hammered into it. Wrapping a dainty fist around the nail, she wrenched it free and instantly reverted to the howling monster that had emerged from the ruined brick wall.

The revenant spun about to face me, a venomous hiss unravelling from its coal-black tongue, its eyes two windows of a burning building.

'Fine,' I said, taking a step back and removing a fresh tool from my pocket. 'Have it your way, Mary.'

She came at me shrieking and I met her with my crucifix.

THE LIGHT HAD DIMMED SIGNIFICANTLY when I returned downstairs, shrouding the lounge in thick drapes of shadow. The sun was heading for a lie-down, bringing us to the close of another dog-end day. The old lady was where I left her, sank into the sofa; two sad old pieces of furniture fast becoming one.

'Well?' she said, clasping a glass of tap water between two shaking hands. 'Is it gone?'

Reunited with my physical form, I took a spot in front of her and nodded.

She placed her drink on the floor and lowered her wrinkled head into her hands. Weeping came next. I knew what for.

'You lied to me, Betsy.'

Tears cut rivers through the old woman's caked-on makeup. 'I'm not a bad person,' she said, her voice dry as bone dust. 'That's the God's honest. I only meant to give those poor sods who lost their boys a bit of comfort, a bit of closure.'

'What about your partner?' I snorted. 'What about Mary? You didn't give her much closure, did you? I told her she had two options —she could stay here or ask for forgiveness—but she found a third. She chose oblivion, and I don't know that I blame her. The person who let her die didn't repent her sins, so why should she?'

I tossed the spent crucifix and it landed with a dull thud at her feet, same place I was laying blame. It sat there, warped from use, curled up like a demonic talon with smoke coming off it.

'It weren't my fault. None of it was. When the coppers turfed me out, Mary got left behind. I didn't know she was stuck in the wall. How could I?'

If Betsy was looking to me for forgiveness, she was looking in the wrong place.

Her hands came together, steepled in an unconscious prayer. 'Far as I was concerned, Mary was the lucky one. I got hauled over the coals but she didn't even get collared. Good for her, I thought.'

'And you never considered that she might be in trouble? Never thought to tell anyone that the last time you saw her she was sandwiched in a crawlspace?'

'And grass on my partner? No, never.'

I stared her down, expecting her eyes to track sideways, but she kept her cool.

'What happened after they arrested you?'

She kneaded her temples, to focus her memories or stem a sudden headache, I couldn't be sure.

'I spent a week in the clink before they put me in front of a magistrate. In the end, they let me off. I only got a warning on account of my age and my barrister doing a good job, but by then it was too late.' She shuffled awkwardly on the sofa. 'I got word from Mary's folks that she never came home after the raid, so I came back here, snuck inside, and went looking for clues. I saw a chair lying on its back, knocked over when the police stormed the place, blocking the secret door that led into the hidey-hole. I figured the rest out by myself. Mary was done for. Sealed up inside the wall and left to die.'

'How could you know that for sure?'

'Because I heard it. Heard this awful moaning. I don't know how to talk to the spirit world—that was all make-believe—but I knew in my guts that the sound coming from behind that wall didn't belong to anything alive. Mary was dead and her ghost was angry. So I ran, and I've been running ever since.'

'What changed?'

She leant forward to better show me her age-ravaged face. 'I got old and I got tired. That's when I decided to put an end to this. That's why I bought this old place and called you.'

'To do your dirty work.'

She shook her head like her brain was an Etch-a-Sketch and the truth was a doodle she could erase.

'I was just a girl back then,' she said. 'Mary was like a little sister to me, and I let her die all alone. At least now she can have some peace. We both can.'

Her eyes cut left to something beside her lap. Wedged between her thigh and the arm of the sofa was a small orange canister. I snatched it up: painkillers, strong ones, and none left.

'Thank you, Mr Fletcher,' she murmured, her eyelids drooping as the drugs took effect. 'Thank you for lifting my burden.'

She slumped forward, her head sagging between her knees like she was bracing for a crash landing, which, in a roundabout way, she was. She didn't speak again, and I didn't stick around to see which direction her spirit went. I already had a pretty good idea which way she was heading, and it wasn't Heaven for Betsy.

CHAPTER THREE: THE BEAUTIFUL DEAD

FRANK and I arrived back at the office feeling despondent. The day had been a write-off. A total non-starter. No money, no karma, no nothing. This business of ours needed to start taking off in a big way, because being stuck here in this quasi-alive state was doing nothing for either of us. If we didn't get some halos hung on our heads soon, our conjoined soul was in danger of drifting away on the celestial ether.

There was nothing else for it. We desperately needed to earn some Brownie points and get right with God. So what did we spend the rest of the night doing? Shooting scrunched-up paper balls into the office bin, that's what. Yeah. Instead of chasing our next case, Frank and me spent the wee hours in heated competition, luzzing rubbish across the room and cheering our athletic prowess.

'Scooooooore,' Frank gurgled, sinking another basket.

I grunted with frustration as I retrieved the paper ball from the bin, which sat elevated on a filing cabinet.

'Yeah, well, it's a whole other game when you're working with these things,' I said, holding up my traitorous phantom hands, which were ill-equipped to handle physical objects. Don't get me wrong, I can perform basic manoeuvres and manipulations with solid matter, but counting on them to score three-pointers was optimistic at best.

I parked a cheek on the edge of the desk I shared with Frank and folded my arms. 'If you want to make this a fair game, you should be playing with a handicap,' I argued. 'Shooting hoops is a lot easier when you have an actual body to work with. Ask anyone.'

Frank's head swivelled and cocked to one side. At first I thought he was looking the other way so he didn't have to engage with my call for sportsmanship, but it wasn't that. Something had pricked up his ears. Something outside the room.

An intruder?

I cut a glance to the office door and saw a dim silhouette appear behind the frosted glass bearing the Fletcher & Fletcher logotype. Someone had broken into the building, but who? I had so many enemies by this point that I was starting to lose count; an endless conga line of bad bastards eager to do me wrong. Or was the intruder of a different bent? Had the Almighty tired of waiting for me to settle my balance and loosed one of his God Squad on me, another angel come to deliver judgment upon my eternal soul?

Before I could reach for my trusty enchanted hammer, the shadowy figure went from being a silhouette outside the office to a presence in the room. I felt the world slow down as the stranger stepped through the door, walking through solid oak to emerge into our place of business.

'Oh, thank Christ,' I said, sagging with relief, 'you're just a ghost.'

The spectral stranger was a young woman dressed for a night out on the town. She was as tall as she was dark, with skin like black silk draped over glass. Streetlight cut through the Venetian blinds, falling on her in stripes and giving her the look of a stalking predator. The effect was only exaggerated by her gait: shoulders back, eyes fixed straight ahead, her steps long and confident. She walked into my office like a lioness walks into a sub-Saharan orphanage, but the thing that struck me the most about her—the thing that dwarfed everything else—was the bullet hole in her forehead. The one peering at me like a third eye.

'Is one of you two Jake Fletcher?' she asked, her voice clipped and to the point.

Frank growled at her, teeth bared. I gave him a quick *pipe down* wave and he took a step back, lips still drawn back over his gums.

To the woman I said, 'I'm Jake, and this is my partner, Frank.

Together, we're Fletcher & Fletcher, paranormal investigators. Show her, Frankie boy…'

He handed her our business card. The logo read, *No Case Too Cold*. I came up with that.

The woman scanned our offering, keeping her distance from my glassy-eyed companion.

'Is he okay?' she asked.

'Yes. Why?'

'It's just… he looks like he clawed his way out of a shallow grave.'

I chuckled. 'Funny you should say that, he is a bit on the dead side. But then who isn't these days, right?'

'Wait… are you saying he's a zombie?'

I made a face. 'Ooh, we don't like the zed word around here. Bit reductive.'

She squinted to get a better look at Frank. 'He looks just like you.'

'Yeah, he's my dead spit. Get it? Because we're both…'

The woman regarded me with a mixture of confusion and contempt. It was obvious that my cheeky barrow boy act wasn't having the disarming effect I'd hoped for, so I switched gears.

'Why don't you make yourself comfortable and tell me your name?'

I took a seat and shot the cuffs of my jacket, enjoying the comforting feel of its embrace around my shoulders. For some, a suit is a drab, suffocating thing, but not for me. My suit is a second skin, black as midnight and crisp as a fresh banknote.

I gestured for our guest to pull up a pew opposite me. She sighed and lowered herself onto Frank's chair.

'My name is Talisa. People call me Tali.'

'Thanks for stopping by, Tali. What can I do you for?'

She leaned forward and spoke with a dark urgency in her voice. 'I need you to find the man who killed me.'

So far, so good. Well, for me, not so much for her. Helping lost souls find their way to the afterlife was my bread and butter, but I had to be careful, I've been burned by shady ladies before. Just because the woman sitting across my desk had the kind of looks that turned every man she met into a knight of old, didn't mean I had to start behaving like some raving Galahad. These days I took extra precautions. I didn't work for anyone unless they passed my screening process.

'How did you find out about this agency?' I asked.

'A police officer told me about you. You know, after it happened.'

After it happened being a polite way of saying, *After I went tits up.*

Tali explained how she'd hovered at the scene of the crime for a while, screaming at deaf police officers until one started talking back to her: a woman by the name of Detective Stronge.

Ah, yes. DCI Kat Stronge.

Stronge had taken the victim aside and given her the skinny. Said she wasn't able to get into her case there and then—that she had to carry out her duty as a police officer and couldn't be seen talking to herself like a loony (her fellow officers being incapable of seeing ghosts). Stronge explained that she'd catch up with Tali later, and that in the meantime she should pay me a visit. That I'd look after her.

So would I?

Tali had passed the first test. I'd set up that filter system with Stronge personally (and it was good to know the arrangement was working). I stole a quick glance at the framed P.I. certificate on the wall—the one Stronge gave me in the spirit of our rebuilt friendship.

Back to work.

'How long ago did you die?' I asked Tali. That last word might seem insensitive, but I believe in the direct approach. Besides, the usual euphemism, "passed on", wasn't appropriate here. The only way Tali was passing anywhere was if we tipped the scales of justice in her favour, and I was still on the fence about taking her on as a client.

'A few hours ago, I think. There's a part I don't remember, right after he...'

She didn't need to finish.

'Can I ask you something?' I said. 'How is it that you're so comfortable with being a goner? Most dead folks I meet at your stage are screaming a big blue streak.'

She wrung her hands. 'I panicked at first—of course I did—but I have some clarity now. Now I know what I want.'

'And what's that?'

'Revenge.'

I could relate. It was the same with me when I kicked the bucket. There's something about being brutally murdered that really puts a bee in your bonnet.

'So none of this supernatural stuff fazes you?' I asked. 'Being a ghost? Walking through walls? All that jazz?'

'I am a bit weirded out by the zombie,' she confessed.

Frank narrowed his eyes.

'Again, we don't like the zed word,' I reminded her.

Tali leant forward and gripped the edge of the desk. The ring she was wearing caught the streetlight that razored through the blinds, making its stone glint: an emerald set into a polished copper band.

'I'm not new to this,' she said. 'I was born with the Sight.'

That explained that. Tali was an Insider, a normal with the ability to see the invisible dance we call the Uncanny. I was that way too, before I became a fully-fledged paranormal phenomenon.

'I see,' I replied. 'And what did you do with that special knowledge?'

'I became a sex worker.'

Not what I was expecting.

'Um, how exactly do those two things...' I interlaced my fingers, '...slot together?'

'I used what I knew to carve out a niche for myself: a regular person who services the freaks.' Her mouth sharpened into something close to a smile. 'It's funny, there are all these nutty creatures in this city, but to them, *I'm* the piece of strange.'

I drummed my fingers on the desk, considering her story. 'Don't you have someone who's supposed to look after you?'

'No pimp, no madam,' she shot back. 'I fly solo, always have.' A realisation dawned and she corrected herself. 'Always *did.*'

Tali seemed genuine enough, but I needed to test every angle of her story: shake it, bend it, see where it buckled, even if it meant asking some indelicate questions.

'So what's it like, sleeping with monsters for a living?'

She flinched at that. 'The money's better but the work's weirder. You take what you can get.'

'And what you got,' I said, eyes drifting to her forehead, 'was a bullet in the nut.'

Her face pulled into a scowl. 'What the hell would you know?'

'About prostitution? Not a lot, I guess. Try not to hold it against me.'

I felt a heavy hand on my shoulder: Frank's. It was accompanied by a small shake of the head, a sign that I'd taken it far enough. Tali's story checked out. She'd come through the screening process clean. I didn't need to grill her any further.

'I'm sorry,' I said. 'I'm not making judgments about your profession—we're all doing what we can to get by. Why don't you get back to your story and we'll see if we can figure out what happened here?'

Her grimace went away and she relaxed in her chair. 'He was just another John. Nothing special. Nothing that set any alarm bells ringing.'

'What flavour of Uncanny are we talking? Vampire? Werewolf? Some horny wizard?'

'Couldn't tell you. He paid, I laid. All I know for sure is that he must have had money, because my services don't come cheap.'

I didn't doubt it. This was no twenty-quid-a-pop hussy. This woman could have charged a king's ransom for what she was offering.

Without taking my eyes off her, I produced a yellow legal pad from a desk drawer and tossed it to Frank.

'Can you describe him to me?'

She gave a half-shrug. 'Dark hair, slim build, fairly tall. Nothing remarkable about him.'

'Any distinguishing features? Scars, blemishes, birthmarks, a big tattoo of the Tasmanian Devil on his arse?'

She laughed dutifully. 'There was one thing. He had purple eyes.'

'Purple?'

'Violet, I guess you'd call them. Quite unusual.'

Frank took up a pen and scribbled down the details, dictating Tali's words in his big looping scrawl.

'Anything else?'

'No, that's it, really. Other than how good-looking he was. A real pretty boy.' She spat the last two words out like they were pieces of rancid meat.

I wasn't too surprised by the news that he was easy on the eye. Killers rarely look like the slope-browed apes you expect them to be. In the real world, the villain doesn't present as a monster. He's the guy who waves when he passes you by, who chats about the weather, who knows how to tip a waitress right. That's why we're shocked when we find out he's a murderer; not just because of the terrible things he did, but because we can't understand how his evil co-existed with the good he showed the world.

'I'll take the case, Tali,' I said, the words leaving my mouth before I was ready to say them. 'I'll find your killer and make sure he gets what's coming to him.'

This was our chance for a do-over. To succeed where we failed with the revenant.

Tali's fingertips went to her forehead and traced the edges of her bullet wound. 'Thank you. You're doing the world a favour, trust me. That man needs to die.'

'Whoa, easy,' I said. 'I'm a P.I., not a bounty hunter. No one's getting killed here.'

She shot to her feet, sending Frank's chair skittering back on its coasters. 'What the hell? You just said you were going to help me.'

'And I will, by seeing to it that the person responsible for your murder pays for his crimes.'

'Pays how?' she demanded.

'That's up to the London Coven, and believe me, they don't muck about when it comes to taking Uncanny killers off the streets.'

Tali's fists unfurled. 'I've heard of the Coven. All right. If that's who's dealing with him, I'm okay with that.'

The Coven had a reputation for treating those who broke the law with swift, brutal justice. Any Insider knew that.

'So what happens next?' asked Tali.

I smiled and reached into a filing cabinet for a bottle of Bushmills.

'Next we have a drink.'

CHAPTER FOUR: LIGHTS UP ON DARKNESS

Used to be I'd take the lazy man's choice when I wanted to get somewhere—pull a Houdini and translocate instantly to my intended destination—but that was before I found Frank. Since we partnered up, I've started walking again. I've even come to enjoy it, at least when I'm not being stalked by a group of shady, unidentified figures that looked like something Stephen King might dream up after a concussion.

There were four of them in total, scattered wide. They kept their distance, hugging the shadows like rats as I pretended not to notice we were being tailed, but the reflections I caught in passing windows showed me our pursuers were something... *other*. Something with unnaturally long fingers connected by fleshy webbing, and arched backs that forced the ridges of their spines to show through their suit jackets. Something with fishbelly white skin and drawn, sunken features studded with eyes the colour of blood clots.

These weren't people, these were monsters.

But then monsters are a common sight in London, at least if you have the eyes to see them. In any case, the problem I had wasn't that the figures at our heels were inhuman. What bothered me was that I didn't know who or what they were, let alone what they wanted. All I had were guesses. Were they out to mug us? Were they old adversaries I'd picked up somewhere along the road, here to settle a score? Or were they connected to the case somehow? Could these things be related to the person who killed my client? It seemed unlikely. The man I was after had been described as a looker, but these hatchet-faced things would make even the most accommodating woman's knees slam shut. No, this felt like a B-story to me. Something separate from the investigation.

'Pick up your trotters,' I whispered to my partner.

Frank quickened his step, but the figures followed suit. How long were these mystery men going to keep after us, I wondered. Would they hound us all the way to the finish line, or were they looking for a quiet side street they could bundle us into so they could do whatever it was they intended to do?

Frank must have sensed my growing unease because I saw his fists bunch and watched his lip curl back in a rictus snarl.

'Calm down, Spartacus,' I told him, placing a cooling hand on his forearm. 'We're not looking for a ruck; they've got us two-to-one.'

I was thinking of ways we could give our pursuers the slip when something strange happened: the figures in our rearview stopped suddenly, turned their backs on us, and headed off in the other direction.

'Weird.'

They'd been following us a good while—so long that the sun was making an appearance now, turning the sky the colour of a migraine. I wondered if it was the approach of dawn that had encouraged our pursuers to cease their shadowy pursuit. Was it vampires hounding us?

Frank ground to a halt and watched the hunched figures peel off into the distance. Whatever it was our stalkers wanted, we wouldn't learn of it tonight.

I gave my partner a sideways look. 'Come on, pal, we've got places to be.'

IT WAS RAINING knives by the time we rocked up at Cath's Caff, a 24-hour greasy spoon considered by many to be a pot of fried gold at the end of a long, grey rainbow. We ducked inside and found Detective Strong hanging her sopping wet coat on a rack by the door. She wore shoulder pads, a sober head of hair, and dark red lipstick. In short, she looked the way she always did: like she was on her way to solve an X-File.

Stronge was on her own this morning. Her partner, DC Maddox, was on sick leave, recovering from the aftermath of our last adventure. His absence didn't make her any less of a force, though. DCI Kat Stronge was tough as nails and sharp as barbed wire.

'Fuck!' she cried as I tapped her on the shoulder, forgetting that I don't make footsteps and scaring the living bejeezus out of her.

A clod of builders sharing a red-top tabloid looked up from their booth to check Stronge was okay.

Stronge composed herself, turned her back on them, and hissed at me from the side of her mouth, 'This is why people don't like ghosts, Fletcher.'

Before I could apologise, the titular "Cath" arrived, sizing Stronge up through piggy eyes framed with tar-thick mascara.

'You eating or you just gonna stand there like a lemon?' she barked through a puckered mouth shaped by decades of tugging on cheap cigarettes.

Stronge did a quick headcount. 'Table for three,' she said, then quickly recalibrated when she registered the confusion on Cath's face and remembered I was invisible to our host. 'Make that two.'

Cath sighed and begrudgingly escorted us to a table covered in a sticky plastic cloth still bearing tea spills from the diners before us. We sat down, and Stronge selected some fare from the blackboard above the counter.

'Cup of coffee and a plate of eggs, chips, and black pudding. Eggs, well-done; coffee the same colour as the pudding. Ta.'

'What about him?' asked Cath, jabbing a carrot-coloured digit at Frank.

'He's not hungry,' Stronge replied on behalf of her companion. 'Bit green around the gills.'

Cath sloped away, rolling her eyes and muttering a string of dire oaths. Only once she was out of earshot did we get to business. I brought Stronge up to speed on what Frank and I had learned so far, and she shared her notes with us.

'A guest in the neighbouring room heard the gunshot and phoned reception,' she said. 'A hotel porter was first on the scene.'

'And what did he stumble into?' I asked.

'Nothing too messy. Whoever killed that girl didn't fetishize it. Didn't cut her up or play with her blood or anything weird. It was a clean kill: one tap to the head. *Pop.*'

'You make it sound like he did her a favour.'

'Come on, you know what I mean. Compared to some of the bodies we've seen, this one was a prom queen.'

Our waitress returned with a cup of mud and dropped it in front of Stronge like it was radioactive, which it might well have been. The way Frank grimaced at the smell of it certainly suggested so, and he was no potpourri himself.

'Any sign of the murder weapon?' I asked, getting back to it.

'Not present,' Stronge replied.

I scratched my chin. 'I need to get a gander at that crime scene.'

'Not necessary,' she replied. 'My team already conducted a thorough search. Everything that needs finding has been found.'

'Okay. So what did you turn up? Did you lift any dabs you can run through the HOLMES suite?'

Her scant lips formed a smile full of spice and mischief. 'Well, look at you. That's real detective talk, none of that super sleuth, Dick Tracy shit. You're really getting the hang of this, aren't you, Fletcher?'

She'd have put me in a headlock and ground her knuckles into my crown if she could. Instead, she just laughed, leading Frank to join in the fun with a gurgling chortle that added a small lagoon of drool to the already mucky tablecloth. I gave my partner a cuff to the back of the head before he attracted any more unwanted attention.

'You don't even know what you're laughing at, you big lug.'

'Leave him alone,' said Stronge.

'How about we get back to work and leave out the piss-taking, eh?'

She put her frown away, but it didn't go easy. 'Fine. Back to the fingerprints. We were expecting to find two sets—'

'Only two? What about prints from previous guests?'

'Not in this place. The John booked a suite in a Mayfair hotel. The cleaning crew had that room sparkling before him and the victim got anywhere near it.'

'Okay, so just two sets of prints then.'

'I said we were *expecting* to find two sets. Fact is, we only found the vic's.'

It could never be simple.

'Could the killer have been wearing gloves?' I asked.

'It's possible.'

'Or maybe he wiped the scene down before he took off.'

Stronge returned a head wobble. 'And only removed his own dabs?'

Fair point.

Cath arrived with a serving of undercooked eggs, a scattering of anaemic chips, and a slice of blood sausage. She delivered it to the table with a cacophonous clatter that put my teeth on edge, then sloped off to the kitchen without making eye contact. The phrase "customer satisfaction" had never been high among Cath's watchwords.

'Okay, so no dabs. What about blood?' I asked.

'Only the victim's.'

'Any other DNA?'

'How do you mean?'

'The girl was an escort.'

'I know that.'

I cocked my head. Stronge wasn't getting it, but then she had been up all night combing a crime scene.

'What I'm saying is, were there any other… deposits left at the scene?'

It clicked. 'Oh. No, we swabbed, but the vic was clean.'

That struck me as peculiar. I mean, why hire an escort if you didn't plan on having sex?

At the risk of catching the rough side of Stronge's tongue, I said, 'So what you're basically telling me is you've got bugger all.'

She hoisted a razor-thin eyebrow. 'Did I say that?'

'You might as well have. Look, you and your boys did your thing, but I have some tricks of my own. The sooner I get a look-see at that crime scene, the better.'

'If you hadn't interrupted me, you'd know I wasn't finished talking.'

I stared at her a while. 'Okay, I'll bite. What have you got?'

She leaned back in her chair. 'A mirror, taken down off the wall and left on a tabletop with traces of powder on it.'

'Coke?'

'No, this wasn't some cheap gack you can pick up anywhere. This was a rare designer drug, street name: "clad", short for "ironclad". Extremely hard to come by and extremely dangerous.'

'So what are you thinking? The suspect banged some up his snout to get himself in the killing mood?'

'Maybe, maybe not,' said Stronge. 'Honestly, we don't know what the stuff does besides make dead bodies. We've had our tox boys look into it but all we get back is *Unknown Compound*.'

'Could there be an Uncanny element to it?'

'Could well be.' She tucked into her black pudding. 'God, this tastes like a dog's back.'

'You're eating congealed blood, woman. What did you expect?'

Stronge shrugged and returned to the case. 'Here's an idea: what if it wasn't the perp snorting the powder? What if it was the vic? A lot of users in her profession, a lot of damaged people. Drugs help them blot out the pain.'

I had a muse on that. 'I don't think so. I offered her a drink back at the office and she turned me down.'

'What does that have to do with anything? Any woman with a brain in her head would turn *you* down.'

Stronge was missing the point, but willfully so.

'I'm saying she didn't strike me as an addict. Too in control. Too collected. No, that gear belonged to our man, I'm sure of it.'

While Stronge thought on that, Frank sought to seize on the distraction and attempted to sneak some black pudding off her plate; black pudding being one of the few things he eats beside brains (no doubt because of its offal-like quality). His thievery was met with a sharp slap to the back of the hand. He recoiled from Stronge wearing a face like a dog caught with a chewed-up slipper in his mouth, head hung with guilt, eyes askance.

'I thought you said that food tasted bad,' I put in.

'It does,' Stronge replied, plugging a mouthful of pudding into her gob and barely managing to talk around it, 'but I didn't say I wasn't hungry.'

While she chowed down, I cogitated on the drug clue. Tali never said anything about her killer huffing dust, and she would have mentioned it if she'd seen it. I had her give me a blow-by-blow of the evening after I agreed to take her case, and nothing like that came up. My thinking: the killer must have broken out his stash after he put a bullet in her head but before her soul exited her cadaver. So he wasn't amping himself up for the murder, he was rewarding himself for a job well done. Except… why would he stick around at the scene of the crime after he fired the shot? Who could celebrate with that much heat coming around the corner? Something didn't add up, but since the drug was the only lead on offer, it needed chasing down.

'This ironclad stuff; we need to find out who dealt it to the suspect and lean on them. Get them to tell us everything they know about the bloke.'

If the drug was as rare as Stronge said it was, that meant the supply of it was limited, and the number of outlets to purchase it from was scarce. So long as there were only a few people slinging the stuff, there was a good chance our guy was no stranger to his dealer. Maybe even more than that. Could be the two had built up trust and traded some personal information. The kind of information I had a real yearning for.

As usual, Stronge was a step ahead of me. She produced a slim manilla envelope from her handbag.

'What's that?' I asked.

'Our dealer.' She emptied out the envelope and placed a stack of paperwork in front of me. It was a rap sheet, thick as my thumb. 'The only source of ironclad in London, far as we can tell.'

'Hang about, if you've brought along a grubby little dossier on this bloke then you already know he was dealing to the perp, not the vic. So what was all that stuff about, "damaged people blotting out the pain"?'

'Just testing to make sure you had your eye on the ball.'

I could have railed against that, but I chose to take it in the spirit it was intended. 'Always happy to show you a keen mind in action.'

Stronge tipped me a well-natured nod then removed a paperclip from the corner of the stack of paper. She spread the leaves out across the table so I could get a better look, and I leaned forward to examine them closer. Among the notes I saw mugshots of a short, unsightly man with a bulbous, bald head. When I say "short", I mean he looked like he was kneeling on his shoes. And by bulbous, I mean absolutely huge: a sniper's dream.

'Eaaaaaaves,' groaned Frank, jabbing a stiff finger at the ugly mug on the table (the photo, not the chipped crockery Stronge was drinking from, which—on closer inspection—had lipstick on the rim that didn't match the colour she was wearing).

'What's he on about?' asked Stronge.

'He's saying your man there is an eaves.' I waited for a reaction but got nothing. 'They're a race of information gatherers. They look like this feller—like a man and a mole-rat were in a car wreck and got mashed together. Gobs full of itty-bitty fangs.'

Stronge gave me a withering look. 'I've been in this game long enough to know what a bloody eaves is, thank you very much. That's not what my silence was in aid of. What I'm saying is, if the bloke we booked had a mouthful of razor-sharp teeth, don't you think we'd have picked up on that?'

Again, a fair point. An Uncanny selling gear to another Uncanny made a certain kind of sense, but their needle-like fangs did leave a definite impression, both in the mind and in the flesh of anyone unfortunate enough to cross them. No way there wouldn't be a record of that on his blotter.

'Okay, forget the eaves thing. Why don't you save me some reading and tell me what you've got on this shitehawk?'

Stronge necked a bolt of coffee and filled me in. 'The drugs squad booked him a couple of months back for slinging 'clad, but couldn't get a conviction. We know he's dirty, though, and we know he's up to his old tricks. We also know where he's operating from.'

'Okay, now we're motoring. We find this dealer, grill him, and see what he knows about our perp. So where's his spot?'

Stronge didn't need to consult the rap sheet for the answer, she already had it committed to memory. 'He works out of a hardcore fetish club called F*I*S*T.'

That rang a bell. A loud one. 'I know that place.'

Stronge's eyebrow kicked up for the second time.

'Don't give me that look,' I cut in quick. 'I was there for a job, that's all.'

A smirk slithered through her lips. 'Whatever you say, friend. Whatever you say.'

Frank laughed his dumb laugh again and received another slap to the head for his trouble.

CHAPTER FIVE: NOCTURNAL SAFARI

'TELL me again why we need to have your warmed-over corpse with us,' Stronge whispered, shuffling uncomfortably in Frank's shadow as we waited our turn in the heaving queue outside F*I*S*T. 'No offence,' she added, giving Frank an apologetic pat on the back of his hand.

'Me and him are partners now,' I replied, hovering invisibly by her side, 'the brains and the brawn. I'm good for the sneaky stuff, but if we're going to walk into a place full of perverts with whips and chains, I'd sooner go in heavy.'

Frank grunted in agreement and ground his hands together, one a pestle, the other the mortar.

The queue lurched forward a step and we followed. It would be a while before we made it to the door. Thankfully, the rain had taken the night off, so my companions were spared a drenching. Me, I dance between the raindrops.

'What if someone figures out there's something wrong with him?' said Stronge, nodding at Frank. 'Again, no offence.'

When I inhabit Frank, his skin takes on a rosy glow and his muscles behave better, which has the effect of straightening up his gait and stopping his face looking like he suffered a stroke. Working in tandem, we look, to all intents and purposes, alive. Separated, Frank looks like what he is: a walking dead man.

'No one freaked out when they saw him in the café this morning, did they?' I pointed out, 'and the strip lights are so bright in there it's like getting an X-ray. This is London, Kat. No one cares about anyone but themselves. Besides, Frank's hardly going to raise eyebrows in a place where people are openly having it off and torturing each other. No one's looking this way now, and you're basically standing under a streetlight having an argument with yourself.'

Stronge cast a look around at the assorted weirdos and deviants we were shuffling in line with, none of whom gave the bloke in the trenchcoat with the spidery black veins showing through his raw chicken skin a second look. 'Fair enough,' she said, conceding the point.

'The bigger issue here is how we handle this once we get inside. Assuming the dealer's home, we need to think about how we get him to spill the beans.'

'How do you mean?'

I gave her a flinty look. 'The bloke we're after is dangerous. If the dealer knows him, he'll know that too, and he won't want to get in his bad books.'

'You get that I interview criminals for a living, right?'

'Yeah, under lab conditions, but this little chat ain't happening in a police interrogation room. We can't be working to the letter of the law here. We're going to have to colour outside the lines if we want to bring this killer in, because we both know he's not going to stop at one dead hooker.'

Stronge didn't like the sound of that, I could see it written all over her face.

'Yes, we have a killer on our hands, but that doesn't mean we get to go rogue.'

I laughed. 'You're working with a ghost and an upright corpse, mate. I reckon the boat's already sailed on that one.'

Stronge rubbed her temples, a sure sign that she was reaching her limit with me. 'I intend to play by the book in there, and I need to know that the both of you will do the same. So?'

Frank nodded like a pigeon pecking at a hunk of fresh bread. Stronge turned her attention to me, convinced that I was ready to cut corners if it meant getting to our killer faster, which, of course, I was. Thankfully, I was spared having to admit that by the sudden appearance of the club's doorman. It seemed we'd finally shambled our way to the front of the queue.

'Two?' asked a corned beef statue with a samurai topknot and the jawbone mic, looking to Stronge and Frank, his eyes passing right through me.

'Yes,' said Stronge, taken by surprise but adjusting quickly.

She'd chosen not to announce that she was police in case the bouncers were aware of the dealer's activities and were willing to usher him out of the back door at the first sign of trouble. It wasn't uncommon for club staff to turn a blind eye to dealers operating on their premises in exchange for a cut of the profits.

The bouncer sized Stronge up. 'You know what kind of place this is, sweetheart?'

'Yes,' she replied curtly.

'You don't look the type.' And she really didn't in her sensible trousers and practical shoes.

'Sorry to disappoint.'

The goon squared his impressive shoulders as he gave Stronge and her companion a look like a scientist peering through a microscope at a particularly troubling specimen. 'Is he all right?' he asked.

Frank returned a crooked grin. 'Hiiiiiii,' he groaned, one eye swivelling unnaturally in its socket.

'He's fine,' said Stronge, snaking an arm around Frank's waist and pulling him close.

Must be nice, I thought, a bit of actual human contact. Some guys get all the luck.

The bouncer looked like he might have more to say on the matter, but the night was young and the line was long.

'Go on then,' he said, forgoing a pat down and waving them in.

No doubt he assumed Frank was off his nut on something, which, going by some of the gurning faces we'd seen on our way in, was par for the course at this place. It also made Frank a potential customer if we were right about the dealer being on site, which probably meant a nice bung for the bloke at the door.

I followed Stronge as she headed inside, paid for two tickets, and led Frank to the basement. The noise coming up the stairs was a kind that didn't exist back when I was pulling air: an ear-mangling bedlam that sounded like a gunfight in a bell factory.

The stairs bottomed out into a cavernous room crammed with bodies squeezed into leather and rubber. A grey blanket of dry ice hugged the ground, and up above, a mirror ball shaped like a human skull swarmed the scene with pinpricks of silver light. A heaving dancefloor writhed with porn stars and drug fiends and performative Satanists, all of them letting loose like the end was nigh, like demons were marching on the streets of London and hellfire had boiled the Thames away. Bodies nuzzled and licked and grinded, packed together like some insane meat puzzle. I'm telling you, Buffalo Bill could have crafted a Milan fashion parade out of the amount of skin on show.

Seeing these people made me glad they'd found one another. Not because I was being community-spirited, but because I liked the idea of them all being contained in one place. This was where they belonged. Not out there in the wider world, but here in this sordid den of iniquity where they could only hurt each other.

If that sounds prudish, I'm sorry. You have to understand, a lot has happened to the world since I died: technologically, politically, and especially culturally. I've only been dead since 2007, but to me it feels like a century ago. Sometimes I look at the things going on around me and I don't even know where I am. I'm still on this earth, but I'm not really a part of it anymore, not the everyday life part, anyway. I don't mingle with normal people now, and even if I did, I doubt any of our preoccupations would overlap. I'm a ghost who hunts killers for a living; that's something not many folks can relate to. And so, soon enough, I gave up trying. I lost touch. I let the world slip away and buried myself in my work.

But I'm trying. Trying really hard to become a better, more open-minded ghost. To stow away some of my more enduring prejudices and get with the times. I don't want to wind up on the scrap heap, some knackered old relic. I refuse to go out that way: expiring at a rate of inches, a slow, creeping extinction. A death inside a death. And besides, who am I to judge these people? Sure, the woman in the pig mask gyrating around a stripper pole wasn't the conventional sort, nor was the bloke in the nappy snorting cocaine off the back of his pet boa constrictor, but in a lot of ways, I had more in common with these freaks than I did the people outside. I was a phantom, a doomed soul, a creature of the night. That made me more like the patrons of this club than it did the buttoned-down souls on the street above, checking their socials and hurrying to their appointments.

Together with Stronge, we took a recce of the club, pushing through—or, in my case, *passing through*—the throng, trying to lay eyes on the bulb-headed pusher man. We covered every inch of the dance floor and its surrounding area, probed every corner, nosed our way into every nook, booth, and annex. The tour came to an end in the last place anyone would want to be: the blokes' lav.

The bogs were just what you'd expect of a nightclub convenience: walls covered in ugly graffiti and a floor that was more swamp than tile. The sound of a couple going at it hammer and tongs leaked out of a nearby cubicle, but that was nothing unusual, it was that sort of place. The only thing that really stuck out was the toilet attendant in a waistcoat who stood in front of a row of miniature aftershaves and a tip jar. An attendant who was a dead ringer for the mugshots Stronge had shown us back at the café.

We had our dealer. Posing as a bathroom attendant seemed like an odd choice for a pusher of high-end product, but on second thought, it was the perfect disguise. I mean, who looks twice at the toilet guy? He could work this place, scope out clients in an intimate setting, and remain completely invisible. At least, that was the idea. At the moment we walked in on him, his presence was anything but discreet. In fact, he was the most noticeable thing in the room besides the couple going at it in the toilet cubicle, being as he was engaged in a tense disagreement that had turned physical.

A slim young man dressed in jeans and a bulky hoodie towered over him, fingers wrapped around his neck, veins on the back of his hands bulging.

'You conned me,' he cried, spittle flying as he screamed into the attendant's big, moony face. His voice was thick with menace but gilded with class. Whoever he was, he grew up a long way from the gutter. 'This is your fault,' he barked, tightening his grip further still. 'Do you get that? This is on you.'

The red-faced attendant fought back, pounding his fists against his attacker's chest. When that didn't work, he slipped a hand into the pocket of his waistcoat, pulled a switchblade, and plunged it into the man's belly.

It happened so fast. There was no chance to intervene. One second we were rounding a corner to where the sinks were, the next, a man had a knife sticking out of his guts. He staggered back a couple of steps and turned to us with watery eyes.

Watery violet eyes.

'Help me,' he gasped.

'That's him,' I said. 'That's our guy.'

Not only had we tracked down the dealer, by a total fluke we'd cornered the suspect too, hand in the cookie jar, right up to his frigging elbow.

'Both of you on the ground, right now,' Stronge hollered, pulling a Taser (the hand-held, whack 'em and zap 'em variety).

The dealer did as he was told, but the perp stayed upright, clutching his stomach. I could hardly blame him, either—that floor was grim, and he was wearing an open wound.

Stronge was about to repeat her demand when the toilet door burst open and we swivelled around to see a trio of bouncers pouring in, all of them dressed in black, each sporting thick arms and raw knuckles.

Seemed we were right about the security in this place being dirty.

CHAPTER SIX: THE HARD STUFF

FROM THAT POINT, things went downhill faster than a greased bobsled.

Stronge was pulling her badge and preparing to identify herself when the girl going at it in the toilet stall kicked open the door and legged it, knocking the detective's ID from her hand and sending it rafting through the sludge below. The bloke she was knocking boots with was quick to follow, accidentally hoofing the wallet under the door of a separate cubicle as he bolted from the bathroom, tackle flying in the wind.

Stronge got as far as saying, 'Stand down, I'm an off—' before the wind was knocked from her lungs by the man in the hoodie, who—despite being wounded—barged into her from behind and slipped between the bouncers, disappearing into the belly of the club.

Again, Stronge attempted to let security know that she was an officer of the law, and again her words were cut short, swallowed up by the din coming through the toilet door. The only message the bouncers received was that an armed woman was making trouble in their establishment, and that message was received loud and clear. The three of them closed in on Stronge and Frank, but despite the numbers, I knew they could take care of themselves. Priority one was apprehending the suspect.

'Go,' Stronge ordered, and I didn't need telling twice.

I phased through the wall of meatheads and gave swift pursuit.

Back in the club, I caught a glimpse of the man in the hoodie, peeling out like a scalded cat. He cast a look over his shoulder and saw me emerging from the body of an overweight woman wearing nothing but a couple of bits of strategically-placed Gaffa tape. We locked eyes. Whatever this bloke was, he could see ghosts, which meant he could most likely damage them, too. I wasn't about to let that slow me down, though.

I cut through the crowd like a knife, closing the distance between us, gaining ground. He wasn't going to make it to the stairs before I was on top of him, least of all with a gut wound, but he didn't need to. From the waistband of his jeans he pulled a pistol, no doubt the same one he'd used to plug my client. He levelled the gun at me and its metal flashed under the frantic pulse of a strobe light. For a moment I thought he was about to waste a bullet on an apparition, but he had other ideas.

Crack.

A shot rang out, spitting red and blowing a hole through the mirror ball above. Chaos reigned as glass showered the dancefloor and panicking clubbers caught sight of the weapon. A surge of sweaty bodies made a stampede for the exit, breaking my sightline to the suspect. By the time a gap I could see through appeared, the man in the hoodie had evaporated.

But all was not lost. Using the power of translocation, I could take a shortcut to the club's front door, cutting him off at the pass. Emphasis there on the word "could", because for some reason my disappearing trick short-circuited, leaving me right where I was standing. I tried again but remained rooted to the spot. What the hell?

So I went after the perp the old-fashioned way, bounding up the stairs two steps at a time, but when I arrived in the lobby I saw he'd already cut and run. No sign of him on the street outside and no one around to tell me which way he took off. I looked for a blood trail but the spots he left ended at the coat check area. A clothes hanger lay discarded on the counter, suggesting he'd grabbed a garment on his way out—a scarf maybe—and used it as a makeshift bandage.

The suspect was in the wind. Instead of letting him bleed out on a filthy toilet floor—which you might consider a fitting end for a murderer—I'd inadvertently allowed him to escape and most likely saved his life. Not my best work, I think you'll agree.

'Fuck,' I cried, taking a swing at a lamp post and meeting zero resistance.

Still pissing blood but regaining some degree of restraint, I remembered my colleagues, last seen doing battle with three security guards in the men's facilities. I raced back downstairs, across the crushed remains of the mirror ball, and saw the door to the gents explode outwards. The bouncers toppled out like bowled skittles and Frank came after them, chin tucked into his chest like a charging bull. The doormen staggered to their feet to collect their senses and were quickly joined by two more meatheads with the smell of blood in their nostrils. The music was switched off, leaving behind a brittle, ominous silence. For the last time, Stronge attempted to assert her credentials, but the ship had well and truly sailed by this point. The archangel Gabriel could have flown down bearing a scroll from God Himself and this lopsided ruckus would still have gone ahead.

Time to even the odds. I took a run at the burliest of the bouncers (the one with the topknot we met at the door) and went to take possession of his body. Instead of fusing with the bloke's corporeal form and seizing control of his walnut brain, I met him like a brick wall and made friends with the floor. First translocation failed me, now it seemed my possession powers were on the fritz. Something was seriously wrong, but there was no time to run an MOT. For now, I'd have to hope it was a temporary glitch and make do with the classics.

Time to take a ride in the Frank tank.

I stepped into Frank and the two of us became one. It was only once I'd taken a seat in the back of his mind that I realised what I'd done: taken control of a physical form. How was it that I was able to jump into Frank's skull but not the other guy's? Was it strength of will on the bouncer's part, or was it something else? Merging with Frank was something I didn't even have to think about at this point, like shrugging on a comfy old jacket. With a stranger there was more to it; I had to force my way in and kick them out of the driver's seat. With Frank, I called shotgun and the two of us shared the wheel. Maybe that's why I could possess him, because he was a willing participant. Because Frank knows that we complement each other. Together, me and him are what you might call a Gestalt entity: greater than the sum of our parts. He provides the muscle and I add a little extra mind.

Speaking of which…

One of the bouncers came steaming at me, all wide like an angry pufferfish. Rather than tackle him head-on, I employed a bit of savvy, used Frank's gorilla strength to wrench a stripper pole from its moorings, and gave the bouncer a bloody good hiding with it. He kissed the ground goodnight and sent some teeth spinning across the dancefloor.

I rounded on the next muscle Mary in line. 'Come on then, you got the sprouts for it?'

He dithered, but one of his colleagues decided to take the plunge. Stronge gave him a taste of her Taser and sent him down with a few more volts than he needed. I was about to thank her for the assist when a third bouncer snuck up from behind and laid a real peach on me. The pain ricocheted off my high teeth, but it wasn't enough to turn my lights out. I swung my makeshift quarterstaff in a wide half-moon, sweeping my attacker's legs out from under him and leaving him on his ear.

The next guy I was ready for. He threw a hefty dig, but I backed up a step, leaving his fist tugging air. Before he could follow up with a left, I swung the pole down at the top of his skull, dropping him to his knees like a James Brown closer.

Topknot was the last man standing, but he'd seen enough.

'Fuck this,' he said, and turned tail.

Apparently, his salary didn't justify the cost of taking this thing all the way, so he toddled off and took his poncy haircut with him.

CHAPTER SEVEN: LOW-LIFES AND NO-LIFES

IT WAS JUST us white hats left in the game now, or at least that's what I thought before I heard a pitiful moan on the other side of the dancefloor and saw someone splayed out across the ruins of a busted chair. I took him for a bouncer at first, coming to from his drubbing, but when we approached the groaning figure we found the bulb-headed dealer, curled up foetal style and gripping his leg. He was obviously in a good deal of distress. Closer examination revealed that the lower portion of his right leg was broken.

'What happened to you?' I asked.

He didn't answer, but he didn't need to. It didn't take a genius to figure out that he'd been sucked under the tide of escaping revellers and trampled.

The suspect was gone, but we got what we came for. Maybe this evening wasn't going to be a total wash-out after all.

I peeled away from Frank, stepping out of him like a hermit crab vacating its shell.

'Do us a favour, Frank, go shut the door upstairs and make sure we don't get any visitors.'

Frank nodded and ambled away, but the dealer's eyes stayed on me. Something wasn't right with this feller. Either he had the Sight or he wasn't human, and with his oddly-proportioned body and skin the colour of rancid lard, something told me it wasn't the first one.

I dropped to my haunches, hooked a thumb under his top lip, and peeled it back.

'Frank was right,' I said, beckoning Stronge closer.

She took a knee and examined my find. The dealer's teeth had been blunted, filed down to stumps so he could pass for human.

'He's an eaves after all,' said Stronge.

The filed-down teeth explained why the police blotter didn't say anything about him packing a set of piranha fangs.

'Well, what have you got to say for yourself?' I asked him.

He let go of his leg and held his hands out in front of him, fingers twitching like a gunslinger in a spaghetti western.

'What is that?' asked Stronge, stiffening and drawing back. 'Is he casting a spell?'

I cocked my head to get a better look. 'No, that's not magic. That's sign language.'

'You know sign language?'

I cut her some eyes. 'I can read ancient Aramaic. Why wouldn't I know a bit of Makaton?'

Stronge's shoulders hitched in a *fair enough* way. 'So what's he saying?'

'Right now he's saying he needs a hospital, which adds up.'

Stronge nodded and slid a hand into her gilet, searching for her phone.

'Put it away, will you?' I said. 'We've got questions to ask before the ambo gets here.'

'Look at him. He needs medical—'

'I've got this, okay?'

Stronge's lips turned paper-thin. 'Go on then, get it over with.'

I returned my attention to the eaves and showed him some signs of my own. After a bit of broken back and forth, I determined that he did what he did—dealing drugs—because he wasn't able to do much else. He was deaf. An eaves trades gossip for magic, which they need the same way most people need food, and when you're born without a working set of ears, gossip ain't easy to come by. You need to find some other way to earn your fill. It's do or die for a deaf eaves, and this one chose *do*.

I hadn't even asked him about the suspect yet, but I'd already learned our man had magic at his disposal. That was a start. I wondered what else I could turn up if I gave the thumbscrews a twist.

Who is the man with the purple eyes? I signed.

The eaves didn't reply. It seemed he'd suddenly developed a bad case of finger cramp.

I was considering my next move when Stronge cut in.

'Why don't you just possess him and get some answers that way?'

It was a fair question. Just because I couldn't make it work with that bouncer didn't mean I couldn't feather a nest in this guy. Except, as it turns out, it did. I tried to infiltrate him, but his body was a closed shop. My disembodied spirit and his mortal form collided like two positively-charged magnets, repelling each other and bouncing in opposite directions.

'Something wrong?' asked Stronge, seeing the face I was making.

'Having a bit of trouble with the old mind-over-matter right now.'

'But you managed with Fran—'

'Yeah, I know.'

I turned back to the squirming eaves and gave him a no-nonsense stare. 'Are you gonna tell me what I need to know or am I going to have to start snapping fingers?' I asked, mouthing it in such a way that even a blind person could have followed along.

Stronge raised a concern. 'Given that sign language is his only way of talking, is that such a good idea?'

Honestly. Everyone's a critic these days.

'Fine.' I stood up and raised a foot. 'Last chance, Sonny Jim. Speak now or forever hold your peace.'

He returned a two-fingered salute that required no translation, so I ground a heel into his injured leg. The eaves' mouth fell open and a scream punched out of his throat.

'What the hell are you doing?' cried Stronge.

'Just a spot of light torture.'

She placed herself between me and the eaves; a symbolic gesture, really, given that I could go through her like a bulldozer through a cobweb.

'I'm police, you idiot. I can't be part of this, and definitely not in this climate.'

'Okay, I'm sorry, that was wrong,' I said, showing her my hands. 'We should just kill him.'

I drew my claw hammer and raised it high, lining up a swing at the eaves' skull.

That got him talking.

Signing so fast that I had to ask him to slow it down, the eaves told us what he knew about our guy. It turned out to be very little. Apparently, this was only the second time he'd had dealings with the man in the hoodie. The first time, he bought a wrap and paid on the spot, no problem. The second time—tonight—he came in raving about being sold a bad dose and trying to strangle him. The eaves told me that was bullshit, that the 'clad he sold was primo, uncut stuff. I told him I wasn't interested in his Yelp score.

What did he mean when he said it was your fault? I asked, remembering the overheated conversation in the toilets.

The eaves said he didn't know. That the guy probably did something he regretted and wanted to make it someone else's fault.

What is he? I asked, *And where do I find him?*

The eaves told me he had no idea what he was or where he was, and I believed him. If he knew more he'd have coughed it up the second he saw that hammer bearing down on him.

'What's he saying?' asked Stronge, uncomfortable with my methods but eager to hear what I'd extracted.

'Not a lot,' I admitted.

Stronge was beginning to look as fed up as I did. 'If he doesn't have an ID on the killer, get him to tell you some more about the drug he's slinging. If we know what the perp's getting out of it, we might be able to use that to build a profile.'

It was worth a shot. The eaves' knee was the size of a ripe watermelon now, and I had a feeling he'd say just about anything to be left alone.

What does ironclad do? I asked.

The eaves explained that the drug got its users amped up; made them feel invulnerable, removed all sense of fear. In the head of someone high on the stuff, they could never die. Big whoop, I thought. Being everlasting was my day-to-day, but I didn't go around slotting escorts.

What's it made of? I asked.

He signed back, fingers going nineteen to the dozen. *You don't know? It's Uncanny. Made of fairies.*

I learned that 'clad was the latest strain of a drug that first started doing the rounds in Brighton. I'd heard barside rumours about the stuff making its way from the coast to the city, and it seemed this was the proof. The drug's active component was ground-up fairy brains, the kind belonging to the rotten little toe rags that swarm the sewers beneath most major cities, especially this one. I also learned that the eaves really, really wanted to pay a visit to the hospital, and since I'd exhausted my line of questioning, I saw no reason to keep him. A quick catch-up with Stronge and she made the 999 call.

Okay, so here's what we'd learned so far: the person we were after was three things:

- A spell-slinger
- someone who got high on fairy dust
- and someone who definitely wasn't shy about offering customer feedback.

That really didn't give us much to go on. I was about ready to call this bust… well, a bust, but then Frank showed up with something in his hand.

'What have you got there?'

He unfurled his mitt to reveal a smartphone. He gave it a sniff.

I smiled. 'Is this what I think it is?'

He bobbed his head.

'Good boy,' I said, laying a slap on his back.

'What's going on?' asked Stronge, as baffled as she was aggravated.

'Seems our man dropped his mobile on the way out,' I replied.

'And we know that how?'

'Trust me. Nose of a bloodhound, this feller.'

Stronge took the device from Frank and swiped a thumb over it, but it refused to open without face ID. 'I need to get this to the station and have our tech boys crack it open.'

I scanned the corners of the room and found a CCTV camera pointed at the dancefloor, right at the spot the suspect had unloaded his gun.

'I've got a better idea,' I said.

CHAPTER EIGHT: A SHORT, SHARP SHOCK

THE BEEHIVE PUB is hidden behind a magical construct that acts as a sort of supernatural paywall. Unless you're a patron, or know someone who is, you're not getting into the place. That's how things are around these parts: impenetrable barriers stand between the ordinary and the Uncanny, between the city that's on show and the secret streets beyond. One step is all it takes to move between these worlds, but unless you know how to make the jump, it may as well be a million miles. You might only be a hidden door away from the impossible, but that doesn't mean you get to see it. Not unless you know where the doors are and how to get them open.

Stronge marvelled at the blind alley that revealed itself behind the improbable facade Frank and I guided her through.

'You know what gets me most about all this?' she said, eyes gaping. 'It's that the nutters in tinfoil hats were right all along.'

'Doesn't mean they're not dickheads, though.'

She nodded sagely. By the time we arrived at the pub, which was marked only by a nondescript door decorated with the faded image of a beehive, Stronge was all business again.

'Okay, so insane alley that doesn't exist on any maps aside, what are we doing here?'

'Patience, my apprentice,' I said.

Ever the gentleman, Frank pushed open the door to the boozer and we stepped inside.

Nothing about the place had changed since the last time I was there, but that was nothing new. Trying to mark progress at The Beehive was like watching a video of something that moved so slowly you'd swear you were looking at a still image. All the same faces were present, perched on the same old weathered stools and chairs. A group of gamblers rolled bones in one corner, while another chucked arrows at the dartboard on the opposite side of the saloon, just like always. The locals were a motley assortment of oddballs and ne'er do wells—a stacked Pokémon deck of freaks and monsters—but despite their differences, a sense of solidarity reigned. Always did. The Beehive reminded me of a behind-the-scenes story I once heard about those old *Planet of the Apes* movies. Apparently, the actors playing the titular apes ate lunch wearing their makeup, and without ever talking about it, would instinctively sit with their own kind. Orangutans ate with orangutans, chimpanzees with chimpanzees, gorillas with gorillas. That's just the way of the world. People are tribal, they stick with their own kind. It's no different with Uncannies and normals. We tip our elbows in our world, and you do the same in yours.

And yet, tonight a little of the outside had found its way into The Beehive's hallowed walls. Not just Detective Stronge, but something even more unusual than that: a 75-inch flat screen TV. Lenny, the pub's towering landlord, was busy mounting the incongruous device on a wall bracket; a process overseen by a congregation of dissatisfied faces and shaking heads. Apparently, the introduction of a television was causing no small amount of consternation to the regulars, who were leery of anything newfangled finding its way into their favourite drinking hole.

'Never thought I'd see the day,' griped a boozy satyr, stomping a hoof in frustration.

'What's next?' asked an irate troll with slate grey skin and a nose that had been broken more times than an office printer. 'A fruit machine?'

'A pox on your teevee,' screeched a drunken hag making ancient signs with her gnarled hands and laying a hex on the detested contraption.

I didn't see the problem myself, but the way this lot was behaving, anyone would think Lenny had painted a floating corpse on a Monet.

'Pipe down,' he growled, turning to face the crowd and wielding a screwdriver like a prison shiv. 'You don't like it, you know where the door is.'

Lenny knew he had the upper hand. The Beehive was pretty much the only game in town as far as working-class Uncanny drinking holes went, so there was no chance of him losing any customers no matter how much they griped and groaned.

'Thought so,' he said, staring down the dissenters, who went back to their drinks and their games of chance before they wound up getting barred.

Lenny switched on the TV, found a channel showing the snooker, and returned to his place behind the beer-soaked bar. His coarse hair rubbed the ceiling as he traversed the saloon, raining flakes of stucco into people's drinks, none of whom said a word about it.

I approached the bar and got a round in. 'Evening, Lenny. A pint of O'Ghouls for me, a Guinness for Frank, and a shandy for the lady.'

Without breaking eye contact with the TV, Lenny used his walnut-knuckled hand to work the pumps and draw off three glasses. Having topped one off with a bolt of flat lemonade, he leaned over the counter and set the drinks down. I placed a note in front of him and he scraped it into the till as if providing change was a foreign courtesy.

'I always look forward to our little chats, Lenny.'

Nevertheless, I decided to cut our thrilling dialogue short and rejoin my companions. Frank did the honours, carefully transporting our drinks to the pub's last empty table, where the three of us sat ourselves down.

'Chin chin,' I said, clinking my glass against my companions'.

Frank downed his stout in one smooth motion and let out a satisfied burp. I'd seen him do that with eight pints in a row and not seem any worse for wear, but then he was a staggerer by nature.

Stronge took a sip of her drink. 'Shandy? Seriously?'

'You're welcome,' I replied, ignoring her ingratitude.

'Are you going to tell me what we're doing here?' she asked. 'I hope it's not for the atmos, because there's a very threatening aura about this place.'

'How do you mean?'

'Haven't you noticed that everyone's bogging at us?' she said, peering over the rim of her pint at the natives eyeballing our table.

'Oh, they're not looking at us,' I replied.

'They're not?'

'No, they're looking at *you*.'

I explained how bringing a normal into The 'Hive was considered a bit of a breach of protocol, but that she shouldn't worry. Though the reception was likely to be a bit frosty, I was there to vouch for her if push came to shove.

'Let me get this straight,' she said, 'these people are fine with a rotting corpse and a ghost hanging about the place, but me they have a problem with?'

'Yup. So be on your best behaviour, eh?'

I had a butcher's of the room and spotted someone I'd never seen gracing Lenny's gaff before. Hunched over a corner booth and dressed in a cheap suit was a stick-thin figure with webbed fingers the length of steak knives. His blood-red eyes were aimed my way, but darted to the snooker match the moment he clocked me looking back at him. He was one of the dodgy toe-rags I'd caught tailing me the other night, I was sure of it.

'Hey, Frank, see over there, is that—'

But before I could seek my partner's counsel, something flat and black came crashing down on the table, obliterating Stronge's shandy and soaking ten square feet of pub. To my immense surprise —and I'm sure everyone else's—the head of a garden shovel laid in front of us. Attached to the other end of it was a squat, muscular figure wearing a pointy cloth cap and a white beard stained nicotine yellow at the tips. Apparently we'd gone and pissed off a gnome, and a particularly belligerent one at that.

He aimed a stubby finger at Stronge. 'Gerrer out of 'ere,' he slurred, obviously well into his cups.

Stronge went to give him some verbal, but I stopped her before she could open her mouth. You have to pick your words carefully in these situations. Your chances of being killed by a gnome are low, but never zero.

'Why don't you sit back down and we'll forget this happened?' I suggested, turning my hand temporarily corporeal and hitching it to his shoulder.

He batted it aside and made a face like a smacked arse. 'Gerrer out of 'ere or you and me are gonna 'ave ructions.'

Something told me Stronge wasn't the real issue here. It seemed to me that the gnome was taking his anger at the unwanted appearance of a TV set and transferring it to the next available target, in this case, the out-of-towner.

'Keep your shirt tucked in, mate,' I told him. 'No need to get in a flap.'

I looked to the bar to see what Lenny intended to do about the trouble brewing in his establishment, but going by the look on his face—eyes coloured green by the reflected baize of a televised snooker table—the answer to that question was, "Not an awful lot".

'I come 'ere to 'ave a drink in peace,' the gnome went on, little bits of spit forming in the corners of his mouth. 'If I wanted to mingle with scum, I'd have gone to Wetherspoons.'

His fingers tightened around the handle of his shovel. Frank rose to his feet and shot him a look so clear that it didn't need backing up with words.

I stayed seated and kept my eyes on the gnome. 'How about you toddle off to the bar and get the lady another drink? Unless you want my friend here to forget his manners.'

But the gnome wasn't backing down. Instead of doing the sensible thing and crawling back under his rock, he took up his shovel and hefted it over his head like a fairgoer swinging a test your strength hammer. Frank wasn't having that. Catching the feller unawares, he grabbed his chin with one hand and his opposite temple with the other before cranking his head 180 degrees. There was a sickening crunch, then the gnome hit the ground with his noggin facing the other way.

'Jesus Christ,' cried Stronge, firing out of her seat and staggering backwards into a table of card players, upsetting their game.

With no hurry in his step whatsoever, Lenny ambled over from the bar, sighed, and ejected the gnome's limp body through the pub's front door and into the half-light of the dank alleyway beyond, where it landed with a dull crunch.

'Keep your hair on, will you?' I told Stronge as Frank led her by the elbow back to her chair. 'You're showing us right up.'

'*Showing us up?*' she said, her mouth wide as a guppy in a desert. 'A man just got murdered.'

'Don't be such a drama queen,' I replied, pointing to the grimy window that looked out onto the alley.

Outside, the gnome was peeling himself off the cobbles and staggering to his feet. He grabbed his head and gave it a sharp twist, setting it back in a forward-facing position.

'Be off with you,' boomed Lenny, one giant hand cupped to his mouth. 'And forget about your shovel, I'm keeping it until you learn to behave.'

Outside, the gnome grumbled something inaudible, hitched up his trousers, and sloped off down the alley.

I turned to Stronge. 'Tough bunch of lads, gnomes.'

Lenny visited our table, his great shadow falling upon us like an ill omen. 'What about you lot? You gonna keep your noses clean, or do you want chucking out as well?'

For some reason it was this line of questioning that spurred Stronge into action. She took to her feet and gave Lenny a firm poke in the ribs (there was some tiptoeing involved to achieve this).

'Talk to me like that again, I dare you,' she said.

'You what?' Lenny growled, taken aback.

Stronge produced a black leather wallet and flipped it open to show her police ID. 'See that? That says you better adjust your attitude unless you want to accompany me to the station. Got it?'

Lenny's face went blank as a weather-bald tombstone, then the slightest smile quirked his lips. A smile that was quickly followed by gales of uproarious laughter. Soon enough, the whole pub was joining in with the kind of unadulterated, pure hysterics that you'd be lucky to hear more than once in a lifetime.

Still laughing, Lenny headed back to his post behind the bar and drew off three fresh pints. 'These ones are on me,' he said, clutching his gut to calm the convulsions.

Stronge's behind landed heavily in her seat, her shoulders slumped. 'What just happened? Did I say something funny?'

'Are you serious?' I managed, slapping my knee. 'The last time Lenny laughed like that, the miners were striking. Drop the mic and step off the stage, Joan Rivers.'

I felt my eyes welling and wiped away a stray ectoplasmic tear. It was only then that I realised the long-fingered lurker in the corner booth had vanished from the pub and slinked off into the night.

CHAPTER NINE: THE GHOST IN THE MACHINE

By this point, Detective Stronge's patience had worn gossamer thin.

'Are you going to tell me what we're doing in this godforsaken place, or do I find out where you're supposed to be buried and stuff you back in the coffin myself?'

Stronge was something of a control freak, by which I mean working with her could often be less of a partnership than a dictatorship.

'Chill out, Kat,' I replied, raising my hands in surrender. 'We're here to meet someone: a friend of mine who can help with the case. An informant by the name of Shift.'

'Shift? Is that a he? A she?'

'Yes.'

'What do you mean "yes"? she asked icily.

'I mean both.'

Stronge pinched the bridge of her blade-thin nose and squeezed her eyes shut. 'What?'

Right on cue, Shift made a show, waltzing into the bar with an effortless saunter like the whole world was her red carpet. Heads turned and eyes tracked her progress across the saloon as she made her way to our table, flicking her poker-straight blonde hair over one shoulder as she went.

'How's it hanging, Fletcher?' she drawled in her cowpoke American accent.

'By a thread,' I replied, offering up a seat.

I cut a glance at Stronge and saw her eyebrows had almost disappeared into her hairline. Most likely she was busy wondering what this so-called friend of mine could possibly add to our investigation; a woman she'd no doubt already decided was half-idiot, half-tits.

Shift slipped into the vacant chair and placed a friendly hand on Frank's shoulder, her cherry red nail polish a stark contrast to the faded khaki of his stained trench coat. 'And how are you doing, Cookie?' she asked.

Frank grinned back at her, showing off his almost black gums. 'Hiiiii.'

'Don't take this the wrong way, handsome, but you're looking a little under the weather. Next time you're going by a salon, why don't you treat yourself to a glow up? Ain't nuthin' wrong with a little TLC.'

'He's a private investigator, not a contestant on *Drag Race*,' I said.

Shift feigned shock and emoted all the way to the back row, 'Is that a contemporary pop culture reference I hear? My Lord.'

Even though Shift has an innate ability to drive me around the bend, I really couldn't do without her. What she doesn't know about the things that go on in this town ain't worth knowing, but she provides much more than that. Shift is my sherpa through the minefield of modern life. Without her guiding hand, I'd be the relic of a bygone age, consigned to the metaphorical scrapheap.

Bringing our banter to a close with a good-natured wink, I moved the conversation onto more pressing matters. 'Don't suppose you saw a long-fingered geezer slip by you on the way in here, did you, Shift?'

'No, why?'

'I've picked up a tail: some ugly tosser and his ugly tosser mates following me and Frank about. Possibly vampires. Second time I've caught them sniffing my arse.'

Shift returned an uncertain look. 'I'll look into it. But before I get to that, who is *this* rare beauty?'

Stronge did a double-take before she realised she was the one being referred to. 'What? Me?'

'Yes, you, gorgeous! My, my, the boys must be tripping over

themselves to get to you. So long as they can get over the girls, anyway.'

Stronge's cheeks flushed flamingo pink. 'Oh, please...'

Shift went on, continuing to butter the detective's bread. 'Look at that face. You ever think about modelling, sweetheart?'

That was Shift: the kind of person who made everyone around her feel good about themselves, whether they wanted to or not.

Stronge hid her embarrassment behind the curtains of her bob. 'I think you need your eyes tested, but thank you anyway.'

I made some late introductions. 'Where are my manners? Shift, this is DCI Kat Stronge. Kat, this is my good friend, Shift.'

'So, you're a detective, huh? Brains *and* beauty. Ain't you the whole package.' She chuckled and patted the back of the detective's hand. 'You need to learn to take a compliment. From one gal to another.'

That last part had Stronge cutting eyes at me.

'Oh right,' I said, realising the source of her upset. 'You're wondering why I told you Shift was a her and a he.'

'I can take this one,' said Shift. 'See, I'm not a woman, Detective. Not technically. What you're looking at right now is a shapeshifter. A changeling.'

Stronge gave her a cool eye. 'A what?'

'A fetch. A skinwalker.'

'I don't understand,' said Stronge, her brow corrugating.

Shift offered me a shrug as if to say, *Shall I?* I gave her a nod back, and without further ado, she transformed.

The flesh that adorned her skull rippled like a lake dashed by a flat stone and settled into an altogether different arrangement. In the bat of an eyelid, Shift had metamorphosed from a white woman into a black man. The only thing that remained of the person who waltzed through the pub door was the blonde hair, though this was now cropped close to the skull and worn in tight afro curls.

Stronge looked even more astonished by Shift's transformation than she did when she saw the gnome with the broken neck get back up again. 'That's incredible,' she said, her half-full pint glass forgotten in her hand.

'Oh, that's nothing,' Shift replied, speaking in gravel-throated masculine tones now. 'Give me a minute and I'll do the whole Benetton rainbow for you.'

As fascinated as Stronge was by that prospect, she spoke with a note of caution. 'Wouldn't that be a bit... I don't know...?'

'Racist? I wouldn't know. I'm not human, so to me it's the difference between a horse and a zebra.'

Stronge barked a laugh. It was clear from the look of wide-eyed wonder she wore that she found Shift absolutely fascinating.

I leaned forward. 'Is that a smile, Kat? Careful, you'll pull a muscle.'

'Shut up,' came the double-barrelled reply.

I turned to Frank, shaking my head. 'Women.'

He avoided my gaze, refusing to be complicit—a traitor, maybe, but not an idiot.

Once again, Stronge steered us back to the matter at hand. 'Look, it's been lovely meeting you, Shift—'

'Ditto—'

'—But can someone please tell me what we're all doing here?'

'I was starting to wonder the same thing myself,' said Shift, turning to me. 'Well, why was I summoned, Fletcher? Surely not just for my sparkling personality?'

'I need your help on a case,' I explained.

'You sure you can afford me?'

'Don't worry. You'll get your fee in full.'

The truth was, funds were running pretty low. Most of the money I had socked away had been spent renovating the office, and work had been thin on the ground lately. Matter of fact, I was starting to feel like someone had dug an alligator-infested moat around the business to keep the punters away. None of which Shift needed to know.

'All right then, what have you got for me?' he asked.

I produced my phone and presented a photo I'd taken back at the nightclub. It was a photo of a monitor, or more specifically, a man on a monitor who'd been captured by a CCTV camera.

Shift looked at the image then back to me. 'What do you want me to do with this?'

I nodded to Frank, who produced a second phone and placed it on the table in front of Shift.

'That one belongs to a man we're looking for,' I explained. 'The man in the photo.'

Shift went to open the new phone and got shown a padlock icon. 'Locked, huh?'

'Yeah. Only opens up if it's shown the right face.' I wiggled my eyebrows. 'Don't suppose you know a good mimic, do you?'

The corners of Shift's lips drifted upward. Stronge's were quick to follow.

CHAPTER TEN: UP JUMPED THE DEVIL

FROM THE PHONE, we extracted an address marked *Home*. We were at the place within the hour. No sense hanging about; since we bungled our chance at a capture before, the suspect would be on high alert now. Might even be considering skipping town. We had to act fast if we wanted to bring him in this time.

The address the phone led us to was a sinkhole estate: a no-go site that had been scheduled for demolition for years but never torn down. It had been that way for a generation now, a Brutalist horror dusted with filth and shattered glass. Then again, the place was always an eyesore. The way the complex was laid out made it look as if it had been devised by an architect who designed prisons for a living. Squinting up at the imposing five-storey block, I could imagine burning mattresses raining down from its balconies and onto the open yard below.

If the suspect saw us coming he'd have ample opportunity to do a runner, and we couldn't afford to drop a bollock this time. Thankfully, it was late and raining by the time we reached the estate—the perfect setting for an ambush.

Stronge and I passed a puddle of melted tar that used to be a bin, jimmied open a boarded-up doorway, and made our way up an echoey concrete stairwell. According to the information we'd gleaned, our man lived on the building's top floor in a corner apartment. In any other place, that would have counted as a penthouse suite. Here, it would have been as much a source of shame as the rest of the block's miserable dwellings.

We arrived at the fifth floor and crept along a corridor littered with used syringes and other drug paraphernalia until we found what we were after. The apartment door was covered in chipped brown varnish and hung on a single rusted hinge. Through the gap between the door and the frame I could make out a flickering light, but no sound. I made a sign for Stronge to hold her ground, then ghosted through the front door and emerged on the other side.

The apartment was not what I expected. Not at all. Instead of a derelict squat I found a forest. A mass of thorny brambles with stalks as thick as my fingers had grown in through an open window and quilted almost every surface. Lumps beneath the thick briar suggested a smattering of furnishings, but I couldn't make out anything definitive. Then again, seeing wasn't exactly easy. The only illumination the apartment had was provided by tiny flames dotted strategically about the place. Set on the floor between gaps in the brambles, fresh candles stood upon the congealed, molten messes of their fallen comrades, struggling to shed light on the surroundings.

I noticed a convenient aisle running through the centre of the knee-high hedge in the lounge and cut a path through it, more out of habit than necessity. Breezing through the overgrown apartment, I moved from room to room until I'd made up my mind. The place was empty. Whether the killer was hiding elsewhere or had already blown the city, I couldn't be sure. All I knew for certain was, the bloke wasn't home.

'You might as well come in,' I said, calling to the corridor outside.

Stronge pushed open the apartment door—no small feat given the amount of foliage blocking it—and pressed her way inside. 'Bloody hell,' she said, taken aback by the indoor jungle. Taser in hand, she went about checking the corners. 'Any sign of him?'

'Not a sausage,' I replied.

Stronge grunted with frustration and clicked the button on a pocket Maglite. 'What is all this?' she asked.

'Buggered if I know.'

As Stronge's torch beam browsed the undergrowth, I could have sworn I saw the vegetation moving, swelling up and down like the rise and fall of a heaving chest, almost as if the room was breathing. A trick of the light. Had to be.

I stuck my head through the adjoining wall to get a look at the apartment next door and saw nothing unusual. 'Seems to just be this unit that's gone rural.'

Despite the coop being flown, neither of us was willing to admit defeat. There could be something here, some clue that led us to the next breadcrumb along the trail. We'd come this far; surely we were owed something for our effort.

'What part of the flat is this?' Stronge asked as we followed a path through the brambles and arrived in a cramped room so blanketed with flora that its function could only be guessed at.

Searching for an answer, I concentrated on making my hand more like flesh and bone and less like smoke and nothing, then used it to sweep aside a patch of vegetation clinging to an upright unit of some sort. The greenery fell away easily, as though it had only recently grown to cover the appliance, which turned out to be a kitchen refrigerator.

'After you,' I said, showing Stronge the fridge's exposed door handle.

Who knew what lurked inside the thing? Portions of human flesh wrapped in clingfilm? Milk bottles thick with congealed blood? A stack of heads with black tongues lolling from their unhinged mouths? I didn't know. All I knew was, I didn't want to be the first one to clap eyes on the fridge's contents.

With an audible gulp, Stronge reached out a tentative paw, wrapped her fingers around the handle, and gave it a sharp tug. 'Oh my God,' she gasped, 'did this bloke only shop in the treats aisle?'

Huh?

I peered inside the lukewarm fridge and saw shelves heaving not with body parts, but with food. Junk food, to be precise: chocolate bars, peanut butter, packets of biscuits, bottles of pop, buttered popcorn, all loaded with enough sugar to make Jamie Oliver cry himself raw.

'Blimey,' I said, digging around in the back of the fridge but only finding more snacks. 'Must have a hell of a sweet tooth.'

Stronge closed the fridge and we resumed our exploration of the flat.

'I'm guessing this is the boudoir,' I said as we landed in a room with a flat, overgrown mound of brambles that could only be concealing a bedstead.

'I don't get it,' said Stronge, chewing her bottom lip. 'He went to all the trouble of lighting the place, he kept his food here, but where did he sleep?'

It was a good question. Aside from the narrow path through the vegetation that allowed access to each room, there wasn't a square foot not covered in jagged thorns. Where the suspect laid his head was a mystery, at least until the beam of Stronge's torch glanced off a couple of bright spots buried amongst an upright mass of vegetation in the far corner of the room. A mass that I'd assumed until this point was enveloping a wardrobe.

'What was that?' I asked.

Stronge redirected her torch at the tangle of tightly-knit brambles and caught two small reflections. Violet reflections.

Someone was watching us.

CHAPTER ELEVEN: READY. FIRE. AIM

THE MASS of brambles parted with a stiff creak and a figure stepped between the two curtains of vegetation. The perp had been with us the whole time.

He was dressed in his underwear, and was younger than I first took him for; late teens, early twenties at most. With his pretty boy looks and slight build, he didn't seem like he'd put up much of a fight, but looks can be deceiving, especially when magic's involved.

Speaking of which, I noticed the knife wound in his belly had all but gone. Instead of an ugly red hole there was only a pale pink mark, barely visible. No one healed that fast. No one normal, anyway.

'You two,' he hissed, eyes pinging between me and my companion.

Stronge didn't waste any time. Rather than read him his rights, she gave him a taste of her left, which was wrapped around the handle of a police-issue Taser. But the suspect was fast, so fast that he had his hand around her wrist before the weapon made it anywhere near him. He gave Stronge's arm a crank and the sparking stun-stick spiralled to the floor, vanishing beneath the carpet of brambles.

My turn. I made a fist and sent it at his jaw, where it landed with a sound like an ice cube cracking in water, only a good deal louder.

He staggered back a step, head whipped to one side. When he turned my way again, the look he gave was dangerous and dark.

'Oh, you didn't like that?' I asked, my voice high and mocking. 'Then you're going to hate the sequel...'

I chinned him again and he went reeling, stumbling towards the far wall in the direction of the room's broken window. His fingers dug into the window frame, raising splinters, and for a second I thought he was going to use the leverage to propel himself back at me. Instead, he checked his cards, decided he didn't like the hand he'd been dealt, and cashed his chips. Taking up his heels, he jacked his body through the window, using it as an escape hatch and landing on the fire escape balcony outside.

Thankfully, I had that avenue covered.

His feet had barely kissed the ground before a pair of arms wrapped around his midriff and hoisted him into the air. Being as he'd rabbitted on us before, I wanted to make sure we had our exits covered this time, which is why I posted Frank on the balcony, ready to cut off any sudden departures.

I went to help my partner wrestle the fugitive to the ground, but before I could join him outside, the suspect's fingers glowed green and began to dance as if playing an invisible piano. I made it one more step before my feet took root, and looked down to find the creepers carpeting the floor had snaked around my ankles and were holding me in place. It seemed I wasn't imagining things when I saw the vegetation shifting before. These were no ordinary brambles, they were loaded with magic and working at the behest of our target.

Stronge was similarly stricken, her feet fixed in place by another creeping knot of vegetation. Determined to break free, she took to tearing at the tendrils with her bare hands, but the thorns they were studded with made short work of that plan.

Out on the balcony, rain lashed down on Frank as he battled to get the suspect on his back. For a little feller, the squirrelly bastard was putting up a hell of a fight. I fought to tear my leg free of the tightening trap but it was like trying to step out of a block of quick-drying cement. What I wouldn't have given for the power of translocation in that moment, or even a set of secateurs. But then I remembered, though I hadn't come packing gardening supplies, I did have one tool at my disposal: my trusty claw hammer.

I slipped the lump of iron from its place in my jacket (in case you're worried about all these heavy tools I lug about spoiling the cut of my suit, fear not: the magic I specialise in, kleptomancy, allows objects to fit places they shouldn't and weigh next to nothing). I dropped to a crouch and used the claw part of the hammer to gouge at the tendrils wrapped around my front leg. It was tough work, but the tool was up to the task, and after a bit of frantic sawing, I had a foot free.

While I busied myself with the second shackle, I cast a look outside and saw Frank still fighting the fugitive. He squirmed and thrashed and kicked, and though Frank's hands remained chained beneath his rib cage like a pair of iron links, it wouldn't be long before he slipped those surly bonds. Frank's fingers were about to give out, practically creaking under the strain.

The brambles around my other leg loosened up just enough for me to liberate myself from the trap, and I was off, sprinting for the window. I hadn't made it two feet before the suspect managed to throw back his head and flatten Frank's nose. His grip gave out and the suspect slipped our trap, vaulting the edge of the balcony and landing on the one below, bypassing a flight of zig-zagging stairs in the process.

I phased through the window without needing to hop the sill. The weather had really picked up now; being out in it was like being trapped inside an angry cloud. I wasn't about to let that stop me, though.

'I'll take it from here,' I told Frank, his eyes watering from the wallop he'd been dealt.

Moving at a rate of knots, I hot-footed it after the perp, leaping to the next balcony down, only to look through the grille of the stairs and discover he'd already put two more between us. The kid was a strip of wind. How he could eat all that junk food and move so fast was anyone's guess, but he was leaving me for dust.

Then again, I still had my hammer.

I lined up a shot, swung it up to the side of my head, and hurled it at him like a wannabe thunder god. I don't know whether it was my marksmanship, a quirk of the wind, or just plain good luck, but the hammer struck the back of his skull and flattened him. I wondered for a second if I'd been a bit overzealous, but I'd only made it down one more flight before he was finding his feet and preparing to make off. Whatever this bloke was, he was made of tough stuff.

With his wheels in motion again, the suspect scrambled down the final flight of steps and mounted the pavement. He was struggling, though. The hammer blow had him running like a newborn fawn, weaving to and fro. At this rate, I'd be on top of him in no time. I ran flat-out, my dead heart going a mile a minute, but my quarry had an ace up his sleeve.

Suddenly, he just... vanished. And yet he hadn't gone anywhere, just camouflaged himself. Thanks to the downpour, I could make out a human-shaped void in the rain. The killer was there all right, but using some form of camouflage magic, had redacted himself from the picture. I wondered briefly why he'd gone to the trouble of pulling a gun at the night club if he could turn invisible. Unless maybe something was interfering with his powers there, same as mine.

But this was no time for philosophising. I chased the indistinct hole in the rain as it cut a wild zig-zag across the courtyard. I almost lost it a couple of times as a sheet of rain obscured my vision, or the hole found a shadowy patch between streetlights, but I kept my eye on the prize and ran the bastard down. With a flying tackle, I got my arms around his ankles and brought him crashing to the ground in a vacant backstreet, where he became coherent again.

I had him. At least for a moment. Before I could get a knee on his back and put him down for good, he flipped me over and had me facing the sky. The rain beat down on my face, but not as hard as his fists, which landed with such force that it felt like he was taking lumps out of me. You don't need a blow-by-blow account of what happened next. It was ugly, and it was fast, and it didn't end with me coming out on top.

As I squinted through the rain at the figure looming over me, I saw something unexpected. His face was striped with long blue streaks that ran from his scalp to his chin. I thrust up a hand and wrapped it around his mush, but he forced my arm back down and used his spare mitt to reach for something out of view. I twisted my head to see what he was going for and spotted a half-brick lying there, probably used as a doorstop by one of the restaurants that backed onto the alley. A brick wouldn't usually do me any harm, but in the hands of a magic-user it could be as deadly as… well, a brick.

His fingers closed around the block and his arm shot up like he was raising his hand to ask a question: *How many chunks will this clown's face break into when I hit it with a brick*, maybe. I considered calling for help, but screams were like crickets in this part of town: background noise.

I saw the muscles in his hand tighten, ready to bring down the rock, but a sudden shrill beeping pricked up his ears and made his arm go slack. A large vehicle was backing into the alley—a lorry coming to empty the restaurant bins. The rumbling six-wheeler pulled to a stop right by us, the noxious breath of innnercity fumes pumping from its exhaust pipe like dragon smoke. All of a sudden, the suspect cast the brick aside, scurried off me, and bolted out of the alley, still weaving as he bled into the night.

'The hell…?' I gasped.

I lay there for a bit, gathering my senses until a nearby noise announced the arrival of my companions, splashing through an inch-deep puddle of rainwater.

'Are you okay?' asked Stronge, catching her breath.

'I'll live,' I said. 'Well, to a fashion.'

Frank helped me to my feet and I propped against him like a drunk at a pub urinal. I gave him a goosey and saw that he was wearing a blood goatee from the busted nose he'd been given.

'Looks like we've both been in the wars, eh?' I said.

'What happened?' asked Stronge, shouting to be heard over the hydraulic hiss of the rubbish lorry, which was busy emptying the contents of a bin into its rear end. The man operating the lifting mechanism was either oblivious to the drama that had unfolded, or utterly indifferent. I was willing to guess the latter.

'Fucked if I know,' I shouted back. 'He had me on the ropes.'

My best guess was that the lorry must have spooked him. Why else would he have legged it when he did?

'Did you see which way he went?' Stronge asked, swiping a curtain of wet hair from her face.

'I did, but it doesn't matter. He's long gone.'

She threw her hands up in frustration. 'So that's it? We're right back where we started?'

'Not quite,' I replied, and used a finger to daub a long pink stripe along the back of Frank's coat.

The killer was using makeup to cover blue skin.

CHAPTER TWELVE: LISTEN TO YOUR NOSE

THE MAKEUP MEANT SOMETHING. Only thing was, I had no idea what. I'd never heard of an Uncanny coloured blue, at least none that could even remotely pass for human. But there was one thing I did know.

'This is a cocoon.'

We were back at the suspect's overgrown apartment, picking through the wreckage. We'd searched the place top to bottom but found little of interest—some discarded clothes, a mildewed copy of *Don Quixote* that looked as if it had been dragged out of a canal, and a pistol that we didn't need ballistics to tell us had been used in a murder —but the cocoon... that added a whole new slant to the proceedings.

'So what?' said Stronge. 'What difference does it make now he's gone?'

Frank tipped his head to one side, also confused.

I explained why it mattered. 'The knife wound that eaves tagged him with was all gone, and I think this fixed it.'

I beckoned them over and they peered into the hollow the suspect had vacated. Among the mass of vegetation was a single cone-shaped purple flower positioned about waist-height, its petals stained red with blood.

Stronge clucked her tongue thoughtfully. 'Okay, let's assume you're right and this thing patched him up somehow... why do you sound so happy about it?'

I smiled. 'Don't you get it? I dinged him with a hammer so now he's going to have to heal all over again. He can't come back here, which means he's going to have to make a fresh cocoon.'

Stronge completed the thought. 'Which means he can't skip town.'

'Biiiingo,' drawled Frank, getting into the spirit of things.

'He'll need to find somewhere new to lie low and nurse his wounds,' I said, 'somewhere close to vegetation, and when he does, we'll find him.'

'How do we do that?'

I wasn't sure exactly, so I pressed my fingertips together and hoped it made me look smarter than I felt. 'We need to learn more about him. About his habits. And there's really only one place left to look.'

NOW *THIS* IS A PENTHOUSE SUITE, I thought as we ducked the blue and white police tape and stepped into a hotel room large enough to have its own weather system. Slap bang in the heart of Mayfair and boasting a jaw-dropping view of Green Park, this place was not for the thrifty. This was for people who could afford to stay in a hotel room decorated with pictures that weren't just cheap reprints. The art on these walls was specially commissioned and lit in a way that drew attention to their every brushstroke.

'I'm telling you, this is a bullshit move,' said Stronge, setting foot in a crime scene she already considered ice cold.

She didn't like the insinuation that her people were incompetent. That the men in bunny suits she'd watched comb the room had missed something vital. But I'd insisted we re-examine the place. Stronge may have the Sight, but that didn't mean she always knew what she was looking for. There was a chance I might spot something her and her people left behind. That I might sniff out some truffles the pigs hadn't.

'The place has already been tossed top to bottom,' she went on. 'If there was something here, we would have found it.'

'We'll see,' I replied.

Frank blundered into the room after us, bursting through the police tape like a marathon runner crossing the finishing line.

'Watch it, you lummox,' I said, getting his attention before he stuck his size-twelves somewhere they didn't belong.

He stopped just short of the pool of dried blood on the carpet at the foot of the bed, lit clearly by the chandelier above. Right by the puddle, a red splatter decorated the wall like some grisly accent piece. I watched Frank's glassy eyes track from one to the other and saw his already colourless cheeks go a shade whiter. For a walking corpse, he was surprisingly squeamish.

'Right then,' I said, cracking my knuckles.

Arranging my fingers into the appropriate configuration, I untangled a knot of word-vomit and began an arcane invocation.

There are all kinds of magic. There's primitive shamanic magic with funny dances and totems. Then there's sophisticated, refined magic in the hermetic tradition, with carefully orchestrated rituals and finely-crafted symbology. They're all different ways of doing the same thing: tapping into the aether, opening a trapdoor in the fabric of reality, dialling a phone number to another world.

'Let's shed some light on this situation, shall we?'

I lifted my arms like antennas to Heaven and unleashed the spell. A neon wind washed from my hands and flooded the room, bathing it in a heliotrope glow.

'What did you do?' asked Stronge, blinking, her teeth glowing white as a toothpaste salesman's.

'A little home-brew spell I knocked up. It's sort of like the ultraviolet light your SOCO boys use, only with a bit more welly.'

Stronge took a closer look at our surroundings and saw what I meant. Fingerprints were visible to the naked eye and blood glowed violent and white, including smears and spots that hadn't been obvious before. But the real trick of the spell—the cherry on the trifle—was that it highlighted psychic imprints no UV light in the world could have picked out.

'Magic is everywhere,' I explained, 'and when we cut through it, we leave footprints.'

The evidence was plain to see. Blurred bodies traced through the room like acid trails—the victim and our perp, I assumed—crisscrossing the space, sometimes in tandem, sometimes apart, occasionally coming together in clumps where they'd remained static for a while. The figures were indistinct, unfinished, like plaster casts of the victims of the Pompeii eruption. Their faces were unidentifiable, their bodies lacking any real definition. There was nothing on show that could be used to form a definite ID, and yet the movements of the figures were clear.

There was a firmer imprint of the two bodies on the bed, relatively sharp, indicating that they'd remained in a fixed position for upwards of an hour. They weren't engaged in anything salacious, though. They were curled up together on their sides, the killer playing big spoon.

'Creepy,' said Stronge.

The trails diverged after that. The bodies appeared to unfurl from their positions, then embarked from each side of the mattress and came together at the foot of the bed. After that, there was no telling what happened. The trail had come to an abrupt end. Any evidence of how the encounter between the killer and his victim concluded had been erased, suggesting a psychic explosion so violent that it created a sort of metaphysical black hole.

'What happened here?' asked Stronge.

'A bullet in the head,' I replied. 'That's what.'

The spell I'd employed wasn't perfect. Far from it. The imprints it revealed were vague and delicate and prone to being muddied. The trauma inflicted on my client in her final moments had unleashed a psychic cascade that obliterated every imprint in her locality, rendering the spell pretty much useless. Then again, the cause of death was already a dead cert. I'd already heard from the victim what happened to her, and seen the bullet hole with my own two eyes. What I needed was fresh evidence. Something the killer left behind that helped us track him down.

I snapped my fingers, terminating the spell and returning the room to normality.

I looked to Frank. 'You wanna take a run at it, big man?'

He nodded and went down on all fours.

'Now what?' said Stronge, at her wit's end with our shenanigans.

'I told you: nose of a bloodhound, this feller.'

Frank went to work, crawling about the room, getting his snout into all the corners and crevices.

He sniffed the marble-topped honour bar.

He rubbed his beak over a tasteful floral arrangement set upon an expansive oval table.

He even got up on his tiptoes to get a noseful of the crystal chandelier.

'I could really do without your fat-footed partner blundering all over the scene of a criminal investigation,' said Stronge.

'Just let the man work.'

And so she did. It went on like that for a while—Frank rooting around on his hands and knees while Stronge watched through splayed fingers, occasionally shaking her head and muttering profanities—but soon enough, something got my partner's antennae twitching. He sniffed at the valance of the king size bed and followed it up to the luxury mattress, the tip of his bent nose trailing across the ruffled silk bedspread.

'He's wasting his time,' said Stronge, crossing her arms. 'My men already performed a fingertip search of that thing.'

But Frank wasn't one for the light touch. He took the mattress in two hands, hefted it over his head, and hurled it through the room's art deco window like a rock star of old.

'What the fuck,' cried Stronge.

'Calm down.'

'Calm down?' She rushed to the shattered window so she could check the street below. 'He's lucky he didn't flatten someone.'

'Frank's enthusiastic, that's all.'

This wasn't the first time Stronge had questioned our methods, and it wouldn't be the last. And yet, as ever, Frank's instincts were spot on.

There on the bedstead, no longer shielded by the mattress, was the object of Frank's interest: a mysterious glowing bug. It was beating its membranous wings so furiously that it gave off a high-pitched drone, but despite its best efforts, failed to get airborne. From what I could make out, it had become tangled in the fibres of the canvas stretched across the bed frame, and couldn't free itself.

'See, I told you we should have given this place a once-over,' I said, wishing I'd pressed the matter harder back at the café.

Stronge returned from the broken window to get a look. The bug was so tiny it was hard to make out, so she fired up her phone and framed the thing with its lens. I inspected the magnified insect on the screen and saw that it wasn't an insect at all, or at least not one from around these parts. The creature had a skull-shaped head studded with eight eerily human eyes. Its cranium was affixed to a mismatched, semi-translucent body that looked like the kind of thing Kafka might have called, "A bit bloody much".

Frank grinned at me, pleased with his find.

'Not just a pretty face,' I said, giving my doppelganger a playful cheek slap.

Stronge massaged the back of her neck. 'What is that thing?'

'I've got a better question: how the hell could you miss it?' I asked, staring in wonder at the otherworldly beastie.

'Hey, you didn't catch it either,' she shot back. 'Frank's the star player here.'

'We're a package deal, okay? His victories are my victories, and vice versa.'

Stronge did her fed-up nose-pinch thing again. 'All right, enough. Let's get that thing under a jar before it flies away.'

Frank went searching for a glass behind the honour bar, but evidently they'd been removed, most likely to be dusted for prints. Looking for something else he could use, he opened the mini-fridge and produced a miniature bottle of whiskey. He shrugged as if to say, *Waste not want not*, knocked back the contents of the bottle, then carefully captured the bug inside it.

It bashed against the walls of the bottle for a bit before it gave up and went for a lie down. The bug was out for the count. Whether it was the lack of oxygen or the alcohol fumes anaesthetising it, we couldn't be sure, but Stronge thought it prudent to give the thing some ventilation. She took the bottle from Frank, located a corkscrew on a silver tray in the bar area, and used the sharp end to punch an air hole through the lid. She held it up so we could see the bug closer and the three of us gathered around to inspect it. Though we couldn't see it breathing, it gave off a rhythmic pulse of light that told us it was still alive.

Whatever the creature was, it was more alien than insect, and just about hummed with supernatural energy. The killer must have brought it to the hotel with him, because it sure as hell didn't belong there. Good old Frank. Even with a busted nose, he'd delivered the goods. Thanks to him, we had a piece of evidence that could give us a much better idea of what we were hunting. And once we knew what the killer was, we had a chance to figure out where he'd hang his hat next.

A sharp knock on the door announced the arrival of some very angry members of management. How Stronge explained away the defenestrated mattress, I have no idea. I was too busy thinking about our next move.

CHAPTER THIRTEEN: SPRITE NIGHT

IN SOME WAYS, the most shocking thing about our visit to Legerdomain—the magic shop owned by my good friend/sometimes enemy, Jazz Hands—wasn't what we learned there, but what we saw when we rocked up.

'Is that...?'

Frank bobbed his head.

'What?' asked Stronge, confused. 'What am I missing?'

Having not been to Legerdomain before, Stronge was failing to recognise the sheer madness of what we were witnessing.

Jazz Hands was dealing with a customer.

Not someone who'd wandered into the shop by mistake, or come inside to get out of the rain, but an actual, real life patron. This was a first, and no wonder—Legerdomain was a dank, uninviting pit sandwiched between an adult book store and an out-of-business jeweller. A gloomy rat hole so thick with dust that crossing its aisles felt like walking through the ashy aftermath of a volcanic eruption. And here was this man, standing at the counter with a grin on his face and his wallet open, making a cash purchase.

Jazz took the man's item—a magic wand of the *actual* magic persuasion, not the kind stage magicians tap against top hats—wrapped it, and placed it in a brown paper bag. The satisfied customer then took his purchase, thanked her, and received a smile for his courtesy. That was the thing that really got me. Seeing a smile

on Jazz Hands was like seeing a 360 degree rainbow: a once in a lifetime phenomenon.

The customer gave us a nod as he exited through the shop door,
setting its bell tinkling. Across the counter, Jazz adjusted her spectacles and saw me. Immediately, her smile melted. I offered her what
many describe as a smirk, but I prefer to call a slanting smile.

'Bloody hell. Bit crowded in here, ain't it, Jazz? You must have
tripled your annual profits there, girl.'

'What do you want, Fletcher?' she groaned, raking a hand
through her bird's nest of greying hair.

I approached the till and placed a whiskey miniature on the
counter, right next to the *You Break It, You Bought It* sign.

'Do I look like I need a drink?' she asked.

The obvious answer was, *"Yes, always"*, but I kept schtum on that
and stayed on point.

'I need your help with something.'

Jazz looked right through me. This was something that I should
be used to by this point, what with being a ghost, and yet when it
occurred as a result of deliberate, scathing disregard, I couldn't help
but take it to heart. The surly proprietor of Legerdomain squinted
across the shop floor and spied two figures lurking amongst the
sagging cabinets leaning sideways under the weight of how-to
guides, copies of *Magicana Magazine*, and stacks of snide playing
cards.

'Who's back there?' she demanded.

'Oh, I forgot you two haven't met,' I said, calling Stronge over.
'Jazz Hands, Detective Stronge; Detective Stronge, Jazz Hands.'

The two women shook hands as though it was a competition to
decide who cared less.

'Stronge here is an Insider, but she's pretty new to the game, so
go easy on her.'

The look on the detective's face told me she wasn't exactly
thrilled by the introduction I'd given her, but before I could colour
in the details, Jazz had moved on.

'Is that who I think it is?' she asked, her face brightening as she
peered through the gloom and saw who else I'd brought along.

Frank came bounding over like a goofy golden retriever.

'There's my boy,' trilled Jazz, giving him a tickle behind the ear. She clocked his wonky schnoz and frowned. 'What happened here?'

'Contretemps with a wanted killer,' I explained. 'Speaking of which…' I gave the whiskey bottle a shake, agitating the glow bug within, but Jazz had already ducked under the counter.

'Got something for you,' she said, but she wasn't talking to me.

When she stood up again she was holding a Tupperware box. She popped the lid and slid it across the counter to Frank, who snatched it up with a big dumb grin on his face.

'What the hell is that?' asked Stronge, holding her nose.

'Just some meat,' Jazz replied.

Frank took a fistful of something pink, shoved it into his gob, and returned a cockeyed grin. Stronge plucked a piece from the box and held it between her forefinger and thumb like she was desperately wanting for a pair of tongs.

'What kind of meat?' she asked.

I leant over and whispered in her ear, 'Brain meat.'

With a dry heave, Stronge flicked the offending article across the room and it struck the forehead of a ventriloquist's dummy. It stayed glued there, and would remain that way for years to come.

'Why do you have a box of brain bits?' she asked, squeezing an entire tube of sanitiser gel into her hand and rubbing her palms together like Lady Macbeth after a spirited spot of murder.

'Don't be such a prude,' I said. 'It's just cow brain.' I tossed a look to Jazz. ' It *is* cow brain, right?'

It was, and Frank needed it. Since we joined forces I'd discovered that, as well as providing sustenance, ingesting cerebral matter helped him recover from damage. Case in point, it was fixing his head injury up a treat. With each bite of brain meat, his nose got a little straighter, a little less bruised. By the time he'd finished his meal, our hooters were pretty much a matching pair.

Stronge turned my way. 'Okay, I'm going to ask you to explain what we're doing here.'

'Jazz here is an expert in all things Uncanny. I come here when something stumps me, or I need her to job me together a magical knick-knack.'

'*Job together a knick-knack?*' Jazz parrotted, her voice hiked high and loud. 'I'm a magical artificer who produces high-grade enchanted artefacts, not your bloody gadget lackey.'

'Sure, sure. Anyway, I'm hoping you can tell me what this little bugger is so we can figure out what the bloke we're chasing is made of.'

Jazz took a long, cleansing breath, located a magnifying glass from a drawer, and studied the creature buzzing about inside the whiskey bottle.

'The killer left it at the crime scene,' Stronge explained. 'So what is he? Some kind of demon?'

'It's always a bloody demon, isn't it?' I chimed.

Since the London Coven's wards fell a few years back, infernal invaders were forever breaching the walls and slipping into our realm. It was up to people like me to make sure they received a hostile reception.

'How long have you been chasing this killer?' asked Jazz, placing the magnifying glass back in its drawer.

'A while,' I replied.

'Fletcher, I have here the most detailed bestiaries in all of the Uncanny Kingdom. If you needed to query an unknown creature's provenance, why didn't you come to me earlier?'

'Because I'm an idiot?'

'You'll get no argument from me there.'

Frank nodded in agreement.

'Oi!' I said, giving him a dig in the shoulder. 'Traitor.'

Stronge rapped a knuckle on the shop counter, snapping us all to attention. 'How about we get what we came here for before someone else gets shot, eh?'

'Shot?' said Jazz, surprised.

'In the head.'

'That is strange.' She seemed thrown. 'Why don't you tell me what you've learned so far?'

I got the ball rolling. 'Here's what we know: he's the colour of the cookie monster, but he covers it with flesh-coloured makeup—'

Stronge interjected. 'We don't use "flesh-coloured" to describe pink makeup anymore.'

'Why not?'

'Because flesh comes in lots of colours.'

Now it was my turn to pinch the bridge of my nose. 'Christ Almighty, you sound just like Shift. No wonder she likes you so much.'

'Please can the pair of you stop prattling and get back to the point?' Jazz insisted.

I gave her everything else we had on the perp: how he was into a designer drug called ironclad, how he could turn invisible, how he lived in an indoor forest that featured some sort of life-regenerating cocoon. 'That enough for you to go on?'

She considered the evidence. 'I have some questions that should help me reach my verdict.'

'Shoooot,' said Frank.

I'd been subjecting my partner to a lot of old detective pictures— the kind that featured men in trench coats trudging through rain-slick streets to the sound of a plaintive saxophone—and apparently, he'd started to absorb the lingo.

Jazz gave him a pat on the head then turned her attention back to me. 'You mentioned that he was living indoors. Did you happen to find anything unusual there?'

'Besides a magic forest, you mean?'

Stronge had more patience. 'He had a sweet tooth, at least going by the contents of his fridge.'

That caught Jazz's interest. 'What are we talking? Marzipan? Custard tarts? Honey cakes?'

'Something like that, only a bit less medieval.'

'I see. One last question: was this killer abnormally good-looking?'

'I don't know if I'd say *abnormally* good-looking,' I cut in.

Stronge side-eyed me. 'Are you serious? You could have cooked a Pot Noodle on him, he was so hot.'

'Come on. He was no better looking than I am,' I insisted.

Kat shook her head. Jazz, too. Even Frank was on their side, licking his finger and making a hissing noise.

'Can you please just tell us what we're dealing with?' I asked Jazz, my patience beyond thin.

'Let me see... you're looking for a blue-skinned man who lives in a magic forest, has a chronic sweet tooth, and is supernaturally handsome. I think the answer is pretty obvious, don't you?'

The look on my face told her it wasn't.

She sighed. 'It's not a demon, I can tell you that.'

'Then what?' asked Stronge.

Jazz peered at us over her spectacles. 'I'd say your killer is a fairy.'

CHAPTER FOURTEEN: BEAST INFECTION

'HE'S A WHAT?' I was laughing so hard that nothing was coming out of my mouth anymore. If I was the kind of person who needed to breathe, I'd have been in real trouble.

'A fairy,' Jazz Hands repeated, her expression hard and serious.

'A fairy? As in the little flying bastards that live in the sewer? Oh, that is rich.'

Not wanting to feel left out, Frank joined in, honking away like a mad seal.

'No,' she retorted, shutting us both up. 'I'm talking about an Arcadian. Thoroughbred fae folk. Sewer fairies are rabid daschunds by comparison.'

From beneath the counter she produced a leather-bound tome and blew a coating of grime from its cover. Unfortunately, she neglected to turn away from Stronge as she did so, leaving her choking on a swirling grey blur of dust.

The tome landed on the counter top with a resounding *bam*. I read the cover, which was embossed with the words, *The Modern Encyclopaedia of Faeries and Otherkin*.

I snapped my fingers. 'Damn. This was the next book on my To Be Read pile, I swear.'

Stronge flicked through the first few yellowed pages, each packed with a spidery scrawl that looked as if it had been penned with a feather quill. There was no telling when the book had been written, but I was sure of one thing: the "Modern" in its title had expired a long time ago.

'Not exactly a beach read, is it?' Stronge remarked. 'Any chance you can just tell me what an Arcadian is?'

'I suppose I can't blame you for not knowing,' said Jazz. 'Unlike vampires and zombies, fairies don't have their own TV show. Not that I'm aware of, anyway.'

I gave Stronge what I knew. 'The Arcadians are fae folk, enigmatic and fickle beings who traffic in chaos; supernatural royalty who arrived here back when this place was called Albion.'

'Arrived?'

'Yeah. The stories say they come from another place, a wide-open wonderland called Arcadia, hence the name.'

'If it's such a wonderland, what are they doing in this shithole city?' asked Stronge.

'Good question, particularly seeing as they haven't set foot in our realm for hundreds of years.' I threw it out to Jazz. 'So go on, clever clogs, why would an Arcadian show up in London now? So he can shoot a prostitute and leave a glow bug behind?'

'This isn't a "glow bug",' she replied, giving the top of the whiskey bottle a tap and waking up its prisoner. 'This is a will-o'-the-wisp.'

With a clumsy swipe, Frank took up the bottle and pressed a milky eyeball to it, studying the creature inside.

'Again,' said Stronge, seeking swift clarity, 'what's a will-o'-the-wisp?'

'Elemental spirits that buzz about in marshes,' I explained.

'Entirely wrong,' said Jazz. 'Will-o'-the-wisps, or hinkypunks as they're sometimes known, are quite unlike the description you so obviously read on Wikipedia. Though they are known to lead prey off of their intended path and into treacherous ground, the meaning is a metaphorical one.'

'How's that?' asked Stronge.

A glint played in Jazz's eye. She was always at her happiest playing teacher. 'Instead of physically leading their victims astray, the wisp does so by attaching itself to their person and making them a host. With that accomplished, the wisp then implants the suggestion in the host's mind that they seek out a partner who is similarly infested. Thus the wisp is able to reproduce.'

'You're saying they're parasites?' Stronge cut in.

'Yes. Or, more precisely, an STD.'

'Ugggghh,' spat Frank, and flicked the bottle across the shop.

'Careful,' cried Jazz, lifting a section of the counter and swinging it up on its hinges. Moving at surprising speed, she located the still-intact bottle and scooped it off the floor.

'Hang about,' I said, 'are you telling me will-o'-the-wisps live in a fairy's short and curlies?'

'In a manner of speaking, yes.'

'Then why are you so worried about saving the dirty little bastard?'

She gave me a look that was saltier than a mermaid's kiss. 'Because it's a living creature, but also because it can help you.'

'Help me how?' I asked, and saw my incredulous expression reflected twice in the lenses of her spectacles. 'What possible use could I have for fairy crabs?'

'The will-o'-the-wisp is attracted to magic like a moth to flame,' she explained.

'But there's magic in just about everything, isn't there?' said Stronge.

'She's a quick student, this one,' said Jazz, impressed. 'Yes, there's magic in all natural things, but not *fae* magic.'

She opened a display case and fished out a jar of loaded dice. Having tipped its contents into a pocket of her frumpy jumper, she twisted the lid from the whiskey bottle and transferred the will-o'-the-wisp into the empty container.

'Pay attention,' she said, and the three of us gathered around to see what we were missing.

With more room to buzz about in, it was obvious that the wisp's movements weren't as aimless as they first appeared. It was clear now that the creature was straining in a particular direction.

'What's it doing?' I asked.

'The wisp is attracted to the fae whose… nest it took residence in,' Jazz replied.

'That's another thing I don't get. How come the Arcadian didn't know he was lugging this thing around between his legs? I mean, look at it, all lit up like a Christmas tree.'

'The wisp doesn't glow when it's on its host. It only does that to ward off predators. Anyway, you're missing the point here.'

'What point?'

'My God, Fletcher, it's not exactly four-dimensional chess.'

Stronge got there before I could. 'It's a homing device.'

'A *very* quick student,' said Jazz, doubly impressed.

The penny dropped. 'You're saying we can use the wisp as a compass to find the killer?'

'Very good,' she replied, clapping slowly. 'Have yourself a participation trophy.'

Jazz handed Stronge the jar as if hers were the safer hands. Okay, so technically they were, given that mine were ethereal, but it still got my goat.

'Okay, let's go,' said Stronge.

'Before we do that, there's something else I came for,' I said. 'My powers are playing up and I need to know why.'

'Can you be more specific?' Jazz asked with all the conviction she could muster.

'Translocation: that's the first thing giving me gyp. The other one is possession. Well, except when it comes to old blue lips here—I can climb into his bonce no problem.'

'Braaaaiiiins,' said Frank, who always knew when he was being talked about.

'So you're able to possess your better half here but no one else?' said Jazz, drumming a finger against her chin. 'Interesting.'

'Interesting how? Interesting I'm dying? Is that it?'

Was my soul starting to degrade? Had I spent so long stuck in this limbo land that I was finally beginning to fade away?

Jazz returned to her station behind the counter and parked her derriere on the well-polished seat of her stool. 'Tell me, how do you feel when you spend time apart from Frank?'

It wasn't a question I anticipated, but I answered it as honestly as I could. 'It's weird; I get sweaty when I spend too long inside Frank's head, but I miss him when we spend too long apart. He's like a duvet that's too warm on you, but when you throw it off, you get cold.'

'Aww,' said Stronge, one hand flat on her clavicle. 'You know what that is? Separation anxiety.'

I ignored her and returned to Jazz. 'So what's the verdict? How stuffed am I?'

She measured her words carefully. 'You need to think of this less like a handicap and more like an evolution.'

'You what?' Translocation and possession were two very important weapons in my arsenal. How could losing them possibly be a benefit?

Jazz resumed her lecture. 'How did it feel before, possessing strangers?'

'Depended on the person. Sometimes it wasn't too hard, other times it was a fight.'

'And how does it feel possessing Frank?'

I looked to my partner, who also seemed keen to hear my answer.

'I don't know if I'd even call it that. With Frank it's more like merging. Like stepping into an old pair of slippers.'

Some might have taken umbrage at being compared to a set of well-worn footwear, but not Frank. He looked on with unabashed pride.

'And when I connect with him I stay that way. Before I was on the clock; a couple of hours and I'd get catapulted out of whatever body I was wearing. Now I can do three times that. Maybe more. And I don't have to wait ages before I get back in the saddle.'

Plus, when I combined with Frank, I got to take advantage of his freakish strength, which put a real horseshoe in my glove.

'Sounds to me like you and Frank make a good team,' said Jazz.

'Yeah, we do, but that's not the point. The point is, I'm down two powers, and I could really use them right now.'

'You might want to make peace with the possibility that those powers aren't coming back.'

Panic swelled inside of me, sticking to my ribs. 'What are you saying?'

'I'm saying you've merged with Frank so many times now that the pair of you are becoming soul-bonded. Together, you constitute a powerful force, but the bond you share comes with certain sacrifices.'

'You're telling me I can never possess anyone else? Not ever?'

'Correct.'

'Or translocate?'

'You can catch the bus like the rest of us,' she replied with a shrug. 'Or walk. From the looks of it, you could use the exercise.'

I was reminded of that old saying: when God closes a door, He opens a window. Except, in my case, it's more like He slams the door shut on my dick and sits back laughing.

'I'll need my powers up and running again if I'm going to bring in that Arcadian. There has to be some way of undoing this soul bond.' I turned to Frank. 'Nothing personal, mate.'

Frank formed his fingers into an awkward OK sign. 'S'allriiight.'

Jazz gathered her thoughts with a weary sigh. 'It's possible that something could be done to loosen the bond, but I wouldn't pin my hopes on it.'

It wasn't much, but it was a start. 'So you'll get right on that?'

'Of course. After all, what else do I have to do besides single-handedly running a niche business in the middle of the worst economy this country has seen in decades?'

'That's my girl.'

Stronge injected herself back into the narrative. 'If you two are done chit-chatting, can we please make a move?'

'By all means,' said Jazz. 'But before you do…' She opened a wall safe hidden behind a portrait of James Randi and produced an item wrapped in a square of muslin.

I thought maybe I was getting a resupply of holy nails, or perhaps another enchanted hankie for Frank to console ghosts with, but Jazz had other ideas.

'Your Arcadian won't come in quietly,' she said. 'Consider this insurance.'

I unwrapped the package and found an antique rosewood box with a keyhole in its side. I flipped the lid on the thing and found a thin brass disk set upon a spindle and punctured with a pattern of tiny holes. Laid over the disk was a steel comb covered in jagged little teeth.

'A music box?' I said. 'This is meant to bring the bloke to his knees, is it? What does it play, Nickelback?'

Jazz's eyes were a pair of harpoons. 'Your target is a magic-user, and a proficient one at that. The tune this box produces emits a pulse of anti-magic that will dispel any arcane activity within its locality.'

'Sort of like a magic EMP?' said Stronge.

Jazz's hangdog face made it clear that she had absolutely no idea what that meant, nor cared to know. 'Once this is wound and the box is activated, the anti-magic it produces is instant. The effect is only temporary, however—the length of the song the box produces, thirty-two seconds precisely—so make good use of the time it provides you.'

She handed me the wind-up key that fit in the side of the box and I passed the goods along to Frank, who stuffed it into his coat pocket for safekeeping. Jazz also provided him with the Encyclopaedia of Faeries, which he tucked under one arm.

'Thanks, Jazz. You're a diamond.'

'No problem at all,' she trilled. 'Now kindly fuck off out of my shop, would you?'

CHAPTER FIFTEEN: YOU SHOW ME YOURS AND I'LL SHOW YOU MINE

SO THE KILLER WAS AN ARCADIAN. Even under the microscope of Jazz's relentless logic, it was hard to fathom. Arcadians lived in a land of daydreams and legend. What could they possibly stand to gain by coming to London? That would be like living in Hawaii and spending your holiday in Grimsby. Utter madness.

And there were other things that didn't add up. For one, why would an Arcadian be packing a shooter when he had magic at his disposal? And what was with the place he was living in? Alone. Arcadians were royalty. Royalty came in packs, and they lived in great big castles, not grubby little squats. If he was part of the well-to-do set, why was he slumming it in the arse-end of nowhere? I had no idea, and something told me enlightenment was a way off yet. This case was starting to look like Donald Trump's hair: the longer I stared at it, the more questions I had.

We made tracks from Legerdomain—heading after the Arcadian I thought—but the moment we left the shop, our paths forked.

'Wrong way, Kat,' I said, noting how the glow bug in the jar Frank carried was straining north-east, yet Stronge was heading in a different direction.

'We need to make a stop first,' she replied.

'What are you talking about? We need to strike while the iron's hot.'

'Not until I've spoken to the vic.'

I laughed. 'Are you off your chump, Kat? We've got a direct line to the perp here. Why would we take a break now?'

'Because I think she's holding out on us.'

This time I didn't laugh. 'What possible reason could my client—a dead person—have for lying?'

'You're dead. Do you always tell the truth?'

I threw my hands in the air like an evangelical preacher. 'When it comes to how I ended up that way, yeah. Look, the woman's counting on me to find her killer and bring him to justice. Why would she throw a spanner in the works? That's not cutting your nose off to spite your face, it's chopping your whole head off and feeding it to a wood chipper.'

Frank made a face that said, *Oh no, Mum and Dad are fighting again*.

'If your client is so honest, explain the makeup.'

The demand came so far out of left-field that I didn't know what to do with it. 'You what?'

'The suspect was wearing makeup to cover his blue skin. How come she didn't figure that out?'

'Same reason we didn't until I got a hand on his face.'

'That was in an alleyway at night. You saw the inside of that hotel room; it was bright and they were together for hours. There's no way she wouldn't have noticed he was made-up, no matter how well he put it on. Slap a bit of mascara on a guy and people will notice it; cover him in foundation and he'll stick out like a sore thumb.'

She had a point, though I failed to see how it was our most pressing concern right then. We had a beeline to the killer and we'd be mad not to make use of it while we had the chance.

'It's been bugging me ever since we revisited the crime scene,' Stronge continued. 'I put it aside at first, but now I can't let it go. Something's up with the vic's story.'

The bug Frank was carrying settled at the bottom of the jar, its glow dim as a dying ember. If I didn't know better, I'd think the conversation I was having with Stronge was making it as weary as it was me.

'I don't want to get into an argument about this, Kat.'

'We're not arguing, we're just experiencing diverging viewpoints.'

If that wasn't splitting hairs, I didn't know what it was.

'Let's say you're right and the vic knew about the makeup,' I said, humouring her. 'What difference does it make?'

'It means she's being elastic with the truth. She told you she didn't know what kind of Uncanny did her in, right? If she had information that could plug that gap, why would she keep it to herself?'

'You're being paranoid, Kat. She's just a call girl who took the wrong call, that's all.'

She rolled her eyes at me. 'You're being naive. There's a hole in her story bigger than the one in her forehead, and I want to know why.'

'She passed my smell test fine.'

'Great. Now let's have a real detective question her and see what happens.'

She was starting to piss me off now. 'You know what this sounds a lot like? It sounds like victim-blaming.'

'Oh, please. All that's happening here is me crediting your client with a bit of intelligence instead of treating her like a brainless damsel in distress.'

I was done debating. Time to put my foot down. 'She's been through enough already. I'm not having you treat her like a suspect. End of.'

For a moment, Stronge's jaw went tight. When the muscles loosened again, so did her demeanour. 'Jake, when it comes to being fooled by women, you've got form. You're a soft touch, you know that. What I'm asking isn't unreasonable. Before we put ourselves in harm's way, let's find out if she passes *my* smell test, too.'

'I don't know, Kat…'

'And I didn't know about letting you revisit the crime scene, but I went through with it anyway and look what happened.' She gestured to the bug in the jar. 'All I'm asking is that you keep an open mind and extend me the same courtesy.'

I supposed it did only amount to a minor diversion in the grand scheme of things. We had the means of finding the Arcadian now, and he wouldn't be going anywhere soon. He'd need to build another cocoon to recover from the whack I'd given him, because he sure as shite wasn't getting patched up in an A&E.

And there was another reason to stop by the office: the welfare of my client. Tali had been left alone for too long. If she didn't get some human contact soon, there was a chance she'd become insubstantial and be lost to the ether, or worse, turn feral. Tali hadn't had a sniff of company since I agreed to take her case—who knew what state she'd be in now? She'd been a model of self-control when I left her, but if I stayed away for much longer, the bitterness would soon creep in. Left unchecked, she could become an unquiet spirit who wreaked havoc on the living, same as the one I was forced to obliterate after I disturbed her walled-up bones. And what would the point in catching Tali's killer be if taking him down meant her becoming a mindless revenant? No, I couldn't have another doomed spirit on my conscience.

'Okay, Detective, I'm giving you the lead.'

She opened her mouth as if to say something unsavoury, thought better of it, and extended a hand instead. I made mine solid enough to get a grip of it and we shook out a deal.

'Friiieeends,' said Frank, grinning like a kid at the second wedding of his divorced parents.

CHAPTER SIXTEEN: DEAD RECKONING

Tᴀʟɪ just about jumped out of her skin when I came walking through the door (technically speaking, ghosts can already be said to have jumped out of their skin, but you know what I mean).

'Where have you been?' she asked, her voice a raw, chain-smoker's baritone.

The question was aimed at me with the precision of the bullet that had passed through the centre of her forehead.

I showed her my palms. 'I'm sorry, all right? I should have dropped you a line, but we've been chasing your killer non-stop since the moment we left this place.'

'And?'

'And we'll have him any minute now.'

She looked as doubtful as she did hurt, lips pursed, eyes narrowed. 'I can't stay here any more. I'm going insane trapped in this place. I have to get out.'

Shafts of moonlight pierced the blinds of the office window, casting silver bars on the walls that could only have added to the feeling of being a prisoner.

'I wouldn't recommend it,' I replied.

Going walkies would only put her more at risk of turning feral. I needed to keep her contained if I was going to stand any chance of helping her pass on to the next place.

'What am I supposed to do then?' she cried. 'Hover by the front door waiting for you to show up, pinny around my neck, cocktail in hand?'

The bullet hole in her forehead flared like the opening of a furnace, hot and red. When I'm dealing with a ghost, I'm on the lookout for signs like that. Signs that they're losing their grip on reality and becoming something monstrous.

Frank shuffled forward and offered Tali a hankie. She took it with a "thanks" and dabbed her eyes dry.

'Christ, even the zombie's better at comforting a woman than you are.'

I didn't challenge her for using the zed word. Didn't seem like the time.

'I promise this will all be over soon, Just hold on just a little while longer, okay? Can you do that for me, Tali?'

She softened. Not by much, but there was some give. 'I get that you don't want me roaming around, but do I have to stay here? The place freaks me out.'

'Well, it would. It used to be a funeral home before we moved in. Still got the coffins.'

'All right, enough chit-chat,' said Stronge, taking a seat at my desk. It was the first thing she'd said since she stepped into the room, so it landed with a thud.

'You're the detective I met at the hotel, aren't you?' asked Tali, sizing up the other woman as if noticing her for the first time. 'The one who sent me here?'

'How about I ask the questions for now, eh?'

'It's okay,' I told my fellow phantom. 'Kat's assisting us with your case. She just wants to help.'

Despite these words of assurance, she regarded Stronge with steel in her eyes. The detective's brusque pronouncement had signalled a shift that was felt by all: one that changed the mood in the room completely. This was no longer a conversation, it was an examination.

'I think there's stuff going on here that you're not telling us,' said Stronge, offering Tali a seat. 'And I want to know what it is.'

Without breaking eye contact, she took a seat—not on the chair, but on the corner of the desk opposite Stronge, maintaining the higher ground. She crossed one umber leg over the other and cast a withering look at her interrogator. Meanwhile, Frank and I were left standing around like a couple of tourists in our own home.

'What is it you think I know, Detective?'

Stronge set her palms down flat on the desk and hooked her feet around the legs of her chair. 'What do I think? I think you know the man who killed you was an Arcadian. That's what I think.'

I'd seen Stronge employ more tact than this in the station's hospitality suite: her nickname for the interrogation room at the cop shop she worked out of.

Tali shook her head, agitating her storm of hair. 'An Arcadian? I don't even know what that is. What kind of a detective are you exactly?'

'The kind that wants to know how you and the man we're chasing came to meet.'

'Same way I meet all my Johns: by email.'

'I see,' replied Stronge. 'So what do you do, scrawl your address on the walls of pub toilets?'

'Okay, that's enough, Kat,' I put in.

Stronge let out a harsh breath that I took as a warning. She carried on. 'Answer the question. Please.'

Tali answered, 'I advertise my services on a corner of the dark web Uncannies like to go. I don't ask my customers about their creed or colour because that's none of my business.'

'How honourable,' Stronge pinged back.

'It's not about that. It's about money.'

'Right. And tell me, do you often get paid to lie on your back for hours and not have sex?'

'More often than you'd think.'

Stronge ran her eyes over the woman's body, which seemed to have been built expressly for lewd acts. 'Sure you do, princess. And I fart wind chimes.'

The backchat was flying around like paintballs at a teambuilding weekend. If this carried on, someone was going to lose an eye.

'Is that everything, Detective?' I asked, placing my hands on the back of her chair, doing my best to bring the interview to a close.

'Not by a long shot.' Stronge's head snapped in Tali's direction. 'I think you're full of shit. I think there's no way an independent escort who moves in a world of monsters doesn't vet her Johns before she gets into bed with them. Thoroughly. And even if you didn't know what you were dealing with until the two of you were in the room, there's no way you wouldn't have figured out he was hiding something. So admit it. Admit that you knew he had blue skin, and that the only reason you didn't say so is because you knew what that meant.'

Tali's spine straightened and her fists went hard. 'You're wrong.'

'If I am, you're either stupid or suicidal. So which is it?'

Finally, Tali snapped, exploding from the desk and landing in front of Stronge, her finger wagging an inch from the detective's face. 'Stop acting like this is my fault,' she yelled, jerking a thumb at the pit in her forehead, which was spitting sparks now. 'I died. I'm the victim here.'

Stronge folded her arms, refusing to tip her chair back so much as a single degree. 'Very convincing. That's the thing with hookers though, isn't it? They know how to fake it.'

Tali let out a strangled sob. Jesus. Stronge was grilling the poor cow so hard it's a wonder she didn't catch fire. Tali looked to me for help and Stronge did the same. I had a choice to make: comfort the dame or aid the bull. God help me, I chose the latter.

Holding my nose, I went along with Stronge and turned up the heat some more.

'The detective's right,' I said. 'You're not telling us everything you know, and if you're not going to work with us, you don't deserve our help.'

She looked back at me with tears in her eyes. 'Please, Jake…'

I choked back a swallow so dry I could actually hear it. 'Fine, have it your way. Good luck out there, Tali, because you're on your own. You know where the door is, but feel free to head through the wall if you'd prefer.'

Tali stared at me in disbelief, her bottom lip trembling, then she broke, not with anger, but with aching howls that wracked the whole of her body. 'I knew, okay? I knew he was an Arcadian.'

And there it was. I'd been so convinced she was telling the truth, but it was like Stronge said: I was being played. I'd treated my client as a damsel, an innocent, a face in a locket, but she wasn't some pretty little thing sitting on the sidelines. She was a player. The question that remained now was, what was the game?

'Why would you lie about that?' I asked.

She found her breath. 'Because we both know how powerful Arcadians are.'

I did now, thanks to Jazz, but how did she?

She explained, 'Your detective friend was right: I do my research. When I saw the blue in the creases of his skin, I knew what I was dealing with.' She let slip a bitter sigh. 'I didn't care. He was a good talker and he seemed harmless enough.'

'Even though he was in disguise?' I persisted.

'Aren't we all trying to be something we're not?'

I looked to Frank, my friend, my partner, but also the human suit I stepped into when I wanted to fool people into thinking I was alive.

'You said you lied to us because Arcadians are powerful,' said Stronge. 'What did you mean by that?'

Tali wouldn't look at her. Instead, she addressed me. 'I was worried you wouldn't take the case with fae involved. And if you wouldn't help me, who else could I turn to? No one else cares that I'm dead. Nobody.'

'And that's it?' I said. 'That's the only reason you lied to me?'

'It's a pretty big reason.'

It was.

'Okay, fresh start. Is there anything else you're not telling us? Anything at all?'

'Nothing, I promise.' She held up her fingers honest injun style, and the copper ring she wore captured the light of my desk lamp, making its emerald sparkle.

'Is that an engagement ring?' asked Stronge. I'd noticed the jewellery when Tali first came to me, but hadn't followed up on it at the time. 'You got a man out there?'

'Used to,' Tali replied.

'What was he like, your fiancé?' The hard edge in Stronge's voice had blunted, but it wasn't gone completely.

'He was sweet. Wanted me to get out of the game. I should have listened to him.'

She rotated the stone away from us and placed her hands one over the other, hiding the ring in her lap.

I looked to Stronge as if to say, *Satisfied*? Eventually, she gave me a nod. The interview was at an end. No further questions, M'lud.

I thanked Tali for her honesty and apologised for being rough on her, explaining that we only had her best interests at heart. Now we knew what we were dealing with and that we could trust her, bringing in the Arcadian would be that much easier. At least that's what I told her. Frank and I both knew that having a lead on a suspect was a very different story to apprehending one.

All the same, we were going to do our utmost to bring him to justice, so I said goodbye to Tali, promising that I'd do a better job of keeping her in the loop as we closed in on her killer. It was only a matter of time now, and the sooner we got to work, the better.

'Good luck,' said Tali, putting on a brave smile. 'Make it back soon and maybe I'll mix you that cocktail after all.'

I gave her a nod and we took off, but not before Stronge pulled me into the room next door with a hushed, 'Can I have a word?'

Frank and I followed her into the showroom, a dusty hangover from when the building was still a funeral home. Stronge closed the door behind us and the sound disturbed one of our houseguests, sending a spider with legs as thick as pipe cleaners scuttling out of a nearby coffin and scurrying under a skirting board by Stronge's foot. She let out an appalled yelp.

'What the hell, Fletcher?'

'Next room on the refurb list, promise,' I replied, hand on my heart.

Once she'd recovered from the shock, Stronge turned serious. Well, more serious. She was always some degree of serious.

'Do you believe her?' she asked.

'I do.'

'I was talking to him,' she said, nodding to Frank. 'Well, is she telling the truth?'

Frank considered the question. The effort made his mouth slowly drawbridge open until it hung so low that his tongue fell out and he had to suck it in like wet spaghetti. After another minute of deep contemplation, he finally said, 'Yeeeeeeeesssss.'

Fletcher & Fletcher were in accord, leaving DCI Stronge the lone cynic.

'There's something not right here, mark my words,' she said.

'Kat, you came in here with a question and the question's been answered. Let's move on.'

She chewed her bottom lip. 'Okay, but only because Frank agrees with you. He's the one with the good nose.'

Frank smiled. I did, too. We were all on the same page. All that remained now was to follow the will-o'-the-wisp's lead and nail the grotty little bastard it used to nest in. And we would have, too, if it weren't for one problem: the wisp was lying on its back at the bottom of its jar.

'Is it dead?' asked Stronge.

I took a closer look and saw that it was still giving off that faint, throbbing glow. 'No, just sleeping.'

Frank gave it a rattle but the bug wouldn't stir.

'Leave it,' said Stronge, staying his hand. 'We need it too much to risk killing the thing.'

'What are you saying? We just let it sleep?'

'Yeah,' she replied. 'Me, too. I've been up for two days straight—I'm no good to anyone right now. Give me a couple of hours of shut-eye and we'll take a fresh run at the suspect then.'

I supposed she wasn't asking for much. The sun wouldn't even be up in that time, and the killer still had some recuperating to do.

'All right, deal. You wanna take the sofa?'

'No thanks,' she replied with a shudder, most likely recalling the enormous coffin spider.

'Suit yourself. Just make sure you meet me back here in three hours. No more than that.'

Stronge zipped up her gilet. 'Fine. Stay put until I get back, okay? Promise you won't go off half-cocked without me.'

I promised.

The promise wasn't kept.

CHAPTER SEVENTEEN: REALITY BITES

When you don't sleep, you need to find ways to occupy your mind, to keep the dark thoughts at bay. In the small hours of the morning a man is apt to search his soul, and often what he finds there ain't pretty. So I fill that time. Mostly, I spend it the same way the living spend their waking hours: watching movies, playing games, wandering aimlessly. Procrastinating, in other words.

Then there are nights I use that extra time productively. For instance, I might swot up on a subject I'm unfamiliar with, study a new language, or hone my magic. On this occasion, I chose to spend the twilight hours reading the book Jazz Hands loaned me: *The Modern Encyclopaedia of Faeries and Otherkin*.

It was a big book. A whopper, really, but it was loaded with interesting titbits. I was only a short way in and I'd already learned a couple of beauts. For instance, did you know that fae don't have navels, or even fingerprints? I didn't, but now I understood why the suspect didn't leave any dabs at the crime scene. Another thing I wasn't aware of: the fae have a habit of robbing babies and turning them into slaves. Also, fairies can't lie, though they are master manipulators and can do incredible things with a few withheld truths. But the big reveal, the thing that really caught my attention, was learning why the Arcadians vacated our realm all those years ago.

Apparently, the reason was twofold: the first being that people stopped believing in magic, and in doing so, negated their existence. The second was an ecological issue. As the world advanced, the growing pollution became too much for their delicate constitutions, and the fae were forced to relocate. Thinking about it, that was probably why the Arcadian we were hunting grew himself that little indoor forest: to filter out some of the city's impurities. Didn't do him much good when he caught a lungful of exhaust fumes from that bin lorry, though, did it?

But it wasn't just the smog that sent the Arcadians packing in the olden days, it was an allergy to modernity itself. The poor lambs were intolerant to the industrialised world in general, and most products of it. The first thing to get their knickers in a twist was steel. For them, that stuff was a giant no-no. Legend has it that fae are wounded by iron, but according to Jazz's tome, this assessment was a little off. It was the bulk manufacture of crucible steel—a modern alloy—that made this world unsafe for their kind, that turned it into poison. And so the Arcadians stopped visiting our realm altogether and returned to their homeland, never to be seen again. Until now.

So why come back? And why London? What was here for this fae besides even more pollution and modernity? I had no idea, but I knew this much: if the bloke who killed my client was having a hard time dealing with the city, things were only going to get worse for him when we had our rematch.

My reading was interrupted by a familiar buzzing noise: the sound of the will-o'-the-wisp voicing its discontent. I cast a glance to the jar on my desk and saw the creature had taken flight. It was bumping against the walls of its prison, desperate to find its way home, back to the Arcadian that had brought it to this strange and unfamiliar land.

I turned to Frank, who'd been assisting me with my reading, turning the pages of the book as necessary.

'We shouldn't, right?'

He stared back at me, eyes vacant, no clue what I was talking about.

'Go after the Arcadian, I mean. Without Stronge.'

Frank's expression remained absolutely unchanged.

'Then again, haven't we wasted enough time already? What if he slips the net while we're back here sitting on our arses?'

The look on Frank's mush changed not one iota.

'We should get after him, right? Kat won't care that we jumped the gun so long as we get results.'

A continuing look of blank serenity.

I climbed to my feet and pounded Frank on the back, knocking a small avalanche of dead skin from his shoulders. 'Thanks for the assist, partner. You always know the right thing to say.'

My mind was made up. We'd strike while the iron was hot, or better yet I thought—checking my trusty hammer and finding a stamp on its head that identified what it was made of—we'd strike with good old-fashioned UK steel. Stronge was liable to be spitting feathers when she showed up here and found we'd ditched her, but she'd get over it. She'd already played her part. She'd got us this far down the road, now all Frank and me had to do was slap on the cuffs. The Arcadian didn't stand a chance. We had the home advantage, the right equipment for the job, and we'd already dealt the guy a good drubbing. What could possibly go wrong?

It would be a few hours yet before dawn coloured the streets, so the intrepid Fletcher & Fletcher superteam headed into the night to bag themselves a sleeping fae. The wisp pulled north-east and we followed, heading in the direction of Newham. We were moving through a rough part of town—a place the police cars don't stop—when something caught my eye. Reflected in the only unbroken window of a dilapidated building, I saw a figure. He was a good thirty yards behind me but his silhouette alone gave him away, his spine bowed like a flower in desperate need of water. My stalkers were back, or one of them at least.

I caught another flash of him in a parked car's wing mirror. He was all done up in his Sunday best, his long hair tied back into a neat ponytail that swung like a pendulum with each footfall. From the way he was walking—unhurried and confident—he had no idea we were on to him. I wondered how come the bloke was flying solo. Was it budget cuts, or were my mysterious tagalongs just short-staffed this evening? I landed on *who cares*? Frank and me had the numbers this time, that's all that mattered.

I slowed my pace and gave my partner a signal to do the same, which caused our tail to draw closer still. I stole a casual glance over my shoulder as we rounded a corner and got a better look at him. My suspicions were correct. The figure had the same hollowed-out features, blood red eyes, and unnaturally long fingers as the strangers I'd caught in our rearview a few nights ago. I gave Frank a knowing look. This was our chance to discover who these stalkers were, and work out why they'd taken an interest in us.

We took a swift right into an alleyway narrow enough that I could have stretched out my arms and touched both sides. Naturally, our secret admirer did the same. I'll bet the last thing he expected when he turned that corner was to find Frank standing there, looking right at him with murder in his eyes. Actually, scratch that, the *absolute* last thing he would have seen coming was a ghostly hand reaching through the alley's solid wall, grabbing him by the ponytail, and cracking his nut against the brickwork.

The blow left him on the cobbles, but not for long. Frank hauled him up by his tie, clamped a hand on either side of his canister, and turned his face to mine. He wasn't exactly what you'd call a looker. Our stalker had a snub nose, eyes capped by a thick black mono-brow, and giant, pointy ears covered in downy beards. He hissed at me, spitting like a cobra, two white fangs protruding over thin blue lips.

So, the people following us were vampires after all. That was always my guess given the hours they kept, but it was nice to know for sure. When I saw that he cast a reflection I was given doubt, but now I thought about it—fun fact, kids—his kind were only invisible in mirrors backed with real silver.

Anyway, the length of the chompers he was baring told me he was at least a hundred years old, so no newcomer to the game. Best not take chances and treat him with the respect he deserved.

'Tell me who you're working for or I'll kick your arse all the way back to Transylvania,' I said.

Okay, maybe not too much respect. You can overdo these things.

The vamp struggled but Frank's grip remained firm

'Have you got cloth ears?' I said. 'Why are you and your mates tailing me?'

He shut his mouth and went as tight-lipped as an uncooked mussel.

I gave Frank a nod and he dealt the vamp a squeeze hard enough to shift the plates in his skull. Our stalker's mouth came undone but the scream stayed trapped in his throat.

'Ease up a bit,' I told Frank, 'I don't want to end up wearing this numpty's eyeballs on my loafers.'

Frank loosened his grip a smidge, allowing the vamp to let slip a great, pained gasp.

'Fancy having another go at answering my questions?' I asked.

His expression was hard, his eyes two narrow slits. 'I'll tell you nothing,' he snarled in an accent that was hard to place.

'That's a shame,' I said, glad that Detective Stronge wasn't about to see me extract a confession in a way that *definitely* wasn't kosher.

I launched a fist at his face that connected with his jaw and left him wearing a *Hammer Horror* chin trickle worthy of Christopher Lee himself.

'Whoopsie. Sorry about that, pal. I'm all thumbs today.'

'I'll gouge your eyes out and skull fuck your soul,' he screamed.

'Pack it in,' I said, giving him a sobering slap across the chops. 'Getting on my wrong side right now would be the biggest mistake of your life, and I'm factoring that haircut into the equation.'

'Fuck you.'

'We covered that ground already,' I replied. 'Tell you what, why don't we switch things up a bit and you tell me why you and the rest of the Lost Boys are creeping on us?'

Once again, the vamp developed a bad case of lockjaw.

'Suit yourself.' I turned to my partner. 'See if you can change his mind, would you?'

Frank adjusted his grip on the vampire's skull, but doing so gave the rat bastard his moment. He arrowed out an elbow, catching Frank in the bollocks and folding him in half. I was quick enough to throw the vamp a dig before he made a break for it, but it didn't do much damage, in fact, it only served to rile him up.

Quick as a wink, he took my legs out from under me, then his feet were going at my ribs like he was trying to kickstart a busted motorbike. Despite his age, the vampire fought like a young man, nothing held back, no slowing down. Doing what I could to get back in the match, I placed my palms on the ground and made it up to one knee, but that was the best I could manage. While I was wobbling, the vamp cocked a fist and took a swing. Thankfully, Frank had caught his breath by that point, and grabbed the feller by the wrist before he could land the hit.

What happened next is a bit of a blur. There was a tussle that I thought was going to end with Frank duffing the vamp up a bit, only it turned out a bit more serious than that. Growling with ape-like fury, Frank yanked at my attacker's wrist and lurched back a good three feet. It took me a second to understand the strange object he was holding, that's until I saw the ruined mess of the vampire's shoulder and realised Frank had wrenched his arm out at the socket.

The vamp pulled a face like a man at an airport caught with a balloon of heroin up his jacksie, then opened his mouth and let out a scream louder than any I've heard before or since.

'God Almighty,' I gasped.

Usually, old Frank's good as gold, but he's got a temper on him, especially when it comes to someone raising a hand to yours truly.

The vampire shrank back clutching the unplugged hole in his torso, then turned tail and hobbled away. I didn't have the heart to go after him. Honestly, I was too stunned to give chase—we both were, standing there shaking our heads, mouths agape.

Finally, after I don't know how long, I came to my senses and realised Frank was still clutching the vampire's severed limb.

'Drop it, for Christ's sake,' I told him.

He let it go and the arm hit the ground with a wet slap. Gravity rolled it over, and as it did, the long, webbed fingers on the vampire's ex-hand unfurled like a blooming flower. I saw something on the palm: a black mark of some kind. When I crouched down to get a better look I saw felt-tipped words scrawled across the inside of the hand like an open mic comedian's setlist. The handwriting spelled out an address and a time. Also included was a single word, written in capital letters: CONCLAVE.

Most vampires, like fae folk, have a tendency to be technologically adverse, so I wasn't too surprised to learn that the one following us had committed important information to his person instead of maing a note on his phone. More surprising was the richness of the information he'd provided us with, and that we'd been jammy enough to retain it.

A conclave, for those of you not in the know, is another word for a vampire powwow. They're typically convened so members of a clan can come together and discuss matters of importance. What those matters were and whether they had anything to do with our business, I had no idea, but I did know the meeting was happening tonight, and that I felt compelled to stick my nose in. A vampire had lost a limb to provide me with this tip-off; I had to honour that sacrifice, right? Then again, there was a homicidal Arcadian still on the loose, which was surely more pressing business.

And yet.

And yet...

What if the vampires were wrapped up in this somehow? They started following me right about the time Frank and I took the case of the murdered escort. Was it possible that the vamps and the fae were in cahoots somehow? That my client's death was more than some random killing? That her murder had a purpose I didn't understand? A purpose that would forever remain a mystery unless I earwigged on this secret meeting?

Or was I putting two and two together and coming up with a shepherd's pie? There was every chance that the vampires were nothing more than a distraction. Something that had nothing to do with our investigation and would only send us spinning off in the wrong direction.

I looked to the arm on the ground, then to Frank. 'What do you say? Do we check this thing out or what?'

I needed to know. Should we stay the course or take this fork in the road? Was it a good idea to act on this new information or would peeling off at this point be like going on holiday in the middle of a car chase?

Frank's forehead puckered as he considered the question. Finally, he replied with a long and thoughtful, 'Braaaaiiiiins.'

So much for seeking my partner's advice. That's the thing with

Frank, when his brain-lust is up, he's no use to anyone. Getting him to focus on a task is like asking a hungry dog to balance a biscuit on his nose: you won't get what you want, and you might lose a finger trying.

I needed to make an executive decision. I could only hope, unlike the film of the same name, that it wasn't shit.

CHAPTER EIGHTEEN: FLY IN THE WALL

IN THE END, I decided to chuck a frisbee into the abyss and see what this conclave was all about.

The part of town our expedition took us to was even worse than the area we were passing through when we caught a vampire riding our arse. Seriously, you wouldn't want to raise a jackal in that neck of the woods. Derelict buildings lined potholed streets like rows of broken teeth, dossers scavenged for food in overflowing bins, and the whole manor stank of regurgitated booze. I didn't need Frank to tell me that—the stench was palpable with or without a nose.

'Show me that note, would you?' I said.

Frank reached into his coat pocket and pulled out a legal pad, upon which he'd written the address the conclave was taking place at. I had him copy it off the vampire's hand, which we left back in the alleyway, along with the limb it was attached to. Frank had wanted to eat the thing, but I told him no. I didn't want him getting a taste for human flesh, even if that human was a nosferatu. It was already hard enough keeping reins on Frank without him going full Romero on me.

I checked the pad against the address we were at and found a match. By the looks of it, the building had been a storefront at some point, though its signage had long ago been lost to vandalism and apathy. Even the For Sale sign fixed above the boarded-up front door was on its last legs, hanging by a single nail and covered in a decade's worth of exhaust soot and grime. Unlike most properties in London, it seemed this wasn't one that buyers were particularly eager to invest in. Even the city's vulture developers had stayed away from this grotty end of town. Out here, when a place was abandoned, it stayed that way.

We skirted around to the rear of the building and found that the back door, like the one at the front, had been boarded over. Closer examination revealed that the wooden planks here were a front, though. In fact, they were nothing more than a fake skin covering a functioning door that would have granted us easy access if only it wasn't locked.

I put my ear to the door and heard the faint burble of conversation beyond. Someone was home for sure. Going by the time, I had to assume the conclave was already in progress, which meant we were missing out on what might prove to be some juicy gossip.

'I've gotta get in there,' I told Frank.

He nodded once and raised his fists, ready to beat down the door.

'No,' I said, stepping in his way. 'Just me.'

He cocked his head and looked at me cow-eyed.

I placed a friendly hand on his shoulder. 'This is a stealth mission, mate. If you go in there's a chance they might hear us, then this whole trip's been a write-off.'

Which was my polite way of saying that Frank's best attempt at sneaking was likely to sound like the entire drum section of the London Philharmonic falling down a rickety staircase. And yet despite my diplomacy, Frank remained decidedly down in the mouth.

'I know, I know, we're supposed to be partners. It's not fair leaving you out.'

'Twiiiiiiice,' he moaned.

'Right, twice, but you have to trust me, this is for the best. And look, if shit goes down in there, you'll be the first to know about it. I'll need my muscle if things go sideways, so don't go running off anywhere, okay?'

He bobbed his head solemnly.

'Oh, and Frank, one more thing... no eating anyone's brains while I'm gone, okay?'

He bared his teeth and growled. Not in a threatening way, just to let me know he'd had enough.

'All right, going now,' I said, and phased through the door.

It took a few seconds for my eyes to adjust to the building's shadow-drenched interior. I'd landed in a hallway that looked like a hundred years of dust held up by a century's worth of paint. Cobwebs laced a ceiling lit by a few feeble light bulbs, and warped floorboards lined the floor. I glided over them, thankful that I'd chosen to leave Frank outside. The second his clodhoppers landed on one of those creaky boards we'd have had every vampire in the building on us.

Following the hallway, I heard the sound of conversation growing louder with each step until I came to a staircase that plunged sharply into a cellar. I headed down the steps and found each one set at a different height from the last, making it hard to judge how low I needed to dip my foot each time. At the bottom of the stairs was another corridor, its ceiling low and held up by rotting beams. I hung my head and continued along it, noticing a warren of small rooms either side of me. The rooms were stacked with wooden racks heaving with tall green bottles laid on their sides. Wine, I assumed, at least until I took a closer look. With no small amount of effort, I firmed up a hand, uncorked one of the bottles, and poured out its contents. The liquid that slopped out was red, but vino it was not. I briefly wondered how many innocent people these vamps had tapped to fill a whole cellar, then decided I'd prefer not to know.

I walked on as far as I was prepared to go; any further and I'd have crashed the conclave. Going by the noise they were making, there had to be at least twenty vampires around the next corner. I had a hard time against one of them—getting caught by that many would be suicide. So I ignored the corner and made my own path, taking a shortcut through brick and mortar and emerging inside the crawlspace of the wall surrounding the conclave's meeting space.

Through a narrow crack in the brickwork I was able to spy on the clandestine chinwag, which was taking place in a dungeonesque chamber spotted with fungal growths. There was a whole mess of vampires in attendance, even more than I'd guessed at, maybe as many as forty in total.

From my hide I was able to get a good look at the congregation. With their matching stoops and scarecrow frames, these vamps were obviously of the same bloodline as the ones that had been stalking us, though I had no idea which clan they belonged to. I'd never seen vampires like this lot. They barely looked human. Their ratty facial features, pointed ears, and webbed fingers, made me think more of bats than people. If vampires shared some genetic ancestry with flying rodents, this was the strain that never fully evolved. The missing link, if you will. These weren't your misunderstood heartthrob kind of vampires. They didn't sparkle and they weren't given to writing poetry or keeping diaries. These were the sort of vampires that wore high collars and glided out from walls of dry ice. They lived on the fringes because they had no choice in the matter. They couldn't mix with humanity because they were too many steps removed.

So why come to London, you might wonder. A couple of reasons I could think of, but first and foremost, the climate. The UK gets next to no sunshine and spends a good chunk of its time in darkness, which most vampires rely on to survive. The second reason was that vampires have a taste for the finer things in life. Sure, they could set up shop in Antarctica, but try finding a Harvey Nics out that way.

Still buried in the wall, I listened in on the unfolding conversation, or rather conversations plural. There seemed to be no agenda in play, with clusters of clan members chatting amongst themselves as they pleased. That was until one vampire called order on the proceedings by banging the skull-shaped handle of his walking cane against a wall. My wall. The crack I was peeking through widened as a chunk of masonry spilled out. I shrank back, and held my breath (metaphorically speaking). Thankfully, the vampires were too focused on the sudden call for attention to notice me cringing inside the crawlspace.

'Thank you all for coming this evening,' said the vampire with the walking cane. 'And at such short notice.'

His voice was a cocktail of accents: an unholy mixture of British, Slavic, and Germanic. I craned my neck an inch to the left and snuck a goosey at him. He didn't look like much—same ugly face as his brothers, same bent back—but it was obvious from the way he held court that he was top dog here.

'It is my honour to host this conclave, gentlemen. Please, gather round.'

The vampires fell silent and formed a circle about him. With their attention acquired, he placed the foot of his cane on the ground, laced his hands together, and leant upon the handle.

'It is my sincerest wish that by sharing what we have learned these last few days, we will discover the whereabouts of the man we seek.' He made a chest-to-fist salute. 'For the Vengari.'

The last part was echoed loudly by everyone in the room.

The Vengari.

I had to trawl the muck in my skull to find it, but I dredged it up soon enough. The Vengari were a vampire clan like no other. They were bottom feeders among their kind, and yet, like me, they were survivors. They'd endured all manner of purges and scourges over the centuries, and persisted come what may. It was said that the reason they'd developed those long fingers was because they'd spent so long clinging to immortality. Where so many other vampire clans had fallen, the Vengari had refused to let go, determined not to be beaten, determined to carry on.

I suddenly felt very crowded. I'd intruded upon the den of a clan of deadly vampires. Vampires that had survived for centuries. What was I thinking coming here alone? Why hadn't I brought the Nightstalker in on this? Dealing with vampires was her job. Abbey Beckett did the Van Helsing thing for a living; it's why they called her stabby Abbey. But instead of her, the Vengari clan were getting me, a walking memory who could barely uncork a wine bottle.

I held my nerve. I hadn't learned anything yet besides the identity of my stalkers, and that information alone didn't amount to much. I still didn't know what they wanted with me, or whether it had anything to do with my investigation.

And then it came, served up hot on a platter.

The top dog turned in a lazy circle, taking in each of the vampires girdling him, and said, 'So, which of you can tell me where the Arcadian is hiding?'

CHAPTER NINETEEN: CRUMBS FROM THE DEVIL'S TABLE

THERE IT WAS. The vampires were just as interested in the killer fae as I was, though I had no idea why. Not yet, anyway.

The top dog picked out a fellow clan member, seemingly at random. 'What do you have to report, brother?'

The chosen vampire sniffed and cleared his throat. 'We discovered a bolt hole the Arcadian was using—overgrown with vegetation and drenched in fae magic—but by the time we got there, he had already fled.'

The top dog nodded and turned to the next member of the circle. 'What about you?'

'My men have been on lookout detail, covering train and bus stations in case the Arcadian tries to escape the city.'

'And?'

'No sign of him yet,' the vampire conceded, so quietly as to be barely audible.

'I see,' replied the head honcho, rubbing his red eyes. 'And what about the rest of you? Can anyone here tell me where the Arcadian is located?'

The room stayed quiet.

'Do we have any leads at all? A single clue that could point us to his whereabouts?'

Total radio silence.

'So what I'm hearing is, we have nothing. Is that about right?' He went on, the edge in his voice hard but brittle. 'Need I remind everyone why it is so important we capture the Arcadian?'

I got the distinct impression that he didn't need to, but he went ahead anyway.

'He jilted one of our own. That cannot be allowed to stand. He must be brought back to the altar, by force if necessary.'

Well, bugger me sideways. An arranged marriage—was that what all this malarkey was about? Some fae/vampire merger gone to pot?

'This is unacceptable,' cried the top dog, hammering the cellar floor with the foot of his cane. 'You must find the Arcadian and apprehend him at once.'

He laid a baleful look on the congregation. Most bowed their heads in shame, but one vampire was brave enough to meet his icy gaze.

'Who are you to dispense orders, old man?'

A gasp rippled through the crowd. The Vengari at the centre of the circle fixed his blood-red eyes on a vampire with a harelip and shoulders so pointy he looked as if he'd forgotten to take out the hanger when he put his suit on.

'Who am I?' barked the man in charge. 'I am the chair of this conclave and you will do as I—'

'Enough,' said the vampire with the harelip and the take-charge attitude. 'We need action, not ceaseless prattle.'

Whoever this bloke was, he had some balls on him. Vampire hierarchy was clearly delineated and brutally enforced. Speaking up to a superior like that could have cost him his neck, but he obviously didn't care.

'How dare you,' roared the head vamp, spitting like an angry camel. 'This meeting is more than just talk. It's about pooling our resources... working together as a clan.'

'If you really wanted to find the Arcadian you'd be out there right now instead of conducting this pointless ceremony.'

I could tell from the way he carried himself that this was the smartest feller in the room. I think everyone could.

'If you're such a man of action, what are you doing here?' asked the chair.

'That's a very good question,' replied the upstart.

He snapped his fingers and a vampire by his side helped him into his coat.

'Where do you think you're going?' demanded the chair, nostrils flaring.

The vampire with the harelip shrugged on his coat and buttoned it up. 'You stay here and have your little knitting circle. I'll be out there finding the Arcadian and bringing him to heel.'

'Come back at once.'

But the upstart paid him no heed, heading out of the cellar and taking three vampires with him.

The congregation had become agitated now. The chair was losing the respect of his brethren. He let out an awkward cough.

'Surely someone must have something. Anything...'

A vampire who hadn't been brave enough to chip in before filled the vacuum. 'Speaking on behalf of my chapter, I can report that we have located and continue to shadow Detectives Fletcher and Fletcher, who are also tracking our target.'

So that was it. The only reason the Vengari were keeping tabs on us was to get to the Arcadian. Far as I was concerned, that was just rude. A total lack of professional courtesy. Now I didn't feel the least bit bad about Frank ripping their man's arm off.

'And?' said the chair, leaning forward on his cane. 'Have the detectives' findings proved useful?'

'So far they've failed to lead us to the Arcadian, but we're confident it's only a matter of time.'

That was it for the chair. He snapped his cane over his knee, his face a mask of pure rage. 'Idiots. Idiots!'

One of the other chapter heads spoke up for himself. 'Perhaps we should consider cutting our losses. It's clear that the fae are no longer interested in honouring the terms of our pact, so why are we so determined to recover their runaway groom?'

A murmur of agreement bounced around the room.

The chair's eyes went wide. 'Have you lost sight of what this union could do for us? An opportunity like this comes along once in a millennium, if that. This is our chance to rise up, to take our rightful place at the top of the totem pole.'

I couldn't make hide nor hair of this. The Vengari were already looked down on by their fellow clans—how was marrying off one of their own to a foreigner going to change that? And more to the point, what was in it for the fae? The Vengari were the lowest of the low, and the Arcadians were card-carrying royalty. Why would they be interested in forming a coalition with these cockroaches?

And then there was the real poser, the one that had me utterly stumped: what did any of this have to do with my client?

I broke it all down, the story so far. It really was a whale of a tale. Going by what I'd learned, it went something like this: the killer fae left Arcadia to come to London, got involved with a clan of vampires, and promised to marry one of their women. Then, for reasons entirely beyond my understanding, he abandoned their bride and did a runner. Having done the dirty on the Vengari, he then killed a random call girl, roughed up his drug dealer, and holed up in a sinkhole estate. What kind of behaviour was that? The bloke was all over the place. Maybe the drugs he was on had driven him doolally.

Whatever he was up to, it was obvious that the Vengari had no more of an idea where he was hiding than I did. And yet, hiding in the wall had taught me more about them than they'd have liked me to know. Enough that they'd sooner kill me than let me slip away with their secrets in my head. Which seemed to me like my cue to leave.

Without waiting around for the wrap up, I phased through the other side of the wall, crept back up the cellar stairs, and left through the back door. Frank was waiting for me by the exit.

'Let's go,' I said, nudging his elbow.

Instead of falling in step, he remained motionless, arms crossed, a sour look on his face.

I persisted. 'Come on. We've gotta scarper.'

But Frank dug in his heels. 'Shaaaare,' he moaned.

Which was his way of telling me he wasn't going anywhere until I told him what I'd seen.

'Later.'

Frank turned his nose up at me and snorted.

Perfect. A pack of vampires could come pouring through that door at any moment, and instead of making good with our legs, moody bollocks was holding me hostage. All because he felt a bit left out. Christ. Don't get me wrong, having Frank around has been great, but there are times he can feel like a real albatross around my neck. This was definitely one of those times.

'Have it your way then, you stroppy sod.'

In the spirit of compromise, I merged with Frank and downloaded what I'd learned into his rotting brain. This really wasn't the time for it, but sharing information this way was quicker than a regular conversation, not to mention quieter.

Our minds became one and I felt the two-way exchange of our thoughts crossing paths. Frank was miffed. More than I realised. I'd sidelined him more than once since this case began, and he did not appreciate it. We were partners, he reminded me. Equals. Where I went, he went. I wanted to tell him that the only reason I froze him out just now was because the vamps would have heard him coming from a mile away, but I was too busy filling him in on the Vengari's secrets, so instead, I stayed schtum and let him say his piece. I was just about done passing along what I knew when the sound of a creaking hinge spelled out my worst fears.

A lone vampire stepped out of the building's back door, cigarette in one hand, a Zippo in the other. It was the Vengari chair, still raging from the disrespect he'd been shown downstairs. It wasn't until he'd sparked his smoke and the door closed behind him that he realised he wasn't alone. He stared at us, open-mouthed.

Frank got there before I did, lashing out a fist and putting the stuffy old bastard on his arse. Not before he put him through the door, though, which broke with a sound like a starter gun and with much the same effect.

'Intruders,' shrieked the vampire.

His cry was quickly followed by the sound of feet hammering warped floorboards as the rest of the Vengari raced up the stairs to see what they were missing. Frank didn't take any cajoling after that. Without separating, the two of us picked up our feet and stole away into the night.

We were barely three blocks away when we stepped into a brand new pile of shit.

CHAPTER TWENTY: THE BOYS IN BLUE

THANKS TO THAT LITTLE DETOUR, the Vengari not only knew who I was, they knew that I was onto them. I thought the conclave would be a piñata I could crack open for juicy gossip, but instead it had turned out to be a nest full of angry wasps. Even worse, I was about to discover that the vamps weren't the only bad bastards my investigation had succeeded in stirring up.

We rounded a corner and ducked behind a wall with bits of broken glass embedded in the cement on top. Using Frank's eyes, I checked back the way we came and confirmed we'd shaken our pursuers. The squeezing fist of dread that held us both in its icy grip seemed to loosen for a moment, at least until I cast Frank's head in the other direction and saw some new figures heading our way.

The three strangers moved simultaneously, each footstep landing in perfect synchrony like a trio of dancers performing a well-rehearsed routine. It wasn't clear who or what they were, but I was certain they didn't belong to the Vengari clan. With their upright posture and peacock strut, they were a total contrast to the crooked, hunched vampires we'd just outrun.

The figures crossed beneath a street lamp buzzing with fat moths and I saw them for what they were: Arcadians. So, the fae I was chasing hadn't come to the city alone. That put a whole new complexion on things. Speaking of complexion, with their azure skin on full display it was clear that these Arcadians—unlike the one I was chasing—had no respect whatsoever for the Accord.

The Accord is what us Uncannies call the agreement we have: the one we adopted centuries ago to keep our supernatural business separate from the workaday world. I wondered briefly whether the fae were oblivious of the agreement or just contemptuous of it, but as they drew closer I could tell by the look on their smug blue faces that it wasn't due to ignorance. The Arcadians knew the rules, they just considered themselves above them.

'My name is Draven,' said the Arcadian flanked either side, his voice smooth as a meadow river. All three fae were dressed smartly, but the cut of this one's jib was a little tidier than the rest. He was suited and booted and wore a coat with a collar made from the fur of something rare and expensive. He lifted his chin and peered at me imperiously. 'I assume you know who we are?'

I scratched my cheek stubble. 'I'd say the Blue Man Group, but you're a fuck of a long way from Vegas.'

I saw Draven's face stiffen and wondered if pissing him off was really in my best interest. Inside my head, Frank was equally concerned, and with good reason. Even wrapped up in his body, I was as vulnerable to creatures who wielded magic as I was to other undead. I've learned over the years that the list of things that can kill ghosts is a long one. Aggravatingly long.

'We're here to find our missing brother,' said Draven.

So they were looking for the killer, too. It seemed even his own people didn't know where he was. What happened, I wondered. Did he go rogue? That would explain why I found him roughing it. Just how ugly was this vamp he was meant to marry that he was prepared to ditch his own family and live like a derelict?

'If you're asking after the other blue pretty boy, you're wasting your time,' I said. 'Because I don't have a Scooby.'

'A what?'

I sighed. Why does no one take the time to learn the lingo anymore? 'Scooby Doo: clue,' I explained.

'I see.' Draven returned a sinister smile. 'Well, that's odd, because a deaf eaves told us very much the opposite.'

Shit. The bulb-headed dealer must have done some digging and grassed me up as a thank you for the grilling I gave him at the night-club. Poxy eaves.

Draven continued, 'Having learned about the so-called Spectral Detective, we decided to stop by your office. We've been following you ever since.'

I guess they figured I knew this city better than them, so why not let the cat lead them to the mouse? That meant I had two groups piggybacking my investigation now. Honestly, the cheek of these people. On the other hand, two sets of stalkers; a bit flattering.

While his companions remained mute, Draven spent a moment taking in his surroundings. 'You know, the last time I was here, this place was fields as far as the eye could see. Now look at it.'

A sudden cough rattled his ribs. He plucked a silk handkerchief from his coat pocket and dabbed at his mouth. Clearly, the city agreed with him about as much as it did the Arcadian I was chasing.

Draven returned the hankie to his pocket. 'Now, are you going to tell us where we find our brother, or do we need to extract an answer from you some other way?'

I didn't like the sound of that, and neither did Frank. Matter of fact, he floated the idea of telling the fae what we knew and leaving them to deal with the matter themselves. He only said it out of love for me, mind you. Frank knew, even though we were certain to catch a beating for it, that we weren't giving the Arcadians shit. Not when we had a murdered woman relying on us to take down her killer.

'Sorry, lads, no can do,' I said.

Draven's mouth curved into another fishhook smile. 'Such a shame,' he said.

He popped the buttons of his fur-lined coat, peeled back a flap, and produced a weapon. Not a common shooter I noted—like the type his kin had used on my client—but something not of this world. In his hand, he held a short iron rod topped each end by a lump of crystal the size of a doorknob. Embedded in each of these crystals was what looked like a miniature swirling thunderstorm. He passed the rod to his other hand and a crackling white tentacle trailed behind it. I tasted static on Frank's tongue and gulped involuntarily.

Draven's smile turned dangerous. 'I'm going to enjoy this.'

He lunged at me with his rod of ruination, but I pulled back just in time and it slammed into the wall beside me, missing my skull with barely enough space for a Rizla paper. The other two didn't wait for me to take my turn. The fae pounced in my direction, but before they could get to me, I evened the odds by parting ways with my corporeal form. As I peeled away from Frank, he took a swing at the nearest fae, caught him in the jaw, and introduced him to the pavement.

'Hm,' said Draven, tutting. 'That explains where your partner got to.'

As we backed away, the floored Arcadian staggered to his feet, blood shading his blue face purple. Eager to return to the fight, he fell in line with his companions and the three of them came at us as one.

I turned to Frank and saw from the look in his eyes that he was thinking the same thing I was: no way we were going to take on the Arcadians in a straight fight. We'd need to box clever if we were going to stand any chance of walking away from this, and that started with getting the hell out of their orbit.

For the second time that evening, Frank and I ran. We ducked by the Arcadians and made good with our legs, Frank's shoe leather slapping the ground hard, my phantom loafers making no sound at all. As we barrelled down the side street I snatched a look over my shoulder and realised the fae were gaining on us with ease. We wouldn't outrun them. The best we could do was face them in an arena of our choosing; some place that gave us an edge. I had no idea what such a place would look like, but I saw a door on our right and decided being inside was a start. Out here we ran the risk of running into some vegetation the fae could use against us—a patch of ivy creeping up the wall ahead being a likely culprit. Indoors, the worst we'd have to face was a pot plant.

'Quick, through there...'

Frank caught my meaning. Ducking his head and turning his shoulder, he steamrolled through the door and laid it flat on the ground.

CHAPTER TWENTY-ONE: A FREUDIAN SLAP

THE ROOM we found ourselves in was large and grey and littered with pallet trucks. Evidently we'd barged into the loading dock of a warehouse. We forged on into the main storage area, a massive space lined with rows of industrial racks that stretched up high to a corrugated iron roof. The warehouse was dark and contained plenty of places we could hide and spring from. Because if there's one thing ghosts are good at, it's springing on people.

'Come out, smog-drinker,' called a voice I recognised as Draven's. It was followed by another racking cough.

I hoped the environment I'd chosen, combined with the fae's intolerance for the modern world, at least gave me and Frank a fighting chance.

'Allergies playing up?' I called back. 'Maybe you should get out of London and bugger off back to the Midsummer Night's Dream candyland you came from.'

'So quick-witted,' came Draven's disembodied voice. 'And yet what are you, really? Just the absence of a person. A void.'

'Better that than a fucking displaced wood nymph,' I retorted.

We were fighting for our lives, so forgive me a bit of fae-cism. That's racism against the fae. Get it? Okay, let's move on.

I decided to stop taking Draven's bait and shut my trap before I gave away our position. Frank and I ducked behind a rack loaded with nondescript cardboard boxes and watched the three Arcadians split up to cover more ground. Obviously, these guys had never seen a horror film before.

One of the lackeys—the feller that Frank had leathered outside—ended up wandering in our direction, more by luck than judgment. Bad luck as it turned out.

Without waiting for my permission, Frank plunged a fist through one of the cardboard boxes stacked between us and the fae and connected with his temple. His knees unhinged and he went down, but the bloke wasn't out for the count just yet. He tried to get up but failed on the first attempt, one foot sliding out uncontrollably and sending him back down. The floor beneath him had turned slippery and shone like an oil slick, only this wasn't Texas tea, this oil was see-through as a cartoon ghost. I noticed broken glass scattered among the mess, and attached to a portion that still bore a half-jar shape, a label. It read FRISKY BUSINESS SEX LUBE. With a rapidly dawning realisation, I came to understand exactly what kind of warehouse we were occupying, and what it was doing parked in this shit part of town.

The fae was getting back to his feet. If we stayed in this spot and let him square up for round two, his friends would come running for sure. We needed to retreat and make another attack from the shadows, guerilla warfare style. So Frank and I fell back and found a new hiding place among a forest of assorted fetish gear hung on mobile clothes rails.

I caught sight of the creeping fae, who looked pretty much recovered from Frank's punch and was once again heading our way.

'Hiding, eh?' he said. 'Two can play at that game.'

With that, he vanished. I don't mean he took cover or stepped into a shadow, I mean he disappeared without a trace. It was the same invisibility magic I'd seen the Arcadian I was hunting use, only there was no rain to give this one away. This camouflage was one hundred percent effective.

Feeling exposed, I reached into my jacket and felt the reassuring weight of my hammer. I took the weapon in my fist and pressed my back to Frank's. Together, we turned in a slow circle, eyes darting this way and that, searching for the first sign of danger.

I almost didn't spot it at first, it was so subtle: a barely significant detail that I almost mistook for a floater in my eye. A shiny spot had appeared on the ground in front of me, accompanied by a low squelch. Behind the spot were more of the same, a breadcrumb trail of small, wet marks. Something invisible was leaving behind footprints like a man tracking dog shit through the house. Only this wasn't shit, it was lube.

I lashed out with the hammer and felt the flat end connect with something mid-swing. The fae struck the ground as large as life, blood leaking from his ear. I looked down and saw the hammer had snapped in half, the part with the steel head lying on the floor some distance away.

'Fuck you, Thumbelina,' I hissed, 'and the unicorn you rode in on.'

One down, two to go.

I hooked a hand under Frank's elbow and steered him to a new hiding spot, a shady nook in a narrow aisle of marital aids. I felt good. I felt lethal. I felt like my blood was on cocaine.

'Listen,' I whispered to my partner, 'I need you to lie low here while I get the drop on the next one.'

Frank went to say something but I clapped a hand over his wet mouth before he could start grousing.

'Don't take it personal,' I assured him, 'it's just that you make a fuck of a lot of noise. Me, they won't see coming.'

Frank clearly had more to say on the subject of being benched, but he let me have this one and stepped aside with a minimal amount of grumbling.

'Thank you,' I said. 'Whatever you do, don't go anywhere. Just stay here, okay?'

He nodded once. 'Oookay.'

I took off, patrolling the aisles in search of a new weapon. I was on the lookout for something with a bit of heft to it, something I could do some real damage with: a janitor's mop, or maybe I could detach the handle from one of those pallet jacks and use that. I felt confident. I felt emboldened. And then I felt a fist in the side of my head.

The punch landed hard and left me swaying like a drunk at his ex's wedding. An Arcadian snapped into focus before me. It was the other lackey: the second of Draven's footsoldiers. While I was still floundering, he socked me with a left that had my head singing like a bell.

I got cocky, that's what I did. I was so amped up after taking down the first fae that I forgot the golden rule—the same one I only just chided the enemy for breaking—don't split up unless absolutely necessary. There's strength in numbers. Frank knew that, but instead of cooperating with him, I went stag and got myself into this mess.

The fae gave me a kick in the guts before I could call for help, and then another. A third punt caught me in the head and threw a fistful of static blooming across my vision. There was nothing I could do to stop him; if the fae carried on like this, I was going to end up a leaky bag swimming with loose bone splinters.

And then came my knight in shining armour.

A pair of arms girdled the fae's chest and lifted him off his feet, bearhug style. Frank to the rescue. He'd disobeyed my order and snuck up on my attacker in a pincer movement, and thank Christ for that. If he hadn't tagged in I'd have gone belly up for sure. And no, the irony of telling Frank that he was too clumsy to be useful in this fight, only for him to sneak up on my assailant after I blundered into his trap, was not lost on me.

The Arcadian tried to call out to his superior, but Frank was hugging him so tight he couldn't breathe air into the words. Still, there was no telling when he might break free and bring more heat on us, so he needed taking down. I considered taking a swing at him, but if Frank's best punch only fazed these guys, chances were I'd only break my knuckles on his face. I needed something stronger than a fist, something that really left a dent.

Or maybe not.

Maybe what I needed didn't need to be tough at all, just poisonous. The Arcadians had a weakness to steel, but how were they affected by truly modern materials? Say something completely synthetic, like—my eyes searched the shelves either side of me and settled on just the thing—a silicone dildo the size of a grown man's arm.

I snatched it up, tore off its packaging, and belted the fae across the chops with it. It worked like a charm. His eyes crossed on impact and he crumpled to the floor in an ungainly heap, all trace of his former poise lost. As I stared at the livid mark decorating his cheek, I asked myself whether there was such a thing as a dignified way of being knocked out by an oversized sex toy, and decided probably not.

I high-fived Frank. 'Good lad,' I said.

I'd thank him properly later; for now there was the matter of the third fae, Draven. But before we could mount another hit and run, the final Arcadian blinked into existence behind Frank and dealt him a crack across the back of the skull that made him collapse like a failed soufflé. An eardrum-molesting crunch accompanied Frank's fall. I thought for a second it was the noise of bone shattering, at least until I saw broken glass on the ground and realised it was the jar he was carrying, crushed beneath the weight of his body along with the will-o'-the-wisp it contained.

Draven flashed me a grin like a monkey about to fling a fistful of fresh shit, then brought down his magic rod.

A black wave folded over me, plunging me into a dark dreamless nothing.

And that was that.

CHAPTER TWENTY-TWO: OFF WITH THE FAIRIES

I WASN'T EXPECTING to open my eyes again, but I did, at least in flashes. As I drifted in and out of consciousness I caught disparate glimpses of my surroundings, snapshots of an unfamiliar world.

I saw a steep grass verge and a weed-choked path.

I saw birds circling overhead, screeching like no bird I ever heard before.

I saw the yawning mouth of a gated tunnel covered in crude graffiti. One of the paintings was of a black skull topped with a pair of large round ears. Underneath it was scrawled the words MICKEY MORTE.

Then off flicked the switch and I was left in the dark again.

When the lights came back on, the first thing I saw was my own face. I thought I was looking at my reflection for a second, then I realised I was lying next to Frank. We were splashed across the floor of a small room. More of a cell, really. A cell so small it was like a coffin with headroom.

'Frank?' I whispered.

He wasn't breathing (reanimated corpses tend not to), so it was hard to tell if he was unconscious or whether he'd earned his epitaph. I was starting to panic when a twitch of the eyelid and a tic in his cheek told me he wasn't done kicking yet.

I rolled over and saw a flickering light filtering through the gap underneath our cell door. I scooched up to the gap, placed an eye to it, and saw a cold blue flame burning in a metal sconce outside, illuminating the corridor beyond with eldritch fire. There was magic at work here. Fae magic.

Where were we? Was this the realm of the faerie? Had we been Shanghaied to Arcadia? Before I could get a sense of which way was up, three fae carrying slim swords arrived and unlocked our cell. One of them gave Frank a poke and he sat up, tongue lolling from his mouth, looking even more confused than he generally did.

'What do you want with us?' I asked, but the terrible trio weren't taking questions.

The fae ordered us to our feet and frogmarched us from our cell along a low tunnel with arching walls. My head felt like a balloon on a string, and from the way Frank walked—teetering and oozingly slow—he wasn't feeling much better. Hardly surprising since we'd been tranquillised like a pair of bloody zoo animals.

'Where are we going?' I asked, my voice echoing down the tunnel. 'Let me guess, you're taking us to Buttercup Junction so we can meet King Lollipop.'

I got a slap for that, which seemed about right.

As we traipsed along the tunnel at swordpoint, I studied our surroundings. Tangles of thick tree roots forced their way through cracks in the roof like hands reaching through sleeves. It was as though the fae were magnets to nature, attracting nearby vegetation to their vicinity with enough force to penetrate solid rock.

Something among the clusters of tree roots caught the blue light of one of the nearby torches. From the looks of it, one of the twisted tentacles had dragged something through the earth with it and brought it into the fae lair. Closer examination revealed it to be a bottle, and as we passed beneath it, I made out something written on its side. Embossed in the cloudy glass were the words PEPSI-COLA.

We weren't in Arcadia. We hadn't been dragged through some fairy portal, we were somewhere beneath the city streets. The fae had set up shop in London. But why? What was the sense in coming all the way to the big smoke if you couldn't handle the smoke?

The Arcadians bullied us around a corner and into a much larger tunnel, wide enough to drive a car through and just as tall. Rainwater dripped down from the ceiling above, landing in fetid puddles

at our feet that collected pools of blue light from the torches placed
intermittently on the tunnel walls. I threw a look over my shoulder,
past the Arcadians at our back, and saw a gate some way down the
tunnel behind us. It was the same gate I caught a flash of on the way
in, the one at the lair's entrance with the MICKEY MORTE graffiti
on its other side. From what I could tell, this was the main drag of
the fae lair, with various tunnels and chambers branching off on
either side. Where we were, though, I had no idea. An old war
bunker maybe? A cave system? Part of a decommissioned sewer?

I felt a sharp poke in my kidney and turned to face the right way,
back in the direction the Arcadians were marching us. Ahead of us
were a pair of large wooden doors. Well, sort of. In fact, they were
made of more tree roots—so tightly-packed that I doubted a single
drop of water could have slithered through their sturdy weave.

The fae brought me and my partner to a dead stop; "dead" likely
being the operative word. Frank looked at me with those big doe
eyes of his and I wondered for a moment whether the doors ahead
would end up being our final curtain. Certainly, the way our escorts
scurried away like beetles from an upturned rock suggested nothing
good lay beyond them.

Finally, inexorably, the giant doors began to part, slowly
swinging inwards, seemingly of their own volition.

'See you on the other side, pal,' I told my partner.

Not for the first time, I wondered how that was going to work. In
the event of our untimely end (okay, pretty timely, given that Frank
and me turned up our toes years ago) what would our afterlife look
like? Assuming we got one, that is, or that there was even a "we" to
speak of. I mean, we were fundamentally the same person, only
divided. If we somehow succeeded in paying off the sins of my
misspent youth and squeaked past Saint Peter, would we continue
on as separate identities, or be reunited in spirit? Frank had evolved
so much since he showed up that I'd grown to think of him as his
own man. A personality independent from my own. The idea of us
becoming lumped together as one indistinct blob, or worse, that I
absorbed Frank like some greedy twin in utero, seemed unfair to say
the least.

A wedge of cold light escaped the opening doors, revealing what lay beyond. At the far end of a massive bramble-swamped chamber, a cobalt throne sat beneath a canopy of (you guessed it) more brambles. The empty throne was flanked either side by a fae guard. One I recognised as Draven, the Arcadian who knocked us out. The other was the fae I broke my hammer over. The one I dickslapped with a giant dildo was notable by his absence.

I was expecting more of a welcoming committee. With our escorts gone, the odds here were even. There was hope for me and Frank yet, a chance for us to overcome our captors and bust out of this place. Or so I thought.

With a curt *c'mere* motion, Draven summoned us to his end of the chamber. Something was off. I sensed the makings of a trap. Even Frank could tell something wasn't right about this setup. I considered turning us around and going the other way, but a sense of grim inevitability sucked me further into the chamber. Following my lead, Frank accompanied me along a central aisle until—about halfway to the throne—we arrived at a large circular grate on the ground. An oubliette, I think you'd call it; not part of the original architecture, custom-built. I saw Frank's nose twitch and followed his gaze as it drifted to the floor. I heard a snuffling sound in the gloom beneath our feet and tentatively peered through the grate to get a better look.

The first thing I saw was the leathery hide of two giant wings, then scales the colour of polished sapphires. The creature at the bottom of the oubliette padded in a circle around its pit, an arrowhead-tipped tail swishing behind it like a charmed snake. The beast craned its muscular neck and brought its bulbous head up to the grate, showing us a pair of thin slits that belched twin plumes of steam. I didn't need to see the horns or the long mouth full of razor sharp fangs; I already knew what I was looking at. A dragon. A bloody Saint George special, here in modern-day London.

Any feeling of bravado I felt evaporated instantly. The dragon changed everything. Frank and I didn't stand a chance in a fight now. We were two tadpoles in a shark tank. The only thing we could do was wait to see what happened next and look for a chance to wriggle free of the mess we were in.

Draven raised a fist and made a booming proclamation. 'Hear ye, hear ye,' he roared, punching the air. 'Announcing the arrival of His Royal Highness, King Merodach the First...'

So we were in for an audience with royalty, were we? Seemed I wasn't too far off the mark with that King Lollipop crack.

Draven went on. 'All rise for the first of His name, ruler of the Unseelie Court, the protector of the realm, Lord of the endless hinterland...'

He banged on like that for a while, but this is about the point I tuned out. It's not that Draven was a bad hype man, but when it comes to fancy titles, it's in one ear and out of the other with me.

The King came swishing through a side door at the throne-end of the chamber. He wore a fine gown and enough jewellery around his neck to give Midas conniptions. Atop his head he wore a crown of thorns lined with rich blue velvet.

Given that there were only five of us in the room (six if you included the dragon) it seemed like a lot of excess pomp to me. Which made me wonder, why was this grand hello such a private affair? Was it because Frank and I were deemed unworthy of a larger retinue, or was this conversation being held behind closed doors to keep it private from the rest of the court?

The King took a seat upon his throne. I waited for him to speak but he said nothing. Instead, he just stared at Frank and me like he was trying to blow holes through us with his eyeballs.

I knew I should wait it out. That talking out of turn would only get us in trouble. I'd learned from Jazz Hands' book that fairies respected the laws of hospitality and punished poor guests. If I knew what was good for me, I'd be on my best behaviour. And yet I was running low on an already stringent supply of fucks to give.

'Nice gaff you've got here, Papa Smurf. An actual safe space. You know, for folks who hate the modern world, you're surprisingly in touch.'

Frank laid a defeated look on me. The King white-knuckled the armrests of his throne.

'How dare you speak to me that way!' His head twitched to the man on his right. 'You there, bring me his head at once!'

A smile spread across Draven's face. It was the kind of smile you'd have seen even if you were looking at the back of his head. 'With pleasure, Sire…'

Frank stepped in front of me as the Arcadian drew a sword from a ceremonial scabbard strapped to his side.

'Thank you, Lieutenant, but that won't be necessary.'

A woman entered from a doorway opposite the one the King had waltzed through.

'Now then,' she said in a voice like dry leaves blowing across a crypt floor. 'What are we going to do with you two?'

CHAPTER TWENTY-THREE: YAS QUEEN

THE QUEEN of the Unseelie Court wore a cloak made of smoke and walked with footsteps as soft as a snowfall. She eschewed any hyperbolic introductions, and unlike her husband, wore only modest jewellery upon her person. Her jet-black hair was piled high and fixed in place with an ivory pin, her head unadorned by fancy headgear. This lass had no need for a big jaggy bonnet. It was clear right away that she wore the trousers around here, and that the bloke sitting in the throne behind her was very much the Dennis Thatcher of the house.

'Sorry I'm late,' she said, addressing her guests. 'I wanted to look my best for you both.'

I said nothing and kept my expression neutral. Frank did the same, but more by default than choice.

'So, this is the famous Fletcher & Fletcher?' Lady Muck went on. 'Thank you for coming. I'm sure you're wondering why you were summoned.'

'The thought had occurred,' I replied, answering on my partner's behalf.

The Queen's mouth curved into a smile. 'You're aware that one of our kind has gone missing.'

It was presented as a statement rather than a question, so I didn't feel the need to respond.

'Good,' she said, happy not to have to beat around the bush. 'Then it might interest you to know that the missing person in question is my only son.'

Her son. No mention of her hubby, King Whatchamacallit of the Frozen Wastes, or whatever it was he called himself. Poor bloke. All that build-up, and now his missus had shown up he was barely getting a look in. Anyway, that was by the by. The real news was that the killer I was chasing wasn't just any blue-skinned blueblood, he was a bonafide prince. Next in line for the throne. That put a very different spin on things.

The Queen prowled down the aisle towards us, dragging her smoke cloak behind her, and arrived at the opposite side of the oubliette. She wore leather-strapped sandals, which allowed her naked toes to curl over the edge of the grate, the only thing separating her from the dragon lurking below. She couldn't have looked less bothered.

'I know from what my subjects tell me that you have already encountered my boy.'

'In a manner of speaking, yeah,' I replied, remembering our ruckus at the council estate. 'Nice feller. Bit murdery.'

The King twitched in his chair but his old lady remained the very picture of calm.

'How very droll. You know, for two dead men, you make for most lively company.'

'Thaaaaaaanks,' droned Frank, who never could tell the difference between a compliment and veiled threat.

'Can we cut to the chase here?' I asked. 'You went to the trouble of bringing us all the way to your little Never-Never Land; why don't you tell us what for?'

Despite my dig, the Queen's smile stayed plastered perennially across her face. 'We invited you to our court because we require your assistance.'

Didn't see that coming. I was convinced that this was all a bit of foreplay before the fae turned me and Frank into dragon food.

'Sorry, love, can't help you there,' I said with a shrug. 'There's nothing I can tell you that you don't already know.'

'Perhaps not yet, but in time.'

'What are you saying?'

'I'm saying—*we're* saying—(she gave a little nod to the King, just about remembering he was present) that we wish to procure your services.'

I matched her smile with my own. 'You're not going to execute us?'

'You held your own against three of my best footmen,' she replied, causing Draven and the other soldier to bristle. 'I find that impressive.'

'And our reward for impressing you is what? Getting to work for you?' It was all I could do not to turn to Frank and twirl a *cuckoo* finger beside my head.

'I suggest you tell us everything you know about our boy's whereabouts,' growled the King. 'That's if you want to see daylight again.'

The Queen stepped in to soften his offer. 'Anything you can tell us would be most helpful, Mister Fletcher. For instance, how was he during your encounter? Did he seem well?'

'Not after I brained him with a claw hammer, he didn't.'

The King was up on his feet now, screaming until spit flew. 'Pluck this whore-son's tongue from his skull and throw him to the dragon. His meat puppet, too. I demand to see them both devoured.'

The Queen turned to him with a placating smile. 'Remember our agreement, dear.'

Breaking royal protocol, Draven offered his tuppence worth. 'I implore you, allow me to dispatch this motley twosome and give *me* the honour of recovering the prince.'

The Queen silenced her lieutenant with a look and returned to the King. 'Our boy being wounded is no bad thing. He'll need to stay in the city while he recuperates, which will only make it easier for us to locate him.'

Ah, the old royal "us", meaning me and Frank, of course.

'I've got a question for you,' I said, addressing Her Majesty. 'Why did your lad do a runner in the first place?'

'Oh, you know how it is,' she replied with a watery chuckle. 'Boys will be boys.'

So, ditching a bride at the altar and going on a murder rumspringa was just par for the course, was it? Bollocks. There was nothing normal about what was happening here. The Arcadian scion had gone rogue and his family needed him brought in from the cold no matter what. That gave me leverage.

'What if I say no to working for you?' I asked.

It was a risky move and I knew it. Here they were extending me an olive branch, and I was eating the fruit and spitting back pips.

'If you choose not to assist us you will be killed,' said the Queen. The smile never left her lips.

I saw a gulp travel up and down Frank's throat. He was made of tough stuff, but this bitch was stone cold.

'Okay, new question: if we get your boy back, what then?'

'You want to know that he'll be punished, don't you? I can assure you that once the prince is returned to us, his crime will be dealt with according to the full extent of Arcadian law.'

'I see. And what about the wedding? I know a bunch of vampires who are pretty gutted about your boy standing up their little princess.'

The Queen cocked her head. 'You know about the Vengari? My, my, you have done your homework, haven't you? I'm impressed.'

'All part of the Fletcher & Fletcher promise: two brains for the price of one.'

'Braaaaaiins,' moaned Frank.

'Not now,' I said.

The Queen returned us to the topic at hand. 'You need not concern yourself with the Vengari,' she replied. 'Our contract with them has been torn up.'

'Is that right? Because that's not what they seem to think. Matter of fact, they're set on marching your boy back down the aisle, toot suite.'

Beneath our feet, the big blue dragon huffed, sending a belch of tremendous heat through the oubliette that momentarily turned the throne room into a furnace. I staggered back a step, shielding my face. Frank shrank from the withering heat like a man who'd opened an oven door with his head too close. The Queen didn't so much as flinch.

'If the Vengari wish to hold a grudge, that is up to them,' she said. 'Once we have our son back, this city is behind us. That is a promise.'

Interesting. Provided Jazz Hands' dusty old tome was on the money, that promise was gospel. Arcadians couldn't lie, even the rotten ones. Once the prince walked back through those big double doors, the union was off.

Again, I wondered what a wedding between the Arcadians and the Vengari would have accomplished. It seemed like the vamps would be getting the better end of that deal, and to a serious degree. The Arcadians must have been stark raving to even consider the idea, though making that point at this moment would no doubt have earned me a spot at the bottom of a dragon pit, hence the swift change of subject.

'Righty-o then,' I said, cracking a smile. 'If you want your prince found, you'd better let me and Frank get to work. No time like the present, eh?'

The Queen's smile reached its broadest span yet. 'Agreed. But do not seek to elude us, Mister Fletcher. You will locate my boy or suffer the consequences.'

She gave her guards a nod and they skirted the oubliette to join us. Draven's fingers itched at the pommel of his sword.

'Kindly escort our guests from the premises,' said the Queen, waving a limp hand as she breezed by the King hauling her smoke train, leaving him sitting there like a lump on a log.

Draven went to show me the way out.

'I can find the door by myself,' I told him. 'Don't worry, if I need you I'll tap your food bowl.'

I was three steps toward the exit, maybe four, before the cosh came down and I was off for another disco nap.

CHAPTER TWENTY-FOUR: THE SPIRIT IS WILLING

MY POCKET WAS SINGING.

Why was my pocket singing?

And more to the point, why was it singing the theme tune to *The Munsters*?

Wasn't that my ringtone?

It *was* my ringtone.

So that wasn't singing.

That was ringing.

Someone was ringing my phone.

Yeah, that's about how long it took me to figure out what was going on there. In my defence, I had been beaten over the back of the bonce by a magical sleepy stick. Frank, too, though he's pretty slow on the uptake at the best of times.

I peeled my head off the floor and my partner did likewise. Nearby, a couple of mangy pigeons fought over a puddle of sick. It seemed the fae had dropped us off pretty much where they found us: the shitty patch of urban sprawl we went to looking for a vampire conclave.

I fished out my phone and pressed it to my ear.

'Hello?' I croaked.

Stronge answered. 'Where the hell have you been, Fletcher? I've been calling you for hours.'

I checked my phone and saw sixteen missed calls. The thing had been ringing red hot.

Frank widened his eyes at me and did his owl impression. 'Whooo?'

I cupped a hand over the receiver. 'Stronge's on the blower,' I explained. 'Sounds a bit miffed.'

'Miffed?' she barked, clearly not fooled by my subterfuge. 'I'm bloody livid.'

'You're livid? I've got a clan of pissed off vampires up my back-side, and now the Arcadians have got me on the hook to find their missing prince.'

There was a long pause before Stronge spoke again. 'We need to talk. Now. Meet me at Cath's Caff in half an hour.'

ONCE THE HUMAN cigarette who ran the café had taken Stronge's order and slunk away, we were free to chat.

'Isn't that the same meal you had last time?' I asked, pointing at a sad-looking plate of eggs, chips, and black pudding. 'The one you said tasted like a dog's back?'

Stronge shrugged. 'Better the devil you know.' She forked a helping of undercooked egg white into her mouth and winced. 'Now how about you forget about my breakfast and tell me why you've been dodging my calls?'

The woman was on a hair-trigger, so I decided to be straight with her.

'Hear me out and don't get angry. I went looking for the Arcadian...'

Before I could say another word she pounded a fist on the table, making Frank jump. 'I knew it. I knew you'd go sneaking off without me.'

'Can you blame me? What was I supposed to do? Last time we worked together you told me you were sick of fighting monsters.'

'So what? That doesn't mean you get to leave me out of the loop. I want this collar just as much as you do.'

Somehow I doubted that. Stronge wanted to see the Arcadian pay for what he'd done, but it's not like her eternal soul was on the line.

Failing to bring in the killer wouldn't sit well with her, sure, but for me and Frank it could mean a reckoning. The pair of us were only ever one cocked-up case away from a nudge into the great lake of fire.

'Well?' said Stronge. 'Why did you ditch me? What have you got to say for yourself?'

'Sooooorry,' said Frank, surprising us both.

Stronge's frown melted. Her animosity towards me came easily, but no one would stay angry with Frank. People just liked him. Even though it's obvious he's not the full shilling, they know he's sound as a pound.

I decided to take advantage of Frank's powers of placation and bring Stronge up to speed while her guard was down. 'Here's what I picked up,' I said, leaning in and speaking low despite the fact that her and Frank were the only people in the café aware of my presence. 'The Arcadian didn't come to London alone, he brought a whole dynasty with him. They've set up a base in the city somewhere—we went there, but we were sparked out, so I couldn't tell you where it is. Anyway, it turns out the fae left Arcadia so they could marry their son off to a vampire bride—I overheard that part hiding in a wall at a vampire gabfest. Apparently, the wedding didn't go ahead on account of our man leaving the bloodsucker in the lurch.'

Stronge placed a hand on either side of her head as if to stop it from splitting in half. 'You're telling me you learned all of that in just a few hours?'

'It's been a night.'

'And there's more?'

'Oh, I've barely scratched the surface. See, after our man did his runaway groom act and shot my client—don't ask me how those two things add up—he went missing. Not just from the law, but from his own people. The Arcadians don't know where he is and neither do the vampires, but they're both pretty keen to find out. The Vengari—that's the vamps—want to drag the fae prince—did I say he was a prince?—back to the altar, but his mum's decided the wedding is cancelled.'

'And you believe that?'

'I don't know, but either way, this is going to make for an interesting entry in the old casebook.'

Stronge rested her chin on her palm. 'Here's what I don't get: what's a fairy doing marrying a vampire? Could that even work? Physically, I mean?'

'I guess so. The vampires kept calling it a union, the fae too, so the horizontal tango must have factored into the arrangement somewhere.'

Frank pulled a face. He was surprisingly squeamish when it came to the mention of anything carnal, which was strange. Out of the two of us, he was the only one who could really partake in a bit of the old in-and-out, and yet he had no urge to do so. If I had what he had I'd have been at it like a rat up a drainpipe. And before you get any ideas, no, I haven't made use of Frank's body just so I can… well, make use of a woman's. The thought has never even occurred to me, so get back in your box, you pervert.

Blissfully unaware of my inner dialogue, Stronge picked up where I left off. 'So the grand plan in all this is to make vampire-fairy babies?'

'Sounds that way, but mainly these things happen so two factions can consolidate power. The weird thing, though, is the fae already have all of it. The Vengari are a gutter clan. I can't for the life of me work out what they'd be bringing to the table, or why the Arcadians would traipse all the way to London to get it.'

Stronge nodded thoughtfully, took another bite of her brekkie, and was immediately reminded how bad the last mouthful had tasted. 'Well, it doesn't sound like there's any chance of this union going ahead now. The second we catch the fae he's off to the London Coven for some comeuppance.'

I sucked some air through my teeth. 'About that… the Arcadians made me and Frank an offer. Well, less of an offer than a demand, really. An *on pain of death* sort of thing.'

One word: 'What?'

'They asked—insisted, really—that when we find their prince, we hand him over to them. They promised they'd dole out the proper punishment.'

Stronge laughed. 'Right. A slap on the wrist and a, "Don't do it again", no doubt. If that.'

When I failed to laugh along with her she knew something was amiss.

'You can't seriously be considering throwing in with the Arcadians?'

I fidgeted in my seat. 'You didn't meet their matron. The woman gave me the heebie-jeebies. I might be better off disappointing God than her.'

'I really hope you're joking. I'm not in love with the idea of palming the bad guy off to some magic lady I've never even met, but I don't have much choice since he's not human.'

As I'd explained to her previously, the Accord insists that Uncannies aren't filtered through the common law legal system and are dealt with by the London Coven instead. It's not an ideal arrangement, but it's the only one we've got, at least in this city.

Stronge continued, 'If you think I'm handing a wanted killer over to his own family, you've got another thing coming. I'd sooner throttle him with my own hands than let that happen.'

'All right, chill your boots, Kat. I didn't say I was going to actually do it, did I? Besides, it's all a bit academic at this point since we don't even know where the fae's hiding.'

'What do you mean? What about the wisp?'

Frank's expression puckered and he looked to his trotters.

'Why is he making that face?' asked Stronge.

'The wisp's gone,' I confessed. 'Splatted.'

Stronge rubbed her eyes with the heels of her hands. 'Of course it is. So what now?'

'Honestly, we were hoping you might have something, because we are shit out of ideas.'

She pushed her plate of unfinished grub aside as if clearing a desk, making it ready for work. 'I'll head to the station and check the HOLMES suite to see if any suspicious crimes have been reported—something that might be attributed to the perp.'

'Great. What can we do in the meantime?'

'Oh, I think you've done enough already, don't you?' she said, snatching her coat from the back of her chair and heading for the door.

Frank turned to me with an expectant look on his face.

'Go on then,' I sighed.

He shot out two hands and tucked into Stronge's leftover black pudding like he was feasting on fresh brains.

CHAPTER TWENTY-FIVE: THEY ONLY COME OUT AT NIGHT

OUR CLIENT DESERVED to be apprised of the new developments in her case, so we headed for the office to fill her in. Only we couldn't get inside to talk to her. Not with a car full of vampires lying in wait.

The Vengari had the place staked out (excuse the pun). If we wanted to get in there, we were going to have to throw them off the scent. I gave Shift a bell.

'Shift, my man.'

'Woman right now,' she replied.

'Whatever. Listen, I need your help with something.'

'Well, since you asked so nicely, what can I do for you?'

I laid out my plan. She laid out her fee. An hour later, Shift was on the scene.

'SO LET ME GET THIS STRAIGHT,' said Shift, peeking her blonde head around the street corner to snatch a glance at my office. 'You want me to pretend to be you so I can draw a pack of vampires away from your door?'

'We went over this already,' I replied.

'Yeah, but… am I missing something? If you need bait, why not have your twin here do it?'

'Frank's… not exactly built for black ops,' I explained, placing a hand on my partner's shoulder.

Frank nodded meekly. Since our blow-up at the conclave, he'd changed his tune about being left out of things—about being benched when the need arose. There were things I was good at (sneaking into places), and things he was good at (beating the ever-living shit out of anyone who stood in our way). We both had a talent for going through things, we just used different methods.

I chanced a look around the corner and saw the vamp-mobile parked exactly where it had been an hour ago. 'You know, it's drop-ins like this that make me think I should stop advertising in the Yellow Pages.'

Shift tossed a look my way. 'You think?'

'Don't be like that. I need to get the business noticed, don't I?'

'Then advertise on the dark web like everyone else who sells something that shouldn't exist.'

'Do me a favour. I only found out chat rooms aren't still a thing last week. You should see my laptop; it's the size of a Volvo. Now come on, are you going to help me out or what?'

'For what you're paying? Consider it done.'

Shift did her Mighty Hermaphrodity thing, her face becoming a blur as it reshaped itself into mine. Well, a bit like mine.

'Hm,' I said, squinting at Shift's effort. 'Not bad, but not quite there yet. Why don't you have another crack at it?'

'What's wrong with this?'

'Don't get me wrong, it's not bad. It's just... you haven't quite captured my roguish good looks.'

Shift let forth a long sigh then the features she was wearing swam as she morphed again. I waited for the face to settle and studied it a second time.

'Did you even change it? It looks exactly the same to me.'

I turned to Frank for his opinion—it was a face he knew as well as I did, after all—but he was staying Switzerland on the matter.

'Trust me, this is fine,' said Shift, getting aggravated now. 'Even the hair's a match.'

I supposed it would have to do. To my eye, the effect needed some finesse, but I reckoned it should work at a distance.

'Fine,' I said. 'Moving on...'

I told Shift exactly what I wanted him to do.

'I have a question,' he said, raising a paw. 'What am I supposed to do if these vamps take the bait and grab me?'

'You're the shapeshifter; if they get too close just shed your skin and blend into a crowd.'

'Oh, so suddenly you're an expert on evasion, Mister I-Put-My-Home-Address-in-the-Phone-Book?' He took a breath. 'Sorry about that. I can get a little aggressive when I'm pumping testosterone.'

'Get those bloodsuckers off my doorstep and all is forgiven,' I replied, giving him a friendly slap on the back.

He took one last look down the street to check that the vamps were still camping by my front door (they were), gathered his courage, and cut a path past their car. To my mind, the manner of his gait was a little off—I don't want to say mincing, but I'm at a loss to describe it any other way. In any case, the ruse worked. The Vengari exited their vehicle and went after Shift on foot, leaving Frank and me to slip into the building unseen.

Home sweet home.

We headed for the back office, pushed open the door with our name stencilled on it, and found Tali standing by our desk, her big brown eyes wide with anticipation.

'Well? Did you get him?'

One look at my face and she knew. Her backside landed in my chair and she buried her hands in her afro.

'He's going to get away with it, isn't he?'

'Hey,' I said, taking the seat opposite while Frank fetched her a hankie. 'We're going to get him, trust me. I've got all the pieces of the clock laid out in front of me. I just need to figure out how to put them together and get the thing ticking.'

She looked up at me through her lashes. 'What's that supposed to mean?'

'It means we're closing in on the bastard. He's got three different parties looking for him right now, and we're closer than any of them.'

Her back straightened. 'Three?'

'Yeah. I'm telling you, it's like *Catch the Pigeon* out there.'

She returned an uncertain smile. 'Who else?'

'Besides me and Frank, he's got a bunch of vampires on his tail, plus his own family.'

The vague smile she was wearing deflated like a punctured tyre. 'The Arcadians?'

'Yeah. Mummy Dearest had the pair of us kidnapped and taken to their home from home. Made us an offer, too.'

'What kind of offer?' she asked, her stare turning distinctly hostile.

'The kind you don't refuse,' I replied. 'Either I find their boy and give him to them, or they turn Frank and me into a couple of charcoal briquettes.'

'So what are you going to do?'

'Still making my mind up about that.'

'No!' The word ripped out of her like a hog hurtling down a slaughterhouse chute, sending me and Frank rocking back on our heels. 'I came to you for help. You can't do this.'

'I haven't done anything yet,' I said, holding up my hands, a move mirrored by my partner.

'What do you think they're going to do if you hand him over?' she cried, fighting back tears. 'Wag a finger at him?'

'Listen, I know you don't want to hear it, but not fighting the Arcadians on this might be for the best. London's got enough hoodoo already without adding them to the mix. Having fae folk in the city might be the thing that tips the scales and wrecks the Accord. But it doesn't have to be like that: so long as they get their boy, they're off over the rainbow and back to the old country, out of our hair for good.'

'And you believe that?'

'They made me a promise, and the fae don't lie—I've read the book on them and it's right there in their manifesto.'

The tears were flowing freely now, bursting from Tali's eyes like a river through a busted dam. I placed a placating hand on her back.

'It's not fair, I know that, but getting shot of these bastards is the real endgame here. The fae are bad news, Tali. This is about the greater good.'

'Even if it means letting the man who killed me go free?' she shot back, her voice loaded with acid.

I was searching for an answer to that question when the doorbell rang.

CHAPTER TWENTY-SIX: MY ENEMY'S ENEMY

THE VIEW through the peephole of my front door wasn't at all what I was expecting. I was hoping to see Shift with his thumb in the air assuring me of a job well done. Instead, I found him wearing his blond male form and surrounded by four Vengari vampires.

Fuck. There was another knock. The vamps wanted in, and unlike the creatures of myth, these fellers didn't need to wait for an invitation.

'Open up,' said Shift, his voice shaky. 'Come on, buddy, let's not keep these people waiting.'

I had no choice.

I turned to Tali. 'Go hide in the back. In the room with the coffins.'

'Who's out there?'

'The vampires I was talking about. Now go.'

She obviously had more questions—not to mention a giant bone to pick with me—but she knew what was best for her and scarpered anyway, disappearing through the back wall.

Right then. If I was going to entertain uninvited callers, I was doing it with some muscle.

I swivelled to Frank. 'Okay, big man. This is it: Operation Jehovah's Witness.'

I merged with my partner, slipping him on like a prizefighter donning his favourite pair of boxing gloves. The vamps had us outnumbered two to one, so working as separate entities wasn't going to make a difference here. We were better off combining our efforts and taking on the fang gang as a united front.

I tugged open the door and lunged for the closest vampire.

'Not another step,' said a vamp with the muzzle of a gun pressed to Shift's head.

Outnumbered *and* outgunned. Not ideal.

'My name is Enoch and these are some friends of mine.'

I recognised the gunman as the upstart at the conclave I'd snooped on: the cool customer with the harelip. The vampires with him were the crew he stormed out with.

'How about you show us inside, Mister Fletcher? You and I need to have a little chat.'

I shook my head at Shift despairingly. 'See, I told you that morph-job wasn't fooling anyone.'

'Hey, that impersonation was flawless,' he crowed.

'You're right,' Enoch told him. 'But no amount of camouflage could have disguised the smell of the cheap perfume you're wearing.'

'That's Chanel N°. 5!' Shift shot back, only falling quiet when the vampire's gun bit deeper into his temple.

'Easy,' I said. 'Come on in and let's talk this out.' I stepped off the welcome mat to allow the door-stoppers inside.

The Vengari filed through the door. Under the lights of the lobby I was able to get a better look at them. Enoch was a miserable-looking specimen, but his backup were concentration camp-thin, with cheekbones so sharp they were close to piercing flesh. I wasn't about to let their malnourished bodies fool me, though. Vampires were fighters, these ones especially.

'Why don't we start with you telling us why you're tracking the Arcadian?' Enoch said with breath that made halitosis smell like air freshener. This was the first time I'd encountered the Vengari with a working nose, and the bouquet they gave off was absolutely foul.

'That's private,' I said. 'As in private eye.' I hooked a thumb at the door behind me—the one with my name and title stencilled on its window.

Enoch looked at the door then back to me. 'Paranormal Investigator, eh?'

'You can read? Wow, what other tricks can you do? How about rolling over and playing dead?'

His lips stretched thin with hatred.

'Silly me,' I said. 'I guess the horse already bolted on that one, didn't it?'

I expected him to call the kettle black, but instead he nodded in the direction of the office door. '*Fletcher & Fletcher*,' he recited. 'Except I only see one of you. Where's your partner?'

Was he mucking me about? Did Enoch really not know that Frank and I were huddled together like a couple of Russian nesting dolls? Then again, why would he? Him and his boys slipped away from the Vengari soirée before our names even came up; no wonder he wasn't privy to all the gossip.

'My partner stepped out,' I explained. 'It's just me here.'

Enoch nodded agreeably. Okay, I was definitely onto something. First the bloke failed to pick up on the irony of a ghost roasting his lack of mortality, now this. To Enoch, I was a regular Insider: a living, breathing normal who knew about the Uncanny but wasn't of it. When his fingers did the walking through the Yellow Pages and he saw the words "Paranormal Investigators" on our ad, he must have taken it to mean that we were to folks who investigated the paranormal, not that we were investigators who were paranormal.

Come to think of it, this wasn't the first time someone had made that mistake. I once had a potential client visit the office asking me to help him evict a man renting out his cellar. Apparently, the feller had turned it into a laboratory and was stitching together body parts he'd nicked from the local graveyard. Imagine the landlord's shock when Frank stepped in looking like Eddie the Head. Poor bloke must have thought it was Frankenstein season.

All of which is to say that my ad copy could probably use some tweaking. Then again, the misconception was paying off here, so maybe keeping what I did vague wasn't the worst idea in the world. Food for thought.

Another thought: the Vengari not knowing that Fletcher & Fletcher were a double-dead combo meant the vamp whose arm my partner tore off most likely hadn't made it back to the clan. Probably collapsed on the street when he bled out and cooked away when the sun came up. Lucky for us. Not so much for him.

I guess I couldn't blame the Vengari for not putting it together. A ghost merging with his own reanimated corpse isn't something you see every day. In fact, I don't know that it happens anywhere outside of our peculiar partnership. Which was all the more reason to keep my gob shut. If they wanted to believe I was a breather, so be it. Let them be in the dark. It's where vampires belong.

'Are you going to tell me why you stopped by with a gun to my friend's head?' I asked. 'Or is this just your way of saying hello?'

Shift cringed as Enoch cocked the hammer of his pistol.

'We're looking for the Arcadian, too, and we think you might be harbouring him.'

'Then you're on a hiding to nothing, mate,' I replied.

Enoch hissed into his hostage's ear, 'What's he saying?'

'Don't ask me,' squeaked Shift. 'I only understand about half of the things that come out of his Limey mouth.'

Enoch turned the gun on me. 'How about you be a good host and show us around, Mister Fletcher?'

'I'd rather not.'

'What's the matter? Do you have something to hide?'

I knew I had no choice but to cooperate with the home invaders —that's unless I wanted a second ghost with a bullet through the head to avenge.

'Come on then,' I groaned, 'why don't I give you the tour?'

I started off by leading Enoch to the office, which his lackeys tossed from top to bottom, eyes peeled for any sign of the rogue Arcadian. Naturally, they found none. After they were done there, his boys split up and took a shufty at the rest of the premises. After a few tense minutes in the company of Enoch and his hostage, a voice called from down the hall.

'We found something in the back room, boss...'

They must have sniffed out Tali. I was hoping she'd be canny enough to stay hidden, but it looked like they'd rooted her out. Enoch nodded to the office door and off we shuffled to the show-room. We stepped through the ragged curtain that led into the showroom. I expected to find Tali with her hands in the air, but instead I found three vamps with their mitts in my coffins.

'What do we have here?' said Enoch, taking in the room.

The parlour housed six caskets in total, laid across trestles the way I found them when I moved in. If you weren't aware that the building used to be a funeral home, I suppose you might find them a bit suspicious, if not downright ominous. The only reason they were still there—aside from the fact that I hadn't got around to renovating the back end of the building yet—was because Frank used one of the coffins to sleep in. If you could really call it sleep. It's more like he zones out for a few hours at a time, really. Honestly, you'd hardly be able to tell the difference unless you really knew him.

Enoch eyed the one coffin that his cronies had yet to crack open.

'You like it?' I asked. 'Must make you feel right at home.'

Following Enoch's order, the vamps flipped the lid on the last coffin and found it as empty as the rest. I breathed a sigh of relief. Tali had obviously been smart enough to find a better hiding place than that. I cast a glance about the room and caught a quick glimpse of her face peeking out from a wall before it dipped back in again. Clever girl. There was no telling what might happen if the Vengari found her, and from a selfish point of view, my case completely fell apart if she got snuffed out for good.

'You've had a rummage and come up empty,' I told Enoch. 'Now how about you and your boys jog on before the sun comes up?'

Shift winced again. I'm sure he'd have preferred I play nice with the Vengari given that he was the one with the gun to his head, but it just wasn't in my nature to kowtow to vampires. Horrible fuckers. How they've ended up portrayed as gorgeous, brooding fiends is beyond me. All I can say is, they must have a bloody good P.R. team, because there's nothing gorgeous about 99.9% of them. Vampires are diseased relics who breed like an undead pyramid scheme.

Enoch gave Shift a shove, sending him in the direction of one of his men, who caught his neck in a chokehold. I wondered for a moment if it was possible for Shift to transform into someone better suited to a fight—some hench bastard with a short forehead and prison yard muscles—but I guess that wasn't in his toolbag.

Unencumbered now, Enoch turned his attention to yours truly.

He placed the gun he was holding in its holster, a power move, a way of letting me know that the weapon was unnecessary and that he could rip me apart with his bare hands if he fancied it.

'Listen up, and listen well,' he said, giving his voice a real twist of pepper. 'You work for me now, Mister Fletcher, Paranormal Investigator. You're going to find the Arcadian, and when you do, you're going to bring him to me.'

'That's funny,' I said, 'the fae just gave me the same pitch. Better get in line.'

Again, Shift shot me hate rays. Even Frank, who'd been quiet until now, was voicing his disapproval inside my head.

Enoch went on. 'You're going to hand the Arcadian over, otherwise me and my boys will be paying you another visit, and this one won't be so cordial.' He nodded to a lackey, who handed me a card with a phone number on it. 'The minute you lay eyes on the Arcadian, you send me a text.'

'Thanks for the offer, but I'm old-fashioned. I prefer to chat face-to-face.'

A reptilian smile played on Enoch's lips. 'I'm afraid that won't be possible.'

'Oh yeah? And why's that?'

His wicked grin stretched from ear to ear. 'I thought you'd never ask...'

He nodded to the two vamps who weren't busy holding Shift in place, and they lunged forward, seizing me by the forearms. I struggled to break free of their grip, but even with Frank's hulkish brawn I was no match for them. Despite their twiggy bodies, the Vengari were possessed of incredible strength. They were like ants: nothing to look at, but able to perform immense physical feats. I suppose that was the trade-off for being carbonised by sunlight, not to mention looking like cursed waxworks from a condemned seaside attraction.

The vampires slammed me into one of the open coffins, a tasteful number with faux-gold handles and a white clamshell finish. Out came a knife, six inches of cold steel in Enoch's hand. He turned it over, enjoying the play of the parlour's gallery lighting on its cool steel edge. I went to strike out with my feet, but Enoch used his free hand to slam shut the lower portion of the casket lid, protecting him from any stray kicks.

I could have jettisoned from Frank's body and landed a punch or two, but where would that have got me? Chances were Enoch could have taken us as a twosome, and even if we did manage to put him down working separately, he still had three more knee-breakers backing him up. No, I had to stay out of sight—spring the trap only if it was a matter of life or death.

'Get off me, you toothy bastard,' I cried.

Enoch tested the tip of his blade with his thumb and drew a bead of blood.

'Hold still. It'll hurt less that way.'

He placed the knife between his teeth then grabbed my face, digging his sharp fingers into the flesh of my cheeks. With his free hand he forced his spare digits into my mouth deep enough to trigger my gag reflex and bring up some of Frank's last meal. I tasted brains as Enoch rooted around my mouth and fished out my tongue. I fought him every inch of the way, but he succeeded in yanking it between my lips and holding it there, rigid and taut and longer than I knew it could stretch.

Enoch transferred the knife back to his weapon hand.

'Has anyone ever told you that you have a big mouth, Mister Fletcher?'

The edge of the knife met the pink eel pinched between his fore-finger and thumb and began to saw. Cold white light shot through my eyes and down my spine, all the way to the soles of my feet where it ricocheted back again and exploded in my brain. My finger-nails embedded in the palms of my hands, deep enough to draw blood, so deep I thought they'd come out the other side. I tried to scream but it lodged in my throat as a hard bulge.

I wanted to go, wanted to escape Frank's body and leave the pain behind, but I couldn't do it. Not because I didn't want to, but because I couldn't let him suffer alone. Despite my scream being trapped inside of me, my partner's rang loud and clear, an anguished howl, raging through every filament of my being. Frank could feel what was happening to his body just as much as I could. The soul bond Jazz warned us about had seen to it that he could feel pain, so I wasn't the only one affected by our partnership; he'd had changed, too. While I'd gained the ability to smell and taste and touch using the body I was born with, Frank had gone from being a vengeful automaton to a man with thoughts and feelings. It made him human, but wrapped up in that package was the suffering that came with the human condition. You might say I got the better part of the deal, but it really didn't feel that way, not in that moment, because Frank's pain was mine to share. And yet as torturous as it was—the vampire's knife shearing through muscle and tissue in ragged bites— the pain would have been doubled if it wasn't being shared.

I heard an audible snap like a rubber band coming apart and the back of my head struck the bed of the coffin. Through eyes stung with bitter tears I saw Enoch, still grinning. The severed tongue laid across his palm like a fat, bloody slug. The harelipped vampire stuffed the grim trophy into the pocket of his coat, then stooped over me and wiped his bloodied knife across the lapel of my jacket.

'Find the Arcadian quickly, otherwise the next time you see me I'll take more than what's in your mouth.'

With that ultimatum delivered, the Vengari exited the parlour and slipped away into the last of the night.

I stayed crumpled in the coffin, merged with Frank still, squeezing our hands together to stem a frigid tremor.

Tali emerged from the wall to check on us. 'Are you okay?' she asked, even if it was obvious we weren't.

Shift came over and placed a sympathetic hand on my shoulder, his mouth forming a weak smile. 'Oh, Fletchers… what have you gotten yourselves into this time?'

Despite our best efforts to conceal it, Frank and I were trembling all over. I told myself it was rage giving us the shakes, but after what we'd been through, fear had taken the lead from rage by a good few furlongs.

CHAPTER TWENTY-SEVEN: BODY AND SOUL

I WAS GETTING payback for what they did to Frank, that was a promise. The Vengari were dead wrong if they thought they'd brought me to heel. Carving up my partner had only given me purpose. Now I was a wasp at a picnic: I wasn't going anywhere and I was going to make it my mission to fuck up their day.

We left the office travelling two abreast, Frank leaning on me for support, my arm wrapped around his waist. When we arrived at Legerdomain, Frank shot out a hand and grabbed the door handle like a drowning man reaching for a piece of passing driftwood. We stumbled inside, causing the shop bell to tinkle a merry tune that was very much at odds with the mood.

Jazz Hands was sitting upon her usual stool as we entered, busy talking to someone on the phone. She didn't give us the courtesy of looking our way, giving us a *wait* finger, instead.

'We need your help,' I said.

'Not now,' she hissed, refusing to be interrupted, eyes still trained on nothing in particular while she concentrated on a conversation that couldn't possibly be more important than the one unfolding right in front of her.

Jazz wasn't the easiest person to get on the right side of. I often think of her as a maze. Somewhere in the middle of that maze there's a heart—a place of compassion and understanding—but to get to it I have to navigate a complex tangle of corridors and wrong turns. Finding my way to Jazz's gooey centre can take a long time. Sometimes it can feel never-ending. But when I find my way there, it's always worth the journey.

'Jazz, seriously—'

She turned her back on me and continued her phone call. 'You've got it lodged where?... How is that even possible?' A looong pause followed. 'Let me get this straight: you just *happened* to be naked and *accidentally* sat on it? Sat on a magic wand?... No, I don't think stranger things have happened, actually.'

'Jazz, this is importa—'

Without turning to face me, she made a fist and gave it a firm shake, warning me off.

'It's a hospital you want, not me,' she barked into the phone. 'I don't care if they do manage to fish the thing out, you've voided your warranty. Ha! If you think you're getting a refund after that, you're in for a big bloody surprise.'

She slammed down the receiver on her ancient bakelite phone, disconnecting the call. Finally, she swung about to face me, her neck mottled red with anger.

'What? What is it?'

'It's Frank, he—'

I didn't get any further than that before she cut me off. 'You brought Frankie boy?' she chirruped, her mood taking a rapid U-turn. 'Get over here, my little ray of sunshine. Come on, come to Mama.'

Frank stayed where he was.

'What's the matter, boy? Cat got your tongue?'

'A vampire did, actually,' I replied on Frank's behalf.

He opened his mouth to say something but all that came out was blood.

Jazz turned ash-grey and crossed herself. 'What did you do to him?'

'You think I did this?' I fired back, but Jazz was already brushing past me on her way to turning over the shop's Closed sign.

She rushed to Frank's side, fussing over him, steering him gently to a seat (technically not a seat but one of those metal rigs that runs up the trouser leg of a human statue, giving the impression that they're floating on thin air instead of just wasting everyone's time).

'Oh, you poor lamb,' Jazz cooed, stroking Frank's tangled hair.

'Have you got any brain bits handy?' I asked, knowing she liked to keep a stash in the fridge for our visits.

She reached under the counter and returned with a Tupperware container. She popped the lid and Frank tipped his head back like a Roman emperor gorging on grapes while Jazz fed him rubbery scraps from the plastic box.

'How are you feeling?' I asked. 'All better?'

Frank shook his head. I got him to open wide and peered into his mouth like a dentist hunting for cavities. Inside I found a sticky red stump where his tongue used to be.

'What's wrong?' I asked. 'Why isn't he healed?'

'The bleeding's stopped but that's as good as it gets,' she replied. 'If you think a few morsels of grey matter will grow a tongue back, you're sadly mistaken.'

'Why am I?'

I'd seen a brain breakfast set a broken nose straight before, and I was counting on one fixing this mess too, otherwise I wouldn't have made the trip to Jazz's dank boutique in the first place (quick note here: I did try a couple of butchers' shops before I darkened Jazz's doorstep, but the two I breezed into didn't have any head porridge in stock).

'Eating cow brains will help Frank kick in the dents,' Jazz explained, 'but it won't regenerate severed body parts.'

Gravity tugged at the corners of Frank's mouth.

'What about human brains?' I said. 'Would that do the trick?'

'You're talking about necrophagy, Fletcher.'

'I am?'

'Cannibalism to the layman. And if you think I'm getting involved with that, you can give your head a wobble.'

'What if the donor has it coming?'

She stared me down.

I threw up my hands. 'So that's it, is it? Frank's a mute now?'

'I'll tell you what he's *not*, and that's a bloody gecko. He's just like the rest of us: he can't regrow something from nothing, no matter what you stick in his gob.'

'There's gotta be a way to fix this.' I made a circuit of the shop, muttering curses under my breath until a thought popped into my head. 'What if I got the tongue back? Could you put it back in then?'

'Maybe. I don't know.' She stroked her chin, which gave off a thistly crackle. 'Perhaps if I had the original organ I could find some way to reattach it.'

I perked up as I imagined myself storming the next Vengari conclave, guns blazing, vampire bodies stacking up like Jenga bricks. Ah, who was I kidding? I couldn't stand up to the Vengari on home ground; what chance would I have going against them a second time? I needed to face facts. Frank's tongue was history.

'Can I ask a silly question, Jazz?'

'Better than anyone I know, Fletcher.'

I chose not to rise to that. 'Is there really no way to reverse this soul bond?'

'What does that have to do with anything?' she asked incredulously.

'A bunch of vampires came into our home and cut Frank's tongue out of his head. He felt that. *I* felt that, and I wouldn't wish it on anyone. If we can't fix what happened, the least we can do is make sure he doesn't go through anything like that again.'

'By reversing the bond?'

'If we can pull that off we take away Frank's ability to feel pain.'

'I already told you that's not on the cards.'

I firmed up a fist and pounded it down on a stack of magic kits, which responded by spitting out an assortment of wands, balls and cups. I could tell from Jazz's face that I'd be paying for them in full later, but for now, I had her attention.

'Jazz, I've seen you turn an angel's umbilical cord into a lasso that could snare a demon. Don't tell me this is beyond you.'

She turned to Frank and found him wearing the same hangdog expression he came through the door with, mouth buttoned tight to hide his shame. She laid a soothing hand on the back of his and bobbed her head slowly.

'I'll try. I'm not promising anything, but if there is a way to undo the bond, I'll find it.'

'Thanks, Jazz. That's all I ask.'

She wasn't finished. 'But know this, Fletcher: it might mean making some changes to the connection you two have. Some big changes.'

I shared a consoling look with Frank. 'That's a risk we're going to have to take.'

CHAPTER TWENTY-EIGHT: THE STRONGE AND SILENT TYPE

I SPENT the rest of that day in a funk, pacing the office, desperate to find a new inroad into our investigation: some means of getting back on the Arcadian's tail and scoring our client some well-deserved justice. There had to be a way of picking up the thread, but for the life of me I couldn't think of it. Ever since the Vengari paid me a visit my thoughts had been coated in a thick fuzz.

'We could ask around The Beehive,' I suggested, bouncing yet another half-arsed idea off my partner, who was in no position to contribute to the conversation in any meaningful way (even less so than normal).

'Nah, that ain't gonna work,' I said, giving a bottle of scotch a swift kick—an empty one the vamps tipped from the office bin when they ransacked the joint. 'Lenny ain't talking out of school, and neither are any of the other reprobates who haunt his gaff.'

I marinaded on the idea some more.

'Unless... what about another eaves? Razor used to knock around The Beehive, and he's got dirt on everyone. I'll bet you anything he knows where our man's cooped up.'

Frank cocked his head like a dog watching the telly.

'Except the last time I saw Razor, the two of us were rolling around on the floor throwing fists at each other.' I gave myself a sharp slap on the forehead. 'Come on, Jake, use your loaf.'

Every time I thought I'd solved the Rubik's Cube, I turned it over to find one side still fucked. I was starting to think the investigation had hit a total dead end when my phone started up. I snatched it out of my pocket and checked the screen. Stronge. Quick as I could, I stabbed the Answer button and put her on speakerphone.

'Please tell me you've got some good news, Kat,' I begged, chewing on a cuticle as I carried on pacing up and down the office.

'I can't say for sure, but I might have something. After I left you I went to the HOLMES suite looking for homicides.'

'And?'

'Nothing.'

Frank and I deflated like a couple of undercooked meringues.

'Not loving what you're giving me so far, Kat, gotta be honest.'

'Let me finish, you ingrate. After no murders showed up I did a search for other crimes the perp might have been responsible for: sex crimes, GBH, smash and grabs, that kind of stuff.'

I was trooping back and forth across the office so frantically that I'd have worn a rut in the floor had I not been weightless. 'Well? Did anything come up?'

'Nope.'

I was about ready to break my phone over my knee by this point. 'God Almighty, Kat, I'm sure you called for a reason, so can you skip to it?'

'Vehicle-related theft.'

'Eh? Someone nicked a car? So what?'

'So the person responsible had blue skin.'

That pricked up my lugholes. Frank's, too. 'Blue skin? And you're sure this is our guy, not some dickhead in clown makeup?'

'I don't know. All I know is, the suspect wants out of the city and he's got enemies squatting on all the obvious exits. Why not steal a car?'

The idea had legs. Big beefy ones.

'If the Arcadian's managed to tea-leaf a motor and bugger off out of London, that's our investigation pretty much fucked, right?'

I could almost hear Stronge smile. 'Only if he managed to keep hold of the car after he stole it.'

I stopped pacing. 'He's back on foot again?'

'Seems that way.'

I gave Frank a high-five, which turned out to be a mistake.

'Okay, so what next?' I asked Stronge, rubbing a sore wrist.

I heard a horn sound outside. 'Next you step out of your front door and get in my car. We've got a witness to talk to.'

THE STREETS ROLLED by in a blur as Stronge popped on the blues and put the pedal to the metal. The scene of the crime was a multi-storey car park in Euston: a stack of grey concrete slabs built for parking cars, but more commonly used by sexual deviants and mashed crusties selling balled-up toilet paper as weed. We were visiting during the daytime, but the scant amount of light that found its way inside the structure made it seem like night had rolled in early.

Stronge steered us up a spiral access ramp to the third level and put on the brakes. A bunch of uniform coppers were gathered around a young woman, upper-middle-class going by her outfit: a designer dress made of something that looked as if it disagreed with washing machines. She spoke to the uniforms in a plummy accent and appeared to be in a state of some distress.

At this point I should probably talk about how I was presenting myself, or should I say, *we*. I couldn't show up as a phantom or I'd be invisible to the witness, so I had to possess Frank in order to take part in the conversation. Okay, Frank didn't have a tongue, but as I assured Stronge in the car, that wouldn't be a problem. Frank didn't need a tongue so long as I was able to speak through his mouth, and besides—as I've been told many times throughout my life—I spoke enough for two people anyway.

Stronge flashed her ID to shoo the coppers away, but one stayed firm: an overweight constable with excess neck meat spilling over his collar.

'Who's this?' he said, aiming a stubby finger my way. 'Another one of your psychic consultants?'

Some of his colleagues laughed. Stronge was far from amused.

'I suggest you stop asking stupid questions if you don't want to be put on permanent bicycle duty, Constable.'

That knocked the smile off his face.

'Yes, ma'am,' he whimpered, and quickly made himself scarce.

Kat approached the witness.

'My name's DCI Stronge and this is my associate, Mister Fletcher. We're here to follow up on your call.'

'But I already told the other officers what happened,' she replied, panic threading her voice.

'Yes, but we're hoping we can dig a little deeper. Can you describe the man who attacked you? Other than the fact he was wearing blue makeup.'

The witness held a palm to her chest, covering a heart that was still in danger of punching its way through her chest. 'I don't know... about average height, good head of hair—'

'Would you say he was good-looking?'

That tripped her up. 'I wasn't really thinking about that at the time.' She thought on it some more. 'I suppose he was rather easy on the eye. Could have been a model, really.'

That tallied up. This was starting to sound a lot like our guy, even if I didn't think he was really *that* good-looking.

Stronge took down some notes in a pad, more for show than for any practical reasons. Her brain was a steel trap; the notepad was only there to instill a sense of confidence in her interviewees.

'How did he approach you?' she asked.

'It's like I told the other officers, he came out of nowhere.'

Stronge cast a glance about the car park. 'Show me where exactly he came out of.'

'You're not getting it. None of you are.' She was pissed off now. 'I said *nowhere*. Literally. He stepped out of thin air.'

I sent a knowing look in Stronge's direction. This was our man for sure. I was starting to think he'd snuck away like a thief in the night, but this was proof that he was still marooned in London.

'I know how that sounds,' the woman went on, her voice rising in pitch, 'but I promise you I'm telling the truth. Breathalyse me if you like, I'll prove it.'

'That won't be necessary,' said Stronge.

I decided it was my turn to talk. 'What happened after the blue man stole your car?'

The witness looked at me like my head was on fire. Stronge, too. It was only when I asked what the matter was that I realised the problem: the questions were coming out of my mouth okay, but the movement of my lips was completely out of sync.

What's haapnin? asked a voice in my head: Frank's.

I had no idea. Why this sudden disconnect between my jaw and my thoughts I couldn't be sure, but it left me looking like an actor in a badly-dubbed kung-fu movie, which must have been extremely disconcerting to watch.

I clammed up quick. I wasn't going to be able to contribute to the conversation. The best I could do was keep my mouth shut and let the witness think she was imagining things.

'Did you just… what's wrong with your mouth?' she asked.

I shrugged and made eyes like, *Whatever do you mean?*

Stronge cut in, changing the conversation. 'You said on the 999 call that your car was stolen but later returned. Is that right?'

The witness stared at me a few seconds longer before shaking her head and turning to Kat to answer her question. 'Um… yes, that's right. This is my car here.'

She patted the bonnet of a Honda E. The "E" stood for electric. It made sense that the Arcadian would want to go on the run in a clean-fuel vehicle, given his intolerance to pollution. What didn't make sense was what came next.

'Is that…? Stronge peered into the rear passenger window of the car and saw a little girl asleep in a baby seat.

'My daughter,' the witness explained. 'That's why he came back. He didn't realise there was a baby inside when he pulled me out of the car.'

'You're saying he drove away with your kid on board?' asked Stronge.

'That's right,' the witness replied, wincing at the memory. 'When he screeched off I thought I'd never see her again, but when he realised what he'd done he reversed back up the ramp, gave Rosie back to me, and said sorry.'

So far I'd been keeping up with the conversation by offering the occasional nod here and there, but I really had to interject at this point.

'He apologised?' I tried to say, mouthing the words and using body language to get across my meaning.

Except it didn't go down that way. Instead, the whole left side of my body turned into a dead weight that almost dragged me to the ground. I just about managed to shoot out a mitt and steady myself on the car's bumper before straightening my gammy leg and regaining my balance. Frank made noises in my head, just as perturbed as I was, only more vocal about it.

'Are you okay?' asked the witness, her voice echoing about the car park and catching the attention of the lingering uniforms, who looked up momentarily before returning to their conversations.

'He's fine,' said Stronge, giving me evils as she helped me to my feet. 'Aren't you?'

I nodded, but even the act of bobbing my head was difficult. My body was in revolt.

'Do you need to sit down?' the witness asked. 'You don't look well.'

I peered into the Honda's wing mirror and saw she wasn't wrong. The light I gave to Frank's eyes had gone out, leaving behind a life-less void. We were occupying the same space, but the warmth my soul gave his body wasn't touching the sides. There was no harmony between us. I was puppeting a floppy old ragdoll using ten broken fingers. I considered ejecting from Frank's body so I could find some equilibrium, but who was to say he wouldn't collapse in a big sloppy pile right there and then?

'Don't mind him,' said Stronge, plastering on a smile. 'Must be that bug that's going around.'

The witness considered this. 'Maybe you're right. The blue guy didn't look very well either. Kept coughing, could hardly stand up, even.'

'Is that right?' said Stronge.

I managed to take a hand off the car bumper long enough to make a *wind it back* motion at Stronge. She caught my meaning.

To the witness, Stronge said, 'You mentioned before that the suspect said sorry after he brought your car back. Did he say anything else?'

I gave her a thumbs up.

'He did, actually,' said the witness. 'He told me he didn't want to take my car, but said if he didn't get out of the city, he'd die. What do you think he meant by that?'

'Who knows?' replied Stronge, playing dumb. 'Probably on something. We see a lot of that on the job.'

'Anyway, it was right after he gave Rosie back that another car came by. I shouted for help and I guess that spooked the blue guy, because he took off like the wind, thank God.'

Stronge asked the witness a few more questions to make sure she'd juiced her for everything she had, said thanks, then turned her back over to the uniforms. Exhausted from holding myself upright, I plonked my arse down before I fell down, parking it on a metal barrier scuffed by short-sighted motorists.

'What is wrong with you two?' Stronge hissed.

'I don't know,' I said, feeling defeated.

Frank apologised, too, forgetting that he couldn't be heard outside the walls of his own skull.

'Something's up with our connection,' I said, stating the obvious.

'Well, pull yourself together,' she replied, and never had the phrase been more on the nose.

'Leave us alone, Kat. We're doing our best.' I could see myself speaking in the wing mirror. My lips were out of whack with my words still, but much improved. The pink had come back to my face, too. Whatever it was that was messing us up, it seemed to be passing.

'What did you make of all that?' Stronge asked, reintroducing her prop notepad to her pocket.

I rotated one wrist, then the other, pleased to see them doing as they were told. 'That was him for sure, but there's some things I don't get.'

'Like what?'

'Returning the car because it had a baby in it? Fae steal human babies, got a real habit for it, at least according to the book Jazz gave me.'

'Huh. So what are you thinking?'

'I dunno. Maybe he decided he could do without the hassle.'

'Then why not chuck the kid out of the sunroof? Isn't that what a cold-blooded killer would do?'

I had to admit, I was a bit stumped by the good samaritan act. Why do a one-eighty like that? Why take that kind of risk?

Stronge chewed her lip. 'Is there something we've missed here? Something about this guy we're not getting?'

'I don't know.' I rose to my feet, back in control now. 'But I can tell you this much: I've tackled the guy twice, and he's bad news. Maybe he had an attack of the conscience one time, I don't know. The real headline here is that he's trying to skip town, and since he isn't leaving London on foot and doesn't have a motor, what does that leave?'

CHAPTER TWENTY-NINE: HAS ANYONE SEEN THE INVISIBLE MAN?

EITHER THE ARCADIAN choked to death on London's smog or he found a way out of the city fast. The way I saw it, he only had one real means of doing that now: mass transit. He could try to jack another car I supposed, but since that hadn't gone so well the first time—and electric vehicles weren't easy to come by around these parts—the smart money was on him slapping on some makeup and taking a ride on public transport. So what were his options? Coaches belched diesel and rode the motorways, so I could probably rule those out. That left trains.

It was a risky play. Like Stronge said, the Arcadian's enemies would be lying in wait for him at any obvious exit points, which made a train station with routes out of the city a likely trap. And yet what choice did he have? London was killing him. It was shit or get off the pot time.

We decided to split up to cover more ground. Stronge staked out King's Cross Station, while Frank and I made a beeline for Euston. Those were the two most obvious choices, escape-wise, being the closest to the suspect's last known location.

Being as Frank and I were still a bit out of sorts, we decided to stay separate for now. By the time we rocked up to Euston Station it was getting on for 4 P.M. and the sky had already turned off. It got dark early at this time of year—dismal for the living, perfect for vampires. Speaking of which, I spied a Vengari soldier posted at the station's main entrance, stooped over, his long-fingered hands thrust deep into the pockets of a trench coat. His eyes were buried under a pair of shades, diligently sweeping the surrounding commuters for any sign of his prey. Lucky for us, he was so focused on finding the Arcadian that Frank and I were able to slip by unnoticed and take a hiding spot behind a ticket machine. From there we watched over the vampire's shoulder, straining to get the first look at the man we were both searching for.

It was another half hour before anything worth writing home about happened. Frank saw him before I did: the Arcadian, dressed in a black hoodie as he hobbled across the station concourse, coughing into a balled-up hand. He was wearing makeup to alter the colour of his skin, but that's about as far as his disguise went. And yet the Vengari soldier looked right through him. I don't think the vamps realised just how much the city disagreed with the fae. They had their eye out for a proud figure with a stride to his step, not a hacking leper. At least that was my theory.

Frank and I kept a safe distance as we followed the Arcadian through the ticket barrier and onto Platform 9, next train departing for Gloucester. He was heading somewhere nice and bucolic I bet: a sweet little village where no one knew his name, completely off-grid.

The Arcadian continued along the platform, shuffling all the way to its furthest end. There was precious little in the way of lighting along that final stretch, but then there wasn't much there worth shining a light on, either. All the same, there was CCTV all over, covering every scrap of ground, leaving no blind spots. I took care of that with a spot of kleptomancy—a spell of my own design that disabled cameras and returned a jumble of static instead of video.

The Arcadian pulled a Twix from his pocket, tore open the wrapper, and scarfed it down like a piglet, two fingers at once. A thought occurred as we spied on the sweet-toothed bastard: so long as Frank and I could get within grabbing distance without being noticed, we could do pretty much whatever we liked with the bloke. Forget about sparking him out, we could murder him if we wanted. A quick twist of the fae's head and it'd be done. An eye for an eye. Surely the Big Man would forgive us that.

But I'm no killer. Like I told Tali, I'm a P.I., not an assassin. I already had enough souls weighing on my conscience without adding another. The spirits I sent to oblivion back when I was an exorcist were a hod of bricks that I could never put down. Even if God were to one day grant me forgiveness and let me ascend, I'd still know the weight of those ignorant sins.

So instead, I reached into Frank's pocket and took out Jazz's music box, the one that short-circuited any local magic. If the Arcadian caught wind of us, his first instinct would be to turn invisible. I couldn't have that, so I inserted the key into the side of the box and went to wind it back. I was a half-turn in when the Arcadian stopped suddenly, seized by a violent coughing fit. Forget the box. There was no one else down this end of the platform and the suspect was all but incapacitated. Preparation had met opportunity; it was time to act before our target felt the itch of eyes upon him.

'Go,' I whispered.

Frank lurched forward and bore down on the Arcadian, hitting him with everything he had. The fae hit the ground like a sack of hammers, his skull bouncing off the platform so hard it even made me wince. Frank didn't care. Using a move I'd taught him, he cranked the killer's arm up behind his back and got him in an unbreakable hold. The Arcadian let out a pained gasp.

'Whatever they're paying you, I can best it,' he hissed into the concrete.

Even if he hadn't murdered a woman in cold blood, his stupid Little Lord Fauntleroy voice was enough to guarantee a no from this working-class stiff.

'Fat chance.'

Realising he wasn't about to buy his way out of this bind, the fae did his best to wriggle out instead. He may as well have not bothered; when he blinked out of sight, I spent all of a second worrying about it. From the way Frank was positioned it was obvious that our captive hadn't really gone anywhere. As suspected, all the Arcadian had done was pull his usual vanishing trick, which—given that my partner had a knee driven into the small of his back—was about as much use as sunblock to a skeleton.

The Arcadian reappeared, bringing with him an exhausted outtake of breath. He wasn't going anywhere and he knew it. There was nothing he could do to slip away or fight back. Which was a shame, as I was looking forward to a bit of aggro. Catching the Arcadian was the main thing, but giving him a boot up the Aris ranked a very close second. I almost wished he'd had some vegetation to work with so he could have done his Jack and the Beanstalk trick, but the only greenery on offer was the narrow trail of grass that ran between the nearby train tracks, watered into life by the flush of onboard toilets.

Frank slapped a set of heavy-duty cuffs on the Arcadian and rolled him onto his back before giving him a pat down. A quick frisk showed us the fae hadn't come tooled up.

'Where's the shooter?'

'The what?'

'The gun.'

'That thing? I threw it in the Thames. The only reason I took it from the hotel was so I had it when I went after that eaves.'

The bulb-headed dealer he had an altercation with at the nightclub. I still didn't know what that was all about. Didn't much care, either. We had our killer, that's what mattered.

I knelt down to get a proper butcher's at the bastard. He looked even rougher up close. His cheeks were hollow, his skin wreathed in flop sweat, his violet eyes shot with red veins and weighed down by two purple pouches that no amount of makeup could conceal.

'Not so pretty now, are you?' I noted.

London Town had taken a real toll on the Arcadian. He wasn't going to survive much longer in the city. At least not if I had anything to do with it.

I pulled out my phone and dialled.

The Arcadian saw what I was up to. 'What are you waiting for?' he croaked, pulse hammering in his neck. 'Get it over with.'

'I'm not doing anything until my client knows the score. After that, you're off to the Coven.'

A look of genuine confusion crossed his face. 'Coven? As in the London Coven? You mean you're not with the Vengari?'

'Unfortunately for you, no.'

The call connected and the answering machine at my office picked up. Tali wasn't able to handle physical objects or she'd no doubt have taken the call, but that was okay. The machine was one of those old-fashioned types that broadcast out loud, so she only had to open her ears to hear the good news.

'We got him,' I announced, not even bothering to disguise the smile on my face. 'We're going to turn him over now. In the meantime, put on your glad rags and some lippy, 'cause you've got a date with the Big Man.'

Once justice was served she'd be getting her ticket to the great clubhouse in the sky, and my record would get a shade less grubby. A couple of Brownie Points in my pocket and another satisfied customer. A job well done.

I hung up.

'Who was that?' asked the Arcadian, genuinely perplexed. 'Who were you talking to?'

'What's the matter? Did you already forget about the woman whose head you put a bullet in?'

The Arcadian's eyes were the size of saucers.

'That's right,' I said, wagging a finger for emphasis. 'She came back, and she's not very happy with you, son.'

The Arcadian's gaze bounced between me and Frank until he regained control of his vocal cords.

'You're wrong,' he said, his voice thin and reedy.

'Oh yeah?' I shot back. 'What am I wrong about?'

He looked at me with raw conviction in his eyes. 'I didn't murder Tali,' he said. 'She took her own life.'

I'd have laughed it off if it weren't for one niggling little detail. Much like Shakira's hips, Arcadians can't lie.

CHAPTER THIRTY: THE DIRTY TRUTH

THE BOOK JAZZ Hands gave me was wrong. It had to be. The part about Arcadians not being able to lie must have been fae-spun propaganda, like the story they have us tell children about the tooth fairy: the one that teaches kids to willingly invite their kind into our homes.

I gave my partner a nod. He gathered up two fistfuls of hoodie, hauled the Arcadian into a sitting position, and dumped him on a bench. I craned over the fae and pressed a finger to his forehead.

'What did you just say to me, sunshine?'

'Tali shot herself. That's the truth. I was supposed to do the same.'

I pressed my finger into him hard enough to leave a divot, same place he left a bullet hole in my client's skull. 'So you're not a murderer, is that it? This whole thing was just a suicide pact gone wrong?'

'I swear.'

'What do you reckon, Frank?'

Frank growled and dragged a thumb across his throat.

'Oh, come on,' the Arcadian protested, his voice at its plummiest yet. 'He's a zombie, what would he know?'

'Plenty, I'd say. Old Frank here's got a hell of a nose on him. Some say he can even sniff out lies.'

Frank responded with an angry moan, the best he could manage with no tongue.

'What's he saying?' asked the Arcadian.

'He's asking what fae brains taste like. What do you think? I bet they taste like rice pudding.'

Frank's mouth let slip a runnel of drool and the Arcadian's hairline responded with a fresh trickle of sweat.

'We were together,' the fae pleaded, 'me and Tali. My family disapproved, so we chose to die together rather than be forced to live apart.'

I offered a dry chuckle. 'Funny. Back in my day we drove to Gretna Green and eloped.'

'We tried running once but we were caught,' he replied, exasperated. 'My family is dead set on me marrying a vampire. They dragged me back kicking and screaming, but even after that I got away.'

I had to give him credit. The bullshit he was feeding me at least fit the narrative. Some of it, anyway.

'Let me get this right,' I said, toying with the toggles of his hoodie as if I was about to use them as a garrote. 'You and Tali were sweethearts in a sinking ship? Then how come you're still breathing?'

The Arcadian hung his head. 'Because I'm a coward. After it happened… when I saw her lying on the floor of that hotel room… I just couldn't do it.'

'No? Not even with all that 'clad in your system?'

'What?'

'Ironclad. The drug you took that makes you feel like you can take on the whole world.'

The Arcadian was so struck by that statement that he tried rising to his feet. Frank put him down with a shove that almost caved in his ribcage.

'I took it so I wouldn't be scared,' the fae wheezed, struggling for breath. 'It was Tali's idea. She took it, too.'

I decided to play along, to lure him into saying something I knew for a fact to be untrue. To watch him tie his own noose.

'If you took that stuff, how come you lost your bottle? Why didn't we find your brains painting that bedroom as well?'

'Because the powder the eaves sold me didn't work, and now I'm stuck here with you instead of lying in Tali's arms.'

I considered what he was saying. When we caught him in that nightclub toilet, he was raving at the eaves dealer for stitching him up with a dodgy dose. What if there was some truth to what the Arcadian was saying, only it wasn't a bad dose he got, it was that the ironclad was incompatible with his system. The eaves told us the psychoactive substance in ironclad was fairy dust, and seeing as that was part of fae biology already, the Arcadian would most likely be immune to it.

But even if the part about the ironclad had a grain of truth to it, that didn't mean the rest of the story had merit. I'd met some champion bullshitters in my time, and there was a technique they all practiced: use a truth to hide the lie. That's all that was happening here. The stuff about the 'clad was legit, but the only reason I was hearing it was so I'd think his story about a suicide pact was on the level, too. Well, forget it. I wasn't buying what he was flogging.

'You believe this slippery prick, Frank?'

My partner shook his head solemnly.

'Please,' said the Arcadian. 'I swear to you I'm not lying.'

'Sure. You're just an innocent boy who fell in love with the wrong girl, right?'

'The right girl. The wrong circumstances.'

I didn't appreciate the correction, so I had Frank give him a smack in the chops. The backhand left him slouching like a drunk granddad in his favourite armchair.

'If you're so innocent, explain why you left a will-o'-the wisp at the crime scene?'

That shut him up.

'Yeah, I thought so. A fairy STD doesn't quite fit the star-crossed lovers narrative, does it?'

'I must have caught it from one of my father's concubines,' he replied, swiping a trickle of blood from his chin.

I made a face. 'Come again?'

'When my father found out his son was carrying on with a human, he tried to put me on the straight and narrow.'

'By fixing you up with some fae floozies?'

He released a deflated sigh. 'Things work differently among my kind. You wouldn't understand.'

'I understand you caught crabs off your dad.'

The Arcadian fell silent. Turns out he didn't have an answer for everything.

'Give it up, pal. Do you seriously expect me to believe my client caught a bullet because of some forbidden romance? If she loved you so much, why would she come to me asking for your head?'

That was the big hole in the Arcadian's tapestry of lies: what was Tali's motivation in all of this? Why would she want him dead if they were lovers?

'Isn't it obvious?' he said.

'Obviously a crock,' I replied.

The fae's gaze sank to his feet. 'It's the truth.'

'Stop it. You weren't in a relationship with Tali. There was no suicide pact. You're just a vicious little shit with a moral compass that points due twat.'

'That's not true.'

We were going in circles. I needed the Arcadian to confess to his crimes. Not because I doubted his guilt, but because I wanted to hear him admit what he'd done.

'You know what, sunshine, I'm starting to think the Coven is too good for you. Frank, do me a favour and give this tosser a thick ear, would you?'

He did it with relish, snatching the fae up by the scruff of the neck and laying a thump on him that sent his limp body skidding across the platform. Ordinarily, Frank would look to me for guidance before going in for round two, but on this occasion he was just as ticked off as I was. He rolled up his sleeves and stalked over to the Arcadian, who was lying on his front, wrists still cuffed behind his back, struggling to get upright. Frank grabbed him by an ankle and dragged him down, then raised a fist like a mallet about to sink a nail in one.

'Stop,' I cried.

Something on the Arcadian's hand twinkled. I squatted down by his side to get a look at it. He was wearing a ring. A copper ring. I turned the band around to examine it closer and found a distinctive green stone that was a perfect match for the one Tali wore.

'Aw, shite.'

I felt a knot of tension in my chest. Could it be? Was the Arcadian telling the truth? The clues were all there; I'd witnessed them with my own eyes but been too blind to see. First there was Stronge's point about the Arcadian's makeup—how there was no way Tali could have been fooled by it up close. I was five feet away from him on a gloomy station platform and even I could see the joins—the way the makeup crusted in his eyebrows, how his natural blue colouring showed through the creases of his skin.

Then there were the psychic imprints my spell revealed at the crime scene: the spooning figures on the hotel bed that had lain together for hours. I wondered at the time what kind of killer would have waited that long to pounce, and why Tali hadn't mentioned an extended conversation prior to her death. Now I knew why. The scene my magic rendered was their final heart-to-heart before they conspired to end it all.

And finally there was the engagement ring Tali wore. When Stronge pressed her on the matter she said she had a fiancé, and yet she never once asked us to check in with him—to let him know what had become of his lover. Sure, her focus was on catching the man who killed her, but even so, that lack of consideration should have sent up a major red flag.

Talking of red flags, the platform we were occupying was starting to look like its own kind of perilous. An over-the-shoulder glance in the direction of the station concourse revealed the Vengari soldier who'd been lying in wait for the fae, only now he was heading in our direction, and at speed. The vampire was still a way away—far enough that I couldn't make out his facial features but read his body language loud and clear. His shoulders were hitched, head hung low like an animal ready to pounce, and he wasn't alone. Two more Vengari soldiers had joined him, their postures matching his, jaws thrust out, claws bared.

I had options here. This wasn't a fight or flight situation. As far as the Vengari were concerned, I was working for them—the hare-lipped vampire who took Frank's tongue made that pretty clear. There was nothing to stop me acting like I was here doing his dirty work; that I'd intended to hand the fae over to him and not the London Coven. After all, killer or not, I had every right to throw the

Arcadian to the wolves. He wasn't just any fae, he was the prince of the Unseelie Court, and everything I'd read about that lot spelled bad news. So what if he didn't murder Tali? Who knew how many other scalps he had on his belt. He might not be guilty of this caper, but he was dirty all the same.

Then again, how could I really know that? I had no proof that the Arcadian in my custody was a wrong 'un besides some things I'd read in a pile of yellowed old pages. All I knew for sure was that he didn't kill my client. That was the case I got handed: to bring in a bloodthirsty murderer and avenge an innocent woman. Now what did I have? Far as I could tell, I was looking at a lovesick fae who chickened out of a double-suicide. A delinquent who did a runner from a wedding. How could I possibly hold that against him? God knows I wished I'd skipped out on my nuptials, it would have saved me a world of heartache.

I looked to Frank, then to the Arcadian. He was just a sick kid, really, or at least he looked that way. And there was something in his eyes... something that didn't say killer. Try as I might, I couldn't summon up a picture of a crusty machete lying under his bed. Until I knew for a fact that the guy deserved his fate, I couldn't let the vamps get their hands on him, or anyone else. What happened next wasn't up to the Vengari or the Arcadians, it was up to me.

'Come on,' I said, hustling him along the platform. 'We've gotta scoot.'

CHAPTER THIRTY-ONE: TOGETHER FOREVER

THE VENGARI WERE ALREADY through the ticket barriers and cutting off our exit. We weren't getting through them. The best we could hope for was to find a way around.

I was searching for some way to wriggle off the line when a train pulled into the station with a raucous metal shriek. The carriage doors sprang open and vomited up a great flood of commuters, disgorging them onto the empty platform as one congealed mass. As the advancing scrum formed a wall between us and the vampires, I seized on the chance interference. Frank and I rode the tide, heads bowed, forcing the Arcadian to duck down with us as we manoeuvred ourselves to the other end of the platform. The Vengari fought a losing battle against the flow, desperately searching for their prey, but the chaos made us invisible. A quick cut to the left and we were heading for the station's service exit with the vampires none the wiser.

'Nice move,' said the Arcadian.

'Thanks,' I replied, remembering our first encounter at the nightclub. 'I stole it from you.'

We arrived at the service exit: a large shutter separating us from the street outside, chained and double-padlocked. The Vengari would find their way here soon, so we needed to get through quickly. Lucky for me, my corporeal companion had a knack for this kind of stuff.

'Do the honours, would you, Frank?'

He wrapped his mitts around the chain and pulled it apart, sending a snapped link whizzing over my shoulder. With one hand he yanked the shutter aside and sent it screaming along its coaster. We shot through the exit like bullets from a machine gun, and off we went, moving as fast as our legs would carry us. The night was a puppy, but there was plenty to do.

The Arcadian was the first to slow. Despite keeping up the pace for a good half-mile, he eventually succumbed to a coughing fit that folded him in half. He looked so weak. So hard done by. I was having a tough time squaring the bloke coughing his guts into the gutter with the man who got the better of me twice. But then no wonder; all the evidence suggested the Arcadian wasn't the ruthless killer Tali sent me after. That she'd made that man up. And I had a good idea why. Hell, I bet even Frank did.

'She wants you dead so the pair of you can be together, doesn't she? That's why she hired us.'

The fae stopped coughing but said nothing. Even now, after everything Tali had put him through, he was loyal to her. Even after she sentenced him to death, he still loved her. He was on his own there. Tali lied to us—set me and Frank on a bogeyman that didn't exist. She was so desperate not to suffer in limbo alone, so keen to see her lover dragged through the grey veil with her, that she pretended to be the wronged party, the hooker with the heart of gold who died at the hands of another cruel customer. She framed the man who jilted her at death's door and set the dogs on him without a care for me and Frank.

It pissed me off. Tali played me, took advantage of my old-fashioned sense of chivalry, and it had worked. Once again I'd let some dame get one over on me, only this time I wasn't the victim. Because of her, I almost sentenced a man to death for a crime he didn't commit. It didn't matter that it was love, not vengeance, that drove Tali to such extremes. The results could so easily have been the same. Another dead body. Another wasted life.

'What a mess,' said the Arcadian, propping his back against a wall, knees ready to buckle. 'Look at all the trouble I've caused. Maybe I should just give Tali what she wants and put a bullet in my head.'

Frank groaned.

'What's he saying?' asked the fae.

'He's saying you don't want that. Take it from the pair of us, being dead ain't all it's cracked up to be.'

The Arcadian laughed and set off another coughing fit. While he hacked away, I asked myself what death meant for his kind. Were there fae in Heaven, I wondered? Were they part of God's flock? Not that He was much of a shepherd anyway, at least going by the number of deceased souls left stranded here, tangled up like lambs in barbed wire.

On that grim thought, *The Munsters* theme tune kicked off and out came my phone. I checked who was calling, sighed, and dumped the thing back in my pocket.

'Who was that?' asked the Arcadian, still wheezing.

'A detective I know.'

'So why don't you answer?'

'Because I can't be dealing with her "I told you so" right now.'

Stronge knew something was wrong with Tali's story, and when she found out just how right she was she'd be sure to beat me over the head with it.

'There's something still bugging me,' I told the Arcadian. 'How come the vamps are so upset with you?'

A cold sweat had washed off most of his makeup by now, leaving barely a few streaks behind. 'Because I stood up their bride.'

'Yeah, I get that. The Vengari wanted to marry their girl off to your lot and merge houses, only Hugh Grant wanted to muck about with Divine Brown instead. So what? Can't the vamps just fix their bit of totty up with some other geezer? There must be a hundred different flavours of Uncanny to choose from.'

The Arcadian—who probably caught about half of what I said there but figured the rest out using context clues—filled me in.

'It's about blood,' he said, breathing shakily. 'Fae blood and Vengari blood… they're compatible, or at least mine is with their candidate.'

'So you and their princess can breed?'

The Arcadian nodded. Still struggling to catch a breath, he went on to explain that the child of such a union would have none of the faes' intolerances to the modern world and could live comfortably in an urban sprawl. Additionally, they wouldn't suffer the aversion to sunlight that blighted the vampire race, and the necessity to feed on human blood would be a trait that belonged only to their ancestors.

At last I had the full picture of what I was mixed up in. A fae-vengari half-breed would have all of the good stuff—magic, strength, speed—but none of the downsides. No wonder the vamps were so keen to catch the Arcadian and drag him to the altar for a shotgun wedding. And no surprise the Arcadians were prepared to hold their noses and mix blood with those Vengari cockroaches. This was about more than consolidating power. Much more. If the two factions succeeded in formalising their pact and creating a hybrid species, they'd become an unstoppable force. In a couple of generations we'd be looking at an unholy alliance that could rule the UK with an iron fist.

This wasn't about a murder investigation, it was about the birth of a master race. Not for the first time, I'd found myself tangled in something so much bigger than I was. Why could it never be simple? Did every job have to turn into a whole bloody saga? I get that I had to do right by the Big Man, but I was trying to get into Heaven, not audition for Jesus.

'Come on,' I told the Arcadian. 'Rest time's over. Get your skates on.'

He did his best to comply but his legs unhinged and he sank to the ground. 'Just go,' he gasped, his throat tight, his voice cracked almost beyond comprehension.

'No man left behind,' I told him. 'Frank, be a good lad and help the feller to his feet, would you?'

Frank hefted the Arcadian over his shoulder in a fireman's lift, and off we went, wending our way through the backstreets to Hammersmith.

'Where are you taking me?' asked the fae, his voice little more than an arid whisper.

'Same place I was always taking you,' I replied. 'The London Coven.'

That was about the point the Arcadian blacked out.

CHAPTER THIRTY-TWO: THE WITCHING HOUR

WE WERE WALKING the last cobbled stretch to the coven when sleeping beauty peeled back his peepers.

'Good morning, Major,' I said, despite the fact that it was distinctly nighttime.

'Major?' replied the Arcadian, still woozy as Frank set his feet down on the ground.

'Never mind, it's from an old sitcom,' I said. 'It occurs to me I don't know your name. I'm Jake Fletcher and this is my partner, Frank. What do you want me to call you?'

The fae rubbed his eyes. 'My name is Lneshes'sent.'

'Right. Don't suppose you've got a nickname I can say without giving myself a nosebleed?'

He shook his head.

'Kid it is then.'

We came to the coven door. You might expect the entrance to the famous London Coven to be a thing to behold, but it's nothing to write home about. No mystical etchings, no wrought iron bands, no fancy antique knocker, just a plain wooden door in need of a fresh lick of paint and a squirt of WD40.

'Is this…?'

'Hammersmith, yeah,' I said.

The Arcadian gave me a hooded look and completed his question. 'Is this the home of the witches of the London Coven?'

Frank chuckled. Even he knew better than that.

'Used to be,' I told the fae, 'before they got potted by some bad bastard who ate magic for dinner.'

The ancient trio who established the coven were long gone, and with them, the wonder wall they built to protect the city from demonic slags. But they left behind a failsafe—a familiar they built to handle the rough and tumble stuff. Not the kind of familiar you might be thinking of, a cat or a crow or something like that, but a human-looking protector by the name of Stella Familiar. She was the one who kept the peace around these parts nowadays. The one who dispensed justice.

It's funny, when I fantasised about Frank and me handing the Arcadian over to Stella, it wasn't going to be for his benefit. How things had changed. The moment he blew up my world with his big reveal, I realised the kid wasn't the enemy. In fact, he was the only thing standing between life as we knew it and an army of fanged blue fairies running amok. So instead of a perp-walk, I'd come to the coven looking for sanctuary, because this story was way too big for Fletcher & Fletcher. To make it through this one we needed to call in the big guns.

Frank rapped a knuckle on the coven door.

'You're looking better,' I told the Arcadian, passing the time.

I didn't say it to be polite. Even with makeup streaking his face and sweat still beading his forehead he looked much improved.

'It's this alley,' he explained. 'There's magic here. A lot of it.'

'That's blind alleys for you.'

His nose wrinkled. 'Blind what?'

'Secret streets that normals can't access. Can't see, even.'

The Arcadian flexed his fingers and stood taller than I'd seen him stand. 'Whatever it is, it's making me better.'

'No wonder. Pollution can't touch you here. Blind alleys are their own thing, a sort of... wrinkle in reality.'

He shook his head. 'It's more than that. Magic is like oxygen to my kind. The place I come from swims in it. This city is a desert by comparison, but here in this alley... it's like an oasis.'

I nodded politely and shared a secret look with Frank. I could tell he was thinking the same thing I was: *Are we juicing up a bloke who's about to turn on us?* After all, it was only gut instinct telling me the kid was a black sheep among his kind and not just as rotten as the rest. The sooner we brought Stella in on this, the better. She'd have a better idea of who we were dealing with, and be able to nip any problems in the bud if my read was wrong.

Frank knocked again, louder this time. I pressed my ear to the door but heard nothing inside. What was the hold up? Everyone knew the coven's door should be open at this hour; open to anyone who needed the resident's help, anyway. It was common knowledge that tonight was for walk-ins, that visitors were welcome to stop by and request the coven's assistance. So where was its last remaining member? Where was Stella Familiar?

'You're a ghost,' noted the Arcadian, sensing my frustration. 'If you want in, why don't you just walk through the door?'

'And set off about two-hundred magical countermeasures? I'm not ready for the knacker's yard just yet, mate.'

What was keeping that woman? Was she back there having a kip or was she out and about fighting monsters? Maybe something urgent came up that she needed to deal with: some other looming catastrophe besides the one I was bringing to her door.

Frank knocked again and I decided to cover the conversational shortfall with some chit-chat.

'Something keeps nagging at me: The Vengari have been knocking about for centuries. If you and your peeps wanted to mingle, why did you wait this long to come to London?'

'It's not that simple,' the Arcadian replied. 'Just like the door before us, this world was closed to my kind. For hundreds of years, modernity made it impossible for Arcadians to thrive here, but more than that, the magic was gone. Literally. When we first arrived in Old Albion—when Arthur sat upon the throne—magic ran rampant across this land. Then came the Age of Enlightenment and people stopped believing in things beyond the limits of their five senses. Science and philosophy reigned and magic became myth. We Arcadians had no choice but to leave. It wasn't that we couldn't survive here, we couldn't *exist.*'

'Then how come you're back? What changed?'

'You did. Your whole civilisation. This is a post-truth world now, where facts are no longer relevant. And when facts don't matter, the unreal prospers.'

I only half-followed, so I let him go on.

'Take a look around you, Jake Fletcher. This world of yours is so anti-science now that it has become pro-myth. An age of illusion is upon you. Is it any wonder that we Arcadians were able to return?'

'Hold on a sec. Are you telling me because of you-know-who at Number 10 and these bloody anti-vaxxers and flat-earthers, fairies are back?'

'That's precisely what I'm telling you. The skin between our dimensions has thinned. We were held captive in a fantasy, but when reality became a fairy tale, the genie escaped the bottle.'

I didn't know whether to laugh or cry. All I knew was, no one was answering this bloody door, so I decided to let myself in.

CHAPTER THIRTY-THREE: NO REST FOR THE WICCA'D

'HOW EXACTLY DID YOU DO THAT?' asked the Arcadian as Frank closed the front door behind us. 'Didn't you say the coven was sealed with all manner of magical protections?'

'Yeah, but I found a key under the mat.'

Unsurprisingly, the fae wasn't taken in by this.

'Okay, I gave it a bit of the old razzle dazzle, that's all. Nothing fancy.'

'Pardon me?'

'I broke in. I used a spell to disable the security measures and now here we are, bingo-bango.'

I was a dab hand at kleptomancy, but even still, I wouldn't have stood a chance against the protections the coven's original witches employed when they were around. It was only because Stella did the locking up these days, and her magic was geared more toward lobbing about fireballs than bolting doors, that I was able to pick the lock and gain access.

The Arcadian cast a wary look about the hallway. 'Should we really be here without permission?'

I coughed on a laugh. 'It's just a spot of B&E, mate. I thought you were an unseelie fae. Aren't you lot meant to be hard cases?'

All the same, the kid had a point. 'Stella?' I called. 'You home, luv?'

As far as I could tell, no one was home, but I'd just as soon not round a corner and have a flaming fist thrust through my head.

I called out again but no one answered, so the three of us proceeded down the exposed brick hallway and into the guts of the building.

If you've never visited a witches' coven before, let me set the scene for you. First of all, forget about black cats and bubbling cauldrons and flying monkeys—a modern day coven is more like a student flat than the pages of a *Meg and Mog* story. The women (and occasionally men) who occupy these places live pretty much like the rest of us do, so expect to find a fitted kitchen with modern appliances and a bathroom with contemporary plumbing. No pissing in a pot for witches, at least not since Thomas Crapper gave us the U-bend.

I stuck my head into a side room and found a library filled with ancient tomes, some standing on shelves, others splayed out on the ground, covers bowed, pages dog-eared, spines cracked. No sign of Stella, though. I called out one more time.

'Jake Fletcher here. I come in peace.'

The kitchen was empty, the bedrooms, too. The familiar was elsewhere. And yet the place wasn't entirely void of magic. Far from it, in fact.

'This place… it's so rich with mana that I feel as if I'm treading water,' said the fae.

I wasn't able to sense magic in the same way he could, but even a one-trick spell-slinger like me could feel a heaviness to the place, a sensation like a warm coat hung across my shoulders.

'How are you feeling?' I asked the fae, noting the newfound spring in his step.

'Fantastic,' he replied wearing a smile so broad he looked like an emoticon. 'I can't tell you how good it feels to be away from the smoke and the soup of electronic signals you have out there. How do you stand it?'

I shrugged. 'What was it Sammy J said? *When a man is tired of London, he's tired of life.*'

'But you aren't alive.'

'That only adds to my point doesn't it? If a dead man's willing to stick it out in this city, it must have something going for it.'

'I'll have to take your word on that.' He wiped a hand down his face and looked at the pink mess on his palm. 'If it's all right with you, I'm going to clean this muck off my face.'

'Knock yourself out,' I said, pointing the way to the bathroom. 'Just don't try legging it out the window unless you want to get yourself cut in half by a magical guillotine.'

We parted ways as Frank and I headed to the core of the coven: a large common room sparsely furnished with a few knick-knacks and a couple of bits of old furniture. In one corner sat a weathered rocking chair, and against the far wall, a knackered couch worn past the point of distress and peppered with rips. A metre-square slab of black slate was affixed to the floor in front of an open fireplace with a surround patterned by twisting flowers (something witchy like deadly nightshade I think, or maybe plain old garden weeds—I'm no botanist). Upon the black slate was a pentagram inside a circle, drawn in white chalk flecked with shavings of silver. The artist was absent, however. The London Coven was categorically deserted.

'What do you reckon, Frank? Do we hole up here and wait for Stella to show or look for somewhere else to hide His Majesty?'

But Frank wasn't listening, he was too busy traipsing around the room like a stiff-legged Frankenstein, having a nose of the place. Without meaning to, he tripped the five-pointed star drawn upon the slate, breaking the seal and triggering a dormant spell. From the pentagram sprang Stella Familiar, shimmering like stardust.

'Hello, Jake.'

Frank leapt back about three feet, while I reversed a distinctly more manly two.

'Stella?'

But the person I was speaking to wasn't a person at all, merely an illusion that played out like a pre-recorded hologram.

I turned to my partner. 'How did she know I'd be the one to break in?'

'Because you're the only person I know foolish enough to invade the London Coven,' she said, anticipating my question.

'Well, how about that,' I said, marvelling at Stella's foresight as well as the intricacy of her magic. 'A custom-made simulacrum, just for little old me.'

Frank looked a bit put out.

'Don't take it personally, pal,' I said. 'You weren't even on the scene last time me and the magic lady did a job together. I'll introduce the pair of you soon enough.'

You might be wondering what Stella looks like, and given that she was made by a trio of witches, you could be forgiven for thinking green, wrinkly and warty. If that's the case, get ready to have your hair blown back, because Stella Familiar is a looker. Built with a perpetually camera-ready face and hair so thick you could swing from it, Stella has the kind of rarified body you mostly see stepping from the back of slick black limousines. The woman looks more like a catwalk model than London's first line of defence against the Devil's unholy minions, but don't let that fool you—she could kick your arse from here to Timbuktu and not put a hair out of place doing it.

Stella's fancy out-of-office message went on. 'I can only assume things are desperate for you to have broken into my house and put your sticky finger all over my pentagram—'

'You don't know the half of it, darling.'

'—but I'm afraid I'm currently unavailable.

'You what?'

'Right now I'm on a pilgrimage in a faraway land, communing with Galaeta, the First Witch.'

'Are you joking me?'

'Rest assured that my duties are being looked after in my absence—'

'Okay, here we go…'

'—by the Academy of Myth Management.'

And with that, Stella was gone.

'That's it? No contact number? Fuck.'

'Is something the matter?' asked the Arcadian, sauntering into the room shirtless and towelling his chiselled blue face. 'Who are Myth Management?'

'They're a bureau who maintain the balance between this world and the ones beyond. I've done some consultancy work for them before. Bit of an old boys' club, but good at what they do.'

'So what's the problem?'

'Nothing much, only that they were blown sky-high recently when a Greek god tried to muscle his way into the city.'

'They're gone?'

'Might as well be. They won't be operational for months, maybe even years.'

The Arcadian's mouth fell open. 'We don't have that long.'

Frank rolled his eyes in a, *No shit*, way.

The fae paced the room, old floorboards groaning sympathetically beneath his feet. 'Is there anyone else who can help?'

'None that I know of. Or none who'll help us, anyway.'

The fae collapsed on the dented couch. 'So we're fucked?'

It wasn't a particularly regal way of putting it, but it was bang on the money.

CHAPTER THIRTY-FOUR: GETTING TO KNOW YOU

I HAD Frank fetch the kid a tub of something sweet from Stella's freezer, then the pair of us sat either side of him on the couch.

'This is magnificent,' said the fae, stress-eating his little heart out.

'Pretty good, right?'

'Good? It's ambrosia.'

He ate the stuff like he was stuffing a musket.

'If you like that, you should try the one with the little chocolate fish in it.'

I waited until the last of the ice cream was gone then made this suggestion: 'What about going back to Arcadia? If all the people chasing you are here, why stick around? Why not go home?'

I sort of knew there must have been a reason the kid hadn't already gone with that option, but I needed to hear it.

'I can't go back. My people, the unseelie fae... we were banished from our homeland.'

Of course. Why else would they abandon Arcadia? Mixing blood with the Vengari was only a means to an end, a way to survive in the Big Smoke. Given the choice, they'd naturally kick their feet up in the pastoral utopia they called home.

'Banished by who?' I asked.

The kid took the kind of breath you take before telling a painful and lengthy story. 'It wasn't long after we left your world that the discord began. There were those in the Seelie Court who believed we needed to concentrate our future efforts on finding a way to return to Britain, and those who felt we should be satisfied where we were.'

'About that: what were you doing sniffing around our manor anyway?'

'Looking for babies. We stole them, raised them, enslaved them. It is a practice I always abhorred, but one that was embraced by my family, who relied on human labour to build and maintain their palaces.'

Palaces, plural. I dread to think how many kids were snatched to make sure the Arcadian and his evil ilk got to live in the lap of luxury.

'Back to the banishing,' I prompted, eager to get to the part of the story where his folks received their comeuppance.

The kid went on, his voice thick with regret. 'Over the centuries the discord grew deeper and a rift formed. There were the common people who wished to leave human slavery in the past, and those determined to cling to tradition: the monarchy and the aristocracy. Eventually, it led to a revolution.'

'And let me guess; the hoi-polloi won out?'

The kid nodded ruefully. 'We were branded Unseelie and evicted from our palaces, and now here we are, hiding underground and climbing into bed with blood-suckers. Anything to claw back the power that was taken from us.'

'Except you don't play that game. Why is that?'

'Call me old-fashioned, but I believe exploiting the rights of others to further my own ends is wrong.'

I smiled. 'I guess the apple sometimes *does* fall far from the tree, eh?'

We sat on the couch immersed in that thought; a dead man sandwich with a fairy filling. The kid was shivering, and not just because of the ice cream he'd munched his way through. I hadn't realised on account of being a ghost, but the coven was cold through to its bones. Since it seemed like this fireside chat might go on for a bit, I decided to cosy things up by tossing a spell into the hearth. A lively spark arced into the pile of dry wood contained in the firebox and caught with a satisfying *woof*. The virgin flames curled and swayed, flicking this way and that as they bathed us in their warmth.

'Clever trick,' said the kid.

'It's literally the only bit of magic I know besides the stuff that got us in here.'

And even then it had taken me years of sleepless nights and singed eyebrows to perfect.

'We haven't spoken about Tali for a while,' I said, moving the conversation along.

The kid turned to me ever so slowly. 'What do you want to know?'

'Lots of things, but the main one I keep coming back to is how did you two meet? How does a fairy prince end up romancing a London call girl?'

Frank leaned in, ears pinned back. He was a real sap when it came to this kind of stuff. You know he once told me that *Pretty Woman* was his favourite film? Not sure I was supposed to share that, but there you go.

'It began not long after we arrived here,' said the Arcadian, sharing his meet-cute. 'I was in disguise, taking a tour of the city— avoiding my parents, really—when my feet carried me into a hotel; one of those upmarket affairs with a view of the river and a rooftop pool. I was drinking on my own at the bar when I found her, or rather, she found me.'

'Let me guess, she asked if you were looking for a good time?'

He laughed. 'Something like that.'

'Only, the hard-sell didn't last too long.'

'It did not. We talked about our lives—as much as we were willing to share right then—and really got to know each other. It turned out we had a lot in common.'

'The son of a king and a streetwalker?'

'Tali was more than that,' he snapped. 'Much more.'

Frank buzzed his lips, desperate for me to stop interrupting and let the kid finish his story.

'I'm sorry, go on.'

The kid shook off a frown. 'Our roots were very different, but we'd both been dealt a rough hand in life. I was being forced into an unwanted marriage by my family, while Tali had been disowned by hers. We were two loners, drifting aimlessly, but we'd finally found something we could hold onto. Each other.'

Frank practically had love hearts in his eyes, the big Jessie.

'So that was that—you met in a hotel bar and fell in love?'

'Not straight away, no.'

'Right. I mean, obviously it must have taken longer than that.'

He smiled. 'Yes. We didn't actually say the words until later that night.'

I had to hand it to the kid, he could spin a yarn.

'Mooooore,' Frank mooed.

The Arcadian laughed and picked up where he'd left off. 'After some more conversation, Tali let me know she'd seen through my disguise, so I decided to drop the pretence and reveal my true nature. Frequenting a common bar seemed ill-fitting after that, so I suggested we head to a place I knew that better suited the mood: a pub by the name of The Beehive.'

'The 'Hive!'

'Oh, so you've heard of it?'

Had I bloody heard of it? I'd been there once already since I took Tali's case. If just one of the piss-heads that propped up Lenny's bar had mentioned an Arcadian coming in with a high-class human escort on his arm, we might not be in this mess right now.

'Yes, I've heard of it,' I replied, keeping my lid on.

'We played darts that night,' the kid said, reminiscing. 'We had fun. So much fun. We were at the end of a game when I bet Tali she couldn't score a bullseye. She told me if she did I'd have to marry her. I agreed, and she took the shot between her legs, doubled over, upside down.'

And? screamed Frank's mile-wide eyes.

'And... bullseye.' He clapped his hand to his heart as if pierced by Cupid's arrow.

Hell of a shot. I wondered for a moment if Tali had something up her sleeve besides a killer throwing arm.

'No magic involved?'

'None,' he assured me. 'At least not the kind you're talking about.'

It was a sweet tale, spoken by a sweet kid. I was starting to understand why Tali was so reluctant to let him go. Why she was prepared to move Heaven and Earth to get him back.

'Is that a tear I see in your jaded eye?' asked the kid, a smile teasing the corners of his lips.

I swiped a sleeve across my face. 'The fire's drying my eyeballs out, that's all.'

Being as Frank had no tongue to speak with, it sounded as if he was talking with a mouthful of sticky Brie, but the words, 'Youuuu're ghoooost,' came through loud and clear.

'Shut up, meat bag,' I shot back, giving him a quick cuff to the canister for pointing out the impossibility of my deceit.

When I looked back to the kid I expected him to still be wearing the smirk, but it was already gone.

'I miss her. I miss what we had.'

'I know, but come on, a part of you must have known this was doomed from the start. Look at what you had stacked against you: your family, the Vengari, the city itself. How were you ever going to make it work?'

'I don't know,' he whispered. 'With Tali by my side, nothing seemed impossible.'

A lump rose in his throat, quickly swallowed down. What he was going through I could only imagine. His love for Tali had been so bright, so pure, but it had brought about her end. An end he should have shared but was too frightened to face. And now here he was, a hunted man, loathed by everyone.

I saw myself in him. A young me. Naive. Lovestruck. Damned. Sure, he'd made mistakes, but for the right reasons. The kid was prepared to give up everything to be with Tali: his tribe, his crown, his power. All of it, flushed down the crapper. I could respect that. But respect wasn't going to fix this problem. The Vengari and the fae would do anything to get him to the altar and cement their pact. And if that happened... maybe the kid was right. Maybe death was the better option.

'Couldn't we just stay here until the familiar returns?' he said, shaking me from my thoughts. 'Surely no one in their right mind would break into a witches' coven... no offence.'

'Some taken.'

I mulled over his proposition, as did Frank. Or maybe he was dreaming of a piping hot plate of cow brains—the two looks were pretty much indistinguishable from one another.

'We can't stay here,' I said, having marinaded on the idea. 'Stella could be on her pilgrimage for a long while yet. Plenty of time for your stalkers to scope this place out.'

They only had to draw a line between me and Stella—known accomplices—and we'd be facing a home invasion in no time.

'Then there's nowhere left to go,' said the Arcadian. 'It's over.'

'Not until the fat lady sings it ain't. Come on, kid, do you really want to spend the rest of your life stuck in this hole?'

'I suppose not.'

'Then let's go,' I cried, shooting to my feet. 'Forget about hiding. Let's find a way to deal with this mess and put an end to it.'

He laughed a laugh of disbelief. 'You really think I'm safer out there than in here?'

'Maybe, maybe not. All I know is, we can't just sit on our arses and wish this mess away. We have to keep moving. If I managed to chase you down, imagine how easy it'll be for a whole clan to get their claws in you.'

'So what are you proposing? Flee the city?'

'Nah, that plan's totally up the spout now.'

The fae hammered his knees with his fists. 'I need to get out of here. I can't survive in London. If you don't want to help, at least show me the way back to the train station so I can make my own way.'

'You haven't thought this through. The vamps have a tonne of manpower at their disposal. They'll have every exit out of the city stitched up now they know you're a flight risk.'

It was easy to forget that the Vengari were legion. Given their low profile, you could be fooled into thinking they were thin on the ground, but the fact was, they were an infestation. The kind you don't see. The kind that hides in the cracks and crevices.

'We have to face them in the city,' I said. 'At least here we're on home ground.'

'Speak for yourself.'

The Arcadian remained unconvinced, arms crossed tightly,

refusing to budge, at least until Frank rose to his feet and offered a hand. At first the kid stayed where he was, but Frank's puppy dog eyes have a way of turning around even the most stubborn of souls.

The fae put out a hand and Frank hauled him to his feet, uniting us as three. It was a moving moment, or at least it would have been had it not been interrupted by the sound of splintering wood coming from the coven's front door. The kid poked his head into the hallway to see who'd come calling.

'Who is it?' I asked, fairly sure it wasn't the homeowner.

'The Vengari,' said the kid, turning to me with a look of grim fatality. 'They found us.'

Now why did I have to go and disable those security measures?

CHAPTER THIRTY-FIVE: OUT FOR BLOOD

RIGHT AWAY I fused with Frank.

'What are you doing?' bleated the Arcadian, seeing our numbers dwindle by one. 'There's a whole pack of them coming.'

I poked my face out of Frank's head so I could answer the question. 'Just play along and act like it's only me and you here, okay?'

The Vengari were under the mistaken impression that the person they were dealing with was a single, living entity, and I intended to keep it that way. So long as they thought I was a normal and not a ghost packed into a meat man, I'd be harmless in their piggy red eyes. Little did they know I could play Jake-in-the-box and spring from Frank's body with my fists out when the mood took me. Chances were that still left us outnumbered by quite a margin, but I had the Arcadian on my side now, and he was fighting fit again. Working together and using the element of surprise, we stood a slim chance of tipping the odds in our favour and making it out of the coven alive (well, you know what I mean).

I smelled the Vengari before I saw them, filing into the room arched over like a row of question marks. It was the same Vlad pack who accosted me at the office: three vampire knee-breakers and Enoch, the peerless wanker who had away with Frank's tongue.

A spastic thump hammered in my chest like the fevered pump of a racing heart. It felt so real, and yet it had to be my imagination playing tricks on me, because the skin of that old drum had worn through a long time ago. I was losing control. *We* were losing control. Ever since Enoch performed unlicensed oral surgery on Frank—on me—we'd been experiencing connection difficulties, and here it was, happening all over again. We could make fists and disguise our inner disquiet for now, but how long could we be expected to act calm in front of the man who did this to us?

'Greetings, Your Majesty,' said Enoch, performing a bow so shallow as to be insulting. 'And hello again to you, Detective.'

While his lackeys hung back looking hard, Enoch got up in my face, leering at me with that sharp face of his, pale as the chalk cliffs of Dover under the light of a full moon.

'What did I tell you, Mister Fletcher? You work for the Vengari. And unlike the familiar of the London Coven, we don't take holidays.'

Baaad maaan, said the voice in my head.

No shit, Frank.

I fought his urge to recoil from Enoch like a dog shrinking from his master's rolled-up newspaper. Together, we stayed strong. Just about.

'No sign of your partner... again,' Enoch remarked. 'Where is he this time? Getting his hair done?'

I didn't answer. Couldn't answer. The room was quiet but for the gentle crackle of the hearth.

Enoch flashed his fangs. 'Admit it, there is no other Fletcher is there? It just looks better stencilled onto a window, doesn't it? Plus you get to bill twice this way.'

I felt a sensation like mites crawling under my skin and resisted the overriding compulsion to scratch at my forearms. I was struggling to hold the reins on Frank's body. He was starting to twitch, and visibly so. What if we lost it? What if we went into a seizure? What if the body I was occupying spat me out—rejected me like a kidney transplant that didn't take?

'No pithy comebacks?' said Enoch. He slapped his forehead theatrically. 'Oh, I'm sorry, how rude of me, I forgot I took this...'

From his coat pocket he produced something swathed in a hand-kerchief, and unwrapped it before my eyes. There it was, Frank's tongue, dried out and blue.

Inside my skull, Frank expressed a long and pitiful moan.

Having made his point, Enoch took the corners of the hankie and carefully wrapped the organ back up.

'I'm sure you're wondering how we found you,' he went on. This time he didn't wait for me to respond. 'It was a deaf eaves who gave you up, Detective. He approached us; didn't even ask for payment. Said it was personal.'

So the fat-headed dealer had sold me out to the fae *and* the Vengari. To think I let Stronge talk me out of mashing the sole of my shoe into his bust-up leg. What a waste.

'It doesn't matter how you found me,' said the Arcadian. 'You're here now, so let's go.'

'He speaks at last!' scoffed Enoch, his sharp shoulders hitching as he laughed. 'Thank you for your contribution, Your Highness, but if it's all the same with you, I think I'll set the agenda here.'

He pulled his shooter. His mates did, too.

Guuuuns, said Frank.

No flies on you, mate, I replied inside of our collective melon. Though, technically speaking, there often were flies upon Frank's person, as despite my best efforts, he still gave off a slight whiff of the grave.

Enoch curled a spindly finger around the trigger of his shooter. 'Don't bother turning invisible on us, Your Majesty.' He pulled at the skin beneath one of his albino eyes. 'We Vengari don't miss a trick.'

He turned the gun on me and I felt my already gaping grave yawn a few feet wider. Bullets wouldn't kill me, but a double-tap to the head would take Frank down for sure, then the jig would be up and the vamps would tear into my disembodied ecto-form with their claws. As for the Arcadian, he'd be on his own, and since I doubted the kid had seen a proper fight in his life, I was willing to bet Frank's left nut that he'd be off out the door a few seconds later with wedding bells ringing in his ears.

That was the theory anyway, except Enoch had other ideas. With a cold grin on his face he gave a nod to a crony with eyes capped by thick, wiry eyebrows. The crony produced a plastic bag from the top pocket of his jacket and carefully unfolded it. It was the kind of bag the cashier gave you when you shopped at a petrol station: transparent and tissue-thin, so insubstantial that it could be carried off by a gust of wind and washed all the way over the horizon. In other words, harmless. Except in the wrong hands.

While Enoch and the vamp with the eyebrows kept their guns trained on me, the other three rushed the Arcadian. The kid managed to take one down with a knife-hand strike to the throat (thoroughly shooting down my theory about his lack of fighting prowess), but the other two overpowered him, kicking in the backs of his legs and wrestling him to his knees.

While the spare vamp kept me pinned in his sights, Enoch took possession of the plastic bag and made his way over to the Arcadian, nice and casual. He took a deep breath and filled the bag with two lungs of air that must have smelled worse than a cracked hellmouth. Then, without fanfare, he dumped the thing over the Arcadian's head and tightened it around his neck.

The kid fought—Christ, he fought—but he was no match for the Vengari, who kept him riveted in place while the head vamp suffocated the life out of him.

'Goodnight, sweet prince,' rasped Enoch as the bag fogged and the Arcadian bucked and thrashed.

The fae's fingers glowed green and danced the way they did when he used magic to give life to local flora, but there was nothing here for him to animate save for a few jars of lentils in the kitchen and a withered pot plant on the mantelpiece.

There was nothing I could do but watch as the bag shrunk and the kid breathed a final shuddering gasp, vacuum sealing his face.

What was Enoch doing? How were the Vengari going to march the groom down the aisle and ensure the union went ahead if the fae prince was dead by their hands?

With fingers dug deep into the kid's windpipe, Enoch shook and he shook until the neck he was throttling turned limp as a chewed rag. The fae went still as his head rolled backwards, eyes showing their whites.

Help, Frank insisted.

Of course I wanted to, but then what? Even if I threw myself from his body and went surging towards Enoch as a ghost, the bullets would soon start flying. My trick was useless against these kinds of odds. I had a card up my sleeve, but it didn't work with anything in my hand.

'Boss,' said the henchman with the nutty eyebrows. 'Boss!'

Enoch whirled about. 'What? What is it?'

'That's enough. Look at him, he's out.'

Enoch snarled. For a moment I thought he was going to bury his fangs in the eyebrowed underling's neck, but he grunted and released his grip on the fae, letting him flop to the ground like a dropped concertina.

'You're right,' said Enoch, climbing to his feet and smoothing down the line of his coat. 'That's enough.'

I ran my eyes over the kid, searching for signs of life. It was hard to tell whether he was done for, what with him already being blue in the face, but I could just about make out the shallow rise and fall of his sternum.

Inside my head, Frank sighed with relief.

'Pick him up,' Enoch ordered, pointing to the body on the floor.

Two of his men—the ones who'd held the fae in place while he was being smothered—stepped in and took the unconscious Arcadian by the wrists and ankles.

'Time to go,' said Enoch. 'But first...'

He took aim square between my eyes, tightened the trigger—

And blasted a hole through the head of the vamp with the wiry eyebrows.

The bullet exited his body with a stroke of blood that painted the faces of the two henchmen carrying the sleeping fae.

Eyes wide with confusion, they dropped the kid and went for their weapons. They were fast—superhumanly so—but their guns didn't clear their holsters before their brains were coating the coven walls.

The last Vengari, who managed to get a handle on his pistol despite having taken a karate chop to the throat earlier, fell a half-second later with two exit holes in his skull.

CHAPTER THIRTY-SIX: THIS IS NOT A TYPE O

THE SOUND of gunshots rang loud in my ears as I stared in shock at Enoch's crew, lying about the room like a pile of bullet-riddled sandbags, recycled blood leaking from their heads and forming a crimson continent on the weathered wooden floor.

Whaaaat? said Frank, echoing my sentiments exactly.

Enoch held the gun steady, arm outstretched, calm and unshaken.

'The Arcadian was never leaving this place,' he said, lip curled, exposing a single white fang. 'His life was forfeit the second he left my sister weeping in a wedding gown.'

That explained it. The bride was Enoch's sibling. This was personal.

What now, I wondered? What happened once the rest of Enoch's clan found out what he'd done here? I supposed I'd never know.

'Goodbye, Mister Fletcher,' said Enoch, plugging a fresh magazine into his pistol and turning its unblinking black eye on me. 'Better luck in the next life.'

Frank's body braced tight as piano wire as I prepared to make a Hail Mary lunge at the vampire and knock the gun from his hand. It was a plan that was almost certainly destined to fail, but what choice did I have? It was now or never.

'Enough!'

To my surprise and Enoch's, we turned to find the Arcadian struggling to his feet.

'Well, well,' said the Vengari. 'The sleeping beauty awakes.'

The kid brushed himself down. 'I don't sleep in dirt,' he croaked, 'unlike you filthy coffin-dwellers.'

Enoch was outnumbered now, but that didn't change the fact that he had a gun. We could swarm him, but one of us would pay the price for it, most likely the kid, who was still in a pretty bad way.

Enoch addressed the fae's slight. 'Some of us weren't born with silver spoons in our mouths, Your Highness.'

'Just because you don't live in a palace, doesn't mean you have to roll around in the filth.'

The vampire offered a razor-blade smile. 'But Your Highness, I like the filth. I know where I come from, I know who I am, unlike the rest of my clan who would abase themselves to sully their blood with yours. When my sister was given the "honour" of being your bride, I said no, but my protestations went unheard. I was commanded to ensure the marriage went ahead, even after you absconded. Tonight, I right that wrong.'

He aimed his gun at the kid, who laughed in his face.

'What's so funny?' Enoch spat.

'Don't you see? You and I are in violent agreement. You want nothing to do with my people, and I would never in a million years marry into your toilet of a family.'

The vampire's eyes narrowed to slits. 'Watch your mouth, fae.'

'Or what? You'll kill me? Didn't that ship already sail?'

'Yes, but there are ways of killing fast and ways of killing slow.'

The kid shrugged off the threat. I had to hand it to him, he was showing some real pluck.

'Either way is fine by me so long as it means not having to walk down the aisle with your dog-faced troglodyte of a sister.'

Daaaaaaaamn, hooted Frank, reminding me to cut down his intake of Yank sitcoms should we ever make it out of this mess in one piece (well, two pieces).

Enoch's response to the fae's put-down was a lot more direct. The vampire moved without moving, crossing the room in the blink of a hummingbird's eye and knocking the fae to the floor. Suddenly, his gun was pressed to the back of the Arcadian's slender neck, its stainless steel muzzle causing the fae's flesh to sizzle like butter in a hot pan.

'Do it, you inbred relic,' the kid retorted, face-down on the floorboards, too weak to resist the Vengari's vice-like hold. 'Just let my friend go first.'

Friiieend? said Frank.

A bit of an exaggeration, I agreed. Don't get me wrong, I'd developed a fondness of the kid, but we'd only just met. What was he up to? Was there a plan in play here?

Enoch was equally surprised by the "friend" bit.

'What do you mean, *friend*, you fool? He only brought you here so he could condemn you to death.'

The fae shook his head, or shook it as much as he could with a crazed Vengari riding his back.

'You said it yourself: the familiar isn't here. Detective Fletcher didn't bring me to the coven to see me punished, he brought me here for protection.'

Enoch's eyes lit with malice, and suddenly it wasn't the Arcadian he was pinning to the floor, it was me. I wanted to lash out—to break free of Frank's body—but the vampire had me facing the wrong way. I could throw out a blind elbow, but if I fluffed it, Frank was taking a one-way trip to slab city. No, I had to be patient. I'd only get one shot at taking Enoch down. If I was going to strike, it needed to be at the exact right moment.

'So, you two are bosom buddies, eh?' growled the Vengari. He gestured to the roaring hearth as he held me down like some vicious bird of prey. 'That explains this cosy little picture. A couple of sticks and some marshmallows and you'd have yourself a fireside picnic.'

In case it's not clear, I really didn't like this bloke.

'Mister Fletcher is a man of honour,' said the Arcadian. 'Something you could never hope to understand.'

'Oh, I understand. I understand that I'm going to make you watch him die before I put a bullet in your fairy skull.'

I felt the barrel of the Vengari's gun digging to the back of my head. Frank's head. We were going to die. Bra-fucking-vo. What a winning plan that was from the Arcadian. A real corker.

I heard the telltale *click* of a pistol hammer.

A smirk appeared on the Arcadian's face. 'Typical.'

'What?' said Enoch. I couldn't see him, but I could sense the scowl he was wearing.

'The gun,' the fae replied. 'A real vampire would have more class.'

A dry chuckle. 'Do I not seem real to you, Your Majesty?'

'The vampires I know would drink his blood under the light of a swollen moon. And you're going to what... put a bullet in his head? You really are a boorish little brute.'

Enoch's voice hiked up a few decibels. 'You want the storybook vampire, do you? The civilised Count, oozing dangerous romance? I'll show you civilised...'

He rolled me on to my back and closed his claws around my throat. I saw his waxy face lunge at mine and felt twin points gum-deep in my neck. Enoch's foul, limpet mouth sucked at my jugular, hungry, eager, desperate for blood, determined to syphon every last drop from me. I expected pain but felt none. Quite the opposite in fact. As the blood left my body I felt warm and sleepy, the world around me turning blurry and distant. I'm sure I would have drifted off to sleep and never woken up if it wasn't for the screaming.

Enoch was howling.

He backpedalled across the room, his wide-open mouth pouring steam like the spout of a boiling kettle. His long, tapered fingers clawed frantically at his shirt, shredding the fabric and exposing his white belly, which bulged and swelled as if something were alive inside of him and trying to force its way out. As the vampire's scream reached a new, deranged pitch, the tissue of his stomach thinned and gave way, releasing a stench like air escaping a violated tomb. A mess of grey innards slopped out of the bubbling hole in Enoch's belly with a thick stew of gluey, clotted blood, then his torso folded backwards and he capsized to the floor in two sections.

I had no idea what I'd just witnessed, but I could tell from the look on the kid's face that he'd been the one to engineer it.

'You did that. You tricked him.'

The kid knew Enoch couldn't help himself; couldn't resist the chance to make him suffer that little bit extra before he took his life. So he set him on me knowing that my blood—Frank's blood—would do... *that* to him.

I rolled onto my knees and craned over Enoch's body. Despite everything, there was still a flicker of life left in the vampire's eyes. I pushed my face out of the skull I was inhabiting and showed him the second Fletcher he'd been looking for.

'Suck on that, you fucking *Lost Boys* reject.'

His eyes went wide, his mouth even wider, and then he was dead.

I peeled away from Frank completely and slapped a hand on the Arcadian's back. 'I knew it. I knew that plan of yours was a winner, you sly bastard.'

Frank turned to me with a dirty look that said, *Like bollocks you did.*

'Okay, fair cop, I thought we were up the Swanee for sure.' I was gushing, never more happy to be wrong. 'How did you know that would happen if ugly plugged his fangs into us?'

The kid smiled. 'The compatibility research my people carried out taught us a lot about the Vengari. One of the things we learned was that their diet is more varied than that of the average vampire.'

'They can feed on animals?'

'Yes, but more than that, the blood they require needn't be fresh. So long as it is properly preserved, a Vengari can subsist on blood that's decades old.'

That explained the wine cellar I found at the Vengari conclave, or *blood* cellar, more like. What it didn't explain was the vampire with the ruptured stomach creosoting the floorboards.

The kid explained. 'Another thing our research pointed us to was an event in the late fourteenth century that the Vengari dubbed, The Famine of Gothenstein. At that time, one of their clans had taken possession of a Bavarian castle; a matter of some upset to a group of knights templar known as the Order of the Ivory Flame.'

'Ain't it always the way?' I joshed.

'Quite. At any rate, the knights surrounded the castle and cut off the vampires' escape, forcing some two-hundred Vengari to starve. On the sixth day of the siege the knights broke into the castle without resistance. The vampires were dead, every last one of them, but not from starvation.'

'They killed each other?'

'In a manner of speaking. According to records kept by the

knights, they discovered a font—a baptismal font wrenched from the castle's chapel—half filled with blood. Surrounding the font were dozens of vampires with wounds matching those of our friend here.' His gaze sank to Enoch's mutilated body. 'And lying besides those vampires were an equal number of blood-stained goblets.'

I put it together. 'They drank their own blood.'

'Yes. To survive, the Vengari called upon the lower castes of their clan to sacrifice their lives for the greater good. The weakest died so that the strong might live. Only it didn't work out that way.'

'I'll say.'

'The Vengari learned an important lesson that day: while the blood they ingest needn't be fresh from the vein, it cannot be dead.'

'Hence the Bavarian Jonestown Massacre. So that's how you knew the joke was on him.'

The kid showed off that smile again. 'It's how I knew that blood without life—the kind the undead carry—is poison to the Vengari.'

More like hydrochloric acid from the looks of it, but I wasn't about to split hairs. The kid saved my bacon. Any lingering doubts I had about him were gone. Now I'd do everything in my power to make sure he survived the vampires and got out of the city. Just one thing left to do before we made tracks...

Slipping a hand into Enoch's coat pocket, I took out a hankie-swaddled package and unwrapped Frank's severed tongue.

'Better luck in the next life, matey,' I said, giving the vampire a condescending pat on the cheek.

CHAPTER THIRTY-SEVEN: BODY POLITICS

THE SUN WAS CREEPING up by the time we'd finished shovelling Enoch and the rest of his muppets into the hearth. Luckily for us, vampires go up like dry kindling when they're introduced to fire, so it wasn't as big a job as it might sound. Tough on the old nose, though. I could only hope the coven had aired out by the time Stella made it back from her hols, because the place smelled absolutely rank when we skipped out of there. As for the bloodstained floor-boards, well… if she kicked up a stink about that I supposed I could always chuck an old rug her way.

Next stop, Legerdomain. I pushed through the door, ambled up to the front of the shop, and slapped Frank's tongue on the counter.

'One reverse amputation if you will, ma'am.'

Jazz Hands tipped her head back wearing a pronounced frown.

'Why have you brought an Arcadian into my shop, Fletcher? Let me guess, he's a fae turncoat? Or is this your shapeshifter friend playing dress-up? Apologies, but I'm beginning to lose track with all the waifs strays you bring into my establishment.'

'This is the Arcadian we've been looking for,' I explained. 'Turns out he's Prince of the Unseelie Court.'

Jazz stood up sharply. 'Your Highness!' she gasped.

Her deference was so feverish that she ended up curtsying, shaking the kid's hand and doffing an imaginary cap all at once. It was an explosion of manners, and made her look like she was having some sort of a fit.

'Don't you care that he's a murderer?' I said. 'I mean, it turns out he's not, but you don't know any different.'

'It doesn't matter,' she hissed from the corner of her mouth. 'He's of noble blood. The rules are different.'

'A pleasure to meet you,' said the Arcadian, giving the back of her hand a peck. 'What a lovely establishment you have here. So...' he struggled to find the right word, '... charming.'

Jazz stammered, 'Well... that's so... you really are very... what an absolute honour to be... thank you.'

She was grabbing at words like a barbecue skewer picking up the last scraps of meat at a Catholic family buffet. Never in my life had I heard her babble like this. I suppose I shouldn't have been surprised; the woman was a staunch monarchist. She still drank her char from a Charles and Di tea set, so it followed that she'd get the vapours when a card-carrying prince came strolling into her store.

I made the necessary introductions—unnecessary as they were—and we got to business.

'How about it then, Jazz?' I said, pointing to my partner's severed tongue. 'Can you get Frank gabbing again?'

At the mention of his name, Frank's tongue twitched and wriggled, flapping about on the counter like a landed fish. It took us all by surprise, except, it seemed, the man himself.

'Are you doing that?' I asked.

Frank couldn't answer, but he didn't need to: the enthusiastic look on his face matched the movement of the tongue, which wagged like a dog's tail in one of those videos where a soldier returns from a tour in Iraq.

'Easy, boy,' I said, and the tongue slowed from a mad thrash to an excited wiggle.

Apparently, Frank was able to maintain control of body parts even after they'd been pruned off him. This was news to me.

'Please make some space and I'll see what I can do,' said Jazz Hands, taking a magnifying glass to the tongue.

I wondered how differently that request would have been met if we weren't in the presence of royalty. I wondered if I'd have heard that "please". Matter of fact, I wondered if Jazz might have dispensed with niceties altogether, whipped out a smudge stick and cast my ungrateful spirit into eternal shadow.

But instead she went to work. From her toolkit, Jazz fetched a needle and thread, then she sat Frank down, tipped his head back, and guided the severed tongue into his gob like she was playing one of those steady hand tester games. After that, she muttered a bunch of nonsense that sounded like a lost extract of *Finnegans Wake* and got to sewing. The thread she was using glowed like liquid gold then vanished as she placed the last stitch. The tongue looked good as new.

'How's the fit, Frankie boy?'

'Gooooood,' he replied, a soppy smile plastered across his mug.

I pounded him on the back. 'That's my lad. Look at that. No more need for the Marcel Marceau shit.'

The Arcadian interjected. 'Now that's done, I wonder if we might return to my predicament?'

The kid hadn't been the most enthusiastic supporter of this little detour. A couple of times on the way over he'd asked if giving Frank the power of speech was really the most pressing item on our agenda, but I told him I'd made my partner a promise and that I wasn't going to let him suffer any longer than necessary.

Still, he had a point. In the time it took us to get to Kings Cross, the fae had deteriorated rapidly. Gone was the glow he wore at the coven, replaced by a cold sweat and a gauntness that had left him looking like a waxwork in a heatwave.

He coughed into the crook of his elbow. 'My body is giving out and my powers are already starting to fail.'

Talking of failing powers...

'Hey, Jazz, where are we at with that whole soul bond palaver?'

'The what?' the Arcadian cut in.

'It's a me and Frank thing,' I explained. 'Ever since his bones got hauled out of the ground, I've been having some power problems of my own. Used to be I could possess whoever I liked and shoot about the place like a leaf on the breeze, no need for all the legwork.'

The fae threw up his hands. 'Are we back to the zombie already? Seriously?'

'Oi! Without that "zombie" you'd be brown bread, mate.'

'Show His Majesty some bloody respect, Fletcher,' barked Jazz, forgetting herself. When she saw the shocked expression she'd brought to the Arcadian's face she quickly composed herself, wiping a stray fleck of spit from her chin and smoothing down her bird's nest of hair. After a polite cough to reset the mood, she addressed my question in her best telephone voice. 'The soul bond, yes. I've been looking into your dilemma and I believe I have made some inroads.'

'Cracking,' I said, clapping my hands together and giving them a swift rub. 'Lay it on me, sister.'

'Given that we're dealing with matters of the spirit, I began by looking into your former field of expertise: exorcism. In doing so, I discovered a specific liturgy that may be of use to you.'

Frank leaned forward. So did I. Jazz went on.

'I had to dig very deep to find it, but my research eventually led me to a medieval sacrament known as the Rite of Sequester.'

'Never heard of it.'

'Now there's a surprise,' she replied, doing her best to measure her tone but failing to modulate the sarcasm from her voice. 'Allow me to explain. The Rite of Sequester was developed to enable the removal of a spiritual entity from a specific vicinity without casting them into oblivion. By employing this rite, it's possible for an exorcist to move along a troublesome apparition without himself ending up trapped in purgatory, unable to ascend to Heaven until he's burned away all traces of his Earthly sins.'

I had a feeling that that last little nugget was aimed at me. In fact, I knew it was.

Jazz continued her spiel. 'Consider the Rite of Sequester a form of light exorcism. Rather than banishing its target, the rite transfers the spirit to a separate locale on the physical plane.'

'Why would anyone want to do that?' asked the Arcadian.

'Because back in those days, people had more respect for the dead,' I explained.

'Correct,' said Jazz. 'In fact, it is said that the saint who penned the rite did so in order that he might move the spirit of his dead mother from her graveside and back into the family home.'

'Good lad,' I replied. 'No wonder they made him a saint.'

'Actually, he was venerated by the Catholic church for choosing a life of extraordinary sacrifice and piety over one of luxury and comfort.'

'Also good.'

Jazz shrugged. 'Horses for courses. I'll take a pass on a sainthood if it means not having to sleep cross-legged in itchy horsehair undergarments for the rest of my life.' She pushed her spectacles up the bridge of her nose and went on. 'That aside, with further research, I believe I may be able to utilise the Rite of Sequester in such a way that it might sever the link between you and your partner and restore your powers.'

'Really?' I said, flashing Frank a smile. 'So we'd be back where we started?'

'Yes. Precisely so.'

I saw Frank's expression sour. He'd picked up on something in Jazz's tone. Something I caught, too.

'Why did that have a note of the ominous to it, Jazz?'

She considered us with her owlish gaze. 'Because you'd be back to square one. Back to the stage you were at when you first met.'

I clocked what she was saying. 'You're telling me we won't be able to merge anymore?'

'Correct. Though you will be able to possess others, you and your former body will become two distinct entities, unable to cohabit the same space. Permanently.'

So that was the price of admission. I could have my old box of magic tricks back, but Frank and me would forever be oil and water. Pineapple on pizza. No. I was just starting to get comfortable in my own skin. Getting sundered from Frank was too steep a price to pay.

'That's not going to work,' I said. 'Carry on the research. There has to be another way.'

'I'll do what I can,' she replied, which was not at all the response I was anticipating. Had the Arcadian not been present, I expect Jazz's comeback would have been of the four-letter variety and delivered with some vigour.

'Right then. Now that's on the back burner, let's see what we can do about getting the kid here out of this marriage.'

'Finally,' the fae gasped.

Jazz Hands rocked back as if delivered a hard jolt. 'Your Majesty is arranged to be married?' she said. 'And you want to call it off?'

Clearly the old bird needed some catching up, so we sat her down and filled in the blanks. Jazz took in the news, deflating at the notion of a royal wedding being cancelled but understanding the necessity of it.

'Well, what do you reckon?' I asked, having laid out the kid's predicament in black and white. 'Got any bright ideas bouncing around that big bonce of yours?'

Jazz cocked her head and touched a finger to her chin dimple. 'You're wrong to think you can deal with this situation on home ground. Facing the Vengari head-on is a fight you cannot win, and that's without the fae being involved.'

'What else can we do?' asked the Arcadian. 'The Vengari have already proved that we can't hide from them, and we've established that leaving the city isn't going to work.'

'With respect, Your Highness, you are thinking too small. What you need is a real escape hatch. A doorway to somewhere far, far away.'

The kid brightened. 'You know of such a place?'

Jazz lowered her gaze reverently. 'It's not exactly fit for a king, but it is completely off the map. It's somewhere your enemies will never find you. Somewhere you can live out the rest of your days in peace, without ever having to look over your shoulder.'

'Where is this magical place?' I asked. 'Penge?'

Jazz's voice dropped to a whisper. 'I'm talking about Other London.'

CHAPTER THIRTY-EIGHT: IF YOU'RE GOING THROUGH HELL, KEEP GOING

OUTSIDE OF LEGERDOMAIN the sun was high and the sky still and stonewashed. Someone who knew less about vampires might have seen this as an opportunity. Might have been tempted to take advantage of the daylight and make a run for it while the bloodsuckers were tucked up their coffins, arms crossed over their chests, dead to the world. As if vampires were that thick.

Just because vamps live in the shadows, doesn't mean they're impotent in the daytime. Their kind have been around for centuries, and learned long ago that they're vulnerable during the hours the rest of us are awake. That's why they create blood slaves: mortals who guard their sleeping bodies and act in their stead while they slumber. Luckless vassals so addicted to the taste of vampire blood that they'll do anything for it. Anything. Which is why the Arcadian would never be safe in the city, and why we had to get him to Other London right away.

If only it were that simple. The portals to Other London had all been sealed, or so legend had it. In fact, there were a few entrances still available to those who had the know of it, though none of them were easy to access. The portal Jazz informed us of was no exception. It didn't really register as a door, and even if you were canny enough to spot the portal for what it was, it wasn't something you just walked through. The secret threshold to the hidden city could only be made real at the stroke of midnight, and was kept behind locked doors. If Frank and I were going to stand any chance of getting the kid through the portal, we were going to need help.

The Beehive was our first port of call, what with the bar being a recognised safe harbour and protected by a magic-dampening bubble that kept any mystical wrongdoings in check. Lenny's pub was about as secure a place as we could hope for, I figured. What I didn't count on was Detective Kat Stronge.

The look on her face when she saw Frank and me walk through the door of The Beehive with the Arcadian in tow was... well, frightening if I'm honest. Particularly since it was backed up by a taser pointed in our direction, and who knew what 50,000 volts of leccy would do to a man sensitive to a whiff of car exhaust?

'What's going on?' Stronge demanded, turning the heads of the smattering of day-drinkers watching the pub's new widescreen TV. 'Why isn't he cuffed?'

I was about to answer her when a meaty fist took hold of Kat's wrist, accompanied by a voice like a bassoon left out in the rain.

'Are we gonna need to have words again?' boomed Lenny, The Beehive's Ben Nevis-sized landlord.

With his free hand he pointed to a shovel decorating the wall behind the bar, a keepsake from our previous altercation with a surly gnome.

'That won't be necessary, Lenny,' I said. 'Kat, put it away and I'll explain everything.'

Once the taser was back in its holster and Lenny was satisfied that we weren't about to kick off again, I sat Stronge down and gave her the whole saga. Shift, too, who arrived in female form not long after Lenny had installed himself back behind the taps. I told them about the star-crossed lovers and the forces that stood in their way, about the Vengari and the Arcadians and the arranged marriage that could change everything in this town. I told them how this case wasn't a murder, that it was a different kind of Shakesperean tragedy.

'And you couldn't have picked up the blower and let me in on this earlier?' said Stronge, peering evilly at me over the rim of her pint glass, livid that I hadn't given her the courtesy of a phone call in all the time I'd been on the lam.

'You know me, Kat, I'm a people person. I like the face-to-face.'

'If it's any consolation,' said the Arcadian, 'I told him he should have given you a call.'

Kat turned her flinty gaze his way. 'You can stay out of this, sunshine. You might have passed his smell test, but you still stink to me.'

'I get it, Kat,' I said. 'Given the bullshit my client spun me, I half-expected to see devil horns poking out of his head, but I'm telling you he's a good guy. Matter of fact, he's a lot like me, only bluer.'

'...And finer,' Shift purred, biting her bottom lip.

'Thank you,' replied the Arcadian.

'But I don't know,' said Shift, eyes narrowing as she turned to me, 'how can we be sure he's on the up-and-up?'

Frank placed an arm around the Arcadian's shoulder and leaned forward. 'Gooood maaaan,' he said, his face the very picture of sincerity.

'Well, that does it for me,' said Shift.

'Yeah, me too,' Stronge agreed, unfolding her arms and leaning back in her chair, defences lowered. 'He's no killer.'

'Oh, sure, him you listen to!' I cried, but it was for nothing. It was clear from the way things were going that no one cared a jot what I thought about any of this.

Stronge took a sip of her drink. 'Just so I know we're all on the same page here, am I right in thinking that instead of avenging a murdered girl, we're now trying to stop a wedding?'

'And your client, Tali—she's the real baddie in this picture?' added Shift.

'Yes,' I sighed.

Stronge rolled her eyes. 'Well, I hate to tell you, "I told you so", Fletcher, so I'll scream it in your face instead: I TOLD YOU SO.'

'Don't be like that, Kat.'

'I'll be any way I want after you spent the last bloody day ghosting me.'

'I am a ghost,' I protested. 'It's what we do.'

We were losing focus (another thing ghosts are fond of doing). Still, Stronge wouldn't let it lie.

'Forget about the wedding for now. Shouldn't our next step be to deal with the person who sent you on this wild goose chase in the first place?'

'What's the point? I'm the only weapon in Tali's arsenal, and since I'm not doing her dirty work anymore, she's harmless. Let her fester for a bit while we figure out how to get the kid in the clear.'

Shift gave a half-shrug.

'What's the matter?' I asked.

'Sorry, but I'm finding it hard to get excited about this,' she replied. 'I mean, he made his bed, right? Isn't this his mess to fix, even if he is an absolute snack?' She gave the kid a wink.

'You're not seeing the big picture here,' I said. 'Neither of you are. If this marriage goes ahead, the effect will be catastrophic. A couple of generations of breeding and the mongrels they spit out will have this city in the palms of their hands. After that, the whole country. Ain't that right, Your Majesty?'

I swung my head in his direction, only to find him gazing off into space. No, not space—at something across the far end of the saloon.

'Oi,' I said, snapping my fingers.

He looked about like a startled meerkat before realising I was the one after his attention.

'I'm sorry,' he said, eyes glossy, lower lip a-wobble. 'I was just… I was thinking of better times.'

That's when I realised what it was he'd been fixated upon.

A dart board. *The* dart board.

The poor, heartbroken bastard was remembering the night he and Tali first met. The night she became his fiancée. The last scrap of happiness in his otherwise miserable life.

When I turned back to Stronge and Shift I could tell the mood had altered. When I told them the story before, it was academic. The look in the kid's eyes had changed that. Made it real. There was no way they were tossing him to the wind now. Not this broken doll.

'So you'll do it?' I asked. 'You'll help us get him out of the city?'

'Landlord.' Stronge raised her hand and called for a round of shots.

I smiled. Or smirked. Probably smirked knowing me. 'Is that a yes?'

'Yes, it's a bloody yes.'

I looked to Shift, who rolled her eyes and nodded in agreement. 'Yes.'

'Yeeeees,' said Frank, so happy.

'Thank you,' said the Arcadian, brimming with gratitude. 'Thank you all so much.'

What a team: a ghost, a walking corpse, a clued-in copper, a shapeshifter, and a fairy. The broken biscuits of the Uncanny Kingdom.

Lenny ambled over on his telegraph pole legs and set down a tray of whiskies. Stronge bolted hers like her life depended on it.

'I thought you weren't supposed to drink on duty,' I noted.

'Yeah. But then I'm not supposed to aid and abet fairies, either.'

'Cheers,' said Shift, raising her shot and slamming it down.

The rest of us threw back our whiskies and made that gasping sound you're obliged to make.

'So,' said Stronge, 'how exactly are you planning on getting His Royal Highness out of this wedding?'

I told the gang about Other London. About the hidden city Jazz Hands had informed us of, and the portal that led there.

Stronge placed an elbow on the table and rested her chin on her palm. 'I don't like it. Too many unknowns. Why not hole the kid up here? There's a magic-dampening bubble, right? Stick him in a room upstairs and he'll be safe as houses.'

Overhearing our conversation, Lenny came by and loomed over our table like an Easter Island statue. 'The Beehive don't provide lodging, Miss. When the bell rings at the end of the day, it's fucking-off time.'

He scooped up the tray, loaded it with our empties, and sloped off to the kitchen.

'Okay then,' said the detective. 'Other London it is.'

'You mentioned a portal before,' Shift noted. 'Would I be right in saying that getting to it ain't gonna be a piece of cake? That, in actual fact, it's gonna be—as you Brits like to put it—a major ball-ache?'

Frank offered a wonky grin. 'Biiiiingo,' he drawled, neatly managing all of our expectations.

CHAPTER THIRTY-NINE: LITTLE MAN, BIG PROBLEM

I LAID it out as it was explained to me: the portal to Other London was situated on private property, so if we were going to send the Arcadian on his way, we had a spot of trespassing ahead of us.

It could have been a doddle, but since the kid had lost the ability to turn invisible and my possession powers were on the blink, we had no way of bypassing any gatekeepers we might run into. Well, short of giving them a good kicking, but that wasn't going to help me balance my books with the Big Kahuna. No, if we were going to blag our way inside and give the kid the old heave-ho, it was going to mean all hands on deck.

The five of us were packed into Stronge's squad car, pedal down, blazing our way to SW1. The night had rolled in a few hours ago, and we were already edging towards the Cinderella hour.

'I wonder what it's like, this Other London,' said the Arcadian.

All we knew was what Jazz had told us: that it was an adjunct reality only a handful of people in the Uncanny Kingdom were aware of, a pre-industrial parallel dimension free of modern pollution. The perfect place to hide a fae.

There are lots of secret places hidden within London, linked together by a system of hidden doorways and pathways threaded throughout the city, invisible to those without the eyes to see them but there all the same. A blind alley like the one that leads to the London Coven is one example, as is the one outside The Beehive.

But there are other streets, other places that exist beyond the city you know, aside from it, on top of it, underlying and overlying. Some of these places are hidden so well that they're all but impossible to find. Others are only buried skin deep, all but scratching the surface. Those sensitive enough can sometimes hear the call of such places, bleeding into the mundane world like a dubbed-over scrap of music seeping through a new recording on an old cassette. A haunting melody sweating through the humdrum warble that masks it. Some have been driven mad by such music. Others, like me, are drawn to it. They seek it out, they make it their business to uncover that hidden melody and dance to its merry tune.

'And you're sure the portal's in there?' asked Stronge, bringing the car to a stop and setting the handbrake.

We were parked outside of Tate Britain, the world-famous art gallery in Millbank. To our left was the Thames, moonlight playing upon its black, wind-rippled water. On our right was a wide flight of stone steps that led up to the gallery's grand porticoed entrance. Its towering pediment was topped by a statue of Britannia with her Union Jack shield and flanked by a unicorn and a lion, just in case anyone forgot which country Tate Britain was in.

'This is the place,' I said. 'All we need to do is find our way there, say the right words at the right time, and presto-change-o: a doorway to another world.'

Trouble was, the gallery was closed and we needed to get the kid out of London right away, no hanging about. Vampires thrived at this hour, and the morning was a lifetime away. The longer we waited, the greater the chance of running into a pack of Vengari and bungling this whole getaway.

We scouted the perimeter of the building until we found a possible entry point, a fire exit manned by a security guard taking a smoke break. Hanging back in a huddle across the opposite side of the street, we watched and considered our options.

'So what do we reckon?' I asked.

'Here's the plan,' said Stronge. 'I'm going to go over there, show the guard my ID, and get him to let me inside. Once I've done that, you and the kid can sneak in and do your thing.'

I looked to Frank. He shrugged as if to say, *Let the lady do her job.*

'All right then,' I said. 'Let's get a shimmy on.'

'Aren't you forgetting something?' said Stronge, barring my way with her arm as if that would ever stop me. 'Detectives come in twos, and since you're invisible, you don't fit the bill.'

'Take Frank then.'

'If it's all the same with you, I'm going to leave your better half over here. Shift, you up to this?'

'Yes, ma'am,' she replied.

A backpack was emptied, a swift change of clothes made, then Shift transformed into a feller. The Arcadian was surprised, but not in the way you might expect.

'I don't get it. Why not just stay a woman?'

Stronge let out a dry chuckle. 'Two female detectives in the same department?'

Shift shook his head in weary agreement. 'You've got a lot to learn about this world, Cookie.'

They headed across the street and I followed, to all intents and purposes not there. Frank stayed behind and didn't pout about it. He knew there was too much at stake here to involve him in this—he wouldn't risk jeopardising this mission just for the sake of being included.

I followed Stronge as she approached the night guard, badge in hand. Shift kept in step with her, doing a pretty decent impression of a law man, right down to the cocky stroll.

The guard, who still had a fag on the go, was dressed in a black jacket with the word SECURITY printed across the back in bold white letters. Perched on his head was a flat black cap with a short plastic visor, the kind worn by Yank cops. It didn't strike me as being standard issue. In fact, it made me wonder if he'd bought the thing off eBay to accessorise the outfit he was given and give himself a touch of extra gravitas. Fuck knows he needed it, standing at the low end of five foot and wearing a wispy little moustache that looked as if it had been stuck on crooked a second before we arrived. Honestly, I wouldn't have left this bloke guarding my pint, let alone a priceless art collection.

'Good evening, sir. I'm Detective Stronge and this is my partner—'

'Detective Spade,' Shift cut in, shaking the guard's hand.

'Yes, Detective Spade,' Stronge confirmed, suppressing an eye-roll.

'What can I do for you?' asked the guard, taking a drag on his ciggie.

Stronge made sure he got a look at her ID and spoke in hushed tones. 'We received a report of an attempted break-in and we've come to check it out.'

The guard looked flummoxed. 'Break-in? Don't know what you're talking about, Detective. I've been here all night and every-thing's in order. Sounds like someone's on the wind-up to me.'

'Either way, we've got to file a report, which means we're going to need you to show us inside so we can tick the right boxes and be on our way. That all right with you, sir?'

The guard's eyelids fell to half-mast. 'Maybe, maybe not.'

'Pardon me?' said Stronge, taken by surprise.

There was a loud fizzing noise from the cherry of the guard's ciggie as he took another puff. 'If you want in I'm going to need to see a search warrant.'

'Are you serious?' said Shift, or Detective Spade as he was currently answering to.

'As cancer,' replied the guard, inhaling another lungful of smoke.

The bloke had no idea what he was protecting, no clue that he was standing between us and a magic portal, but there were plenty of riches in that place besides a gateway to another world.

Stronge straightened up to her full height, towering over the homunculus of a guard by a good six inches. 'Sir, do you know the penalty for obstructing a police officer?'

He didn't hesitate. 'One month's imprisonment and/or a level three fine,' he replied wearing a shit-eating grin. 'But that's not what this is. All I'm doing is asking for proof that you have reasonable grounds to enter the premises.'

That put Stronge on the back foot. I don't think she expected the bloke to know how to tie his shoelaces, let alone know his rights. But she knew who she was dealing with now. She'd seen plenty of them in her time, I bet: embittered little men who tried out for the force and were shown the door. Petty, grudge-bearing bureaucrats who liked nothing more than to use the smidgen of knowledge they had to stick it to the man, to punish those who'd actually earned their stripes. Okay, in this instance, he was right to be dubious of the detective's intentions, but that didn't make him any less of a prick.

'I'm going to give you one last chance,' said Stronge. 'Get out of my way and let me do my job or I'm writing you up.'

The guard gave her a narrow smile. 'Tell you what, how about instead you show me that ID again so I can take down your badge number? You too, blondie.'

He took another draw on his cigarette and snorted two nostrils of smoke at the detectives. Stronge swiped the acrid fog from her face, one eyelid twitching.

'Come on,' said Shift, taking his partner's arm before she did something drastic.

Stronge shook him off, growled something intelligible, and went stalking off with her fists by her sides.

'Nothing personal,' the guard called after her, thumbing the wheel of his lighter and sparking a fresh cigarette. 'Just rules and regs.'

That's the way this job is. Sometimes you're kicking the Great Beast's furry underbelly, and sometimes the biggest thing standing in your way is a petty little jobsworth with the world's worst case of small man syndrome.

CHAPTER FORTY: THE VERGE OF A BREAKTHROUGH

SHIFT and I followed Detective Stronge across the street, where we reconvened privately with my partner and the Arcadian.

Frank stuck up two thumbs, eyebrows riding high. 'Gooood?'

Sensing trouble brewing, the kid took Frank's hands and tucked his thumbs away before Stronge snapped them off.

'Okay, so who's up for beating him to death?' asked Shift, registering his vote with a raised hand. When no one else did likewise he said, 'Oh, come on, people, he's practically begging for it.'

'I want this done clean,' said Stronge. 'No one gets hurt.'

'We could knock him out,' Shift suggested. 'That's only a little bit of hurt.'

'No.'

'Oh, come on, don't be such a spoilsport.'

'Kat's right,' I said.

'Am I?' said Stronge, surprised to hear the words coming from my mouth.

She was. This was one of those areas where colouring outside of the lines wasn't going to work.

'Sparking someone out ain't like the movies,' I said. 'You don't just judo chop someone in the neck and send them off to the land of Nod. If it's hard enough to floor someone, it's hard enough to give them brain damage, and I don't need any more red in my ledger, thank you very much.'

Shift sighed, pulled a stick of gum from his pocket, and gave it a spirited chew. 'You're right. I'm sorry, it's the testosterone again. Gets me raging.'

Rage I could do without. I already had enough blood on my hands without killing a breather, accidentally or not. Even wrapping a ghostly fist around the guard's heart and giving it a light squeeze— a method I've used to KO people in the past—came with risks I wasn't prepared to take here.

'If he wants this done by the book, that's how we'll do it,' said Stronge. 'We'll go away and come back with a warrant.'

I saw the panic in the fae's eyes.

'You're forgetting the squeeze we're under,' I said, showing Stronge my watch. 'The little hand's almost at 12. We don't have time for red tape.'

Stronge looked like she was about ready to start slashing upholstery. 'What do you suggest then, Fletcher? Because I'm getting pretty tired of watching my ideas get shot down.'

'Okay, here's an idea: how about we seduce the guy?'

Stronge's frown somehow became even more pronounced. 'I thought we weren't doing stupid ideas.'

'This one could work.'

'I don't care. There's no way I'm doing that.'

'Oh. This is awkward, but you weren't actually the seducer I had in mind.'

The detective's eyes narrowed. 'Who then?'

I nodded to Shift.

'Me?' His frantic chewing stopped.

'Yeah. Not like you are now, but like the bit of crumpet you were when we got here.'

He grimaced. '*Crumpet*? Jeez. Just when I think you're starting to evolve, you go and say a thing like that.'

'Come on, Shift, I'm not asking for much here. Just tuck it between your legs and flutter your eyelashes at the bloke.'

He almost spat out his gum. 'No way.'

'You got a better idea?' I said, exasperated. 'I know, why don't you disguise yourself as a blonde-haired Amazon package and we'll post you in there?'

'Get bent, Fletcher.'

The Arcadian let out a troubling cough that only stopped once he'd hammered a fist against his chest and dislodged the phlegm sticking to his ribs. 'Sorry to be a bother, but the portal won't be available for much longer.'

His voice was coarse and gruff, his eyes red-rimmed. The city was getting the better of him again.

Stronge's shoulders slumped. 'I hate to say this, but Fletcher's seduction plan is the only one on the table. I don't like it any more than you do, Shift, but the clock's ticking and there's too much riding on this to go burning your bra.'

Shift gnashed his teeth for a bit but he knew Kat was right. He jabbed a finger into my chest. 'All right, mister, I'll do it, but you better put some gratitude in that attitude.'

'Trust me, you have my undying thanks.'

'I don't want your thanks, I want your green. You're going to owe me big for this one. Double my usual fee.'

'Deal.'

I had no idea how I was going to cover that spread since the Fletcher & Fletcher coffers were pretty much bone dry, but I'd come up with something. Hopefully.

We shook on it and Shift reverted to the blonde bombshell who stepped out of the squad car a half hour back.

'Good luck,' said Stronge, giving her a sisterly pat on the back.

Shift tossed her long, platinum hair over one shoulder, turned on her heel, and headed across the road to the surly midget with the cigarette clamped in his mouth.

'Hey, honey, do you have a light?' she purred.

There followed a brief bit of muffled chit-chat and some arm-touching, then the two of them headed inside.

'Mennnnn,' Frank groaned, shaking his head.

The pinched look on Stronge's face suggested she had much to say on the fragility of the male ego, but the work came first. Leading with her chin, she marched across the road and the rest of us followed, the Arcadian trailing behind, his breaths coming in short, plosive bursts. The side door opened easily, kept ajar by the wad of chewing gum Shift had stuffed into its lock mechanism.

I turned to Stronge. 'You wait here and keep an eye out while we shoot the kid's chuff through that portal.'

'After all that?' she said. 'Forget it, I'm coming with you.'

'Not a good idea. We don't want any more people in there than strictly necessary.'

'What about Frank?'

'I need him to help me prop up old Blue Lives Matter here,' I said, gesturing to the Arcadian, who could barely stand on his own two feet. 'Besides, we could use someone keeping an eye out in case any wrong 'uns show up out here.'

Stronge wasn't in love with the idea, but she couldn't fault my logic. 'All right, Fletcher, have it your way. Just don't balls this up.'

'Don't worry, Kat, the hard work's already done. The rest will be a piece of piss.'

Stronge waved us on and Frank and I escorted the kid inside. A flutter of the hands, a quick bit of gutter Latin, and the building's CCTV was fried. Following the directions Jazz gave me, I guided my companions through the museum and towards the promised portal.

The Arcadian's feet gave out from under him, causing his trainers to drag on the buffed wooden floor with a jarring squeak.

'Sorry,' he gasped, barely able to support his own head.

'S'allriiiight,' whispered Frank, propping him up and lacing an arm around his snake-hipped waist.

I heard the soft, slow patter of footsteps heading our way, followed by a puddle of torchlight leaking around a nearby corner.

'Let's go.'

Moving quickly, we continued through pale grey corridors and to an atrium topped by a grand, windowed dome. Onwards we pressed, sticking to the shadows as we skirted the soapy alabaster monolith of Jacob wrestling an angel. Gold-framed oil paintings of landscapes and military skirmishes passed by in a blur until we arrived at our destination: the Rothko Room.

The space was compact and dark; darker even than the rest of the dimmed-down museum. A single bench sat in the centre of the room, surrounded by a series of large abstract paintings big enough to step through. I've heard people describe these pieces as soothing, as objects of contemplation and meditation. That's never the vibe I got. With their oppressive blacks and blood-red tones—the kind of deep, dark red that's last to pump from a dying heart—they didn't make me feel liberated, they made me feel trapped.

'There,' I said, pointing to the painting labelled, *Red on Maroon*.

It was a large unframed piece on a vertical rectangle canvas. The base colour of the painting was a rich crimson and overlaid with a maroon rectangle, which enclosed a smaller crimson rectangle, suggesting a door-like structure.

I checked my watch. Two minutes til midnight; right on time. I had Frank sit the kid down on the ground then use his brawn to drag the bench across to the painting.

'Here goes nothing,' I said, taking a step onto the bench and placing myself inches from the negative maroon space of the painting's eerie inner rectangle.

I counted down until the time was right—the very stroke of midnight—then carefully recited the phrase Jazz had given me.

'*Imagine a door and a door there shall be. Imagine a door and a door there shall be...*'

Again and again I repeated the line, beating it into submission until a tingle of electricity sparked the air, making the hairs on the back of my neck stand to attention. A spot of black appeared within the centre of the painting's crimson frame, spreading like a drop of ink in water until it had permeated all the way to its borders. The blackness of the rectangle was perfect, absolute, a depthless void that would have stolen my breath if I had any left to give.

The portal was open.

'Come on, we don't have long,' I told Frank.

He hooked his hands under the kid's armpits and hoisted him to his feet, but froze at a sudden sound.

More footsteps coming our way.

'Come back, Cookie, we ain't done...' called a familiar voice in the distance.

'Shh,' chided another voice I recognised—the midget security guard this time—'I'm just checking to see what's up with the cameras. Help yourself to something from the fridge, I'll be back in a mo.'

A lance of torchlight swung around the corner and into the

Rothko Room. There was nowhere to run to this time. Nowhere to hide.

'What the—?'

The guard couldn't see me, but he wasn't blind to the shambling, glassy-eyed figure with his arms wrapped around a blue-skinned youth.

'S-stay right there,' he stammered, fumbling for the walkie-talkie clipped to his belt.

I could already see the portal fading, its perfect black rectangle turning crimson as the void gave way to the light. It was now or never. I leapt from the bench, dovetailed into Frank's body, and hauled the limp Arcadian to the dying portal.

Over my shoulder I stole a glance at the guard, who wore a face like a smacked haddock.

'Stick this up your rules and regs, you fucking clown shoe.'

And we were off to the races.

CHAPTER FORTY-ONE: GHOST TOWN

I FELT a crackle in my ears and an all-over tickle like walking naked into a giant cobweb. Then we were through to the other side. Through to Other London.

Frank laid the Arcadian down to catch his breath and recuperate. The street we'd stepped onto looked as though an elephant had teetered down it wearing stiletto heels, leaving behind great deltas of cracks. Behind us stood the other side of the portal, a door-sized rectangle floating mid-air, black as burnt coffee.

'You all right, kid?'

Without turning to face me, the Arcadian bobbed his head. It wouldn't be long before he was back on his feet and walking again. While I waited for him to recover, I cast a gander about the hidden city.

The night sky was freckled with pinprick stars, obscured only by a mismatched collection of ramshackle buildings that reached toward its black velvet canvas like drunks clawing at the last bottle of hooch on a high shelf. Other buildings—long since collapsed—looked as if they were burrowing into the ground, searching for sanctuary in the subterranean darkness below.

The kid made it into a sitting position and took in a long breath. His violet eyes skimmed the dusty rubble littering the abandoned streets of the ruined city. 'Wow,' he scoffed. 'They should have sent a poet.'

I gave him a nudge and he reluctantly sloped after us as we headed down a river of darkness toward the city centre. Along the way, Frank *oohed* and *aahed* at the zig-zagging structures that craned overhead like vultures eager to peck. We passed through a part of the city that looked as if it was built in the Fifties, then rounded a corner to find a grungy Victorian neighbourhood pockmarked by the kind of broken-down slums that Oliver Twist and his gang might have called home. Other London was the very definition of art by committee: a disordered jumble, an insane mish-mash of architectural styles crushed together to form a muddled, nonsensical whole.

'What *is* this place?' asked the Arcadian.

As Jazz explained it, Other London used to be teeming with people. They came here to escape the city I call home, built the place from scratch, and slotted it together by pure force of will. Now there was nothing. Other London was free of people. Free of traffic and pollution. Free of pretty much anything.

'Beggars can't be choosers,' I replied. 'Come on, let's find you a home.'

Not knowing exactly what we were looking for, we followed our feet along mismatched roads and through a cobbled plaza. We passed a derelict tavern with a weathered sign hanging on a single chain and painted with the words, The Rabbit Hole (a rabbit's head peeking out from the O of the "Hole", a carrot clamped in its greedy mouth).

The three of us continued down the street for another half-mile until it terminated at a grand mansion clad in white bricks. The building stood alone upon a parcel of empty wasteland and was surrounded by a tall rust-eaten fence, parts of which had fallen asleep on duty. A palace it wasn't, but it was something. It was a start.

'Home sweet home,' I said, doing a little spin for effect.

We stepped over the fallen gate and chased a winding path to the mansion's front door. A pair of crumbling fountains flanked the threshold, the marble sea monsters frolicking in their dusty bowls no longer dispensing water from their dried-up mouths.

'How do we know this whole place isn't about to collapse?' asked the Arcadian.

To show the kid how sturdy the building was, Frank slapped one of the pillars supporting its porch, only for the blow to create a crack that almost felled the structure.

'Bit of cement and you'll have that bodged together in no time,' I said, dismissing the seriousness of the damage. 'Step lively, lad...'

I hopped up the short flight of steps leading to the front door and the others hesitantly followed. The entrance opened into a large circular lobby dominated by a flight of stairs that twisted up in a spiral like a child's slinky. A faded fresco of moons and stars decorated the domed ceiling, while the walls were hung with tattered red drapes. I tried to imagine the mansion in its heyday and suspected it had been host to more than one masquerade orgy.

I snatched a look at the kid and caught him gnawing his bottom lip.

'What's the matter?' I asked. 'You don't like the feng shui of the place?'

'Do you seriously expect me to live here?' he replied, his raised voice echoing off the lobby's curved walls and scampering down the building's empty corridors.

'Not to your taste? Fine, we'll find you somewhere else.'

So long as he stayed out of London, I didn't care where he hung his hat.

'You don't get it. It's not just the building, it's the whole place. The whole city.'

I parked my backside on the stairs with a sigh and gestured for the kid to take a seat beside me.

'Look, I realise it's no Shangri-La but you'd better make peace with it, 'cause I ain't gonna be pulling another hidden city out of my arse.'

The kid fiddled with the toggles of his hoodie. 'How am I supposed to live here with no company? And what about food? What am I supposed to eat?'

Just then, a rat the size of an American toddler scuttled past and disappeared through a crack in the wall.

'Bon appétiiiiit,' groaned Frank, who was new to humour and had a tough time reading a room.

I understood why the kid was upset. Who knew more about

loneliness than a ghost? And yet this was the only option left, at least for now.

'It's not forever, okay? This is just until we figure out a way to get the Vengari off your back. And your family.'

'So, forever?'

It was a distinct possibility. Both factions were sorely invested in the kid getting hitched. Still...

'Look on the bright side,' I said, 'there's nothing here to set off your allergies, and you've got the full run of the place. With a bit of elbow grease you can turn one of these buildings into a palace; live in luxury like you did back home.'

The Arcadian wrung his hands as he stared forlornly at the cracked marble floor.

'I get it,' I said. 'It's not ideal. But would you rather live here or get married off to a bloodsucker and be responsible for the downfall of human civilisation?' I made scales of my hands and weighed them up and down.

'Will you visit, at least?' he asked, a catch in his throat.

'I'd love to but it's too risky. Anyone could follow me through, then we're back to square one.'

The kid fought back tears. 'I understand.'

God, he was gonna have me blubbing in a minute. 'Take it easy. Enjoy the peace, get your health back, and one day, if things change and the heat dies down, you can give up the hermit life and return to the land of the living.'

'And then what?'

'I dunno. Move out to the sticks. Get yourself a nice country pile and live in nature like you're supposed to. Eat all that sweet crap you love until your teeth fall out.'

The Arcadian offered a broken little smile. I turned to my partner, who looked just as sad as the kid. I didn't want to say goodbye, neither of us did, but it was the only way. Frank and I still had work to do in London, starting with a visit to the office to deal with Tali. I'd yet to confront her, to let her know her game was up. Maybe it was already too late, but until I did that, until I convinced her to confess her sins, there was no chance of turning things around. No hope of saving her soul.

'Right then, we'd best sling our hook,' I said.

'Don't you have to wait until midnight rolls around again?' asked the kid.

'Nah, it works different going the other way.'

'How come?'

'I dunno. Magic. Don't overthink it.' I climbed to my feet. 'All right, Lurch, let's go.'

Frank offered the kid a consoling handshake before joining me, body sagging, weighed low by pity. 'Byee byeee.'

I clamped a hand on the Arcadian's shoulder. 'Stay strong and keep your pecker up, kiddo. You can do this.'

With our goodbyes said and done, Frank and I reluctantly made our way from the shell of a mansion and back to the portal. It was a tough walk. Frank moved in broken, halting steps, continuously throwing looks to the site we'd abandoned the fae. Me, I didn't look back. God knows I wanted to, but I didn't. Guilt sat heavy in my gut. I couldn't shake the feeling that there was more we could have done. More besides ditching the kid and letting him live out the rest of his days in a forgotten wasteland. What kind of a fate was that, anyway? I was no stranger to purgatory, but at least I had company. At least I had purpose. And here I was, condemning someone—a good someone—to the worst kind of limbo.

The sound of a chippy rock theme wrecked the peace of the silent city. My phone. I groped it out of my jacket pocket and answered Stronge's video call.

'Fletcher…'

'Hey, Kat. Wow, you're coming through crystal clear here. This magic phone Jazz gave me gets *amazing* reception.'

And yet Stronge seemed unimpressed by the performance of my remarkable interdimensional mobile.

'Someone's coming,' she spluttered. 'Coming your way.'

It was right then that I noticed she was hurt. Blood matted Stronge's hair and ran down her temple in a wet red rivulet.

'What happened? Who did that?'

'Came at me from behind. A woman.' She mopped up the running blood with the cuff of her sleeve and winced. 'Knocked me down and went barging into the gallery.'

'Who was she?'

'I don't know, I didn't get a look at her face, but I'm guessing she's not coming to bring your little blue friend a housewarming present.'

Frank's arm went up and his finger unfurled, pointing dead ahead.

'What is it?'

I couldn't even see to the end of the street, but Frank's night vision was a lot better than mine. Cat-like, really.

'Sooooomeone,' Frank moaned.

'Gotta go.' I hung up the call and started backing up, heading the way we came, back to the mansion.

I could just about make out a figure stalking towards us, barely a silhouette at this distance, but very much there. She was average height with long hair and didn't seem to be armed, at least not with anything she was pointing in our direction. Still, we didn't stick around to get the full picture.

As the woman continued plodding our way like the hockey-masked killer from a slasher flick, we turned tail and caned it back to the mansion. Unsurprisingly, the kid—who was still getting used to the idea of living in indefinite solitary confinement—was a bit taken aback by receiving company so soon.

'What's going on?'

There was no time to explain, so I grabbed his wrist and the three of us raced up the spiral staircase to the first floor. We sped across the landing and turned into a spacious room packed with a clutter of clapped-out furniture. Among the mismatched collection I saw school desks, a grand piano, and a knotty wooden conference table, all caked in a generous helping of grime. It looked as if someone had been squatting there, hoarding belongings from all over the city. I wondered briefly who that might have been, then spotted a leering skull among the detritus. Him, maybe?

'Help me barricade the door,' I said.

'Why?' asked the Arcadian. 'Who's coming?'

'I don't know and I'd like to keep it that way for now.'

Frank used his superior strength to grab the end of the conference table and drag it out from beneath a heap of poorly-stacked chairs. The kid took the other end, and together they hauled it across the room and propped it against the room's only door. Meanwhile I checked on the room's two windows and made sure they were shuttered.

'There,' I said, dusting my palms. 'Locked up like a vault.'

I heard a cough that didn't belong to anyone in my crew. In the middle of the room, sitting on a school desk, was our pursuer. She was a brunette woman, young—late-twenties maybe—and wore a grey vest and black jeans with a pair of sturdy bovver boots. There was a cruel smile on her lips and an archness to her features that suggested she was used to getting her way, especially if someone didn't want her to have it.

'You know,' she said, bouncing off the desk and landing two-footed on the floor, 'it's always a good idea to make sure the place you're hunkering down in is empty before you nail it shut.'

She stepped into a shaft of moonlight that sliced through an overhead bay window, and I saw patterns decorating her exposed arms. Tattoos. Tattoos radiating a dark energy that sent a chill wind whistling through my crypt.

CHAPTER FORTY-TWO: THERE GOES THE NEIGHBOURHOOD

WHO WAS SHE? Who was this strange woman with the threatening aura and the magical runes on her arms? Not an Arcadian, and not a Vengari, either. Unless she was a slave to one or the other, although she certainly didn't carry herself like someone under the thumb.

'All right, luv,' I said, keeping it light. 'I give up, who are you?'

'The name's Erin Banks. And you must be the Spectral Detective.'

I gave the old mental rolodex a spin but landed on a blank.

'It's past midnight. How did you get through the portal?'

She shrugged. 'Magic.'

'Dooon't overthiiink iiit,' said Frank.

I played it cool. 'I see. And what can I do for you, Miss Banks?'

'You can start by sending the Blue Meanie over here.'

'And why would I want to do that?' I chanced.

'So I can kick him into next week.' She traced a finger along the line of one of her tats and the supernatural ink buried beneath her skin sparked like a nail dragged over a piece of flint. 'Just business. Nothing personal.'

'It definitely feels a bit personal,' said the Arcadian.

'Don't flatter yourself. You're just a paycheque.'

Frank stepped in front of the Arcadian, making a wall of himself.

'Something tells me you're not here to show him the way back to London,' I said.

She gave me a grin as narrow as a paper cut. 'Then something tells you right.'

If Erin hadn't come to Other London to rough the Arcadian up and drag him back home, she could only be here to kill him. That ruled out the kid's family being in charge of her.

'Did one of Enoch's lot put you up to this?' I asked.

'Never heard of him,' she replied.

Of course she hadn't. Enoch had slotted three of his own to keep his secret. His grudge was his alone, and it died when he did.

So who put us in this woman's sights?

'Don't you get it?' said the Arcadian. 'It was Tali. She's the one who wants me dead. She hired the hitman.'

'Actually, I prefer *assassin*,' replied Erin. 'Less sexist.'

Finally the penny dropped. My own client. She'd hired the third party, she'd sent a killer here to finish the Arcadian off and drag his soul back to her side of the portal. The message I sent Tali—the one I left on my office answering machine telling her I'd grabbed the kid at the train station—she must have taken that as her cue. Taken that as her opportunity to get me out of the picture and replace me with someone willing to get blood on their hands.

'Erin, listen to me. This is a mistake. The woman who hired you, she ain't right in the head.'

'Of course not. She must be hysterical. What woman in her right mind would want her murder avenged?'

'So you know she's dead? Doesn't that bother you? How's she going to cough up your fee?'

'She gave me her PIN number.'

That made sense. Since Tali wouldn't be needing all that escort money anymore, why not use it? And they say you can't take it with you...

'You're not getting it, Erin. Helping murder victims is my bread and butter, but this—'

'Let me save you the bother. You ever read a James Herbert book?'

The sudden shift caught me off guard. 'What?'

'You know. *The Rats*? *The Fog*?'

'Can't say I've had the pleasure,' I said, wondering where this was going.

'I get it. I'm not much of a reader either, but I do like me a bit of murder and mutilation, so I'll pick up a horror every once in a while. Anyway, Herbert does this thing where he spends a whole chapter introducing you to a character until you really feel like you've taken a walk in their shoes. I'm telling you, by the end of that chapter, they feel like family. Then you know what he does?'

'No.'

'He kills them. Has rats eat their eyeballs, or flies them into the side of a skyscraper. All that build-up, all that getting to know you stuff, just to murder them.'

Frank looked to me with a confused expression that mirrored my own.

'What are you getting at?' I asked.

'The point is, that's you. You're a James Herbert character, which means everything coming out of your mouth right now is a waste of my time. I don't need your sad little story because any minute now I'm going to come over there and snap your head off—your terrible twin as well—and when I'm done with you two, I'm going to stick a knife in Tinkerbell's ear. So let's skip the bollocks and get to the good bit, shall we?'

She laced her fingers together and bent them backwards, cracking her knuckles.

'Keep away, you mad cow,' I warned as she started in our direction.

The Arcadian shook his head, disappointed. 'There's no need for that kind of language.'

'Kid, when they're trying to kill you, it's okay to not be PC.'

The assassin's tattoos pulsed with that eerie negative light, then she was on top of us. She cocked a fist and my head flared with pain. Somehow I missed the part where she took a swing, and went from standing up to sitting flat on my arse.

Frank came to my defence, grabbing Erin's head from behind and chewing her ear like Mike Tyson. Before he could do any real damage, she sent an elbow his way that left him veering about like a shopping trolley with a wonky wheel.

Now it was the Arcadian's turn. I don't know what happened to him. One second he was heading Erin's way, the next he was spinning about on his heel with blood gouting from a split lip.

Erin bounced from foot to foot like a boxer grandstanding for the crowd. 'I am feeling the juice!' she hooted.

She was certainly dishing it out, but we had the numbers, and she couldn't hold us off forever. So we gritted our teeth and charged the assassin as one, overwhelming her, piling in en masse. Frank gave her a solid chinning, the kid threw in some nice digs, and I got a couple of sweet kidney punches in. Should we have felt bad about ganging up on a lone woman and taking pleasure in her pain? I don't think so. I mean, she had it coming, right? What someone keeps between their legs is pretty immaterial when they're trying to put you in a drawer.

Speaking of which...

The assassin crouched into a ball, made an X of her arms, and exploded to her feet, bringing with her a concussive wave that knocked me flying. A volcano of dark magic erupted from her tattoos, the world did a somersault, and the floor slammed into my face. Ears ringing from the blast and head filled with sparks, I dragged my eyes about the room and found my companions scattered to the far corners.

Erin cackled. 'That was fun. Check it out, my nips are like iced diamonds.'

She drew a knife from a sheath on her leg. Its blade was stark white and had a row of occult symbols carved along its length.

'Well, it's been a hoot, kids, but I'm afraid this is going to have to be a hello slash goodbye. Emphasis on the *slash*.'

We all had the same idea at once: get out of there. Erin had already taken on the three of us with her fists. Add a magic shiv to the mix and she'd have us in ribbons. So we ran for the door, worked together to pry away the barricade, and made off on our toes.

Erin called after us. 'Ah, come on, don't run. Can't you just take a jump on the pointy end of my knife? It'd make my job a lot easier.'

Yeah, no.

We pelted it down the spiral staircase, across the lobby, and out the front door. I was about to keep going when an idea struck me like a thunderclap.

'Wait,' I said, grabbing Frank by the arm before he lumbered any further.

'What's the hold up?' asked the Arcadian, keen to move on as quickly as possible.

'Hang on a minute, lads. I've got an idea.' I pointed to the crack in the column holding up the mansion's sizable porch—the one my partner did a number on before we stepped inside. 'When I give the signal, you give it a clout.'

Frank nodded and we stepped aside, making sure we couldn't be seen from inside the building. A series of footfalls followed as Erin descended the staircase, then another more rapid percussion as the treads of her boots slapped against the marble floor of the mansion's entranceway

'Now!'

Frank threw his full weight against the ailing pillar and down it toppled, taking the porch with it. The timing was just right. A solid chunk of flat stone smashed our pursuer flat, leaving all but her grasping hand uncrushed.

'Nice one, Frankie boy,' I cheered.

High-fives and back-slaps all round. But it turned out our celebrations were premature.

First, Erin's uncrushed fingers began to twitch—not a death spasm, but with purpose, with determination—then the giant slab of stone began to shift. As we backed away, the slab rose and seesawed until it fell to one side, shrugged off by the figure stepping out from beneath its enormous weight. Erin Banks was alive… to a fashion.

Her limbs were crooked, her skin split and leaking blood, and her head looked like a Halloween pumpkin in late July.

'Ooh,' I said, whistling through my teeth. 'It's going to take more than a bag of frozen peas to fix that.'

And yet, Erin hobbled from the rubble with a wicked grin on her face.

'What is she smiling about?' asked the Arcadian, looking as if he was about to evacuate his stomach.

'Check this out,' croaked Erin, plugging a broken thumb into her mouth, closing her lips around it, and giving it a good blow.

Slowly, horribly, the depression in her skull inflated until it was all filled out, rendering her head whole again. And that was only the half of it. The rest of her body was knitting together too—broken bones snapping into their original shapes, open wounds zipping up, the pitter-patter of blood on the ground turning quiet. I couldn't tell you what this woman was made of, but she had the staying power of a gnome.

'You like that?' she said. 'Then you're gonna love this…'

She rolled her shoulders forward, bowed her head, and pressed her fists together like a bodybuilder throwing a pose. Waves of raw black magic boiled along the lengths of her arms and met at each end, sending sparks of furious arcane energy spitting from her knuckles. When she looked up again she wore a stare like a cobra seeking its prey; cold and unflinching.

You best believe we ran some more after that.

CHAPTER FORTY-THREE: A WOMAN SCORNED

Across the ruins of a flattened building we raced, picking our way through the rubble, desperate for someplace to hide. Crackling bolts of black lightning exploded all around us, polluting the air with the smell of scorched ozone and burning hot enough to char the Devil himself.

Unlike Lot's wife in the story of Sodom and Gomorrah, we did not look back; we charged forwards, eyes dead ahead as the assassin's magic blew potential cover to pieces and turned steel beams to slag. This wasn't my London—just a twisted, hollow imitation of it—but I felt like I was caught outside in the Blitz, running through a bombsite, dodging a bombardment from the Luftwaffe and praying for a fleet of Spitfires to swoop in and clean up the skies.

We beat feet towards the remains of The Rabbit Hole, the derelict tavern we passed by when we arrived in the city. It wasn't far and it stood a decent chance of having a cellar we could hole up in. Other London was big and Erin was only one person; maybe if we kept quiet and stayed hidden long enough, the hellcat at our backs would get bored and move on.

Yeah, I know. Fat chance.

Beneath the tavern's weathered sign we found the trapdoor the dray would have used to make its delivery, just a few planks remaining, held together by rusted nails. Frank tugged it open and tossed the trapdoor aside, revealing a sharp plunge into semi-darkness. The ladder that had once provided access to the cellar had long since fallen into disrepair, meaning we had to jump the six-foot drop to its bottom.

Inside, V-shaped columns constructed from hand-made bricks rose to support a low vaulted ceiling. The walls of the cellar were lined with racks heaving under their weight of iron-banded wooden casks, all buried in dust, all dried up. As the three of us cowered in the darkness like a pack of wounded animals, we heard a sing-song voice calling from outside.

'Come out, fairy boy. Time to die.'

I whispered to the Arcadian, 'Now, *that's* un-PC.'

'You know, lads,' the assassin went on, her voice drawing closer, 'this town really isn't the hiding place you were hoping for. I've killed a target here before and I'll do it again.'

'Don't panic,' I whispered. 'Stay still and she'll soon give up.'

Erin dropped through the hatch and landed in a three-point crouch before us.

'Okay, now panic.'

Frank was first to act, but he was nowhere near fast enough for the supercharged assassin. Erin swung a roundhouse kick his way that sent him spinning to the ground, then she stomped once on his head for good measure.

'Sorry about that, Undead Fred.'

The Arcadian made his contribution with some fae eco-sorcery. His fingers danced and glowed green, but the best weapons his magic could muster were a few brown weeds, which slithered wearily through the brickwork before being turned to confetti by the assassin's ivory blade.

My turn. I came to the kid's defence before Erin could stick a knife in him, grabbing her by the wrist and giving her a solid punch in the mush. She barely noticed it. With a tennis player's grunt, she swung her knife and I felt a *whoosh* of parting air. A millimetre closer and I'd received an impromptu oesophagectomy, but instead I managed to land another punch. This one caught her in the nose and sent her staggering in the direction of the fae, who repaid her with a hefty right hook. Now Frank was up on his feet. Grabbing her by the scruff of the neck, he steamrolled her into a brick column hard enough to make the ceiling rain dust.

Erin wasn't out for the count yet, though. As she struggled to her feet, the rows of runes on her arms sparked to life and emitted that strange anti-light, dark as the heart of a black hole. For a second I thought we were about to be hit by another black magic volcano, but the runes sputtered out and the assassin collapsed onto her front, magic spent, strength gone.

Slowly, pathetically, she rolled over, hands shielding her face, blood streaming from her broken beak.

'Please don't kill me,' she bleated. 'I've got kids.'

I kicked the knife from her grip and peered down at her. '*You* have kids?'

A foot came up and caught me square in the knackers.

'Nope. And now you won't, either, you cockney twat.'

I crumbled to the ground, eyes pricked with tears. The pain stayed in my throat, though; I wouldn't give her the satisfaction of screaming.

Erin snatched up her blade and scrambled on top of me. The other two came to my aid but were held at bay by a couple of thick black ribbons: magic tentacles that shot from the assassin's arms and snaked around their necks, throttling them where they stood.

'I'd love to keep this party going,' said Erin, raising her white blade and placing a palm on the weapon's heel, ready for plunging, 'but I've got a bounty to collect.'

The tip of her knife became the centre of the known universe, then the blade came down—

And my hand shot out, into Erin's chest and through her rib cage. Before she could get over the cold water shock of my phantom fingers penetrating her body, I closed a fist around her heart and squeezed, instantly sending her BPM to zero. She let out a long shuddered gasp and pulled a face like she'd taken the ice bucket challenge in Antarctica before keeling over sideways, stiff as a board.

The black ribbons holding my companions turned to liquid and splattered to the cellar floor like pools of Indian ink. The Arcadian shuffled up to me nursing an injured fist. I was about to put a hand out to stop him getting too close to the body by my side, but it was clear the assassin wasn't playing possum this time.

Erin Banks was done.

'Go fuck yourself,' she wheezed.

'Ladies first,' the kid replied.

And Erin died.

CHAPTER FORTY-FOUR: MAD ABOUT THE BOY

OF COURSE FRANK wanted to chow down on the assassin's skull meat, but I told him no. We don't eat people's brains, I reminded him, even if its owner was more hellion than human.

The assassin was dead, but her being here meant there was a good chance her employer, Tali, knew about this place. That meant Other London was compromised, which made it useless as a hide-out. So we left Erin where she lay, licked our wounds, and made our way through the husk of the dead city, back to the portal.

Getting there was a safe paddle through the shallows, and exiting the gallery no harder. The Arcadian was recharged and could move invisibly this time, same as me, so Frank was the only one on display. Lucky for him, the place was still having CCTV problems, and the only night guard we encountered had his head buried in a sudoku. I wondered what became of the jobsworth who gave us all that grief on the way in, and imagined him venting into the ear of some poor barfly minding his own business, ranting about strange blue men vanishing through magic doorways. The thought warmed my cockles.

The sun was just peeking over the rooftops when we emerged outside the gallery, the birds in the trees singing their chorus, eager to attract a fuck buddy or two. I checked the time on my phone and found a text from Stronge. She was at the A&E getting stitches for the clump Erin gave her, and wouldn't be back on duty for a little while. Not a problem.

We headed for Euston, occasionally passing the odd early bird commuter or nightclub survivor, none of which paid us any attention. While my partner's stiff-legged hobble and the Arcadian's blue skin might have drawn stares in some other city, this was London, where people kept their heads down and minded their own business. In a city this size, with a community this transient, why bother giving your fellow man the time of day? Knowing you'll likely never see him a second time makes London an easy place to be an unfriendly bastard.

There was no car parked outside the office of Fletcher & Fletcher this time, no pack of hunchbacked vampires lying in wait. I figured as much. Coming after me and Frank was Enoch's thing: his side project, to have us track down the fae so he could kill him and redress the insult to his sister. The rest of the Vengari would be looking for the Arcadian too, but their search would fan wider than just my doorstep.

'You wait here,' I told the kid as we set foot in the lobby.

I could sense another ghost on the property. I've been able to detect the presence of disembodied spirits since I was a kid; it's how I found myself in the exorcism game in the first place. How I ended up flipping haunted houses for a living and dooming my eternal soul.

'Tali's still here,' I explained.

I was counting on that being the case. Most ghosts have a tendency to roost. They might complain, might rail against the injustice of being trapped in a single locale, but deep down, they find comfort in familiar surroundings. Tali had spent enough time here that the place would be feeling like a home from home. And besides, where else would she go? What was waiting for her out there but more pain?

'I need to speak to her,' said the Arcadian.

I shook my head. 'Not happening.'

I needed to talk to my client, needed to put her straight about a few things, and having you in the room would only muddy the waters.

'At least let me explain myself,' the kid pleaded. 'I need Tali to know why I did what I did.'

I aimed a stern finger at the bench behind him. 'Sit down. Maybe later you two can kiss and make up, but right now I want that girl nice and calm. She's in a delicate place and I don't need her getting all upset.'

Push a ghost too hard too fast and that's when they lose it; when they go off their trolley and turn into the kind of tormented wraith I had to deal with when I visited the home of the old spiritualist lady. That's if Tali hadn't already transformed into a force of pure evil. I mean, she did set an assassin on us, which suggested she wasn't exactly experiencing Dalai Lama levels of serenity. Then again, securing the services of a hired gun suggested a degree of rationality, so maybe Tali was still compos mentis after all. The only thing I could be certain of here was that I didn't know what I was about to walk into, so I needed to be ready for anything.

I convinced the kid to park his arse while my partner and I headed for the office.

'Good morning,' I said as Frank pushed open the door with our name on it.

We found Tali doing laps around the communal desk. She froze in her tracks, coming to a stop in a slice of dawn light that would have picked out every flaw of another woman, but only served to make her look all the more gorgeous. She really was a stunner. Small wonder I let her get her hooks into me.

'What's the matter?' I asked. 'Surprised to see us?'

'Why would I be surprised?' she said, like butter wouldn't melt.

I held up a warning hand. 'Don't bother. We know everything. We know you weren't murdered, and we know you sent a killer after us.'

She dropped the act. 'So what if I did?'

The turn was so sudden that I could only laugh at the brazenness of it. 'You hear that, Frankie boy? No good deed goes unpunished, eh?'

'*Good?*' Tali seethed, her full lips thinned, eyelids pursed in an angry squint. 'You were going to let him marry that vampire skank. What was I supposed to do?'

'Look, we didn't come here to argue with you, okay, we—'

'Oh, you didn't? Then maybe you should have done what you promised instead of selling me out.'

I banged a fist on the desk, making her jump. 'Don't you dare! You came to us for help then you signed our death warrant.'

Frank shot me a look that said, *Chill out*. He was right, I was getting worked up. That wasn't the plan. Calm and professional was the tone we were trying to strike, so I took a breath and perched myself on the corner of the desk, nice and relaxed. Meanwhile, Frank stayed where he was, no sudden moves, a silent sentinel.

'Where did you find her, Tali, this Erin Banks woman?'

At first it seemed like she wasn't going to answer, then I guess she figured why not, the cat was already out of the bag.

'I know her from my Brighton days, before I went solo, back when I worked in a brothel called the Pink Pearl. We drank in the same pub, got to know each other. She knew my line of work, and I knew hers. Never thought I'd have a reason to use her. Not until you told me you were going to work for the Arcadians.'

She gathered up an unpaid bill lying on top of the desk, scrunched it into a ball, and launched it across the room, only for it to land harmlessly at Frank's feet.

So, Tali was able to manipulate physical objects, was she? I cut a glance to the landline. That explained how she managed to dial up the assassin. The woman had some tricks, but then I might have known. I'd seen this happen before to those who were born with the Sight and came back as ghosts, myself included. Spooky in life, spooky in death.

'Tali, I never said I was going to work for the Arcadians.'

'You said it was an option.'

'Only because I couldn't see a better one at the time, then I met the kid and realised there might be another way.'

The malice drained from her face. 'What do you mean? For us to be together?'

She glanced at my partner and saw the hangdog expression on his face. No, that's not what I meant.

I went on, 'He wants you to know he's sorry for the way things ended between you. He loves you, Tali, more than you could ever know, but what you had… it can't go on.'

'What are you saying?'

I formed the words with difficulty. 'You need to go your separate ways now. He needs to go his way and you need to let me show you the way to the next place.'

The look on Tali's face was cold and unpleasant. 'He's just scared of dying.'

This wasn't working. I came here to smooth things over, to make nice, but I was only salting her grief.

I took a step in her direction, arms wide. 'Tali, listen to me—'

'No,' she cried. 'We had a deal and I'm not going to let him back out of it just because he's a coward.'

'If you really love him you'll let him go. All you're doing right now is hurting him.'

The stare she gave me could have stripped paint. 'I don't want him hurt, I want him dead, just like I am, just like we agreed. If he won't honour that, I'm going to have to make it happen myself.'

'If you mean calling Erin Banks again, you're out of luck.'

'Oh yeah. Why's that?'

'Sheee Deeeeaad,' Frank explained, for what he lacked in subtlety, he more than made up for in candour.

I expected the news of the assassin's passing to come as a bit of a blow, but the report only tickled Tali. She let out a bark of a laugh.

'*Dead*? You obviously don't know Erin very well.'

My phone kicked off and I took the call. 'That you, Kat?' I asked, expecting an update on her stitches.

A familiar voice answered, but not the one I was expecting. 'Who's Kat? Is she the copper I flattened outside of the Tate?'

Erin Banks was on the line. Tali's eyes stayed fixed on mine, underscored by a knowing smirk. I put the call on speakerphone.

'Hello again,' I replied, trying my best to disguise the waver in my voice. 'Gotta say, luv, you don't die easy.'

'Looks who's talking, Casper the Unfriendly Ghost.'

Was this a trick or was I really talking to a woman I watched die in the dirt?

'What's the matter, Detective?' she asked, filling the silence. 'Did you really think I was done?'

'Honestly, yeah, I kind of did.'

She laughed. 'It's going to take more man than you to crush *my* heart.'

I saw Frank's shoulders sink. It was her all right. I don't know how she managed it, but Erin Banks was up on her feet. What was in those tattoos of hers? What kind of deal had she struck to acquire healing powers so strong that she could come back from the dead? Even the Arcadian—a creature practically made of magic—needed to sleep off his wounds in a special cocoon, and something told me that his veggie pods were no cure for a corpse.

'I'm guessing you didn't call for a natter, Erin, so what are we doing here?'

'Well, I can only speak for myself, but what I'm doing is sharpening my knife and getting ready to do something to you and your two mates that the Surgeon General *definitely* wouldn't recommend.'

Frank let slip a pitiful moan. Erin Banks was going to keep on coming until we were all sniffing brimstone. That's unless Tali did the right thing and called off her attack dog.

I thrust out my hand, phone aimed at Tali's mouth. 'Tell her the contract's cancelled. Tell her she's done.'

Tali shook her head. 'You still don't get it. We had a deal. This means something...' She held out her hand, showing me her engagement ring.

I made a grab for her wrist. I don't know what I'd have done if I got a hold of her, but I'm certain it wouldn't have been too chivalrous. Probably just as well she whipped her arm back in time.

The bullet hole in her forehead throbbed and spat fire. A banshee cry ripped out of her. 'Leave me alone!' she screamed, her voice so loud that it felt like knitting needles in my brain.

Frank and I were busy cupping the sides of our heads when Tali turned tail on us and ghosted through the office wall. She vanished, leaving behind a buzzing note that I could feel in my spine long after she'd gone.

The Arcadian came running into the room, summoned by the

awful wail. The looks on our faces told him everything he needed to know. Tali had flown the coop.

'We have to go after her,' he said.

Frank placed a steadying hand on his shoulder.

'Let her go,' I said. 'We've got bigger things to be getting on with.'

'Like what? Keep running?'

'No. There's no place left to run. And when you can't run, you fight.'

CHAPTER FORTY-FIVE: WAKE UP AND SMELL THE SULPHUR

THE QUEST TO lay hands on the Arcadian had become a treasure hunt with a whole host of motley pirates searching for the X that marked the spot: Fletcher & Fletcher, the Arcadians, the Vengari, and now Erin Banks. We'd survived the fae and the vamps for this long, but Erin… she was very much the Bluebeard of the batch. I needed to lure her into some rocks and get her out of our wake before she unloaded her cannons.

But first I had to know what made her tick. She looked human enough to me, and though humans could learn to make magic their bitch, they weren't generally able to cheat death with it. Besides, magic was a scholarly pursuit, and since Erin didn't exactly strike me as the academic sort, that meant something else was giving her the good stuff. The tats were the key, I was sure of it. The question was, who gave them to her, and was there any way of undoing their effect?

'I thought you said we were fighting back,' said the Arcadian as we stood in a car park dotted with street lamps hooded by pigeon-deterring spikes.

Before us was a faceless office block; a great slab of concrete the same colour as the bruised morning sky. It was raining overhead and the raindrops had teeth.

'This *is* fighting back,' I told the fae. I was using Frank's vocal cords. It was bad enough having to cart around a bloke with a blue face, without having to explain away old Roger Mortis. So long as we were combined, we could pass for human. A bit under the weather, maybe, but human.

The kid followed me into the building. A bit of negotiation with the feller on the front desk and we were taking the lift up to the third floor, to a business called Citytex Solutions. The lift doors opened into a dreary cubicle farm with grey-painted walls. None of that fancy Farrow and Ball stuff, just a generic, gunship grey—less a colour than an absence of colour. The office's only notable feature was the floor-to-ceiling window on its north wall, which faced another equally drab office block.

I approached the reception desk, which was presided over by a manicured kraken with duck lips, Groucho eyebrows, and a tan that ended at her jawline. While I dealt with her, the kid hung back, facing the other way, hoodie pulled high.

'Hello there,' I said. 'I'm here to speak with Alan Bridge.'

'He's on a break,' she replied, showing me the white of her chewing gum as it rolled around in her mouth like a sock in a tumble dryer. 'Think so, anyway.'

'Would you mind checking?' I asked, taking a slice of hair in two fists and wringing it dry. 'We've come a long way and it's chucking it down out there.'

She crinkled her nose, gave a weary sigh, and reached for the phone like it weighed two tonnes. 'That Alan? Yeah, you're wanted at front desk.' She pivoted side-to-side in her swivel chair. 'I dunno, some bloke in a dirty trench coat.'

She placed the receiver back in its cradle then started scrolling through her smartphone as though I'd ceased to exist. A minute later, a blond middle-aged man showed up wearing a sleeveless shirt with a bloom of ballpoints in its top pocket. He looked surprised. Well, surprised was an understatement.

'What are you doing here?'

'Thought I'd pop in and see how you're doing, Al. How are you, me old mucker? You winning?'

He grimaced then turned to the kraken. 'I'm going to take a quick smoke break, Lucy. Back in a bit.'

'Whatever,' she huffed.

Alan led us back to the lift then down to the ground floor, where we found a concrete awning to shield us from the downpour. It was only once we were out of sight of any potential onlookers that he finally spoke.

'What in the name of fuck are you doing here?'

'Bloody hell, calm down,' I said. 'You know, I think that's the first time I've ever heard you swear, Shift.'

The person I'd so rudely interrupted was none other than your friend and mine, the wily doppelganger him/herself: Shift. And here he was, working a nine-to-five grind at a firm that dealt in high-end data storage.

'This is the shapeshifter?' asked the Arcadian, giving Alan a squiz.

'That's right, Your Majesty,' said Shift, talking through his teeth. 'So nice to see fae royalty show up at my place of business. What an honour.'

'I don't understand,' said the kid. 'What are you doing here? Are you on a mission of some sort?'

'I'm here because I'm a professional tattle-tale, a job that's made me a lot of enemies over the years. Lucky for me, I'm also an expert at blending in.'

The kid twigged on. 'Alan's your cover.'

'The perfect cover, at least until I'm seen chumming it up with a fairy prince and a couple of deadites, so if you don't mind, would you kindly vamoose? My break's almost over and there's a spreadsheet upstairs with Alan's name all over it.'

'We didn't come here for shits and giggles,' I said. 'We're here for information, and seeing as The Beehive has ears these days, we thought we'd go straight to the wellspring.'

I saw a flutter in Alan's physog as anger made Shift's mask slip for a moment, then he quickly transformed back to the doughy office drone. 'How did you even find out about this place?' he demanded.

'I did some checking around.'

'You spied on me.'

'Hey, if I'm going to put my limited life on the line based on someone else's information, I need to be sure I can trust the source of that information. You get that, right?'

Shift ground his teeth. 'Fine. Say what you came here to say and leave me alone.'

'That's the spirit,' I said, giving him finger guns.

So I explained. I explained about the misunderstanding with my client and the hiring of a supernaturally-enhanced assassin named Erin Banks who was out to do us a serious mischief.

Shift put a hand to his mouth. '*The* Erin Banks? Dark hair, filthy mouth, so much scribble on her that she looks like an old school desk?'

'That's her,' said the fae.

'Oh no. Oh no no no. You don't mess with Erin Banks. Demon or angel, sinner or saint, if the price is right, that woman will take you down.'

'Jesus, what are you, the president of her fan club?' I said.

'No. I just take an interest in people who excel at what they do, and Erin Banks is the best of the best.'

'How is she, though? I need to find a chink in her armour, some place to stick in the knife. Come on, tell me, what's her secret? Where's she getting all that juice from?'

'You mean you don't know? She gets it from a demon.'

I might have known. 'Which one?'

'An old friend of yours,' he replied, a faint smile playing upon his lips. 'Or did you forget about the Long Man?'

CHAPTER FORTY-SIX: FIENDS WITH BENEFITS

MUCH LIKE THE duck-lipped receptionist haunting the front desk of Citytex Solutions, the Long Man also presided over his own little fiefdom. While most chthonic entities lurked in the Nether—Hell as you might know it—some of the more potent varieties have been known to create their own private pocket dimensions. As you might expect, travelling to such places is no mean feat, that is unless the demon who calls one home is open to receiving visitors. Just as well the Long Man was known to accept house calls, welcome them even. Whether he let his guests return home after they stopped by... that was a whole other story.

I'd been to the Long Man's realm once before but had help getting there that time. Vic Lords' magic allowed me to bridge the great divide, but since he was dead now—his tortured soul marooned in the very place I was trying to get to—I needed to find another way. Thankfully, Shift knew something Vic didn't: that gaining access to the Long Man's realm was as simple as voicing your request out loud and asking it of the demon using his true name. After that, all you had to do was be patient and an emissary would turn up and show the way.

But the Long Man didn't do Groupon deals. You went to him alone or you didn't go at all, so I told Frank I was flying solo and asked him to escort the Arcadian to the office for safekeeping. Understandably, he dragged his feet on this (metaphorically, I mean.

Literally speaking, Frank always drags his feet). It took some convincing, but I finally convinced the big lug that there was no other way. Bless his cotton socks, he was only looking out for me. For a bloke who gave the kind of handshakes that could put a man in hospital, he was a soppy old sod.

Having said my goodbyes, I took to the streets and made my request of the Long Man. I paid no attention to where I was going. I roamed the highways and byways, speaking my intent out loud, again and again and again. I scattered appeals like markers in my wake, taking it on faith that the emissary meant to hear my voice would respond soon and be compelled to heed my words.

Just as I was beginning to get the distinct impression that I was talking to myself, I saw a man. The sun was still up, but the backstreet he was squatting in—the one my restless feet had unconsciously led me to—seemed to bleed shadows. The man was sat on a milk crate and surrounded by torn bin bags that spewed their contents across the tarmac like gutshot soldiers leaking entrails across a battlefield.

'Frosty?' I said, squinting my eyes.

I knew it couldn't be him, but his name left my mouth anyway. Frost was long gone. Another lost soul I was responsible for. Another black mark next to my name.

The stranger stood up. 'Greetings, Mister Fletcher,' said the stranger, his voice devoid of emotion. 'I am Gerald and I will take you to the Long Man.'

Gerald was a rhino in a pinstripe suit. The Long Man's emissary was on his way to seven-feet tall and as wide as two regular fellers. He wasn't fat, but covered in a thick overcoat of muscle, and had the kind of arms that could bench press a Volvo. His head was a bowling ball, his eyes devoid of sparkle, his nose so button-small that it looked as if it had been selected from the wrong box of body parts and slapped on as an afterthought.

'So what's your deal?' I asked. 'You just sit here all day waiting for clients to show up?'

'I appear where I am required. Wherever there are desperate men willing to make the ultimate sacrifice, the Long Man guides me.'

While most hellspawn lurked in the Nether ready to lunge into our world and claim their victims like demonic trapdoor spiders, Gerald's master preferred a more formal approach. The Long Man didn't dirty his claws by visiting our plane, he sent an envoy in his stead. An envoy and, as it turned out, a gateway.

'Are you ready to leave?' asked Gerald.

'I am.'

He nodded and removed a dull grey Stanley knife from the pocket of his pinstriped suit. With a flick of his thumb he extended the blade, turned it on himself, and thrust it into his neck. This came, as you might expect, as something of a surprise. Perhaps even more surprising was the fact that the stabbing wasn't accompanied by a great arterial gush. Not a drop was spilt; no blood, no tears. As Gerald dragged the blade down from his throat, through his torso, and right the way down to his undercarriage, he didn't so much as wince. Didn't even blink.

When he'd finished mutilating himself, Gerald sat back down on his milk crate and dug his sausage-link fingers into the vertical slice he'd carved through his body. As easily as parting a pair of lace curtains, he peeled back the two great flaps of his trunk and nodded to the opening he'd created.

'Get in.'

'You what, mate?'

Gerald sighed. 'This is the way.'

'Through there? Through your guts?'

'Yes.'

'Because I don't mind taking the scenic route.'

'There is no other way.'

Right then. Crawling through a bloke's slashed-open torso it was. Never a dull day in this job.

'Before I go, do I tip you or what?' I asked.

Gerald stayed mute.

Right then.

I reached a phantom hand into Gerald's chassis then held my breath (force of habit) and poked in a head. At first I was looking at the inside of his gargantuan body, up to my eyeballs in gristle and guts, but by the time I'd crawled forward far enough that my first foot was in, the anatomy lesson had ended and I was someplace else.

Now I was crawling across a carpet of black sand sprawled beneath a hellish nightscape.

'Okay. Right. Cool.'

I took to my feet and brushed the clinging sticks from my trousers. This had been, generally speaking, more dimension-hopping than I liked to do on a murder case—especially one that had turned out not to have been a murder at all. And yet here I was, in the cursed hidey-hole of a wretched monster, ready to cut a deal that no sane man would dare entertain.

I stopped to take in my surroundings. The colour palette of the Long Man's realm was shades of charcoal with parched earth and barren rock all the way to the horizon. There was an eerie peace to the place, but I felt certain it wouldn't be seeing rave reviews from *Lonely Planet* any time soon. Personally, I'd have given a better write-up to Wormwood Scrubs.

It was time to find the horned blasphemy who called this place home. I trekked across the desolate wastes for miles until I found the Long Man's Forest of Souls, by luck or by the demon's hand, I couldn't be sure. Within the blighted forest, among cadaverous trees whose withered branches curled up like dead insects' legs, I found the Long Man.

He was the size of a cathedral, with thick ram horns sprouting from his giant leering skull of a head. His lanky body was a web of exposed, glistening muscle, his huge hands terminating in claws the size of samurai swords. In short, he was a monstrosity. A nightmare. A creature willed from the pages of a Lovecraft novel and made flesh.

When I came across the Long Man, he was busy in his orchard, deadheading ink-black blooms from the skeletal arm of one of his twisted trees. Each of the demon's many trophies was a soul he had collected over the centuries, planted in the forest's black earth and transformed into a grotesque addition to the forest. Some of the trees were saplings, some were full-grown, but all were doomed, paralysed, cursed to live in a state of eternal anguish.

'You need a new hobby, son,' I told the towering demon. 'Every time I come here, you're doing the gardening. It's murder on your back, you know? Take up yoga before it's too late, mate.'

My introduction was maybe a bit lairy, particularly seeing as the last time I was here I only narrowly avoided extinction, but it's important to be yourself, even if you're standing in the shadow of a baleful behemoth with claws that could shred a tank.

The Long Man didn't acknowledge me. Without turning from his work he moved on to a new tree and tended to its branches, snipping away a few unruly blossoms.

I cupped a hand to my mouth. 'Hello? Didn't come here for my health, chief. You gonna talk business or should I head?'

'Mister Fletcher,' said the Long Man, speaking in a voice that sounded like a mangled foghorn aimed into a rusty metal drum.

'There you are. How you doing, matey? Did you miss me?'

The demon considered the question. 'Why would I ever miss you, Mister Fletcher? You are nothing. A speck of dust upon a speck of dust.'

I shrugged. 'I've heard worse.'

The Long Man took a sideways step and focused his attention on a new tree. This one was even scrawnier than the rest, a pathetic specimen, gaunt and malnourished.

'I didn't realise Posh Spice snuffed it,' I said, gesturing to the tortured soul turned topiary. Yes, my references aren't very up to date. No, I don't particularly care.

'You do not recognise this one?' asked the Long Man. 'But this soul you brought to me. A greedy fool by the name of Victor Lords.'

At the mention of his name, the tree's gnarled knothole screamed in anguish. It was a noise so awful that it made me want to stab out my eardrums.

The Long Man turned to the night sky and quivered orgasmically at the pitiful sound. After a moment of deep absorption he returned his hollow-eyed gaze to me and spoke in a post-coital growl. 'Why did you come here, Mister Fletcher?'

'Why else? To strike a bargain.'

'Oh yes? And what is it you seek?'

I was conscious of him studying me intently with his empty, lidless eyes. I made my pitch quickly.

'It's about a woman.'

The Long Man's grin seemed to stretch, even though he had no lips to make that possible. 'Isn't it always?'

'Not like that. This woman's a minion of yours. Erin Banks.'

The Long Man grew still. 'Ms Banks is known to perform certain tasks for me, yes.'

'Well, she's stepping on my toes right now, and I need you to bench her.'

The demon chuckled. It was hideous and loaded with mucus. 'Whatever task Ms Banks is performing right now, it has nothing to do with me. She is a free agent. I have no say in her actions.'

'You're a thirty-foot tall demon, mate. You can at least ask nicely.'

'And why would I do that?'

'Because I'm prepared to make you a very generous offer.'

The Long man crouched down—way, way down—until we were eye-to-eye. 'You are willing to trade your soul?'

'My soul? Actually, I was thinking of something with a bit more shine to it. How does the soul of a fae king sound? Or a queen if you're that way inclined.'

'You possess such a thing?'

'Sort of. I mean, I could definitely point you in the general direction of one.'

'You offer a thing you do not own. You test my patience.'

'Okay, easy, tiger. How about this: you can have my soul, but not right away. We put it on layaway for now and you take it, oh I don't know, a thousand years from now?'

'A thousand years?'

'What's it to you? You're eternal, right?'

'No deal.'

I was running out of options. It was time to do something drastic. I adjusted my tie.

'Okay. If my soul's the thing you need to make this happen, you can have it. Now.'

I had his interest.

'You are prepared to be planted in my garden? To live for eternity in the Forest of Souls?' He stroked the trunk of Vic's tree and it shrank from his touch.

'Why not?' I replied. 'Do you know what I spend my excuse of a life doing? I spend every waking hour—and there are a lot of them—trying to get back into His good graces. Trying to pay off a bunch of sins I didn't even know I was making.'

The demon stared at me, his empty eye sockets somehow even more vacant than before. 'Is this senseless chatter leading somewhere?'

I changed tack. 'You're a gardener. Do you know what forced rhubarb is?'

The Long Man cocked his head and said nothing. I carried on.

'It's this farming technique where they lure rhubarb out of its winter hibernation by tricking it with warmth and darkness. Makes it grow quicker. It sprouts up, reaching for the light, thinking it's summertime, but the summer never comes.'

'Let me guess. You are the rhubarb.'

'I am. And I am so tired of waiting for my day in the sun. But you know what I'm tired of most of all? The guilt. Because it doesn't matter that my sins were an accident. Ignorance won't bring back the souls I destroyed. Nothing will. So why should my soul have it any better? The truth is, I don't deserve the summer.'

'Your guilt is so great that you would consign your spirit to an eternal winter in this place?'

My head sank into a nod. 'Yeah, I would. So long as you tell your assassin to pack it in, I'm all yours.'

The Arcadian was good. He was pure. Trading my soul for his seemed more than fair.

'So what do you say, Twiggy? Do we have a deal?'

The Long Man scraped a claw along his bony jaw as he considered my proposition.

'No.'

'What?'

'I do not desire your soul, Mister Fletcher. It is damaged goods.'

'What are you chatting about, pal? I'm offering you my immortal essence here. Handing it to you on a plate, skin removed. All of the fruit, none of the peel.'

'There is no point arguing. I have made up my mind. Your terms are unacceptable.'

'Listen to me, you bootleg Skeletor, a soul's a soul, surely—'

'No, you listen to me,' the demon replied in a deep, guttural snarl. 'Your soul is out of date. It has expired. It will bear no fruit. Now take your raggedy remains home and do not come here again.'

Some words were clawing their way up my throat—the kind of words they won't let you say on the radio—when the Long Man waved his hand dismissively and the world was whipped away like a magician's tablecloth.

The demon's Forest of Souls was gone. I was back in the alley-way, back among the bags of rubbish and the empty milk crate. Gerald was gone, no sign of the big lad. Just me on my lonesome, empty-handed.

The Long Man left me in the lurch.

The bargain wasn't struck.

I tried to sell my soul to the Devil, but the cheque bounced.

CHAPTER FORTY-SEVEN: PARK LIFE

I THOUGHT I was taking a big risk wandering into an arch-demon's lair, but the Long Man's interest in me was so lacking that he couldn't even summon up the contempt required to destroy me. It was hard not to take that personally, but wallowing in self-pity wasn't going to help the Arcadian out of his mess, so I put the slight behind me as best I could and moved on.

It was daytime still when I returned from my extra-dimensional trip. The clouds had broken and were tipping rain over the city with a roar. I had to get back to the office, back to Frank and the kid, and figure out our next best move. Unfortunately, I was some distance away and without the ability to translocate, which meant taking public transport or burning some spectral shoe leather. I chose to go by foot. A walk would give me a chance to get my think on, and hopefully scrape together something resembling a workable plan.

I ducked into Hyde Park, a short cut. The rain was lashing down still, turning the going soupy. I was halfway across the park when a shiver tickled the back of my neck; the hairs getting up and shaking it like they were having a fit. I stopped and glanced around, expecting to see a vampire's blood slave heading in my direction with malice in his eyes, or maybe a blue-skinned thug looking to bust a ghost's skull. Instead I saw nothing.

Putting it down to the residual effect of having just returned from a demonic hellscape, I turned back in the direction I was headed and got moving. It didn't take long for that weird feeling to return. Someone, or something, was following me, I was sure of it. I looked around again. Still nothing. Just trees and bushes and more trees. Except one of the trees was behaving in a most peculiar way.

A branch reached down, wrapped itself around my waist, and hoisted me off the ground. A hug from a tree, that was a new one. I wriggled, trying to pass through the tree's limb, but it was imbued with some serious magic. I was held tight. Who was doing this? The Long Man had a way with trees; was it him?

'Mister Fletcher, you're a tricky one to pin down.'

I scanned my surroundings, trying to locate the source of the words, but it looked as if I was alone. Still, I recognised the voice well enough.

'Your Majesty?' I wheezed. It was her, all right: the Queen of the Unseelie Court. 'Don't suppose you could get your friend here to ease up a bit, could you?'

I stopped struggling as I spotted something, well, bizarre happening below me. Two bushes were slushing through the mud and heading in my direction. The bushes reared up like dogs begging for a treat, then their foliage began to stretch and weave together, knitting something new into reality. I squinted down and realised what the bushes were doing; they were creating a facsimile of the Queen. An avatar.

'Now that is a bloody good trick. You should go on *Britain's Got Talent* with that, you'd clean up.'

'Silence,' said the avatar. The face wasn't a perfect likeness for the Queen but the menace was all there.

The branch girdling my waist gave me a quick squeeze, almost causing my eyes to pop out.

'I have questions,' said the Queen, her leaves bristling.

'Me too: like, how did you find me for one thing?'

'We fae have a connection to nature. It's difficult to maintain that connection in this filthy, modern city, but look where we are…'

Yup. I'd walked smack-bang into a giant green oasis in the middle of a car-fume riddled armpit.

'As soon as you entered this park, the natural world spoke to me. Whispered in my ear.'

'So what you're saying is, I got grassed up by grass?'

Not even a smile. Must have been a cultural thing.

I pressed on. 'Look, there's no need for the strong-arm tactics. I'm on the job.'

'Why do I find that so hard to believe?' she hissed back.

'Trust me, I'm on your side,' I said, trying to placate her. I wasn't, obviously, but now didn't seem the best time to bring that up.

'If you're truly loyal to the Unseelie Court, tell me, where is my son?'

I wasn't loving being bossed around like this. I got into the P.I. game so I could pick and choose my clients, not get told what to do. Then again, what else could I expect from the fae: a bunch of snooty, stuck-up, baby-snatchers. Of course they'd think I'd do their bidding for nothing. They were used to having slaves.

'I have leads,' I said. 'Many leads. Your boy's going to be back with you, well, imminently. More than imminently. That's a Jake Fletcher guarantee.'

'Don't think you can brush me aside, Detective. You've been given the honour of working for the Unseelie Court—'

'And don't think for a second I take that lightly,' I cut in.

The Queen's avatar face scrunched together in a look of extreme displeasure. 'It would give me great joy to tear what's left of you apart, Mister Fletcher. To render your spectral form nothing more than smoke on the wind. Perhaps I will, yet. Tell me why I should deny myself this pleasure.'

'Frank! Frank, my partner, he's out there right now shaking trees.'

A branch eyebrow raised.

'He's working an eye-witness lead. I was on my way to catch up with him when you... well, started shaking your own tree.'

'Is this a joke to you, Detective?'

'No. Honest to God, Your Majesty, we're getting somewhere and we're getting there fast. Now, if you want your son back, I suggest you put me down and let me do my job.'

That came out a little more forcefully than it perhaps should have, but I needed to sell this lie so I could get back on my feet and get the hell out of that park.

'If I discover you're lying to me... smoke on the wind.'

'Absolutely. I get it.'

The tree branch withdrew, dropping me unceremoniously to the ground. Head spinning, I stumbled to my feet to find I was alone again. The avatar of the Queen was gone. She bought it. Well, at the very least she was giving me another crack of the whip before she killed me. Either way, it was time to get off the green and onto concrete.

I hoofed the ground, sending a clod of wet turf spiralling through the air—the same turf that had snitched on me to the Unseelie Court.

'Talk about your call of nature,' I said, giving the clod another punt as I went hustling for the nearest exit.

Call of nature.

I really do crack myself up sometimes.

CHAPTER FORTY-EIGHT: MEAT FOR PROWLING BEASTS

THE RAIN WAS STILL HAMMERING down when I made it back to Camden. Being a ghost, I couldn't actually feel the weather, but it had become so oppressive by this point that even I wanted to take cover from it. It was with some relief that I phased through the front door of Fletcher & Fletcher and made my way to the sanctuary of the office. Sadly, that relief was not to last.

'Hi, honey, I'm hom—' was as far as I got before I realised the reunion I had in my head was not to be.

I found Frank tied to the office's cast iron radiator by a length of steel wire, his wrists bound so tightly that his hands would have turned blue if they weren't already that way.

Lying in the middle of the Persian rug was the half-conscious fae, badly beaten but still breathing.

Erin Banks sat languidly in my swivel chair, feet on the communal desk, cleaning crud from her fingernails with the tip of her ivory-bladed knife.

'Well, look who it is: Jake Fletcher, the little engine that couldn't.'

I assumed a relaxed stance, arms wide and unthreatening. 'Let the Arcadian go. He doesn't deserve this.'

She dug a flake of Other London from beneath the nail of her swearing finger and flicked it across the room. 'Sure. I should trust the word of a man who turned my heart into a fucking stress toy.'

'If you really want to kill him, why isn't he dead already?'

Erin formed an impish smile. 'Because I want you to see me do it, that's why.'

'Seems a bit mean-spirited.'

'And what was dropping the front of a house on my head? Because that definitely felt a tad nasty. You know, from where I was standing.'

'I'm sorry about that.'

In truth, I wish I'd carried on hammering until there was nothing left of her but stink, but that probably wasn't going to advance my case, so I kept it to myself.

'The situation's changed, Erin. Take a look around. Your client—my client, too—she's gone. She's fled the scene and she ain't coming back. This job of yours, it doesn't exist anymore.'

Frank nodded in agreement. 'Jobbbb gooone.'

Erin dislodged another piece of dirt from her nail bed and smeared it jaggedly across the surface of the desk. 'The fae dies and so does anyone who gets in my way.'

She swung her feet from the desk and stood upright.

'Can we at least talk about this? I've got money.'

'Sorry, Casper, but if I gave in to every Tom, Dick, and Harry who tried making me a knifepoint deal, my rep would be in tatters.'

Frank strained at his bonds. The kid drooled into the carpet. Erin came at me with her knife.

'What the bloody hell's going on in here?'

Heads whipped around to discover the identity of the party crasher. It was DCI Kat Stronge.

'You!' she said, aiming a stiff finger at the woman who brained her outside the Tate.

The distraction lasted just long enough for Frank to break free of the steel wire fixing him to the rad and clout Erin across the back of the head. The blow should have caved in her skull, but it only put her in a mood.

'You know, I really don't like coppers,' she said, nursing her crown.

The tattoos on her arms pulsed with living darkness, throwing off flickers of demonic energy and making the room thrum. A sudden wind whipped about the office, creating a howling eddy that hauled an assortment of loose papers around in mad loops. As the wind picked up, it dragged a table lamp from the desk and hurled it against a wall, showering the floor in green glass. The vintage phone with its built-in answering machine was sent flying, too, dispatched through the office door, shattering its frosted glass window.

'Careful,' I screamed over the din. 'We just had the place fixed up.'

It was bad enough that the Vengari had already given the place an aggressive redecorating when they went looking for the Arcadian—now this? I was going to have to live with it, though. The maniacal look in Erin's eyes made it clear that preserving the decor was not the uppermost thing on her mind.

Black ribbons snaked out of her tattoos and came slithering our way like serpents slinking from their holes. Stronge reached for her stun gun, but before she could unclip it from its rapid release holster, I made a hand corporeal and seized her by the wrist.

'Not going to happen,' I said, and yanked her across the room.

Frank was quick to follow, scooping up the Arcadian and hobbling after us as fast as his legs could manage. We darted across the lobby, making for the front door, but a cluster of black ribbons fired over our heads along with the office desk, which landed across the exit with a thunderous crash.

Thinking fast, I cried, 'This way,' and steered us through a side door. It led down a hallway and into an extension bolted to the side of the building: a double-wide garage.

Frank set the semi-conscious Arcadian down on a pile of old newspapers and got to work barricading the door. He did this using a step ladder snatched from the rafters, which he propped against a sturdy workbench before wedging its other end under the door handle. The door came under siege immediately and the lump of wood separating us from the murderous assassin rocked and shook, causing tools piled upon the bench to shiver in response. It stayed solid, though. Unless Erin had a steamroller handy, she wasn't getting through that way.

The battering against the door behind us ceased abruptly.

'She must be looking for another way in,' said Stronge, and soon spotted the most obvious choice.

The exit from the garage was the old-fashioned kind: two doors held together by chain and a padlock. Thankfully, they were also *built* the old-fashioned way: made from solid oak and reinforced with thick iron braces. Would they stand up to an onslaught from Erin Banks, though? Not for long.

'Whaaaat nowww?' asked Frank.

I took in the room. It was dank and musty and contained mostly junk: old pots of paint, rusted tins of motor oil, a perished garden hose. But there was one item of interest, namely the vehicle parked in its centre and covered by a vast grey dust sheet.

'You've got a car?' said Stronge.

'Belonged to the previous owner.'

I whipped the dust cover off to reveal an aging hearse. The antique motor was old enough to draw a pension and had windows that were either made from smoked glass or turned opaque by grime. But for all its faults, it had four inflated tyres and stood up in one piece, so might yet have its uses.

'Get in.'

The hearse was our way out of this mess. I ushered Stronge into the passenger side, got Frank to lob the Arcadian in the back, then combined with my partner to take the driver's seat.

'You really think this knackered old thing is going to run?' asked Stronge.

There was only one way to find out.

CHAPTER FORTY-NINE: DEATH DRIVE

THIS WASN'T my first time scrumping for cars. I had a bit of a wild youth—enough that I knew how to hotwire certain older models, and this one was a prime candidate, ripe for the picking.

Since I didn't have a screwdriver to pop the cover off the steering column, I used Frank's brawn to muscle it open. I fumbled with the roils of wiring that plopped out and freed a bundle from its harness.

With a hair-raising thump, the garage doors flew inwards but held firm, kept together by the length of chain looped through their handles. The wolf was at the door.

'Hurry up,' Stronge urged, shaking my shoulder.

'Not helping,' I said, digging the nails of Frank's thumb and fore-finger into the end of a wire and stripping away a short length of rubber tube.

There was another thump as the garage doors flexed and rattled, splits appearing in the wood now.

'I'll huff and I'll puff and I'll blow your house down,' Erin yelled from outside.

I deprived a second wire of some insulation and twisted its copper end around the one I'd already stripped. As the two wires came together the dash lit up and the car's radio came to life. Whoever was in the driver's seat last had tuned the wireless to a classic rock station and set the volume high, leading to a spirited chorus of—I shit thee not—Meat Loaf's *Bat out of Hell*.

'Come on!' said Stronge, shouting to be heard over the thundering din of the tubby rocker's seminal masterpiece. 'What are you waiting for? Are you checking the fluids?'

So far I'd only succeeded in powering the ignition switch. To get the engine running I still had to spark the starter wire.

The garage doors splintered and buckled as Erin laid on another punishing welter of blows. With some difficulty I fished out the starter wire, tore a nub of rubber from its tip, and rubbed the exposed copper against the tied-off battery wire.

A spark. I buried the accelerator with Frank's foot and revved the engine, pleased to discover that there was still petrol left in the tank.

'Yes!'

Only one thing left to do now. I cranked the wheel like I was trying to snap the thing's neck and broke the steering lock. The hearse was ours.

Another wallop against the garage doors. The wood resembled Swiss cheese now. Erin was seconds away from forcing her way inside.

Whaaat nowww? drawled the voice in my head.

Frank had a point. We'd already dropped a tonne of masonry on Erin's nut, not to mention stopping her heart, so what use was running her down going to be? So long as she had her demonic powers, chances were the only thing coming away from this inevitable collision with any real damage was the car.

Erin's fist exploded through the door, fingers reaching in like a fox trying to claw its way through a chicken coop.

I dialled down the volume on the radio and turned to Stronge. 'Gimme your phone.'

'What? Why?'

'Just give it here!'

She handed it over and I frantically punched in a number. The person on the other end picked up. Well, not a person exactly: a demon.

'Who is this?' growled the Long Man.

'All right, chief? It's your old pal, Jake Fletcher.'

A beat. 'Is this your device I am holding?'

I imagined the Long Man clutching my tiny phone in his massive claws and chuckled. 'Yup. Listen, can you do me a favour—I think I left something else behind, too.'

'What?'

Crunch.

Erin had her arm in up to the shoulder. The chain holding the doors shut was ready to rupture. Any second now a link would give in and the fox would have her feast.

'I think I left it in one of your trees,' I told the Long Man. 'In the knothole of the one that used to be Vic Lords. Could you have a look for us?'

I heard shuffling on the other end of the line as the Long Man went in search of the mystery item. Stronge was looking at me like I'd lost my tiny mind. Frank was giving me all kinds of verbal. Sunlight exploded into the garage as Erin dealt the doors the coup de grâce. She stood before us like some evil goalkeeper, a silhouette wreathed in exhaust fumes, a shadow wearing a smile.

On the other end of the line I heard the bright golden tones of clockwork music.

'What is this infernal racket?' growled the demon as the tune plinked and plunked in the background.

It was the music box Jazz equipped me with: the one I was meant to use against the Arcadian before we got all chummy. I'd taken it with me to the Long Man's realm and planted it in Vic's knothole while the demon was looking the other way, key wound and wedged in such a manner that it would stay in place until the box was disturbed. Now it had been, and the device was playing its little tune —the one that delivered a pulse of magic-dampening energy, a counterspell that revoked the demon's magic and cut off Erin's power at the source.

'Till next time, you big dumb bastard,' I cackled, and hung up the phone.

What? Did you really think I dimension-hopped to a demonic plane without a double-cross in my back pocket? I needed to sever the Long Man's connection to Erin, but I knew my soul was no good to him, and that no amount of verbal judo was going to convince him otherwise. So I came up with a plan and held it back for dramatic reasons. While the Long Man was busy getting his jollies to the sound of Vic's tormented scream, I used some sleight of hand to squirrel away the music box. After that, it was just a case of leaving my interdimensional phone where the demon would hear it ringing. Think of it as a kind of *Who Wants to Be a Millionaire?* lifeline, only with actual lives on the line.

But enough of my gabbing...

'Go, go, go!' yelled Stronge, as if I had something else planned.

It was time to get this wagon rolling. I engaged the clutch, shifted into first gear, and popped the handbrake. Before Erin could take another step, I punched the accelerator and the hearse lurched forward, wheels burning hot enough to blister tarmac. Out of the garage we burst, *A-Team* style, folding Erin in half and sucking her under the wheels. The car bounced twice as she passed beneath its axles, and then we were off.

'Heal that, you dozy bint!'

We jetted up the driveway and traded paint with a passing car as we peeled out into Eversholt Street.

'Yeah!'

I turned up the radio and punched the roof of the hearse. We did it. We beat the super-charged assassin.

'That's why you don't play chicken with a car,' cried Stronge, united in triumph.

Braaaaaaaaaaiiiins, bellowed Frank, which I think was his way of saying congrats on executing a well-designed plan. That or he was hungry.

We caned it down the road, belching diesel, hooting like winners. I took a corner, then another, steering us into a tree-lined side street, fingers still choking the life out of the steering wheel. I heard coughing coming from the back of the car.

'You all right, kid?' I asked, looking in the rearview and finding the Arcadian pushing himself upright on the back seat.

He tried to talk but all that came out was more coughing. He raised a shaky arm, finger pointed dead ahead. Finally, the kid managed to force out some words.

'They're here...'

In front of us, smack dab in the middle of the road, were a trio of blue-skinned men. I recognised the one in the middle with the fur collar as Draven, the Arcadian Lieutenant. Shit. I'd been so caught up with bloodthirsty vampires, tattooed assassins, and extra-dimensional demons that I'd forgotten about the Unseelie Court.

The three fae stood firm as they combined their magic to topple one of the roadside trees, which came crashing down on the carriageway, right in our path. I slammed on the anchors but it was too late. We piled into the felled oak, hitting it so hard that the hearse was sent into acrobatics. Chunks of chassis went spinning and I went with them. Not Frank, just me, hurled from my partner's body and sent spiralling into the road. The shock of being wrenched free of my corporeal form, plus the impact on the tarmac, made scrambled eggs of my brains.

I saw a grass verge and a weed-choked path.

I saw birds overhead, screeching like no bird I ever heard.

I saw the yawning mouth of a gated tunnel and the graffiti skull-face of MICKEY MORTE.

And then I was back in the present, spreadeagled across the broken white line of the road.

A leering blue face loomed over me, a predator's smile etched across his chiselled visage. Draven.

'You're dragon food, Detective.'

He grabbed me by my tie and hauled my head from the tarmac, bringing it within swinging distance of his magic rod. I was getting ready to have my brain reset to factory settings when a guttural roar ripped down the street, making the fae's arm go slack. Frank had made it out of the wreck and was wielding a weapon of his own: the bumper of the hearse, which he swung like a caveman's club.

For a moment it looked as if Draven was going to take him on, but cooler heads prevailed, specifically the heads of his soldiers, who pulled him away like a girlfriend holding back her drunk boyfriend in a pub brawl. Draven shrugged the soldiers off but heeded their message.

'Next time,' he snarled, and slipped the rod back into his belt.

Then he dissolved into thin air along with the rest of the Arcadians.

Frank let go of the bumper and helped me to my feet. Together, we staggered back to the hearse, which lay on its back like a flipped turtle. Stronge was belted into the passenger seat upside down, a fresh cut on her head and broken glass in her hair. She was shaken up and a bit bloody, but otherwise fine.

But the kid?

The kid was gone.

CHAPTER FIFTY: THINGS FALL APART

INSTEAD OF SNUFFING ME OUT, the Arcadians had decided they were better off getting their prince to safety and leaving me to rot. Happens quite a bit, that: folks underestimating me. It's part of the reason I've stuck around so long.

Frank was able to flip the hearse upright and get the old girl back on her boots. Amazingly, the car wasn't a write-off. I'm telling you, they *really* knew how to build a motor back in the day.

People came over to see if they could help, others whipped out their mobiles and dialled 999, but the three of us piled back into the car and got it moving before the ambos arrived. The Arcadians had the kid and that couldn't be allowed to stand. Somehow we had to get him back before they could seal the deal with the Vengari, and to do that, we needed a plan with some hair on its balls.

A conflab was required, somewhere familiar, somewhere safe, and above all, somewhere with booze. Since the office was a no-go, that meant a trip to The Beehive. Sure, we'd been spied on there before, but since we had nothing left to hide, I figured what the hell. The pub's dampening bubble kept most strains of offensive magic straitjacketed, and Lenny was always there to keep any other kinds of violence in check. All in all, we were safer within those four nicotine-yellowed walls than anywhere else in the city.

Nighttime. The troops were gathered, Shift included. She'd sloughed off the balding salary man we cornered at Citytex Solutions and arrived in her more familiar (and infinitely more pleasing to the eye) female form. Together we knocked back a round of pints as we tried to figure out a way to avert the oncoming crisis.

Now, some of you might question the common sense of trying to formulate a battle plan with a bellyful of booze, but you should know there's historical precedent for this. In ancient Persia they say men used to debate ideas twice: once sober and once drunk. It was only if the idea stood on its feet in both states that it could be considered a winner. I don't know for sure whether that's true or not, but since I'd rather noodle an idea around my head with a pint in my hand than without, it's what we were doing.

Except… well, the ideas weren't flowing as fast as the beer was. We'd been sitting in a booth for half an hour already, and the most productive thing I'd managed was to make a set of Olympic rings on the table using the condensation at the bottom of my pint glass.

Shift was the first to break the silence. 'I don't want to sound cold here, but what's the big rush on getting the Arcadian back? I get that this union's bad news, but we don't have to worry until he breeds and produces offspring, right?'

Stronge nodded. 'She's right. We should take our time, really think about this, find some allies.'

'You don't get it,' I replied. 'I owe that kid. I promised I'd get him out of this mess, and he's right back where he started. I'm going after him with or without you.'

Frank grunted in agreement.

Stronge drummed her fingers on the table. 'Okay, so how do we get him? Where is he?'

'At the fae lair with the rest of the Unseelie Court would be my guess.'

'And that's where?'

I looked to Frank knowing he had no more of a clue than I did, but hoping against hope that he might have something rattling around in his noggin that had slipped out of mine. The shrug he gave back told us that he didn't.

Shift blew out her cheeks. 'In other words, you two have about as much of a plan as you do a pulse.'

We had visited the fae hideout—albeit against our will—but the only recollections I had of the place were loose scraps of memory that didn't quite patch together. I shared them with the group anyway: the weed-choked path, the screeching birds, the tunnel with the graffiti.

'Mickey Morte?' said Stronge, parroting my description of the urban cave painting I saw on my way to a fae prison cell.

'That's right,' I replied. 'Add that to the other two clues and that's three things we've got. Can't you take those and… what's the word… triangulate? Can you triangulate them?'

Stronge laid a look on me. 'Triangulate them?'

'Yeah.'

'Jesus Christ.'

A sudden cheer went up across the other side of the saloon as a football team scored on Lenny's big new telly.

Stronge stayed focused on the discussion. 'In all the time you had the Arcadian in your custody, did it ever occur to you to ask him where his family were hiding?'

'Apparently not,' I replied.

'Ruuunning otheeer waaaaaay,' said Frank, pointing out the truth of it.

Shift wet her cherry-red lips with some beer. 'I've looked into it but I can't find anything on the Unseelie Court. Their hideout could be anywhere in the city.'

'So now what?' said Stronge. 'We stick a pin in a map and hope for the best?'

I was gathering my thoughts into something shaped like an answer when the room was stilled by a gasp so profound, so utterly aghast, that it seemed to suck all the air out of the place. I turned to see what the commotion was and found everyone looking in the same direction: at the widescreen television on the far wall, which was no longer playing the footy. The news was on now, BBC One, and it was showing something it really shouldn't be showing.

The Uncanny.

Something beyond the realms of possibility had been caught on camera—on lots of cameras, in fact—and the evidence of it was being broadcast live on national TV. There on screen for everyone to see was a blue dragon circling the night sky. A big blue dragon breathing big blue fire.

'Bloody hell,' I whispered.

What is this? the reporter asked. *What are we seeing here? Is it a hologram of some sort? It looks so real.*

Experts were asked to give their opinions but were left dumbfounded. When they failed to offer anything concrete, the doors were thrown open to wild speculation. A member of the public with a camera shoved in her face suggested the sighting might be a promotional stunt for a restaurant in Chinatown. Another spouted some nonsense about Mercury being in retrograde. Finally, inevitably, conspiracy theorists were called upon to provide their harebrained takes. One member of the tinfoil hat brigade claimed the sighting was a mass hallucination caused by 5G phone masts messing with the brain's alpha waves (never mind that the dragon had been captured on video in perfect 4K glory). Another nutter swore blind that the reptilian aliens who controlled the Earth had finally thrown off their human disguises and sprouted wings (wrong, but still closer than the 5G theory).

Shift's mouth was a perfect O. 'What's going on?'

'A victory lap,' I replied.

The dragon belonged to the fae, and this was their carnival float, their big knees-up for getting their prince back. They didn't care about the flying lizard being seen by normals. They didn't care about the Accord. As far as the Arcadians were concerned, this city was almost theirs—so who cared if they celebrated early? It was only a matter of time now. The wheels had been set in motion. Their reign was assured.

It didn't take a genius to see this was a disaster. Sure, the Accord had been broken before, but never like this, never so openly, so brazenly. The Uncanny got glimpsed by the wrong people from time to time, but those who shouted about impossible things were always pushed to the fringe. The rational mind is a world-class sceptic, and ideas that threaten to smash the matrix of reality have a way of being filtered out.

But this? A big blue dragon swooping about the skies of London? How do you filter a thing like that out? One sighting you could maybe pass off as a hologram or something clever with drones, but what about two sightings? What about three? If the fae carried on disregarding the Accord, people were going to learn the truth. They were going to find out that some of the things they'd seen on the internet—the things they'd passed off as made-up nonsense—were real.

That livestream of the talking crow in Hyde Park. Real.

The dashcam footage of the Arkansas woman who got hit by an eighteen-wheeler and walked away without a scratch on her. Real.

The video of the man who dug up his grandma's corpse and gave it a kiss, only for the mummified cadaver to pucker up and respond in kind. All too real.

No pranks, no special effects, just flashes of the Uncanny. Glimpses behind the magician's curtain. And those glimpses were just a fraction of what the curtain concealed. Pull it back completely and people were going to learn that there were monsters in this city. Not men with their heads wired up wrong, but real monsters, lurking in gloomy subway tunnels, watching silently from behind mirrors, staring up from the muddy riverbed of the Thames. And once people knew that, the whole world would unravel.

This was bad. Actually, bad didn't really cover it. Saying this was bad was a bit like the 1945 mayor of Hiroshima saying there was a bit of a warm snap coming.

I downed the rest of my pint and quickly ordered another.

CHAPTER FIFTY-ONE: AS BELOW, SO ABOVE

SOMEHOW I HAD to find a way to roll this turd in some glitter.

We needed to figure out where the fae lair was, and pronto. DCI Stronge headed for the station to see what she could turn up on there. Maybe the HOLMES suite had something to offer—that was her thinking. I told her good luck with that, but Frank and me would be using our own methods. She urged us not to go off half-cocked, to act like real detectives and work within the confines of the law. I told her we'd do whatever it was that needed to be done. The stakes were too high to be playing by the rules. This was war now.

And so the Fletcher brothers went looking for the skinny via a different channel, an altogether less salubrious one than Stronge's: an eaves. The eaves controlled a spy network that ran the length and breadth of the country, and picked up on each and every whisper that passed their ears.

So why hadn't we knocked on their door before? A number of reasons. First of all, they're not the nicest people to work with, as demonstrated by the drug dealer who stuck a knife in the kid then ratted me out. Another problem was that the eaves don't exactly have doors for knocking on. Their dens are hidden by convoluted labyrinths of their own design that make them all but impossible to find. Yet another problem with accessing the eaves network was that the only eaves I knew who wasn't actively trying to get me killed would probably still put me in the ground given half a chance.

Razor was that eaves. I'd only met him once before, but the encounter had ended in him trying to stick a broken bottle in my face. I guess what I'm saying is, we weren't exactly what you'd call best mates. But Razor was good at what he did. Very good. If anyone in this city knew where the Arcadians were, it would be him. The problem was, how did I go about convincing him to share that information?

The solution? Magic.

Eaves love the stuff, and even though magic is a force that exists everywhere and within everything, they're no more able to access it than you are. Since they can't extract magic the natural way, they need the assistance of those who can: magicians, conjurors, enchanters, spell-casters of all stripes. That's how an eaves gets his fix; he wins the favour of someone willing to reach into the cosmos and sprinkle him with a dash of stardust. But no one gives stardust away for free. To get the good stuff, an eaves has to cut a deal. He earns his dose of magic by trading it for the eaves' most treasured possession.

Information.

And information was exactly what I needed. I've never been much of a spell-slinger myself, so I didn't have much of the stuff at my disposal, but I had enough of a rep to pique Razor's interest and convince him to parley. My hope was that the magic I was offering was worth the gossip I was seeking. If it wasn't, I had another offer for Razor: two pairs of fists and a take-no-prisoners attitude.

Back in the olden days you could count on Razor to be lurking about in the shadows of The Beehive, but he'd since gotten on Lenny's wrong side and earned himself a lifetime ban. These days, Razor preferred a more alfresco lifestyle, and liked to hang out under the Hammersmith flyover. That's where he conducted business now, where he met with clients and scored his magic.

I was keen to talk with Razor the minute the fae unleashed their pet on the sky, but the following morning was the earliest slot he was willing to give me. So there we were, Fletcher & Fletcher, up with the larks and headed for Hammersmith. The part of town we arrived in gave me bad vibes right away. They say building the flyover meant clearing a big chunk of graveyard from St Paul's

Church, and that a lot of graves were lost. Maybe that's what gave me the heebie jeebies: the psychic trauma of all of those displaced souls. Or maybe it was just the prospect of breathing the same air as a man who once tried to kill me with a beer bottle.

We found Razor haunting a gloomy, litter-strewn stretch of the elevated motorway, which arched over him like the spine of some ancient and badly-buried behemoth. It was his smile I saw first, small and yellow and made of teeth sharp enough to slice through a finger like it was made of wet tofu. Razor was short, but what he lacked in height he more than made up for with his stocky, well-muscled build. The lad was a hard case, a pitbull, but at the end of the day there were two of us and only one of him.

'Well, if it ain't Jake Fletcher, the Spectral Detective,' he growled. 'Still waiting to get raptured, son?'

'Yup,' I replied. 'Guess the Man Upstairs didn't find my name in the Book of Life just yet.'

The eaves' beady eyes twitched to my companion. 'I see you brought your old bag of bones with you, too. How nice.'

Seemed Razor knew about Frank already. I guess he must have heard on the grapevine that I'd formed a partnership with my reanimated corpse. Good. If Razor didn't know that bit of trivia, what were the chances of him knowing where the Unseelie Court was?

Time to negotiate. 'You've heard about the Arcadians I take it?'

Razor gave me a squint. 'That your question?'

'No, mine's a bit more specific. I need to know where they are; the ones in London.'

His mouth sharpened into a feral grin. 'Now why would I go and tell you a thing like that?'

'Because I've got magic.'

He gave a phlegmy bark of a laugh. 'That's rich. Ghost magic.'

'Good as any other.'

'Not to me it ain't. You think I don't know everything there is to know about you, Fletcher? You're no wizard, you're a birthday party magician at best.'

The boy had done his homework. It seemed there was no wall in this town that Razor didn't have a glass pressed against.

'Okay, fair play. I'm not exactly flush with magic, but I know someone who is, and they're willing to donate whatever you need.'

Razor's arrowhead-shaped ears twitched. Chances were he knew I was telling fibs, but he'd hear me out all the same. That's how much of a draw magic was to an eaves, because it's not just a fix to them, it's a way of life. Without magic, they have no way of building the mazes they use to keep their dens hidden, and as with all snitches (Shift included), privacy isn't just desirable, it's fundamental.

'Who's the lucky donor?' asked Razor.

Frank answered for me. 'Stellaaaaa Familllliar.'

The eaves eyed him sourly. 'What are you trying to pull? Everyone knows that bitch ain't around no more.'

Apparently, Frank and I were the only people in this town who weren't aware of the familiar's walkabout.

'Stella's on her way home right now,' I lied, 'and when she gets here, she's going to top your tank right up. I've had it out with her and she's fully on board, trust me.'

'Why would I trust you?'

'Have you ever known me to be dishonest?'

'No. Never known me to be honest, either.'

This was getting us nowhere. Without being asked, Frank grabbed Razor by his thick neck and hauled him off his feet.

'If I were you I'd start talking,' I said as Razor's feet pedalled air.

'No chance,' he croaked, staring Frank down.

'This is too big a deal for us to be mucking about. Either you tell us what we need to know or we beat it out of you.'

Frank made a fist, pulled back his arm, and prepared to knock the eaves' teeth out.

'You don't have the balls.'

'Listen, sparky, if you think you're walking out of this place without telling us what we want to know, you're in for a hell of a surprise.'

But it was us who were in for the surprise. Eyes appeared in the darkness provided by the shadow of the flyover. Razor hadn't come alone. A crowd of eaves was waiting in the wings, a dozen or more, looking at us like we were food.

With an awkward smile, Frank let go of Razor and smoothed down the lapels of his coat. 'Nooo haaarm donnne.'

The pack of eaves took a synchronised step in our direction.

'Give me one good reason why I shouldn't have you two torn to pieces right now,' said Razor.

Instinct told me to pile on some more bullshit, but since I couldn't think of anything in the moment, I was forced to resort to honesty.

'You saw what happened last night. You saw the dragon.'

'Course I did. So what?'

'Don't you get what's happening here, Razor? The fae are going to tear up the Accord. All of the things the normals used to pass off as delusions are going to crystallise. And when that happens the pillars of order will come crashing down.'

'And? You ask me, this town could use a shake up.'

Cackles from the peanut gallery.

'You're not getting it,' I said. 'When the likes of you and me get dragged into the light, what do you think's gonna happen? You think the muggles will welcome us into the fold? No. There'll be a war. A war that we won't win.'

'We're eaves. Let them have their wars, they can't touch us.'

'For now, maybe. But what about when the war's over and the magic's all dried up? What then? Where are you going to get your supply from when the Uncanny is just a memory?'

Without magicians to leach power from, the eaves were as good as dead, and Razor knew it. He didn't want to know it, didn't want to admit that I was right, but his sense of self-preservation was strong enough to let me keep talking.

'What are you proposing?' he asked.

'I'm proposing you tell us where the Unseelie Court is so we can put a stop to the Arcadians before they bring it all crashing down. If we can blow their pact with the Vengari they'll have no choice but to bugger off and find some other realm to pester.'

Razor's eyes flicked to Frank before swivelling back my way. 'And I'm supposed to trust you Siamese idiots to take down the fae, am I?'

'We've got allies. All we need is for you to point us in the right direction.'

Given the amount of skin they had in the game, you might have expected the eaves to throw in with us, but that wasn't their way. Much like the Vengari, their kind only played their hand when they knew they were holding all the aces.

'All right then, Fletchers. I'll give you what you're after, but this is a one-time offer, capiche?

'Once is all we need.'

Razor nodded slowly, checked the coast was clear, then spoke from the side of his mouth. 'Listen up. If you want to find the Arcadians, you're going to need to—'

A buzzing noise cut him off.

'Whaaaa?' groaned Frank, doing a sudden about-face.

The drone was coming from behind us, jarring and high-pitched like a dentist's drill dragged across a pane of glass. Something was coming our way: a big black cloud, pouring from a sewer grate. The buzzing had risen to fever pitch before I realised what it was. Wings. Thousands of them—maybe tens of thousands—beating in furious rhythm.

Razor figured it out before we did.

'Fairies,' he cried.

Sewer fairies to be precise, an army of them, surging towards us, flying in attack formation. A colony of rabid parasites packed together so tightly that they looked like a deadly, sentient smog.

We were chum in the water.

The swarm descended on the eaves first. Razor's backup scattered like cockroaches chased away by a housemaid's broom, leaving their leader to soak up the damage. We looked on in horror as the fairies went at Razor like a storm of needles, slashing, jabbing, ripping him apart. Within seconds he was on his knees, a pile of screaming ground beef. Blood spilled out of his body like a nest of glistening red snakes. He fought and thrashed but there was nothing he could do to save himself.

'Run… you… idiots.'

The fairies stripped Razor down like a shoal of piranhas skeletonising a cow until there was nothing left of him but rags and bones.

The killer swarm turned its attention to yours truly. The cloud engulfed me, turning my world into a deafening hurricane of flashing wings and gnashing teeth and needling stingers. Through the chaos I saw Frank whip off his trenchcoat and helicopter it about his head, using it to swat the fairies from my orbit. He caught a bunch of them that way, pummelling their twiggy bodies and snapping their fragile wings, but the numbers were still very much against me. The buzzing grew louder as more fairies piled in, consuming Frank too. The swarm was suffocating, lacerating, and refused to let up. The only way we'd survive it was if we could outrun it.

'Let's go!'

I grabbed Frank by the wrist and off we scarpered, beating a hasty retreat. At first my only thought was to get us the hell out of there, but the terrifying sound of the swarm riding our backs quickly wrangled my scattered thoughts.

We ducked between some traffic, jumped a hedge, and sprinted across a small green. All the while the fairies advanced on us, their screeching din rising in pitch as they grew ever closer. After a couple of minutes of frantic pursuit we rounded a sculling club and there it was: the Thames. Frank's legs were beginning to give out but I urged him on, one hand between his shoulder blades, pressing him towards the river. The swarm was in my periphery as we legged it down the final stretch, feathering the edges of my vision. Finally we vaulted a low brick wall and struck the septic green water of the Thames.

Sanctuary.

The fairies couldn't operate underwater, whereas Frank and I— who had no need for oxygen—were more than comfortable in its depths. The blackness enveloped us, a perfect visual silence to accompany the hushing of the angry swarm. Down on the riverbed, among the sludge and the shopping trolleys, we had only our thoughts for company.

CHAPTER FIFTY-TWO: THE SHADOW OF KINGDOM COME

OUR NEAR-MISS and Razor's untimely end were just the beginning of what was wrong back there. Sewer fairies only came above ground to spawn, and even then, only at night. And yet it was still broad daylight. Something was off, and I had a feeling it went deeper than the fae taking a dump on the Accord. This was a targeted attack. Sewer fairies might be rabid dachshunds compared to purebred Arcadians, but they were still of the same blood. The fae were on to us. They knew we still had unfinished business with them and were doing their best to tie up loose ends.

The river carried us a good mile before we dared resurface. When we finally emerged from the black and into the grey of the city, the sewer fairies were gone. They'd lost our scent and dispersed, which was just as well as we were in no shape to go another round with the bastards. I'd escaped the worst of it thanks to Frank, but he was all chewed up. The fairies' stingers had unknotted cloth and flesh alike, leaving him covered in a lattice of weeping cuts. A quick riverside examination revealed that the damage was mostly superficial, however. It looked bad, but everything was still where it was supposed to be, no missing body parts, nothing mauled so badly that it couldn't be fixed by a couple of courses of warmed-up cow brains.

Being as our only lead was now a pile of bones, we headed to the station to see if Stronge had turned anything up in our absence. As we made our way to Kentish Town we flinched at the sight of every sewer grate we passed, each a gun barrel pointed our way.

Given the state the fairies had left Frank in, I'd planned on leaving him outside the station and ghosting my way in alone. Turned out there was no need for that. The station was in a state of utter disarray. The entrance to the building was crammed with officers doing their best to calm agitated members of the public, who breathlessly shared eye-witness reports that belonged less in a cop shop than the pages of a funny book.

A woman with a pinched face ranted about a reflection in her bathroom mirror that didn't belong to anyone in her family.

A mother with two frightened girls was spouting off about a pair of burning eyes staring out of the Wendy house at the bottom of her garden.

An anxious old man harangued a uniform about a puzzle box he'd found in his attic that kept whispering sweet temptations in his ear.

These weren't crackpots, they were decent, salt of the earth members of the community. Sooner or later, the folks in charge were going to have to start listening to them, and when that happened we were all in trouble. It was bad enough that the death of the witches of the London Coven had left the fabric between our world and the Nether more porous than ever, now everyone wanted in on the action. It seemed the aerial display the Arcadians put on had acted as a kind of beacon, a rallying cry. Creatures that would ordinarily stick to the shadows were peeking out their heads, emboldened by the fae's flagrant disregard for the rules.

We had to shut this down. We had to squash the Arcadians and pour cold water on their pact before the people in this country learned that there are some old wives tales you can take to the bank.

Frank and I slipped invisibly through the crowd, past the exhausted desk sergeant, and headed upstairs to look for Stronge. After breezing through a few doors and magicking open some more, we found the detective in her immaculate office, scrutinising a pinboard peppered with notes. She whirled about at the sound of Frank's footsteps.

'Christ. What have I told you about coming here, Fletcher? I almost maced you.'

She immediately went about lowering the blinds.

'No one cares, Kat. Have you seen it down there?'

'Seen it?' she replied. 'It's *all* I've seen. We had a man in just now who filed a report about a flying skull that chased him the length of Camden High Street. I didn't know whether to laugh or cry.'

I knew what I'd have done, and I usually have such a good sense of humour.

'Whaaat thiiis?' asked Frank, pointing at the object of Stronge's scrutiny.

Among the seemingly random assortment of photos and print-outs tacked to the corkboard was a satellite image of a building, plus a print-out of an email with a letterhead belonging to a bat conservation trust.

'Bats?'

'Yes, bats.'

I nodded as though I understood what was going on, then thought better of it. 'Why bats?'

Stronge walked away from the pinboard and took a seat behind her desk. 'I got thinking about your visit to the fae lair. What you told us about it.'

'And?'

'Those birds you saw, the ones circling the entrance that you said sounded funny—'

'You think they were bats?'

'I do.'

'And why do you think that?'

'Process of elimination.'

She turned a laptop our way. On its screen was an image of a path with a steep verge angling upwards on either side. The path was overtaken by nature and fed into a familiar-looking gated tunnel—the same tunnel the Arcadians carried Frank and me into after they put our lights out.

'Thaaat's iiit,' said Frank, jabbing the screen so hard it's a wonder he didn't break the thing.

'He's right,' I agreed. 'That's where they're hiding. What is it?'

'The old Highgate Station,' Stronge replied.

'That's a railway line? Where are the tracks?'

'Thieves had them away years ago and sold them for scrap. The line's been abandoned since the war. Bats have been roosting in its tunnels ever since, but the fae must have driven them out when they moved in.'

'You're telling me you figured out the exact location of the Unseelie Court just from that one little scrap of information I gave you?'

'Not exactly. There were a couple of other things: your description of the surrounding terrain, and the graffiti.'

She opened another doodad on her laptop and showed me a close-up of a patch of urban art on the tunnel entrance. It was a spray-painted skull, black in colour and topped with a pair of big round ears. Underneath it was scrawled the legend, MICKEY MORTE.

I didn't even bother suppressing my smirk. 'So what you're telling me is, you took those three pieces of information I gave you and—what's the word I'm looking for here—*triangulated* them?'

'That's not what triangulating mea—'

Too late. I was already busy doing a winner's jig; at least until Frank's discouraging look convinced me to cut it out. Back to business.

'Okay, so now we know where the Arcadians are hiding, let's do something about it.'

'What did you have in mind?' asked Stronge.

I'd been considering this question for a while, so I already had an answer in the hopper.

'I translocate. I've been to the place once already, and now I know where it is on the map. All I need to do is hop back in there, grab the kid, and pull him out.'

Stronge rose from her chair. 'Are you mental? They'll be watching him like a hawk. There's no way it'll be that easy.'

'Sure it will. Once I'm inside, all I have to do is ghost through a few walls until I find out where they're keeping him. Anyone who gets in my way gets possessed.' I pinched an inch of air between my forefinger and thumb. 'There's just one teensy problem…'

'What?'

'I still can't translocate. Or possess people.'

Stronge collapsed back in her chair, which squealed in complaint. 'Fuck sake, Fletcher.'

'Easy, girl,' I replied. 'It's all in hand...'

Wiggling my fingers theatrically I firmed up my mitt, grabbed the cord of Stronge's phone, and dragged it across the desk. With some difficulty—disguised by practiced nonchalance—I punched in the number for Legerdomain and put Jazz Hands on speakerphone.

'This better be good, Fletcher,' she barked. 'Have you seen the news, for Chrissakes? Dragons buzzing the city! What's next, the sky raining blood?'

Apparently I was lost in that maze again, searching for Jazz's gooey centre.

'Yeah, I saw the news,' I replied. 'That's why I'm calling, to get your help putting the kibosh on it.'

'I see. And how am I meant to do that exactly?'

'That project you were working on... how's it coming along?'

She let forth a withering sigh. 'I assume you're referring to my ongoing research into the soul bond?'

I was. I needed her to reverse it, to unfuse me from Frank, to fix my busted powers so I could creep back into the Unseelie Court and get the kid back.

Jazz continued. 'With a few modifications and a little divine providence, I believe I can adapt the Rite of Sequester in such a way that it can be used to affect the bond connecting you to Frank.'

'Really? And that would give me my powers back?'

'I believe so.'

'No shit? Translocation and possession? The whole shooting match?'

'Yes.'

I gave Frank a spirited high-five and hooted in triumph. Across the desk, Stronge seemed less enthusiastic, as though her cop instincts told her the news was too good to be true. It turned out her instincts were right, because Jazz wasn't even half done.

'Before you go celebrating, you should know there is a drawback to the procedure. A rather sizeable one. Once it's done, you and Frank will no longer be separate entities.'

It took a second to register what she was telling me. 'You what?'

'Unfortunately, the Rite of Sequester cannot be used to loosen your bond. In order to do what you ask, I would have to reverse its effect. In essence, strengthen it. Doing so will restore your powers, but it will come at a price: instead of being individuals, you will combine to become a single entity.'

Frank let out a marble-mouthed cry of discontent. I was equally put out, but remained a tad more stoic.

'That can't be right, Jazz.'

'I assure you it can. While I was hoping to displace the bond's effect and sever the link you share, further experiments have taught me that this won't work.'

I tried not to think about what those experiments involved and concentrated on the core issue.

'So I'd be bonded with Frank forever? Is that what you're telling me?'

'Yes, but probably not in the way you have in mind. You see, you wouldn't bond to Frank in the sense that you're used to, with you occupying his physical body. Frank would merge with you.'

Again, it took a moment.

Kat craned her head to the speakerphone. 'Detective Stronge here. Am I hearing this right? Are you saying Frank would become part of Fletcher?'

'Yes,' Jazz replied.

'Then what happens to Frank's body?'

'It will go back to the way it was before it was magicked out of the ground. It will become a cadaver. Coffin fodder.'

'Noooo bodyyyy?' Frank moaned.

I jumped in. 'I don't get it. So long as you're talking about slapping us together like some Fletcher & Fletcher sandwich, why not do it the other way around? Make it so I merge with Frank and get my body back.'

Jazz scoffed. 'You're talking about permanently returning a soul to its physical form. There's a name for that, my lad, and it's resurrection. I may know a few tricks, but I can't raise Lazarus.'

I took her point. If it was that easy to bring back the dead, this planet would be even more overrun than it already was. Besides, the name of the game was getting into the Unseelie Court; how was I meant to translocate if I was anchored to a corporeal form?

Stronge was on her feet and pacing now. 'Tell me you aren't seriously considering this, Fletcher. Frank's his own man. He's one of us. And you want to just get rid of him?'

'That's not what this is about,' I explained. 'Jazz is talking about a merger. Frank would be around still, but he'd be part of me. We'd be part of each other.'

'It pains me to say it, but he's right,' said the voice on the other end of the line. 'Frank won't be gone, he'll be subsumed. He'll become part of a unified whole.'

'You're a unified hole,' Stronge snapped. 'I'm sorry, that was uncalled for...'

'Your frustration is perfectly understandable,' Jazz assured her. 'Trust me, I have no love for the method I'm proposing, but given the gravity of our situation I believe it to be necessary. Remember, Frank will still be with us, and there's a big positive here worth considering...'

'What's that?' I cut in.

'Frank's sage presence can only serve to make your personality less insufferable.'

'Yup. Cheers for that.'

'You're welcome. So what's it to be, Fletcher? Are we doing this? Shall I go ahead and prepare the rite?'

There followed a blanket of quiet as the three of us in Stronge's office sat wrapped in thought. The whole time Frank's eyes stayed glued to mine, though I couldn't be sure what was going on behind them. Finally he nodded.

I broke the silence.

'We're on our way to you now,' I told Jazz.

And hung up the phone.

CHAPTER FIFTY-THREE: PAINTING THE TOWN RED

IT WAS a long walk to Legerdomain, or at least it felt that way. The sun had reached its zenith and rolled back over the rooftops, leaving the city swallowed by night. The hustle and bustle of the day was over and the evening not yet begun, giving way to a void, a silence that begged for introspection.

The phone call with Jazz Hands had landed like a bombshell. Her proposition came with a huge ask, but it had to happen, right? The fae needed to be stopped. As undesirable as the solution was, surely it was worth it to put an end to the lunacy and save the city? I just had to make sure Frank was definitely on-board with the arrangement—that he fully understood the terms and conditions—but when I turned to him, the answer was already upon his lips.

'Weee doo iiit.'

'We should at least have a proper conversation about this.'

He shook his head and repeated his assertion. 'Weee. Doo. Iiit.'

Was he right? Was this the only way? A crisis as grave as the one we were in always demanded a sacrifice. Then again, was this really even a sacrifice? Frank wasn't going anywhere; Jazz wasn't talking about putting a pillow over his face, she was only proposing to put him back where he belonged. Back with me. Back where he began.

Plus there were other factors that made Jazz's proposition sound like the right choice. Things I didn't much like to admit but were no less true for my denial. The fact was, Frank slowed me down. Not always, but sometimes. If I was honest with myself, there were days I felt like I was carrying the feller, correcting his mistakes, tidying up after him. Frank provided some handy muscle—no doubt about that —but was I really better off having him shambling around in my footsteps? Maybe this change was for the best. Maybe I'd be better off with him inside my head instead of being out there, running amok. Given the circumstances, anyway.

And yet…

'We can't do it, Frank. It's not fair. Why should you get the wrong end of the shitty stick?'

'Muuust dooo,' he replied, his voice creaking even more than usual.

I stopped walking and Frank did likewise. Just because he was willing to accept his fate, didn't mean I had to. Frank was more than some dried-up chrysalis I shed when my soul soared free. He was his own person. He should have his own body. His own mind.

'I don't wanna go back to being a one-man show, Frank. I like having you around.'

It wasn't just that I'd gotten used to Frank sitting across the desk from me; I needed him. He was my best friend. No, he was more than that. They say blood is thicker than water, and Frank had mine running through his veins. My actual blood. That made him family. Okay, a weird kind of family, but still, I couldn't give up on him. Not like this.

Frank gave me a lopsided grin and made a sloppy OK sign. 'S'all-riiight,' he slurred.

I felt a prickle in my eyes. The noble bastard had me blubbing. 'You don't get it, Frank. You're the best of me. I need you by my side.'

But he wasn't having it. Frank was determined to do the right thing. Determined to sacrifice himself for the greater good. And being prepared to so that only proved my point.

'Sorry, Frank, but you're too good to be living inside of this skull.'

Seeing as I no longer had my mobile, I found a payphone (one of those poncy WiFi kiosks they rolled out recently that mostly get used by drug dealers), tapped in the number for Legerdomain, and got Jazz on the blower.

'Forget about the rite,' I told her. 'We'll find another way to get the kid back.'

I swear I could hear the smile in her voice. 'Whatever you say, Jake.'

Was that the first time she'd called me by my first name? I wasn't sure. At that moment, I wasn't sure of much at all.

'Whaaaat nowwww?' asked Frank.

It was a reasonable question, but one I wasn't really qualified to answer. Try as I might, I had no idea how we were going to bust the Arcadian out of the Unseelie Court without my being able to translocate there.

One thing I did know, though: Frank looked a fucking state. There were so many holes in his outfit that he resembled a scarecrow coming apart at the seams, and the wounds beneath the shredded fabric weren't going to heal by themselves. He needed fixing up, and since there was a plate of cow brains in the kitchen fridge that would do the job nicely, that meant a trip to the office.

We were on the home stretch to the engine room when Frank was accosted by a man on the street. Burst capillaries spidered his cheeks, and one of his eyes was hooded by a drooping lid that hung low and loose. He wore a Parka mended with electrical tape, hood up, fake fur trim caked with filth.

'Sorry to bother you, guv,' he said. 'I missed me train home and I don't have enough money for another ticket. A fiver's all I need—I'll pay you back if you text me your bank number.'

He thrust out a grubby mitt and arranged his mouth into a big brown smile.

I've always had a soft spot for the homeless. I'll knock them a couple of quid no matter how rough around the edges their hard-luck stories are, and this one was rougher than a kitten's tongue.

I nodded to Frank and he fished around in his pocket for some loose change.

'Bless you,' said the man, accepting the donation. 'But you can keep it, Cookie.' The last part was delivered in a Southern drawl and aimed my way.

'Shift?'

'The very same.'

Frank was equal parts shocked and delighted.

'What are you playing at?'

'I'm working,' Shift replied. 'See that restaurant across the street with the couple eating together? His wife hired me to make sure the woman he's with is there to talk business and nothing else.'

'What about the office job? What about Alan?'

'He's for the daytime. By night I'm this guy.'

It was a smart ruse. A rough sleeper asking for change is pretty much invisible in this town. The perfect cover for a snooper.

'I've gotta hand it to you, Shift, you keep yourself busy.'

The bloke in the restaurant reached under the table and placed a hand on his companion's bare knee.

Shift groaned. 'Ugh. What is it with married men and their secretaries? This is gonna break that poor woman's heart...'

He pulled out his phone and took aim at the restaurant window. He was busy snapping incriminating pictures when the device started chirping.

'Boy, I am popular tonight,' he said, answering the call.

There followed a conversation that I was only privy to one side of.

'Hey... Oh yeah? Where?... Seriously?... Well, then get the hell out of there... Yeah, thanks for letting me know... Okay, bye.'

He hung up wearing a haunted look.

'What's the scuttlebutt, Shift?'

'The *Scuttlebutt*? You really are a fossil, Fletcher.'

'The gossip, then. The buzz. Whatever you want to call it.'

Shift lowered his voice. 'I just got word from the grapevine that some weirdos crashed a local bar. You should check it out.'

'Weirdos? There's an old man outside the station who wears a nappy and dances to techno all day. This is Camden.'

'You don't get it. These were a different flavour of weirdo. The Uncanny kind.'

'And what makes you think I have time for a side quest right now?'

'Because these weirdos had blue skin. The ones who didn't have fangs, anyway.'

Frank gave me a wide-eyed look. Arcadians and Vengari drinking together? That couldn't be good.

'We'd better check it out,' I told Shift. 'You gonna go like that or do you want to change first?'

He laughed. 'What do I look like to you: Seal Team Six? I'm a snitch, Fletcher, not a soldier.'

'Are you serious? You're not gonna back us up?'

'Damn right I'm not. I wish you and Frank all the best, but you're on your own.'

It wasn't long after we ditched Shift's cowardly arse that Frank and me were moving in on the Black Heart, a tucked-away boozer hidden down a quiet side street not far from Camden Underground. Only tonight, the Heart was anything but quiet. Spilling out of the pub arm-in-arm were a gang of Hooray Henries, except these roaring poshos weren't the kind I was used to, these were Arcadians, and with them, equally mullered, a crowd of crooked albinos with wire hangers for bodies.

As promised, the fae had taken leave of their sanctuary and braved the smog for a night on the town, and they'd brought the Vengari with them. There they were, brothers-in-arms, all fired up on the impending nuptials and the pact that came with it. There was no makeup or magic to disguise this monster mash; the players were out in the open, plain as you like. No doubt a night of Bacchanalian revelry lay ahead; who knew how much damage the pricks would do before they sobered up?

One of the Arcadians, who I recognised as being part of the team that escorted Frank and me from our jail cell and into the heart of the Unseelie Court, caught wind of us.

'Well, look who it is,' he slurred, tilting forward as if he was leaning into a stiff wind. 'Fletcher and Fletcher. Tell us, which of you is the top and which is the bottom?'

One of the Vengari cackled and joined the pile-on. 'They say sodomites end up with men who look like them, but this is ridiculous.'

Yeah. Funny as cot death, these pricks.

We squared up to the mob. 'Have you lot got any idea what you're doing? Do you even know what the Accord is? You're throwing the whole balance out of whack, you bell-ends.'

A Vengari burped acid in my face. 'Didn't you hear, Detective? Forget about balance. The whole world is about to change.'

An effete fae slung an arm around the vampire's shoulder. 'He's right. The wedding is at midnight. Soon the Court will ring with the bells of matrimony.'

'The age of man is over,' hissed the Vengari. 'See for yourself…'

He aimed a finger at the pub window. It was dark inside—the Black Heart was that kind of boozer—but I could just about make out some people moving around. Nothing seemed out of the ordinary at first, not until I put my face through the glass to get a better look and saw that it wasn't people in there but ghosts. The realisation of what I was witnessing sent a wave of dread all the way to the pit of my stomach. Dead bodies littered the pub floor, a half dozen or more, leaving behind pale wailing figures that drifted about, unnerved and untethered. Together, the vampires and the fae had murdered every last punter in the place.

'What did you do?' I said, though the question mark was purely for decoration.

One of the Vengari showed that he'd taken his pint to go, and raised a glass sloshing with blood. 'Cheers!' he crowed, knocking back a hearty belt of the red stuff.

Thank Christ it was only the middle of the week. A handful of regulars had met a sorry end, plus the barmaid who'd been topping them up, but it could have been so much worse. Had it been the weekend, the place would have been a charnel house.

The Vengari polished off his pint and bared his fangs at me. 'The city is ours, ghost. Now step aside and make way for the new order.'

'Over my dead body.'

Frank got the message. Lurching into action, he placed a hand on the vampire's hollowed-out sternum and gave him a shove that sent him reeling.

One of his Vengari brothers propped him back up. 'You're going to regret that,' he said, his teeth sharpening.

But I didn't, mainly thanks to Frank, who chinned the bloke hard enough to send his oversized canines flying down his throat.

Then it all kicked off.

A drunken Arcadian threw himself at us, arms windmilling madly. Frank turned him into a big blue bowling pin, but after that, the mob was on us like stink on shit. Suddenly—I'm not sure how—I was down on the ground, buried by an onslaught of feet and fists. Frank stayed up a little longer than I did, but was soon on his back, laid low by a fierce drubbing.

My vision began to tunnel and the spots in my eyes coalesced into a single white blob. Was this it? Was this the fabled light at the end of the tunnel? Had I been forgiven for my sins? Was I finally going to the Promised Land?

The white light hovered there, begging for my approach, imploring me to step through it and come home. But I knew it was a trick. Heaven wasn't ready for Jake Fletcher. Not yet. This wasn't going home, it was giving up. The tunnel that light burned through wasn't a portal to a better place, it was the hole of a guillotine, and the second I stuck my neck through it, the blade would come crashing down. So I stepped away from the light and swam off in the opposite direction, back to the real world, back to the drubbing.

What I saw next came in blurry snatches...

A blue head went scudding through the air, detached from its body.

A weapon moving too fast for me to identify pulped the brains of a too-slow Vengari, leaving him boss-eyed and certifiably dead.

An Arcadian's legs were swept out from under him and his head punched with such ferocity that it separated his jaw from the rest of his skull.

There was more murder after that. Lots more. So much murder.

Soon the only member of the fae/Vengari pack left standing was the showboating vamp who'd waggled his pint of blood at us. He didn't last long. Before he knew what hit him, he was lying belly-down on the ground between Frank and me, clawing at a slit throat. That was until his assailant arrived and finished him off with a kerb stomp that painted the tarmac in a great gushing wash of red.

It was just me and Frank left now. Me, my partner, and the person who'd single-handedly annihilated a whole squad of Uncannies. I rolled over to greet our saviour.

'Hello, boys,' said Erin Banks. 'Did you miss me?'

CHAPTER FIFTY-FOUR: FRIENDS IN LOW PLACES

WHAT DID it take to put this woman down? How was it that the same universe that saw me pushed under a train for no good reason kept rewarding this cold-blooded murderer?

Battered and bloody but not out of fight, Frank struggled to his feet and put himself between me and the assassin.

'Chill your boots, Igor,' said Erin, 'I'm not here to start any aggro.' She cast a look at the puddle of blood and splintered bones at her feet. 'Well, not much.'

'What do you want?' I said, pushing myself upright, my vision still spitting stars.

'Good question,' she replied. 'If you'd asked me that a few hours ago I'd have said it was your soul fed through a shredder and your mate's head on the end of my knife. Since then, I've mellowed a bit.'

I spat some ectoplasmic blood into the gutter and ran my tongue over my teeth to check they were still there. 'Why the change of heart?' I asked.

'After you ran me over in a car, you mean? Oh, it didn't happen right away, I can tell you that. Not until I healed up, turned on the news, and saw blue Smaug doing fucking loop-the-loops.'

'Why would you care about that?'

'I don't if I'm honest. Not a big fan of London. No elbow room and the whole place smells of piss.'

'Then why get involved?'

'Because whatever happens here won't end inside the M25, and that bullshit right there…' she pointed through the pub window at the ghosts of the dead, who were already starting to vanish to the other side thanks to Erin wiping out their murderers, '…that cannot be allowed to stand.'

Frank relaxed and so did I. Erin wasn't here to kill us. The question was, what was she here for?

'I have friends,' she went on. 'Family. People who aren't part of this world. So I'm not having monsters strutting down the street like they own the place.'

'I'm sorry,' I said, holding up a hand. 'I'm stuck on the idea of you having friends.'

Frank gave a little gurgle that I recognised as a laugh.

'Keep it up and see what happens,' Erin growled, aiming the tip of her knife at his groin. Catching herself, she sucked down a long calming breath, sighed, and lowered the weapon. 'Look what you did, getting me all worked up again.' She wagged her finger playfully. 'I already told you guys I'm not here to fight.'

'Right. So you're not angry at us for running you down with a hearse?'

'Water under the bridge, lads. Totally over it.'

'Really?'

She punched me in the face. Hard.

'Okay, now I'm over it.'

Frank went to retaliate but I called him off. 'What do you want, Erin?'

'I want to work with you,' she said. 'To help you nip this in the bud.'

I rubbed my nose. 'Thanks for the offer but it's all in hand.'

It wasn't, obviously, but the situation was serious enough without throwing petrol on the fire.

Erin gave us a bitchy smirk. 'With all due respect, this isn't a bunch of schoolgirls fighting over a handbag. If you really want to clean house, you need me.'

'We've been doing all right so far,' I said.

Erin's eyes slid over us slowly, taking in each bruise, each cut. 'Sure. You're really sticking it to the big boys.'

I cast a look to the ground, to the blood running down the gutter, to the mess she'd made of our attackers while we were busy getting our heads kicked in. Erin was right. She was a wild card, but she was the only weapon we had against the enemies arrayed before us. Frank and I could ruffle some feathers, but Erin was the real deal. With her help we could drive a wedge into this union and send the fae packing.

'I know where the Arcadians are hiding.'

Erin smiled. 'Look at you, pulling your weight. Go on then, where is it? A gingerbread house? Some enchanted dimension you get to through a ring of magic mushrooms?'

'Nooo,' said Frank. 'In ciiiity. Undergrooound.'

'He speaks!' said Erin, taken by surprise. 'So what are we talking, franken-man? Concealed doorway, heavily guarded, tight as a gnat's fanny?'

Answering this one was going to take more words than Frank knew, so I picked up the slack.

'The fae have taken over a disused tunnel system. The way in is gated but not invisible. It's big enough to drive a car through and hiding in plain sight. Honestly, I don't think the fae are all that worried about being found. They know we're not a threat to them.'

Erin cackled. 'They haven't met me yet.'

A quick look at the diced-up corpses on the ground reaffirmed Erin's worth.

'So then,' she said, a wicked glint in her eye, 'where is it exactly? Where's this rabbit warren of theirs?'

'Before we get to the nitty-gritty, we need to lay out some ground rules.'

Erin cocked a hip. 'Not really one for rules, boys.'

'Then it looks like we won't be working together after all.'

She looked to my partner to see if he felt the same way and was met by a resolute nod.

'Fine,' she said, shrugging her tattooed shoulders. 'What did you have in mind?'

'I need you to cancel your contract on the kid.'

'His Lordship? What are you talking about? I'm here to wipe out the Arcadians; why would I want to leave one alive?'

'Because your client hired you under false pretences. The kid didn't kill Tali. Doesn't that mean anything to you?'

'Nope. I don't get hung up on the details. Show me a target and I'll show you a dead body, that's the deal.'

'Not this time. This is a deal-breaker. Either you cancel the contract or we're done.'

Erin toyed with her knife, balancing it on the tip of her index finger and turning it like a fidget spinner. 'You realise I could just torture you until you tell me where the fae are hiding, right?'

'I do.'

She jiggled her foot while she weighed up her options. Eventually she said, 'Fine. As a show of good faith I'll cancel the contract. Might as well cut my losses on that job anyway since I don't know where Tali disappeared to.' She caught the knife by its hilt, stopping it mid-spin. 'But there's one condition: you have to make sure that little pixie evaporates. I hear about another big blue invasion and it's you two I'll come looking for. Got it?'

'Got it.'

'Gottt iiiit,' Frank agreed.

'All right then.' She pulled aside a flap of her leather jacket and slid the knife into a concealed sheath.

'So, your morals…' I said, 'pretty fluid, huh?'

She threw back her head and laughed. 'Mate, you have *no* idea.'

We shared the location of the Unseelie Court and went about prepping our mission: crashing the wedding and giving the Arcadians their marching orders. According to what we'd learned from the drunk fae lying at our feet, we only had a few hours left before the bells were set to toll, so I suggested we use that time productively and get tooled up.

'First thing we need to do is stop by my friend's place,' I said, steering us in the direction of Legerdomain.

'Oh yeah? What friend's that?' asked Erin.

'Jaaazz haaaaands,' said Frank.

'Did I hear that right? Did Death Breath just say your mate's name is *Jazz Hands*?'

'Yeah. I call her that on account of her having the old spirit fingers.' I gave my digits a wiggle, laying on some imaginary hoodoo.

Erin offered a derisory snort and rolled up a sleeve to show off her tattoos, which pulsed with the power infernal. 'Magic we've got. If we're going to wipe out an Uncanny army we need another kind of weapon.'

'What did you have in mind?' I asked.

She returned a smile as jagged and red as a teacher's tick. 'That hearse of yours... is it still running?'

CHAPTER FIFTY-FIVE: PIT STOP

UNDER ERIN'S INSTRUCTION, we took the company car to a mechanic for what she described as, "A little tune-up". What that entailed I had no idea, but I knew one thing for sure: the under-the-arches garage she took us to was bent as a nine bob note. It was obvious from the disassembled car components lying all over the gaff that this was a chop shop, a place where stolen motors were stripped down and sold for parts.

'What exactly are we doing here?' I asked.

I was just as confused as Frank by all this, and it wasn't my job to be as confused as Frank.

'I told you, a little mod to the motor,' Erin replied.

'Why, though? How's this going to help us break into the Unseelie Court?'

'You said it yourself, Casper: the way into the place is big enough to drive a car through.' She slapped the hearse's bonnet. 'This is the car.'

Frank laughed.

'See, even he thinks that's a joke. Tell me that's a joke.'

Erin shook her head. 'In case you didn't work it out already, I like the sledgehammer approach. No mucking about. Blow the bloody doors off and get the job done.'

It sounded mental—it was mental—but since we couldn't exactly stealth our way inside, a full-frontal attack was pretty much the only option we had. The stretch of tunnel that led from the gated entrance to the throne room was big enough to accommodate a car, and yet a question still lingered: how was driving a motor in there going to improve our chances against the wedding party?

Stepping in from a side office came the owner of the garage, a hairy-handed knuckle-dragger with a primate stoop and leathery skin the colour of something you'd dig out of your nose.

'There he is,' said Erin. giving the ogre a friendly dig in the shoulder. 'Fletchers, say hello to Terry, the best mechanic this side of the river.'

'*Either* side,' Terry corrected in a voice like a rolling boulder. 'Didn't you hear? Danny in Camberwell got his head bitten off by a werebadger.'

'Sorry to hear that,' said Erin.

The ogre shrugged. 'It happens.'

He sloped over to the hearse, spat in his palms, and rubbed his hands together. 'Right then, let's get a look up her skirt…'

Rather than using the pit to get underneath the vehicle, he reached down, grabbed a load-bearing part of the undercarriage, and heaved the hearse up on two wheels.

'Bit battered, but I can work with this,' he said, stroking his chin with his free hand.

'Sorry, can I butt in?' I said, raising a finger. 'What exactly are you doing to my car?'

The ogre set the hearse back down. 'Well, I'm not here to rotate your tyres, I'll say that much.'

'Okay,' I said, growing tired of the secrecy. 'So what then?'

Erin sighed. 'You *really* hate a mystery, don't you?'

'I'm a detective, so yeah.'

'Just roll with it this once, will you? I promise the surprise will be worth the wait.'

While Terry went about his job, Erin steered us from the main part of the garage and into a side room: an all-in-one kitchen/toilet. The space was cramped, filthy, and plastered with ogre porn. Frank ogled the display, eyes bulging from his head like a pair of doorknobs.

'See anything you like, big boy?' asked Erin.

'Can we change the subject, please?' I suggested.

'Fine.' She popped on the kettle and brewed herself a cuppa. 'Let's talk about how you cancelled my tattoos back at your office.'

I supposed it beat discussing ogre porn. 'Paid your boss a visit,' I explained. 'Pinched it off at the source.'

She sucked in a whistle. 'Oh dear. That's you on the Long Man's shit list.'

'About that: would you mind putting in a good word for me there? Help me smooth things over?'

She took a sip of her tea. 'Maybe. Maybe not.'

'Thanks a million.'

'Don't get snippy with me, Spooky. If you'd let me kill His Lordship before the fae snatched him back, we wouldn't be in this mess.'

Eventually, the ogre swung open the door.

'All done.'

We followed him back into the garage, where I gave the hearse a once-over. I had to circle around to the front end of the thing before I figured out what was different.

'So that's what this was all about.'

Frank grinned. 'Gooooood.'

'Pretty sweet, eh?' said Erin.

'You were right,' I admitted. 'It was worth the wait.' I crouched down and gave the modifications a closer inspection. 'And you're sure these are going to work?'

'No idea,' she replied, 'but it's going to be a lot of fun finding out.'

Erin Banks wasn't petrol on a fire. She *was* the fire.

'All right then,' I said, merging with Frank. 'Let's fire this thing up, get into that lair, and James Herbert those pricks.'

'Now we're talking,' said Erin. 'Go on then. Get your purse out and pay the man.'

I felt a tap on the shoulder and turned around to see Terry the ogre presenting me with an open palm the size of a lowland gorilla's.

WITH ERIN RIDING SHOTGUN, I drove the modded hearse from the garage and headed for Kentish Town to pick up Stronge. It wasn't until she stepped into the back of the motor that she realised who I had in the passenger seat.

'You!'

She reached for her hip but I turned and slapped Frank's hand on hers.

'Keep your hair on, Kat. She's with us.'

'Are you forgetting this woman attacked me? That she tried to kill you?'

Erin swivelled in her seat and gave Stronge a shit-eating grin. 'Mad, right?'

'Erin's had a change of heart,' I explained. 'She's not after us now, she's after the bad guys.'

'Oh, that's fine then,' said Stronge, feigning relief. 'Never mind that she's a hired killer, she's had a change of heart. I feel safer already.'

'If this is about me clobbering you over the head that time, I'm sorry,' said Erin. 'At least I left you alive, though. That was pretty cool of me.'

Stronge stared daggers at her.

Erin turned to me. 'Well, this clearly isn't going to work.'

'It has to work,' I said. 'You know what we're going up against here. We need all hands on deck.'

I turned my attention to Stronge. 'Look, Kat, I know she's a bit of a handful, but—'

'*A handful?* I'm not having her be any part of this, do you understand? I'm the law. I know that doesn't mean much in this world of yours, but it's enough to stop me buddying up with an assassin.'

'Ordinarily, I'd agree with you, Kat, but we need her. Frank and me aren't gonna do the soul bond thing, so I can't be ghosting in there and pulling the kid out.'

Stronge squinted at me. 'Why are you making that face? Are you about to say something really fucking stupid?'

'The only way we're going to rescue the kid is by busting into the Unseelie Court and cracking some heads.'

'There it is.'

She placed her head in her hands and kneaded her temples vigorously.

I put on my best teacher voice: calm and soothing but direct and weighty. 'The wedding's at midnight, and if this marriage goes ahead, the Accord is done for.'

The upcoming union was already messing with the city's delicate ecosystem. If the ceremony took place, the Uncanny Kingdom and the regular UK would no longer overlap invisibly, they'd clash together like a couple of cymbals. Magic would reign and the world would be turned upside down.

'We've got one shot,' I went on. 'If we don't stop this wedding it'll be silly season out there. Total anarchy. There'll be rioting on the streets before the sun comes up and magic on every TV station. You okay with that?'

'Of course not,' Stronge shot back, 'but there has to be some way of stopping all that happening without blowing up a wedding.'

'Wise up, girl,' said Erin. 'This isn't a wedding, it's the Thunder-dome. We do whatever needs doing to stop shit falling apart.'

'If there was any other way, Kat. Any way at all...'

Stronge wrung her hands like a Homeric widow. 'Fine. But I'll have my eye on this lunatic the whole time.' She shot Erin an icy glare. 'You hear me? You do anything I don't like in there and you'll have me to deal with. Understood?'

Erin just about managed to keep her smile in check, which was pretty sporting given that she could have murdered the detective in about a thousand different ways.

'Deal. Now can we go kick some dick, please?'

Inside my head, Frank voiced an enthusiastic, *Yeees*.

I fired up the engine, gripped the steering wheel, and slipped the car in gear.

Erin drummed her hands on the dashboard and foghorned like a boxing announcer, 'Leeet's get ready to nuptial!'

CHAPTER FIFTY-SIX: SCHLOCK AND AWE

WE SAT in the hearse facing the old train station, an onslaught of bullet-sized raindrops battering the windshield and smudging the pinpricks of distant streetlights.

Were we really going to do this? Were the four of us seriously about to drive into a fae lair and crash smack bang into the middle of an Uncanny congregation? Surely that was insane. Then again, what was that old saying?: *No risk = no reward*. And yet there was another saying, wasn't there, one that rang truer to me: *The top of Mount Everest is littered with the bodies of people who took risks.*

But what choice did we have? The day was nearly done and the sound of wedding bells was all but in our ears. If we had even the slightest chance of dropping some bleach in this cesspool, we had to take it.

'I'd like to state for the record that I think this is a terrible idea,' said DCI Stronge.

'Noted,' I replied.

She was right, though. As far as good ideas went, this was up there with tossing a fistful of coins into the turbine of a plane for good luck.

Still...

'We ready?' I asked.

Stronge nodded back grimly. Inside my head, Frank answered in the affirmative. The only person who seemed to really be on board with the plan was Erin (not just on board, but giddy).

'What are you waiting for?' she said, punching the roof of the car. 'Let's go, fuckos.'

I gunned the engine, revved her up, and popped the stick in first. The car carved a sudden s-shaped path as we lurched forward, then we were off, wipers frantically scraping aside the never-ending sheet of water that bore down upon us.

The bumper took down a chain link fence as we steamed down a grass verge and barrelled towards the padlocked gate of the fae lair. There was an ear-splitting bang of metal on metal as the gate was flattened under the front end of the hearse and delivered out of the back. The dashboard lit up with every warning light imaginable, but the old girl kept going (they *really* knew how to build a motor back in the day).

Beyond the entrance was a second layer of security: a pack of soldiers standing guard at the gate. Since they were busy playing cards when we arrived, they didn't present us with much resistance and were sent bouncing over the roof of the car in rapid succession. That's what you get for shirking your duties. That said, it's hard to imagine what they would have done to stop us even if they were alert at the time. We wanted in and we were bloody well getting in.

Further down the tunnel we sped, threading the needle, the acoustics of the shaft multiplying the din of the engine and turning it into a war cry. Blue torches flashed by us in a dizzying blur until we hit a puddle of standing water and I lost control of the wheel. The hearse went hydroplaning across the last stretch of the tunnel, through the giant tree root gates, and into the throne room.

In a flash, we skated down a central aisle flanked by pews of attendants, hit the rim of the oubliette like a ramp, and went crashing into a wedding altar. I heard a blue-skinned man with a fancy collar utter, 'Does anyone have any objections?' before I slammed on the brakes and the hearse ground to a halt with him plaited around the axle.

Folks in fancy clobber went scrambling every which way, except for the groom, who punched the air in triumph and gave a celebratory whoop. 'Go, Jake!'

The Vengari bride tore off her veil and screamed, revealing a face even a mother couldn't love.

Surrounded by a panicked throng of wedding-goers both Vengari and Arcadian, the fae king roared with such anger that his bramble crown was thrown from his head, revealing a shiny blue pate underneath.

By his side, though not shrinking one bit, the fae Queen shot me a stare so chilling it glued my tongue to the roof of my mouth. Her husband was all bark and no bite, but this bitch had teeth enough for two.

'I want their heads decorating my bed posts,' she cried, swishing her cloak behind her like a pantomime witch.

With the initial shock of our arrival over, the crowd of attendees —a mismatched assemblage of foppish fae courtiers and Vengari plebs—began to surround the car, closing in like a tide of encroaching lava.

Stronge piped up from the back seat. 'We're going to die now, aren't we?'

'Let's call that Plan B,' I replied.

I switched on the high beams, which were protected by solid steel baskets and operating with brand new bulbs. High wattage ultraviolet bulbs.

'Let's get this party lit,' cried Erin, closing a hand around the passenger side grab handle and gritting her teeth.

'How long have you been sitting on that?' I asked.

'Pretty much since we left the garage.'

'I figured.'

Making use of some skills I learned pulling doughnuts in a supermarket car park at the wheel of a nicked Ford Fiesta, I put the steering on full lock, set the handbrake, and floored the accelerator. The back end of the car kicked out with a rowdy screech as the hearse spun in a circle, pressing me into the driver's door and sending Stronge sliding across the back seat. Around and around we went, the UV headlights lancing across the chamber like deadly laserbeams. Deadly to the Vengari, anyway. Through a cloud of burned rubber, I watched the beams cut through the bride's side of the congregation, ashing at least a dozen of the knife-elbowed albino bastards.

It was, putting it mildly, metal as fuck.

The remaining few Vengari knew better than to stick around for more of that. Cutting their losses, the sinuous figures plucked the bride to safety, taking off through the pale blue gloom of the entrance tunnel and vanishing into the night. The marriage was well and truly annulled.

The kid cheered again, tearing off his suit jacket and whirling it around his head like a lasso. That's until a muscular mass of tree roots snaked down from the roof and took hold of his limbs, hoisting him into the air and holding him there like a malfunctioning marionette.

Draven had arrived, accompanied by a retinue of footsoldiers, a couple of dozen at least. Around his open hand swooped a cascade of shimmering green magic. He closed his hand into a fist and the tree roots tightened their grip on the prince, making him cry out in pain.

'Enough,' commanded the Queen, stopping her lieutenant before he did something to her son that couldn't be undone.

The kid was in a bind—a literal one—and it was up to us to get him out of it. All we had to do was fight our way through a mob of superpowered Arcadians. Simple as that.

'Kill them all and make a mess doing it,' said Draven, spurring his soldiers into action.

The fae hopped to it, drawing their blades and marching towards the hearse. I tried the engine again but it wouldn't start.

'What now?' asked Stronge, watching the soldiers close in, eyes bulging with panic.

'Honestly, this is about as far ahead as I thought,' I said.

Erin drew her knife and popped the passenger door. 'Don't worry, kiddiewinks, this one's on me.'

Black static sparked from her tattoos as she jettisoned from the car and into the impending throng.

The first Arcadian who got in Erin's way received a blade to the neck that passed through him so cleanly that, if she hadn't followed up with a stab to the belly, might not have been noticed until he bent over to tie up his shoelaces and his head rolled off. After that it was ruddy-tinted carnage. Erin went at those poor bastards like a combine harvester through a wheat field, killing in numbers, laying them down.

Blood fountained from necks.

Fresh stumps ran like taps.

The air turned wet with red rain.

I quickly lost count of the amount of fae Erin had whittled her way through. We were facing an unbeatable force one minute and looking at the aftermath of a massacre the next. But Draven had insulated himself from her wrath, hiding behind his soldiers and summoning forth another mass of tree roots that fastened around Erin's neck and left her dangling. Black ribbons sprang from the assassin's tattoos and attempted to worm themselves beneath the creaking wooden bonds, but the hanging continued until Erin's tongue was swollen and poking out from a twisted mouth.

It was our turn to step into the breach. Stronge exited the car and I did the same, still wearing Frank's body. The remaining soldiers, seven of them in total, were there to greet us. Stronge unholstered her Taser and took aim at the nearest. The gun looked ridiculous, this stubby little thing made of yellow plastic, a kid's toy in a child's hand. The fact that Stronge was shaking like a wet chihuahua didn't exactly add to the menace.

'Don't make me use this,' she said, flicking off the safety and tightening a finger around the trigger.

The fae laughed until they were lightheaded, then one of them made a move and Stronge did something that wiped the smiles right off their faces.

Twin probes snagged the soldier in the chest, followed by a burst of electricity delivered down the Taser's connecting wires. Typically, this had the effect of stunning a target, but instead of seizing the fae up, the electricity had sparks flying off him. His skin ripped apart as thermal burns cooked him from the inside out. Blood ran from his nose and his eyeballs burst, turning into runny yolks on his cheeks. Smoke poured out of the craters they left behind, creating a noxious stench that hit me like a hot slap.

'Holy shit,' Stronge cried as the charred remains of the fae hit the floor.

Apparently, that's what happens when an Arcadian gets a fat dose of leccy plugged into his nervous system. In a way, I was glad the Taser didn't have a second shot in it, as I'm not sure my stomach could have handled another poor bastard getting Green Miled.

'Anyone else?' I said, realising the fae weren't to know Stronge didn't have a second round in the chamber.

The remaining soldiers vanished, and I mean that in every sense of the word: turning invisible and flying out the door. And who could blame them? They'd already watched most of their brothers get minced by Erin, and now here they were getting nuked by some other madwoman. This, they collectively agreed, was not what they signed up for when they pledged allegiance to the Unseelie Court. Whatever lay in store for them in the inhospitable world outside, it had to be better than this. Drinking polluted air was surely a step up from being turned into the "After" photo from a PSA about kids who climb pylons to retrieve lost frisbees.

With his soldiers gone, Draven was left playing Billy-no-mates. When he vanished too, I assumed he'd taken his cue from the rest and also given us the Irish goodbye. But no.

'What the f—?' Stronge's face turned into a mask of pain as the hand she was using to hold the Taser folded back on itself, knuckle to wrist. There was a horrible popping sound and the gun clattered to the ground, quickly followed by the detective, who dropped to her knees nursing a busted paw. Draven reappeared by her side, punched her out, and kicked the Taser across the throne room, where it disappeared through the grille of the oubliette.

The remaining members of the wedding party hurrahed Draven's fortitude. The King and Queen saluted their lieutenant's impending victory. It was just me left standing now. Me and Frank. I peeled away from my partner's body, giving us the numbers.

Draven sneered. 'Ah look, the corpse has a shadow. How very frightening.'

He produced a weapon. Not the magical knock-out stick this time—we were way past that—but a sword from the ceremonial scabbard he wore on his hip. I was just starting to wonder how we were going to do battle with a bloke swinging a bloody great chopper when the fae added another layer of complexity to the problem by turning invisible. Frank and I went back-to-back, covering all the angles, hands groping the air in search of a limb, a stray tuft of hair, an eye socket. My body stiffened, stomach tensed, ready to absorb a blow from nowhere.

'You see anything, Frank?'

'Nooo.'

Where had that toe-rag gotten to? I kept my eyes peeled for any odd disturbances, hoping Draven might leave a footprint on the bloodied floor and give himself away like his crony did when he stepped in a puddle of lube at the sex toy warehouse (simpler times). The rest of the fae looked on, holding their breaths in anticipation as they waited for their champion to strike. Time dragged its heels as Frank and I turned in dread circles, expecting a blade to lunge out of the thin blue at any moment. Then I caught sight of something that made the laws of physics look like more of a suggestion than a set of immutable principles.

Pat-pat-pat-pat went a tattoo of rapid footfalls as two invisible feet came charging my way. I had a sliver of a second to defend myself, and I wasted it thinking about the best way to do that. Frank, however, was unencumbered by such intellectual concerns, and threw himself into Draven's path like a Secret Service agent taking a bullet.

It cost him an arm.

The fae's invisible blade chopped the limb through at the elbow and left it lying among the rest of the assorted body parts Erin had left in her wake.

The next thing to happen was a crushing mass of roots punching through the roof of the throne room and bringing down a chunk of masonry that struck Frank in the back and pinned him to the floor.

When Draven turned visible again he was five feet ahead of me, his blade held at full extension, its razor-sharp point tickling my Adam's apple.

'Goodbye, ghost.'

CHAPTER FIFTY-SEVEN: KILLING THE FANTASY

'Wait,' I yelled as Draven raised his blade.

'I think not,' he replied, and took a swing that had "death blow" written all over it.

'Halt,' cried the fae queen, stilling her lieutenant's hand.

'Your Majesty?' said Draven, his blade poised an inch from my throat.

'Need I remind you that we are people of honour,' said the queen. 'If Mister Fletcher wishes to say some final words, allow him that much.'

Draven breathed a frustrated sigh. 'Go on then, human. Spit it out.'

I turned to the queen. 'Actually, I was hoping I could say a quick goodbye to my other half before you send us on our way.'

I nodded to Frank, who lay on the floor trapped and bleeding and feeling every bit of the wounds he'd been dealt.

The queen favoured me with a cold smile. 'Go ahead and say your piece.'

Frank looked up at me with tears in his eyes.

'Well, it looks like this is it, old boy,' I told him, forcing a smile. 'End of the line.'

'Get to the point,' said Draven, prodding the tender flesh of my neck with the tip of his sword.

I dithered a bit, then to Frank I said, 'I'm sorry. I should have put some words aside in case it ever came to this. I always figured I'd think of something in the moment, but now I'm here, the cat's got my *tongue*.'

I placed extra emphasis on that last word, enough that it raised Draven's eyebrow but didn't clue him into the coded message I was sending. The tongue was the clue. I'd witnessed Frank maintain control of the thing even after it was cut out of his head. If he could manage that, it followed that he could do the same with other body parts, say the severed arm lying on the floor behind my would-be executioner.

Sadly, Frank was just as confused by my none-too-subtle hint as Draven was.

I tried again. 'I said, I'm sorry, the cat's got my *tongue*.'

Frank gave me a quizzical look. He wasn't getting it.

Draven scowled and turned to his queen. 'Clearly fear has broken his mind, Your Grace. May I finish him now?'

'Mister Fletcher, I would advise you to say what you mean to say, and quickly.'

I tried again—one last, desperate attempt to get through to my slow-witted partner.

'Tongue, tongue, tongue!'

Finally, he got it. Frank's eyes widened then flicked to his severed arm, which was about six feet in front of him, lying on its back, fingers in the air. The limb was halfway between where Frank was flattened and Draven was standing. Careful not to look directly at the limb and give the game away, I watched from the periphery of my vision and saw its fingers begin to twitch. As suspected, Frank still had control of it. He squinted and strained as he gave the rebel appendage all of his focus, and like a flipped-over turtle trying to right itself, the arm began to rock.

'Enough stalling,' said Draven, and this time his Queen offered no objection. 'On your knees, you piece of human refuse.'

'Kinky,' I replied, giving him the old Cockney wink. 'Should I have brought knee-pads for this?'

Over Draven's shoulder I watched the animated arm gather the momentum it needed to roll onto its front, palm-side down. Using its fingers like spider legs, the limb began a shuffling journey across the floor, slushing through guts and the muck as it slowly crept up on the fae's rear.

Draven gave me another prod and I sank to my knees. The King and Queen looked on eagerly as their lieutenant raised his arm aloft like a prizefighter awaiting the world heavyweight belt. The crowd cheered and jeered.

'Correct me if I'm wrong,' I said, 'but I'm starting to think this isn't going to end in a knighthood.'

Draven laughed. 'Not bad for a walking Halloween costume.'

Frank's arm inched forward some more, gaining a little more ground. I had to keep this up. Had to give Draven the rope he needed to feel big about himself, but not push him so far that he lopped off my noggin.

'Gotta say, this ain't the way I pictured it going down,' I told Draven.

'Is that so? And how exactly did you envision your trespass ending?'

'Well, I reckoned we'd bust in here, kill as many of you as we could, and take off with the fairy prince.' I took a moment to review that sentence in my head. 'You know, it's only when I say that out loud I realise this case took a real turn somewhere down the line.'

Frank's arm was a couple of feet from Draven's heel now and had yet to be detected by any of his admirers, who were too excited by the prospect of my head bouncing off the floor to give their attention to anything else.

'You should never have come here,' said Draven. 'No human could have succeeded against us, least of all a dead one; an old cart horse, put out to pasture.'

I rocked a hand from side to side. 'I don't know. Up until the end there, I reckon I was on a bit of a streak.'

'Indeed. The kind of streak one leaves in his underwear.' He laughed at his own witticism and his adoring crowd joined in.

'Good one,' I conceded. Careful to keep his attention facing my way, I cast a look over my shoulder at the bodies of his fallen men. 'You know, you might not be much at soldiering, but you'd make a lovely court jester.'

A tic took possession of Draven's right eye. 'Are you always this annoying?'

'Not always,' I replied. 'Sometimes I'm much more annoying.'

Draven had tolerated about as much of me as he could. His fingers tightened around the hilt of his sword. 'Your time is up, ghost. For good this time. Give my regards to whatever idiot god spawned you.'

His arm tensed as the blade came up and its mirror-like finish flashed with blue light. The sword was at its apex and about to begin its deadly descent when Draven felt something tugging at the cuff of his britches and whirled about in surprise.

It was all the distraction I needed to grab a fallen sword from the floor. Taking it in both hands, I swung the blade in a half-moon, cleaving through the lieutenant's neck. His eyes went wide as his head left his neck and his decapitated body collapsed to the ground. Bounce, bounce, bounce went Draven's bonce until it came to a stop at the feet of his royal superiors like a glorious hole-in-one shot.

'Maybe *I* should be the court jester,' I quipped, 'because I've got this one rolling in the aisles.'

Classic stuff.

The King was outraged. Well, you would be, wouldn't you?

Draven was dead and so was his magic. The tree roots he'd taken command of immediately went limp and released their holds on Erin and the kid.

The King turned to the remaining wedding-goers. 'What are you waiting for? Kill him!'

Not wishing to further raise the ire of their ruler, the small crowd took up arms and advanced on me. I looked to Frank for help but he remained trapped under a portion of fallen ceiling, wriggling and helpless.

Erin was no use to me either; she'd been strangled to death by Draven's tree roots, so it'd be a minute or two before she was back up and at 'em.

Seemed I'd reached my expiration date after all—

Or maybe not, because it was at that moment I heard an engine turning over. The hearse. The knackered old motor was running again, filling the throne room with pure, unfiltered pollution. Who did I have to thank for this crucial assist? None other than DCI Kat Stronge, who was sitting in the hearse's driver's seat and revving the nuts off the thing.

'What?' she yelled over the roar of the engine. 'You think you're the only one who knows how to hot-wire a car?'

The crowd of fae shrank back as if the exhaust pipe was spewing mustard gas instead of diesel. The air was fairy poison now.

Acting quickly, the Queen limbered up her fingers and began mouthing an arcane evocation. The air crackled and thickened, becoming pregnant with something that strained the stitches of reality. A fissure cracked open in the roof and released a web of tree roots that snaked through the air before interlacing and forming an archway large enough to house a castle gate. The space within the arch shimmered and rippled like a pond disturbed by a skimming stone then revealed an opening to another place. What place I couldn't say, but judging by the landscape on show—a flat expanse of blighted earth dotted with charcoaled tree stumps—it was a long way from the pastoral Eden of Arcadia.

'Go,' she commanded. 'Leave this place.'

The remaining courtiers did as ordered and slipped through the archway, vanishing like thieves in the night. We'd given the fae no choice but to run. Wherever they were headed, they were better off there than suffocating in this toxic pit. And yet the King and Queen hadn't seen fit to leave just yet.

The King turned an accusing finger on his son. 'You did this. You destroyed the pact and doomed your people. You are not fit to be my successor. You are not fit to live!'

A bolt of lacerating blue light sprang from his fingertip and struck the kid square in the chest, lifting him off the ground and smashing him against the far wall. He smacked against the brickwork with a gristle-grinding crunch and landed with all the grace of a fly-tipped mattress.

'No!' screamed the Queen.

In a rage, she plucked the ivory pin keeping her hair in place and thrust it into the King's neck. His throat released a Pollock-like splatter of arterial spray and he dropped to the ground, gurgling his last.

'You always were a useless old fool,' said the Queen, stepping over his body on the way to her fallen son.

She crouched low over the kid's body and placed a hand on his chest. 'He's not breathing,' she said, then turned to me. 'You have to save my boy.'

CHAPTER FIFTY-EIGHT: IF IT'S NOT ONE THING IT'S YOUR MOTHER

WE'D STOPPED THE WEDDING, but it was beginning to look like a pyrrhic victory. The kid was down, and from what I could tell, he was staying that way.

The Queen craned over him, her icy, aristocratic features splintering, emotion leaking through the cracks.

I signalled for Stronge to kill the hearse's engine, then the two of us went to Frank and levered the lump of rock off his back. I merged with him right away, taking on his pain, sharing the load. I could spend a paragraph or two describing how it felt, inhabiting a body that had lost an arm and been hammered by a bloody great chunk of roof, but I reckon you get the idea. Let's just say it wasn't exactly a teddy bear's picnic.

I was busy turning Frank's belt into a tourniquet when I saw Erin back on her feet and surveying the wreckage.

'What did I miss?' she asked, skin flushed pink, her neck not even so much as blemished. She watched as we gathered around the kid. 'What's up with him? Did he snuff it then?'

Ordinarily, I'd have looked for the kid's ghost for a definitive answer to that question, but since none of the mangled bodies littering the floor had left any behind, I could only conclude that the fae weren't the haunting kind.

'Come on, kiddo, on your feet,' I said, patting his cheek with the one hand I had left.

Inside my head, Frank mewled pitifully. The kid wasn't getting up. I grabbed his wrist and checked for vitals. Nothing.

'Can't you conjure up one of your magic cocoon things and fix him?' I asked the Queen.

'There isn't time,' she said. 'You need to help him. Now.'

Stronge pressed an ear to the kid's chest. 'Whatever it was your man hit him with, it stopped his heart.'

In the movies, this is the part where the paramedic would have shown up shouting "Clear!" and stepped in with the chest paddles. But not this time. The end credits were already rolling on this flick.

I turned to Erin. 'What about your tattoos? Can't you magic him better?'

'Do I look like Florence Nightingale to you? The tats fix me, no one else.'

Of course not. Erin dealt the damage, she didn't cure it.

'How about you?' I said, looking to Stronge. 'You've had first aid training. What about CPR?'

'You need a defibrillator to get a stopped heart going. Doing it with CPR is a million-to-one shot.'

'Kat, we just rinsed a small army. There's room for a miracle here.'

She held up a mangled hand. 'It would take more than a bloody miracle to do CPR with this.'

'Come on, we've got two good hands between us.'

She nodded dutifully and placed a palm on the kid's sternum. 'Okay, with me...'

Stronge laced her fingers through mine and I followed her lead, pumping in time with her compressions. Again and again we bore down on the kid, working in tandem, driving the heel of my hand into his chest. After a couple of dozen compressions, Stronge craned over the kid's head and delivered two sharp breaths into his mouth. The fae's chest rose but the rest of him remained an inert bulk.

'It's not working,' said the Queen, tears forming in her eyes.

'Again,' I said, and began another round of compressions, determined to kickstart the kid's heart and make good on my promise to keep him safe.

But it was like pulling the ripcord on a busted lawnmower.

Stronge filled his lungs with another blast of oxygen but the kid stayed just the same, unmoving, lifeless.

'Give it up,' said Erin. 'He's copped it.'

The Queen shot her a death stare.

'Just saying...'

With Stronge's help, I ploughed ahead with the CPR, but after another fruitless couple of minutes, she withdrew her hand and settled on her backside, exhausted. 'We did everything we could but we were too late. I'm sorry.'

I wasn't having that and neither was Frank. We'd keep on going until we got what we wanted, because if this ordeal had taught us anything, it's that fairy tales could come true.

With one hand I went on, pumping at the kid's rib cage. I took over the mouth-to-mouth, copying what I'd learned from Stronge, administering breaths and returning to a steady rhythm of chest compressions. But despite my best efforts, each drive of my palm came quicker than the last, heavier, more desperate. Faith was flying out the window. Erin was right. Stronge was right. The kid wasn't a person anymore, he was a corpse. Soon the flies would come and his body would bloat and decay until one day there was nothing left of him but bones. He was undone. His magic extinguished.

And yet I couldn't stop. One last chance. One more breath.

I reached a phantom hand from Frank's body, plunged it through the kid's rib cage, and took a hold of his heart. It was an insane move. The only reason I'd done anything like this before was to hurt somebody, and here I was doing it to someone I'd promised to save. My fingers closed around the slippery mass of his cardiac organ and squeezed.

A jolt.

The kid coughed and bucked.

His chest rose and fell.

He was alive.

I pulled my hand free of his chest and screamed with unfettered joy. 'You legend! You actual legend!'

Inside my skull, Frank squealed like a Japanese schoolgirl.

'I don't believe it,' said Stronge, shaking her head in disbelief. She'd seen some shit in her time, but this just about took the biscuit.

The kid's mother cradled his head in her hands, openly sobbing. 'My boy, my boy, my boy...'

With eyes half hooded, Erin remarked, 'How about that. Good for you.'

The resuscitated Arcadian had the look of a man clinging to a life buoy after a violent shipwreck, but his heart was beating, his lungs drawing air. We saved him. We defied impossible odds and we saved him. It was enough to bring a tear to a glass eye.

I separated from Frank, adding another grinning face to the kid's impromptu bedside.

'How you feeling?' I asked.

It took a moment for him to gather the strength to answer, then he croaked, 'If that's what dying feels like, you have my eternal respect.'

I laughed. Frank laughed. What an irony, I thought: the only thing that could bring the kid back to life was two dead men. Alanis, get out your pen and write another verse.

'If you lot are finished, I could use a ride to the hospital,' said Stronge, clutching her wrist.

'Fine,' I replied, helping the kid into the back of the hearse, where he immediately passed out. 'Give us a second to grab Frank's arm and we're out of here.'

But the Queen had other ideas.

'Stay right where you are,' she said, barring our way.

'Are you having a laugh? I save your son's life and you're still gonna be a pain in my arse?'

'You've won a stay of execution, Mister Fletcher, but you're not going anywhere with my son.'

Frank stepped in front of me. Stronge did the sensible thing and took up the rear.

Erin took out her knife. 'You really wanna do this, missy?'

The queen bee remained calm despite the forces arrayed against her. Even the threat of Erin—a woman who'd unleashed a wave of havoc upon her people that I can still see when I blink sometimes—failed to put the willies up her.

'What makes you think I'd ever leave the kid with you?' I asked the Queen.

'Because if you don't, my promise not to kill you is rescinded.'

She was so thoroughly outmatched, and yet the confidence in her voice gave me pause.

'Why should I believe a word you say?' I said. 'You've been lying to me since the day we met.'

She fixed me with an owlish gaze. 'How so?'

'You looked me dead in the eye and said you'd torn up your contract with the Vengari. So what's the deal? I thought you Arcadians didn't lie.'

'We don't,' she said, reaching into the pocket of her gown and producing a fistful of shredded paper, 'but just because the contract was torn up, didn't mean we couldn't write an identical one.' Reaching into another pocket, she produced a fresh piece of paper fastened with a royal seal.

'And that's not lying?'

'No,' she said, smiling. 'It's being liberal with the truth.'

Having let us peek behind the curtain of her little illusion, she tossed the shredded contract into the air like the end of a magic trick.

'Clever,' I said. 'Shame that's the only confetti this wedding's getting.'

I watched her smile fade. That was a hit. It felt good.

'I'm sorry,' said Erin, cutting through the treacle. 'Is anyone else finding this *way* too talky?'

That Frank put up his hand was no big surprise, but I was a bit thrown to see Stronge's arm go up, too. Was I the only detective in the room interested in getting some answers?

I thought about some other promises the Queen had made and realised they were easily undone by weasel words and careful distortions. Her son's crimes would be dealt with according to Arcadian law? Fine. Since he wasn't responsible for Tali's murder, he hadn't even committed a crime. And yet there was one promise I couldn't quite shake...

'I asked what you'd do if you got your boy back, and you bullshitted me. You said you'd go back to your homeland.'

'No I didn't. I said—and I quote—*This city will be behind us*. And it will be. Behind us, in front of us, and either side of us.'

'You crafty bitch.'

The Queen grinned like a barracuda. 'Naturally. Now give me back my son before I make good on my threat to cast your spectral form to the wind.'

I stepped in front of the car and Frank did likewise.

'Not on your nelly, Your Highness.'

The kid was going nowhere. Sure, the Queen had me touching cloth, but what chance did she have against all four of us? She was an Arcadian, not a goddess.

'Have it your way,' said the Queen.

Erin's hand tightened around the handle of her knife. 'I don't like the sound of that.'

And she was right not to, because she hadn't even taken up a fighting stance before the oubliette swung open on the Queen's command and disgorged a big blue dragon.

Balls. In all the excitement I totally forgot about the giant fire-breathing lizard curled up in the basement. Freed from its prison, the dragon erupted from the pit and landed at the Queen's side with such force that it shook the surrounding sconces and sent a ripple of blue firelight dancing around the chamber. The creature flexed its muscular shoulders and spread a pair of enormous webbed wings, one of which draped across the Queen's shoulders like a great leathery shawl. The dragon drew back its gums to reveal a set of teeth like icicles from some deep and forgotten cave.

I looked to Erin, half-expecting to see her striding into the fray, knife in hand, tattoos broiling with strange black energy, but even she knew better than to go up against this monster. The dragon was covered in an intricate layering of shield-shaped scales, each as brilliant as stained glass, each as strong as steel. In the presence of the Queen's winged protector, Erin was a Lilliputian with a toothpick.

As I withered beneath the terrifying glare of the dragon's gimlet eye, I wondered why the fae hadn't released the beast earlier. My guess was that the damage it caused would have been too indiscriminate. Erin was dangerous, but she had focus. She was a heat-seeking missile; this thing was an atom bomb.

The dragon's nostrils belched twin plumes of steam as its serpentine tail curled about the Queen's ankles.

'It seems I won't be giving you that reprieve after all, Mister Fletcher. Such a shame.'

She gave the dragon a nod and it flexed its talons, gouging inch-wide grooves in the floor. The monster reared up on its hind legs, nose forward, ears back, mouth wide. From the depths of its bottomless gullet, tongues of blue flame lapped at the air like hungry kittens going at a saucer of milk.

Frank planted his feet and made himself into a human shield. It was a nice gesture, but utterly futile. The heat was already rising, hot enough to make even the dead sweat. As the flames intensified, welling up in the beast's throat like a white-hot furnace, the temperature climbed so high I felt like my brain was going to turn into glass. The blast the dragon was about to unleash would kill me. Would kill us all. It would charcoal our bodies and atomise any trace we left behind, even our souls. The flames rumbled and the dragon puffed out its chest, ready to discharge its deadly payload. I closed my eyes but the fire was so bright that my eyelids might as well have been transparent.

'Stop!'

I dared to open an eye and saw the kid standing between us and the dragon, one hand held out, fingers splayed.

Presented with the fae prince, the dragon's chest fell and the flames it was about to expel retreated into its belly. The Queen pinned her son with a stare so hostile it made her fire-breathing pet seem flat-out amiable by comparison.

'Have you no shame, boy? Get into that portal now and wait for me on the other side.'

'The only person stepping through that thing is you, Mother,' said the kid, arm shaking, stance wide but struggling to support his weight.

She laughed. 'And leave you behind? What makes you think I would do that?'

'Because it's over. The pact with the Vengari is done. There's no need for you to be here now.'

The Queen scowled. 'What happened to you, boy? How could you let these pitiful scrags of life brainwash you into thinking it's your destiny to live among them as their equal?'

'They didn't brainwash me, I just realised I have more in common with them than I do you.'

'You're being ridiculous. Now step aside so they can suffer for their interference.'

The dragon drew in another breath but the kid stood his ground.

'If you want to kill them you're going to have to kill me, too.'

Radiating glacial menace, the Queen hissed, 'Don't tempt me.'

But it was a stand-off. The Queen couldn't mete out punishment so long as her son was barring the way. The kid stood defiant.

'Without me, you have no heir and the Unseelie Court has no future.'

'Then so be it. I would rather our empire crumble to dust than be held hostage by an ungrateful child.'

'Then go ahead, Mother. Burn me down. Murder your only son.'

The Queen's hand came up, index finger pointed to the ceiling, ready to drop like an executioner's axe and order the death of us all.

'You have devastated all hope for our kind,' she snapped, spitting the words like they were made of broken glass. 'And for what? A dead girl?'

The kid returned a melancholy smile. 'Yes.'

His mother lowered her arm, not as a command to her dragon, but in defeat. 'If you're not prepared to think of your family, at least think of yourself. You won't survive on this cursed isle, my son. It's not just the pact you've damned today, you've damned yourself.'

The kid nodded. 'It was worth it.'

Gravity took hold of the Queen's shoulders. There was a sadness in her eyes. An understanding. 'Then goodbye. I hope this world serves you better than ours.'

She hugged the kid, then with a swish of her cloak, turned on her heel and marched towards the portal. The dragon trailed her, folding its wings flush to its body so it could fit through the woven tree roots of the archway, and together they vanished from the realm of men. The archway withered and unwove before turning brittle as old bones and crumbling to the floor in flakes of dust.

For a while the throne room was quiet as a tomb, then came a collective gasp of relief so potent I felt it in my eardrums.

CHAPTER FIFTY-NINE: TRAGEDY EVER AFTER

THE SUN ROSE that morning like a slowly-unwrapped present. As we strolled through town I expected to see aftershocks of the fae's meddling, more evidence of the Uncanny invading our post-truth world. But the headlines on the newspaper stand outside Camden Town station were devoted to the latest goings-on in Westminster instead of dragon-sightings and such.

The Accord had been fractured, but not broken. In the sober light of day, the things the public had seen now seemed ludicrous. Laughable, even. Yes, there were eye-witness accounts, but none of that mattered now. The world had moved on. The folks who'd posted YouTube videos and Twitter threads describing their experiences were shrugged off as kooks. Conspiracy theorists. Grifters thirsty for hits and likes. Even the accounts of the legitimate media fell by the wayside as the incredible sights of the last few days became lost in the endless churn of the news cycle. Another unexplained mystery? Ho-hum. A future piece of pub quiz trivia now. An On This Day reminder that showed up on your social media feed and got reshared with a simple, *Who remembers the big blue dragon?*: four thumbs-up, one smiley face, and a comment from your auntie asking how you're getting on these days. The fantastic had been made credible for a while, but that credibility, eclipsed by banality, had become too frail to survive.

Stronge went to the hospital to get medical attention for her hand, while the rest of us stopped by Legerdomain to get Frank's arm reattached. While Jazz Hands did her thing in the shop (accompanied by the kid, who preferred the indoors to the polluted streets), Erin and I sat on the kerb outside and re-played the events of the last few hours.

'Did you see the state of the place?' she said, recalling the mess we'd made of the fae lair. 'Man, we pulled a real *Game of Thrones* on that wedding.'

I grinned despite not really getting the reference.

'Surprised to see you smiling,' said Erin. 'What about the rest of those vamps? You're all right now, but how about when the sun goes down?'

'The Vengari won't be bothering me any time soon. They've survived as long as they have because they avoid trouble instead of chasing it.'

'And if they do decide to stop by your office one night?'

'Then I'll make sure the place is covered in more crucifixes than a Madonna video.'

Erin chuckled as she got to her feet and zipped up her jacket. 'Right then, that's me off. Good luck with everything, Fletcher, I'm heading back to the coast.'

I got up and shook her hand. 'See you around, Erin. Thanks for the help.'

She went to leave then turned back my way. 'Almost forgot...' She pulled a piece of folded-up paper from her pocket and I firmed up a hand to receive it.

'What's this?' I asked.

'My digits.'

'Right. In case I have work for you?'

'Nope,' she said, wearing a libidinous smirk.

'Oh, I see. Well, thank you very much.'

She made a face. 'Not for you, you wazzock. For your partner.'

'You're telling me you want Frank to have your phone number?'

'A prime specimen like that? Too right I am.' Her last words as she headed off were, 'Tell that stud if he ever finds himself in Brighton, look me up.'

I stared incredulously at the scrap of paper. Seemed I was wrong before when I said the fantastic was back in hiding. Apparently, some wonders had yet to cease.

IF FRANK and I were going to stand any chance of wrapping this case up clean, we needed to find Tali. Trouble was, she'd long since vacated our office, which meant she could be just about anywhere in London. Then again, ghosts tend not to be possessed of the greatest imaginations. Left to their own devices, they do what the rest of us do: seek out familiar locales. Ghosts especially are drawn to places they know well. Places that give them comfort.

We found Tali at The Beehive. Not inside, propping up the bar, but standing in the alley outside, staring longingly through the greasy window. In the warmth of the pub, across the far side of the saloon, a man and woman were playing a game of darts.

'Hello, Tali.'

She turned to find me blocking the mouth of the alley.

'What do you want?' she said, her voice low and menacing.

I took a step back, hands raised as if she'd turned a gun on me. 'I just want to talk, that's all.'

And I did, but though my hands were empty, I could feel the reassuring weight of certain tools I carried about my person: tools to repel, to rebuke, to banish. I didn't want to use them, but since the last time I saw Tali she was on her way to turning feral, I'd come prepared for the eventuality that this encounter might not end in a handshake.

'Well, I don't want to talk to you,' Tali snapped, her jaw clamping tight.

She went to exit the other end of the alley, only to find my partner blocking her way.

'Move,' she demanded.

Frank shook his head.

She considered an alternate escape route, but somehow sensed what I already knew: that the walls of the blind alley were as solid to phantoms as they were to the living. Tali was cornered. There was nowhere for her to run and no one coming to save her. She couldn't escape this place, and there was no magically-enhanced assassin left to hide behind.

'So this is it?' she said. 'You're going to wipe me out?'

It wasn't so long ago that I'd met another lost soul and had to do exactly that: Mary, the spiritualist's assistant, trapped in a wall cavity and left to rot. I tried my best to persuade her to go to the next place quietly, but ended up having to obliterate her. My hope was that I could make up for that failure here. That I could talk Tali down from the ledge before she became a creature rendered from pain and malice. Before she was lost forever.

'I'm not here to hurt you.'

'Then why did you come?'

I looked through the window of the pub. The couple were still playing darts, just as Tali and the kid had done the night they met.

'I came to help.'

Her eyes welled up. 'I can't just give up. We were meant to be together. We still can be.'

'Not any more. I'm sorry.'

'But he promised...'

'Promises get broken and love ain't forever, despite what the songs all say.'

'You're wrong. Love doesn't have a sell-by date.'

This girl really had it bad (as if that wasn't obvious given all the aggro she'd put us through).

'Listen, I've been where you are. I loved someone once. A girl. Because of her, I died too. I was so angry, and I held on to that anger for a long, long time.'

'So what did you do with it?'

'I let it go. Let her go.'

'I can't do that. He's all I have left. Without him there's something missing.'

'That's not true. Just because you can't be together, doesn't mean you're not whole. You're you, Tali, with or without him. The question is, what do you want to do now?'

A tear spilled down her cheek. Frank passed her a handkerchief. She took it warily.

'What can I do?' she asked.

'You can move on. And if you do that, maybe you can leave this place and go somewhere better.'

'Why can't I just stay here?'

'Because you'll become a monster.'

'You didn't.'

'No, I got something else. Something worse, maybe. I got to be myself, but stuck here in limbo. I can feel the pull of the next world, but the door's closed to me.'

Sometimes it feels like living in a refugee camp, neither here nor there. It's distressing. I don't belong here, but since I'm not yet the paragon of morality God expects of me, I have to carry on working.

'The door's open to you, Tali. You just have to use it.'

She dabbed her cheeks with Frank's hankie. 'What's on the other side?'

'Same thing as for everyone. Judgment.'

A bitter laugh fell from her lips. 'I think I know which way the scales are going to tip on that one.'

'I wouldn't be so sure. You didn't actually kill anyone apart from yourself, so it's not a foregone. I say roll the dice and see where they land.'

She toyed nervously with her engagement ring. 'I'm scared, Jake.'

'I get it. The Big Man's not known to look kindly on suicide, but I think He's changed since they wrote book on him. He hasn't sent me to Hell, and I've got a rap sheet thicker than Kim Kardashian's arse.'

Yeah, even a dead man knows who the Kardashians are. What a world.

I went on. 'What I'm saying is, I think He could be made to understand a crime of passion. He made us in His image, right, so He must have some understanding of what you've been through.'

I thought I had her, I really did. At first, a calm seemed to descend upon her as though she'd made peace with her fate. As though she was ready to make the right choice. Then her eyes took on that fevered look again.

'No, I can't go. I've done too much wrong. There's no place for me up there. No place. Nothing, nothing, nothing...'

Her words started as a whisper then the whisper became a shout and the shout became a scream. Her voice was twisting, mutating into something else: a deranged banshee howl. Tali was about to tip off the ledge, just like Mary did before I was forced to cast her spirit into shadow. I wasn't going to save her.

Just as well I brought some help, then.

The Arcadian materialised next to me.

'Hello, Tali.'

Instantly, the fever in Tali's eyes was extinguished and her voice returned to normal.

'You came back.'

Moving at speed, she went to him, wrapping her arms around his torso hard enough to squeeze the marrow from his bones.

'I'm so sorry,' he said, meeting her embrace. He touched a shaky fingertip to the bullet hole in her forehead. 'I am so, so sorry.'

They cried. Frank cried. I'd have cried too if I wasn't able to zip up my emotional sphincter.

'We don't need to be apart,' Tali sobbed, her eyes swollen and red. 'We can be together.'

'I wish we could, but it's too late for that now. You have to go to the next world.'

'Not without you.'

'I'll be there. I just need you to give me some more time, that's all.'

'I don't want to wait.'

'I know. But you have to.'

With tears brimming in his eyes he reached for his engagement ring, slipped it from his finger, and closed a fist around it. 'Go and be happy, Tali. I'll be there when you are.'

This was it. The moment of truth. Tali was either going to let the kid go or start chucking crockery about. She raised a hand. She was going to slap him, and with that final act of violence she'd be gone. Tali would be beyond redemption, and it would be up to me to destroy the howling husk she left behind.

But the hand stayed up, held flat like a pledge. She blinked, sending twin falls tracking down her cheeks, and when she opened her eyes again the ring on her engagement finger was gone. The promise was undone. She was letting the kid go.

The gateway to the Great Beyond appeared that moment, right on cue. It looked about how you'd imagine it would look: a golden portal full of celestial light accompanied by the faint sound of choral music. Ever since my deathday I've dreamt about walking through one of those things and making good with Him Upstairs, but this gate wasn't for me, it was for Tali.

'Don't drag it out,' I said.

She turned to Frank to seek his wisdom.

He nodded back at her with a big soppy grin on his mush. 'Ggggggo.'

Tali wiped a wet smudge from the kid's blue cheek. 'I'll be seeing you,' she said, giving him the kind of kiss they zoom in on in the movies.

And then she was off through the golden gateway, swallowed by the light.

CHAPTER SIXTY: ON THE RIGHT TRACK

ONE MORE GOODBYE TO GO.

Euston Station looked a lot like it did last time we were there, except this time instead of jumping the Arcadian, we were paying for his train ticket. Having spent so long trying to capture him, now we were going to set him free. Free to live out his days in the country-side, away from the stifling pollution of the modern world. Free to live.

We were sitting on a platform bench, me on one side of the Arcadian, Frank on the other. The kid was wearing makeup to disguise his true complexion, and chewing on a Twix. We bought that, too.

'How you feeling?' I asked him. 'You good?'

He didn't look good. Matter of fact, he looked downright miserable. We'd been sitting on that bench for an hour already, watched four perfectly good trains pull in, and the kid hadn't taken one of them.

'Even if I can make a go of it out there, how do I know the Vengari won't come after me?'

'What would be the point? The pact's in the bin, plus we gave them a pretty definitive talking to back there. They'll learn from that. The Vengari are survivors, not avengers.'

The kid nodded solemnly.

'But this isn't about vampires, is it?' I said, sensing something deeper at play.

He went to speak but nothing came out, the words unwilling to take flight. Finally, he forced out the question. 'What if we did all this for nothing? What if my mother was right and I don't belong in this realm?'

'Don't be like that. There's a place for you here.'

Frank patted his knee. 'Yooou beee fiiine.'

The kid wasn't so sure. 'How do you know that? Really?'

I cast a look down the track to the daylight beyond. 'You feel that pull, don't you?'

'I do.'

'Then go to it. You have a way out. Be grateful for that.'

The kid's feet rocked back and forth under the bench. 'All right. I'm on the next train.'

Frank reached inside his jacket and produced a crown of brambles lined with rich blue velvet.

'What's this?' the kid asked.

'Croooown,' said Frank.

'I know, but why are you giving it to me?'

'It's a going away gift,' I explained. 'We picked it up in the throne room, and we figure since you're the last Arcadian royal left in the UK, you should have it.'

'Thank you, but I don't need it. That life is behind me now.'

'Suit yourself then,' I said.

Later on I came to appreciate the kid's integrity even more, particularly since his reluctance to take the crown allowed me to flog it to Giles L'Merrier for a tidy sum. With the great wizard's money I was able to restock the company coffers, fix up the office, and pay off Shift's outstanding fee. Why the fae crown was worth so much to L'Merrier I had no idea, especially since he already had the one the Romans popped on JC's bonce before they nailed him to the cross (the real one, not the one in the Louvre). I don't know, maybe the man just liked crowns.

Anyway.

The platform's electronic departure board showed a new train arriving in one minute. I watched the stops cycle by; all six screens of them.

'You know where you're getting off?' I asked the kid.

'Yes. Why, do you want to know?'

'Better I don't,' I replied, holding up a halting hand. 'That way I've got plausible deniability if some vamp with a rusty set of pliers plucks up the courage to come by the gaff.'

The train arrived and slid up to the platform with a metallic squeal. Without further fanfare, the kid got to his feet and headed for the nearest carriage. Before he stepped aboard, he gave us a final wave.

'Goodbye, Fletchers. I only hope the living prove to be as kind as you.'

He boarded the train and the doors hissed shut behind him.

What he'd done had cost him everything: his title, his wealth, his family, his love. Tali had made her sacrifice, too; she'd let go of the hate that had almost consumed her, almost turned her soul black and rancid. And now it was time for me to let go of something: guilt.

I'd saved so many souls, steered so many lost causes to the light, and yet there wasn't a day that went by I didn't think of the ones I took before them. The ones I let my ignorance destroy. The ones I was still being punished for, even in death. But just because God hadn't forgiven me, didn't mean I couldn't forgive myself. There was no changing the past, so why keep punishing myself for it? Carrying this guilt was a choice; a choice I could undo. The idea of giving it up seemed hard—nigh on impossible, even—but really it was simple. I could keep clutching the nettle or I could let it go. So I chose to let it go. To let the past be the past. To let the things I did in life die.

A part of me expected something to happen then. A revelation like that—the audaciousness of it—tempted a response, a sign from the heavens. How dare I absolve myself of my sins? How dare I consider my account settled when the Great Arbiter Himself hadn't closed the books on me? It's a wonder I wasn't struck down by a bolt of lightning, scrubbed from the Earth. But my revelation went unpunished.

I turned to my partner. 'From now on I say we're our own bosses. We help the needy because we want to, not because we have to. What do you reckon?'

Frank nodded. I'm not sure he understood what he was agreeing to, but I appreciated the support all the same.

'Who cares what He thinks, eh? If the only thing fuelling our good intentions is the promise of a divine reward, what does that make us?'

The nodding continued. Frank got it. So what if we were never redeemed? So what if the only thing we were doing down here was shuffling dirt around our grave?

'We can't spend the rest of our days looking for a sign that we're on the right path. You know what I say, Frank? I say we don't need a sign.'

He nodded and so did I, the both of us in full agreement.

And then the message on the electronic departure board changed to a row of halos—an unmistakable message from Him Upstairs that our stock had just gone up.

'Oh, thank Christ for that,' I cried, and high-fived Frank until my palm was sore.

The train pulled away from the platform, taking the kid wherever it was he was headed. For the first time in his life, the Arcadian wasn't living under the tyrannical yoke of his family. He could make his own decisions from now on. Live the life he always wanted. The sting Tali left in his heart wouldn't leave him, but the hurt would fade in time. And maybe he was right. Maybe one day, if God was willing, they'd be reunited in the afterlife. Wouldn't that be nice?

The train turned a corner, sending its rear end kicking out like the tail of some great metal serpent, and then it was gone.

LEAVE A REVIEW

Reviews are gold to indie authors, so if you've enjoyed this book, please consider visiting Amazon to rate and review.

STILL HAVE QUESTIONS?

Like, how did Erin Banks become a supernaturally-enhanced assassin for hire?

Who's Stella Familiar when she's at home?

And what exactly happened at the bureau of Myth Management?

For answers to all of these questions, sign up to the *Uncanny Kingdom* mailing list and become an Insider. Membership includes the free mini-story, *Deathday*, which kicks off the first Jake Fletcher series. You'll also get the complete *London Coven* saga, which intersects with Jake's story.

Sign up at…
WWW.UNCANNYKINGDOM.COM

ALSO SET IN THE UNCANNY KINGDOM

The Spectral Detective Series
Spectral Detective
Corpse Reviver
Twice Damned
Necessary Evil
Deadly Departed

The London Coven Series
Familiar Magic
Nightmare Realm
Deadly Portent
Other London

The Hexed Detective Series
Hexed Detective
Fatal Moon
Night Terrors

The Uncanny Ink Series
Bad Soul
Bad Blood
Bad Justice
Bad Intention
Bad Thoughts
Bad Memories

The Dark Lakes Series
Magic Eater
Blood Stones
Past Sins

The Branded Series
Sanctified
Turned
Bloodline

The Myth Management Series
Myth Management

Printed in Great Britain
by Amazon